Praise for bestselling author Lora Leigh

MIDNIGHT SINS

"Has everything a good book should have: suspense, murder, betrayal, mystery, and lots of sensuality. So rarely do you come across a book that you can lose yourself in and *Midnight Sins* is definitely one of them. Lora Leigh is a talented author with the ability to create magnificent characters and captivating plots." —*Romance Junkies*

RENEGADE

"Leigh delivers . . . erotic passion. This is a hot one for the bookshelf!" —*Romantic Times BOOKreviews*

"Smoldering romance, suspense, and mystery. Add to that the cast of interesting characters—and their pasts—and you have the perfect recipe for one amazing novel."
—*Night Owl Romance* (4½ stars)

"Will have you breathless . . . gets your blood running hot with the physical attraction." —*Romance Reviews Today*

BLACK JACK

"Overflowing with escalating danger, while pent-up sexual cravings practically burst into flames." —*Sensual Reads*

HEAT SEEKER

"Leigh's pages explode with a hot mixture of erotic pleasures." —*Romantic Times BOOKreviews*

MAVERICK

"A phenomenal read."   *—Romance Junkies*

"Scorching-hot sex, deadly secrets, and a determined assassin add up to another addicting Leigh thriller. Leigh's ability to credibly build damaged characters who are both intriguing and intense gives her stories that extra punch."
                                    —Romantic Times BOOKreviews

"Sex and violence power the satisfying second installment of Leigh's Elite Ops series."   *—Publishers Weekly*

"Full of wrenching emotion and self-flagellation by the hero, the new series of Elite Ops promises to be even better than the sexy SEALs at this rate."
                                              —Night Owl Romance

"With her customary panache for emotionally intense, sensual characters, the author attracts readers into every world she creates. This fabulous follow-up to *Wild Card* is no exception to the rule."   *—A Romance Review*

WILD CARD

"Highly emotional and addicting . . . an intoxicating first installment of a brand-new series."   *—Romance Junkies*

"Ferocious passion!"   *—Romantic Times BOOKreviews*

KILLER SECRETS

"A smoldering-hot, new espionage tale. This chapter of Leigh's SEAL saga reverberates with deadly danger."

—*Romantic Times BOOKreviews*

HIDDEN AGENDAS

"Treachery and intrigue combine with blistering-hot sensuality in this chapter of Leigh's SEAL saga. The title of this book is particularly apt, since many of the characters are not what they seem, and betrayal can have deadly consequences. Leigh's books can scorch the ink off the page."   —*Romantic Times BOOKreviews*

"An evocative and captivating read."   —*Romance Junkies*

DANGEROUS GAMES

"A marvelous novel of suspense and raw passion."

—*Romance Junkies*

"Lora Leigh ignites the fire . . . with steamy heat added to a story that makes you cheer and even tear up."

—*Fallen Angel Reviews*

"Leigh writes . . . tempting, enchanting romance[s] that readers are certain to devour."   —*Romance Reviews Today*

St. Martin's Paperbacks Titles by
Lora Leigh

SINS series
MIDNIGHT SINS
DEADLY SINS

ELITE OPS series
LIVE WIRE
RENEGADE
BLACK JACK
HEAT SEEKER
MAVERICK
WILD CARD

SEALs trilogy
KILLER SECRETS
HIDDEN AGENDAS
DANGEROUS GAMES

~~~

FORBIDDEN PLEASURE

~~~

Anthologies
LEGALLY HOT
MEN OF DANGER
RESCUE ME

Wicked
PLEASURE

LORA LEIGH

St. Martin's Paperbacks

This is a work of fiction. All of the characters, organizations, and events portrayed in this novel are either products of the author's imagination or are used fictitiously.

WICKED PLEASURE

Copyright © 2008 by Lora Leigh.

All rights reserved.

For information address St. Martin's Press, 175 Fifth Avenue, New York, NY 10010.

Library of Congress Catalog Card Number: 2008003152

ISBN: 978-1-250-00590-8

Printed in the United States of America

St. Martin's Griffin trade paperback edition / May 2008
St. Martin's Paperbacks edition / May 2012

St. Martin's Paperbacks are published by St. Martin's Press, 175 Fifth Avenue, New York, NY 10010.

10 9 8 7 6 5 4 3 2 1

For a very dear friend.
I miss our morning chats.

PROLOGUE

Her daddy had told her to stay away from him. That he was bad news. That those Falladay twins were boys good girls didn't mess with.

She was a good girl, but she didn't think Cam Falladay was a bad boy. He was hurting, and she couldn't stand to see him hurt.

She was thirteen, and boys were just starting to flirt with her. She liked the flirting, but she didn't like how dumb they acted. Cam was eighteen, a man, but sometimes she just wanted to hug him, because she swore she could feel him hurting.

Not that he ever showed it or spoke of it. Unlike other boys, Cam didn't tell anyone when he hurt. And he didn't flirt with her either. When he saw her he talked to her, and when the older boys bothered her, he always seemed to be there. Those light green eyes of his would pin the other boys in a way that always made her shiver with dread. And evidently, it made them shiver, too, because they ran, and they rarely bothered her anymore.

She sought Cam Falladay out every chance she got, despite her daddy's warning. But now, it seemed he had sought her out.

She tipped her head to the side, brushing back her long auburn hair as she stared at the rusty old pickup he drove.

It was parked on the back road to her daddy's farm, far away from the house and in an area where the cattle hadn't yet been moved to.

He was sitting there silently, just staring out the windshield as she drew her horse to a stop and slowly dismounted.

"Stay, Critter." She patted the horse's mane as she wrapped the lead to the bridle around a branch of a nearby tree and moved toward the truck.

He couldn't have known she would be here. Her father rarely allowed her to ride far from the house.

She watched as he moved, his arm lifting to bring a bottle to his lips, and she winced. It was whisky. And it was really early in the day to be drinking.

She moved to the passenger side of the truck and knew the moment he realized she was there. No, he hadn't come looking for her, because his entire body seemed to tense.

"Go away, little girl." His voice had a rough, growling tone as she opened the door slowly and lifted herself into the vehicle.

He was so sad. He looked so alone right now. With his shaggy black hair framing his wild face, and those light green eyes swirling with emotions that made her chest ache, even though she didn't know what they were.

He sat stiffly, his left arm down by his side, against the door of the truck, his opposite hand holding that bottle of whisky.

"Not a good place for you to be right now." He lifted the bottle again.

Her daddy had warned her to always be careful of a man while he was drinking. But Cam broke her heart. His expression was ravaged, as it had been at his parents' funeral three years ago.

She reached out and gripped his wrist, feeling the heat of his skin as he stiffened.

"Don't, Cam," she whispered. "You're going to hurt yourself like this."

"So?" His gaze pinned her now, and she had to force herself not to be frightened of him.

She stared back at him desperately, hurting for him, hurting with him.

"Wait on me, Cam. I'll grow up and I'll take all the bad things away." She didn't know where the words came from, or the tears that filled her eyes. She just knew she was going to lose him. Right here, right now, she would lose him forever, and it was terrifying her.

His gaze flickered with agony then. "Damn you, Jaci. You're just a kid. You don't know what the hell you're talking about."

"And you're just my friend," she whispered. "Who's going to run those bigger boys off when they bother me, if you don't wait for me? If you leave, I won't have my dark knight anymore."

She tried to smile, but she wanted to cry.

He shook his head and stared out the windshield again. "Dark knights are bad news," he finally muttered. "Dumb little fairy tales. You'd do better to look for a white knight."

"They're boring." She tried to smile, but his face was so still, so grief-stricken, she couldn't find it in her to make her lips curve.

"They're safe." His voice echoed with an aloneness that suddenly frightened her. Frightened her, not of him, but for him.

"You're going to leave, aren't you?" A tear fell from her eyes. "And I'll never see you again."

She didn't know why it was so important that Cam not leave. Shoot, he could do better anywhere than he could in this dusty little county they lived in. But she didn't want to lose him. Not yet.

"Maybe." He finally cleared his throat. "Maybe I'll just leave for a little while."

His voice was faint, aching with pain. She wanted so bad to ease that pain, and she didn't know how.

"I'm your friend, Cam," she told him fiercely. "I'll always wait for you to come back. I'm not like Laida Jones, always wanting to hang on you and run your friends off. I want you to have lots of friends. And I'll always be here when you come back."

He turned and looked at her again, those eyes piercing inside her.

"What do you want from me, little Jaci Wright?" His voice was hard, like her daddy's got when she said something he didn't approve of.

Her hand tightened on his wrist then pulled away as she stared back at him in confusion.

"I don't want anything from you, Cam. I just want to see you smile. And I don't want you to go away."

"Why?" his voice was ragged. "Why does it matter?"

"Because you're my friend, and because I love you. I love you better than anything, Cameron Falladay. I love you enough to know that if you left, one of these days I would find you. And when I do, I'll show you what being a friend really means."

And he was her friend. A friend she never wanted to lose.

He blinked back at her and she realized how fierce she sounded. Like her mom sounded when she was telling her daddy how much she loved him. Sometimes, Jaci heard them talking at night when she shouldn't. And her mom's voice sounded just like that.

Cam shook his head then. "You're dangerous." He sighed.

Her eyes widened. "Shoot, Cam, then we're best friends. 'Cause that's what Daddy says about you."

* * *

Cam watched as Jaci Wright rode her horse back toward home, and he breathed out roughly. The fingers of his left hand were still clenched around the pistol, the single bullet lodged inside just waiting to be released.

He lifted it and stared at it. It was his father's service weapon. The military pistol he had used before his death.

One bullet. But he'd only need one.

He stared back to where Jaci had ridden off. Dumb-ass kid. She was wilder than the wind. Her father didn't have a hope in hell of keeping up with her and keeping her out of trouble.

Somehow—he hadn't figured out how—it had fallen to him to keep the molesting bastards in town away from her. The boys that were too old for her, and sure as hell old enough to know better than to fool with a baby. But she was right. Who would run them off if he left?

He laid the pistol on the dash and capped the whisky.

If he was too fucking weak to take the easy way out, then that left the hard way. Son of a bitch. The hard way sucked, too.

Eight Years Later

It was the bad boy party of the year, held outside the small Oklahoma town Jaci Wright had been raised in. The music was a hard, throbbing pulse through the night air. A bonfire burned in the center of the clearing, huge speakers were set up in the back of a pickup, the rocking music pounding through them as the beer and moonshine flowed freely.

Bodies danced in abandon, whoops and yells could be heard through the clearing as the scent of burning wood filled her nostrils.

It was her first year attending, not that she hadn't tried to slip in over the years. Unfortunately, Cameron was usually here, and he never failed to pull her out within the first few minutes. Cameron might well be here now, but his excuse for pulling her out no longer applied.

She leaned against the bed of one of the pickups, her beer in hand, and watched the antics of the partygoers. The first faint chill of fall was in the air, the university would be beginning its first semester next week, and the yearly party to celebrate the end of summer was under way with all the excitement and desperate exuberance of the crowd and the vacation that was soon to end. Many of those here had been attending for years and no one wanted to miss out on it.

She let her gaze rove over the crowd once again, searching for the tall, dangerous form of her tormentor. Cameron had been pulling her out of this party since she was sixteen, when she'd tried to attend for the first time. He was always here.

In the center of the clearing bodies gyrated, male and female, dancing with abandon. She wondered if Cameron danced when he was here. With his tall, hard-muscled body, the graceful way he moved, he would be a sexual fantasy come true out there. But she doubted he did. Cameron wasn't the type of man to shake his booty for the crowd.

She smiled as she lifted her beer to her lips, intent on taking the first drink of the cold, bitter liquid. She had been putting it off as long as she could.

As it touched her lips, a hard, well-tanned hand came from behind her, gripped the bottle, and held it still. She could barely taste it against her lips, barely felt the icy sensation of liquid. But behind her, the heat of the man seared her back.

"Your father would have a cow if he saw you here."

Trepidation surged in her stomach at the sound of the

dark voice in her ear, the feel of a broad palm covering her hip, and the sensation of being surrounded with heat.

He pulled the bottle from her hand and passed it to another woman passing by them. The blonde flashed him a smile and a wink as she took it and continued on with her companion.

"That was just rude," she told him.

She didn't turn; she couldn't force herself to turn. For the first time in all the years she had been teasing and tempting Cameron Falladay, he was finally touching her.

His chest pressed against her shoulders, his hand gripped her hip, his arm rested on the side of the truck beside her. She felt surrounded by him. Heated by him. She felt sinfully aware of the hard press of his hips against her lower back and the erection beneath his jeans.

"That was common sense." He nipped her ear and she felt her pulse ignite with a heat that burned across her nerve endings. "You shouldn't be here."

"I'm legal," she reminded him, suddenly feeling more feminine than she had in her life.

"By all of three months?" The rasp of his rough cheek against her ear nearly had her coming undone.

She was breathing hard and fast, and she knew it. She couldn't stop it. Her heart was racing in her chest, her thighs felt weak, her clit was swollen, her nipples hard. She could feel every inch of her body readying itself for him.

"Three months, three years." She shrugged with an attempt at a laugh. "Does it matter?"

As she spoke, his arm lifted as though in a signal. Within seconds the pulsing, hard drive of the music eased away to be replaced by a slower, softer tune.

It was late, it was normal. The music turned sexier, pounding with sex and excitement rather than anticipation.

"Dance with me."

Jaci stiffened in shock as Cam's hand tightened at her

hip and he drew her back toward the shadows at the front of the truck, which had been backed toward the circle of partygoers.

She turned in his arms, hands pressing against the dark T-shirt as he stared down at her, his broad chest sheltering her, warming her as his arms moved around her.

"Cam." Wonder filled her voice. She had been dying for this for too many years. To be held against his large body, his arms around her.

She felt the rasp of his cheek against the top of her head, the sliding of his pants against her bare thighs beneath the short hem of her skirt.

He wasn't wearing jeans. He was wearing the camouflage pants he usually wore when leaving for or returning from duty. How long had he been home? It couldn't have been for long. Had he come straight here for her? Just for her?

"You shouldn't be here, sweetheart." His hands slid over her back. Up. Down. Then, his hand slid beneath the bottom of her shirt and touched her bare flesh.

Oh God. His hands were broad and calloused, warm, impossibly arousing. She could feel the shudders working up her spine from his touch, tearing at the control she had promised herself she would have around him.

At twenty-six, Cam was a world ahead of her in experience. A warrior, a conqueror. It was in his dark face, in those light green eyes.

"Where should I be?" She lifted her head to him, he with his gaze imprisoning hers as he stared down at her. He swayed to the music with her, rubbed against her.

"Safe," he answered.

"At home, playing with my dolls?" she suggested sweetly. "Those days are long gone, Cam."

His expression was hungry. She teased him, though she knew better. She tilted her hips toward him, then gasped in shock as his hands slid to her rear, clenched the rounded flesh and jerked her to him.

"Cam?" Her nails dug into his shoulders as the hard wedge of his erection pressed tight against the sensitive flesh between her thighs.

"You can go home with me, or I can take you back to your parents'," he rasped. "Which one?"

Her lips parted as she fought to breathe, to make sense of this abrupt change in the man she had been flirting with and teasing for so many years.

"The party—"

"You're not staying here." He backed her against the front of the truck, lifting her until he was wedged fully against her, his hands sliding beneath the skirt to the bare flesh revealed by the thong she wore.

No, she wasn't staying here. She stared into his eyes, instinct clashing with feminine need and fear, until she fought to breathe through the sensations racing through her.

The party was a catalyst, nothing more. It always had been—since that first party, when she was sixteen. He was the dark visage that moved from the shadows, caught her wrist, and dragged her from the date she had arrived with, and had made certain she never stayed.

He had taken her home that night. Tonight, he would take her to his home. Since she was thirteen and found him in that truck at the back of her father's land, Cam had been her protector in ways he had never been before.

He pulled her to his pickup, unlocked the passenger door, and lifted her to the seat. Before she could turn forward, one hand slid into her hair, the other clamped to her hip, and he was staring at her. His gaze bored into hers, the tension building until Jaci felt as though it would eat her alive.

"My house or your parents'?" his voice was hard, demanding.

There was no question of which.

"Yours." She had waited too long, fantasized for too many years.

No sooner had the words left her than his lips covered hers. Possessive, demanding. He made no concessions, no apologies. His tongue stroked into her mouth, nudged against hers and in those seconds she learned more about a kiss than she had learned in her entire life.

She learned a kiss could burn from the top of her head to the tips of her toes. That it could slam into her womb, convulse it and release inside her a hunger for more that she didn't know she was capable of.

Her arms wrapped around his shoulders, her head tilted to his, mewling cries leaving her lips as he nipped at them, sucked them, then pressed against them once again.

He kissed her like he was dying for her taste and hers alone. He kissed her with an experience, a knowledge worlds away from hers.

When he pulled back, she stared up at him, dazed and uncertain and wanting so much more.

"You know what coming home with me means?" he asked her then. "Everything it means?"

She nodded. Oh yes, she knew what it would mean. She wouldn't be tossing alone in her own bed. She would be in his bed, beneath his hard body.

"Everything, Jaci?" His fingers tightened in her hair as he jerked her closer, his thighs spreading hers, her skirt riding up until the hard proof of his arousal pressed dead center between her thighs.

"Everything," she gasped.

He could have her here, right here in the front seat of his pickup, if that was what he wanted. Whatever he wanted. She was dying for more, primed for it.

"You shouldn't have come here tonight." His fingers

caressed her cheek, his expression darkening. "Any night but tonight."

"But I knew you would be here tonight," she answered. "I came for you, Cam. I always come for you."

He grimaced, a hard flex of his expression as his hands slid to her thighs, curved on the bare flesh and his hips pressed harder against her.

Jaci felt her lashes droop, sexual weakness filling her, pumping through her. A drugged awareness of the fact that he was more man than she could handle, but the only man she wanted.

"Get in there before I end up fucking you here." He jerked back, slid her around on the leather seat and slammed the door.

He didn't drive sedately back to the house he shared with his brother on the other side of town. He took the back roads with a speed that should have been reckless, but instead felt controlled.

He handled the vehicle the same way he had handled her earlier. With confidence and determination, he drove the truck into the two-car garage where he drew it to a stop and cut the motor.

He wasn't giving her a chance to change her mind. He turned, opened his door, and stepped out before reaching back for her. Lifting her against his hard body, her toes barely touching the floor, his lips stole her kiss, and stole her senses.

His lips devoured hers, his tongue slid past them, licked against her tongue and danced over it as she strained to get closer. Wrapping her arms around his neck, she held on tight, lost in a sea of such incredible sensations that she never wanted to emerge from it.

Her senses were tossed amid the lust burning out of control between the two of them, but there was more, she thought. There was a lifetime of waiting, of knowing this was coming. Years of saving herself for this one night, for this one man.

One arm remained around her back while the other gripped the side of her rear, holding her against him as he walked, maybe stumbled a bit to the door that led into the house. Her eyes were closed and desperate mewls of pleasure were echoing from her throat.

His hand clenched on her butt as he braced her against a wall. She didn't even know which room they had stepped into.

"Take this off." He pulled the shirt over her head, disposed of it, tossed it behind him, and a second later he was laying her back on a wide, leather couch as he knelt on the floor beside her.

She wasn't wearing a bra. She had deliberately not worn a bra, and now, as Cam stared down at her, as those light, bright-green eyes narrowed on the swollen, hard-tipped mounds of her breasts, she was fiercely glad she hadn't.

Her nipples ached. They hurt with the need for his touch, the stroke of his tongue, his lips.

"You're beautiful." He said it so simply, his voice so husky and rasping with hunger that she felt her lower stomach tighten violently in reaction.

"I'll never get enough of you." One broad hand cupped a breast. "Ever."

Then his lips were covering her nipple, sucking it deep inside his mouth, as her back arched and a cry fell from her lips.

She was only barely aware of his other hand pushing at the elastic band of her short skirt, pushing it over her hips. The black skirt was amazingly daring, the thong beneath it so brief that she had nearly not worn it.

But this was Cam. There was no shame with Cam.

She writhed beneath his mouth, his tongue flickering over her nipple, flaying it with heat as she kicked the skirt from her ankles and his large hand pressed between her thighs.

His fingers pushed under her panties, found her slick and wet, as a cry ripped past her lips and her fingers tightened in his hair.

The tip of one finger rubbed at the entrance to her body, drawing more of the silky wetness from her. Jaci felt as though she were burning from the inside out, lost in a vortex and fighting to find her way.

"Hold on to me, baby," he whispered, as though he knew, understood. "Just hold on to me. It's all okay."

But it wasn't okay. She had waited too long, needed too much.

Her hands tore at his shirt until he jerked it from his shoulders with one hand. The fingers of the other continued to stroke, to massage the swollen folds of her pussy.

Her hands pushed down on his chest as she fought to breathe, her fingers fumbling with his belt, then the zipper of his pants.

A minute later, the hard, impressive length of his erection was free.

He knelt beside the couch, his fingers doing erotic, wicked things between her thighs, and all she could do was stare at the hard, swollen head of his cock.

It was dark, throbbing, the heavily veined shaft twitching under her fingers as she curled them around it. Not that they could meet. There was a lot of flesh there.

"Jaci," he growled her name—a rough, thick sound—as she lifted her head and placed a kiss at his thigh.

"I've dreamed of this." And she had. Endless nights of dreams.

"All of it, Jaci?" he asked her then. "Everything?"

"Everything." She lifted her head and licked over the engorged cock head, the taste of stormy male and dark lust meeting her tongue as she moaned at the knowledge that he wanted her. Cam wanted her.

"Like this." His hand caught in her hair, held her head still, then his hips pressed the thick length closer. "Open your mouth, baby. Slow and easy. Take me there."

Slow and easy. She let her tongue flicker over the head, feeling his hands tighten in her hair as he filled her mouth with the hard flesh.

Jaci couldn't help but cry out. She stared up at him, her lashes heavy, heat consuming her as she began to draw on the sensitive crest, sucking and licking it. Reliving all the fantasies she had ever wove in her head when it came to Cam.

As she drew on him she felt her thong slide down her legs. Felt his hand part her thighs. His tongue lapped at the moist flesh of her pussy, sliding through the narrow slit, circling her clit.

She stared up at Cam. He had one hand buried in her hair, the other circling her hand, guiding his cock in and out of her mouth.

And between her thighs . . .

A whimper left her, as knowledge slowly penetrated her as surely as that tongue penetrated her vagina, and calloused male hands spread her thighs wider.

She tried to jerk back, but his fingers tightened.

She cried out, staring up at Cam in shock as his eyes opened, the pupils suddenly flaring as something akin to agony twisted his features.

His cock slid from her lips and her head jerked, staring down to watch his twin, Chase, lift his head from between her thighs.

His lips glistened with her juices. His eyes, so like Cam's, his features identical, suddenly tightened with shock and knowledge.

"Cam?" His voice was hard, powerful. "She knew this was coming. Right?"

Jaci shook her head, shuddering, torn between begging them to stop and begging them to finish. A roller coaster of sensation was tearing through her. Her senses were alive with too many impulses, too much pleasure, and too much awareness.

It wasn't just Cam.

Everything. He wanted everything. And then she remembered. Like a splash of cold water, she knew that the rumors of the two brothers sharing their lovers wasn't just rumor. It was truth.

"This is everything," Cam whispered, touching her cheek, drawing her gaze back to him, his eyes tormented, somber. "I thought you knew, Jaci. I thought you were warned what everything meant."

Watch Cam. Everything means giving it to him and Chase. The warning, given by a friend that she had ignored. That Jaci had denied. Petty gossip, she had told herself. Jealousy. But it was truth.

"Damn it, Cam!" Chase was on his feet, jerking his shirt off and pushing it into his brother's hands.

Shaking his head, Cam slowly eased her arms into the shirt as she stared back at him, trying to make sense of what she wanted, what they wanted.

As he drew the edges of the shirt together she whispered miserably, "I'm a virgin, Cam."

She had saved herself for him. For as long as she had remembered, she had known there was no one else for her but Cameron Falladay.

He froze as his eyes widened, his fingers at the buttons of the shirt.

"What did you say?"

"I'm a virgin."

As Chase stomped from the room Cam breathed out with a ragged breath.

"I'm taking you home now, Jaci."

"I waited for you," she whispered. "Just for you."

He cupped her face in his hands then and stared back at her, pain and shadows swirling in his eyes.

"I'm taking you home. Stay away from those parties, because I won't be there again, and no one else will bother to try to protect you, sweetheart. They'll hurt you. And as God is my witness, I'll kill the man who dares to hurt you."

She shook her head, confused, aching, uncertain what she had just allowed to slip through her fingers.

"Wait." She gripped his wrist as he pushed his erection inside his pants and pulled the zipper up. "Cam, tell me why. Why this?"

She was going to cry. She didn't want to cry. She wanted Cam, she wanted the heat, the wicked intensity, and a part of her wanted what she knew everything was now. That part of her terrified her.

"I thought you knew," he said again, his voice soft, filled with regret. "God, Jaci, I thought you knew what I wanted. Come on." He slid her skirt over her legs then pulled her to her feet and replaced it around her hips as he knelt in front of her.

"Cam?"

He was too silent, an air of grief surrounding him as he slowly laid his cheek against her stomach. And Jaci felt the first tear fall. She didn't know what she had lost tonight, and she was suddenly terrified to ask, to let herself wonder.

"Go home, Jaci. For both our sakes, for my sanity, go home."

CHAPTER ONE

Sometimes life just came full circle, whether a woman wanted it to or not. It was inevitable. And life had definitely come full circle for Jaci Wright.

The party was different. The stilted, gossipy political crowd was nothing like the raucous booze-laden crowd that had inhabited the last party where one of the Falladay twins had waylaid her.

She wasn't a woman-child now. She was a mature woman with more hang-ups than a closet and just as many reasons for running as hard and as fast from them now as she'd had seven years ago.

But this time, she knew she wouldn't run.

"It's definitely a party your mother would approve of." Chase Falladay stepped up to her. She had always been able to tell the Falladay brothers apart. Chase was dressed in an evening suit, his thick black hair brushed back from his strong features, his light green eyes watching her with a hint of laughter as a smile tugged at his sensual, sexy lips.

Sun-darkened flesh was stretched tighter over his face, it seemed, than it had been seven years ago. There were laugh lines at the corners of his eyes, but those eyes—such a light green they were mesmerizing—seemed more shadowed now. Haunted. And he still looked much too much like Cameron—the one man that haunted her dreams and her thoughts, even when he shouldn't have.

"Yes, Mom would approve of this party," she murmured, staring around for a second before her gaze was drawn back to him.

He was just as handsome as he ever had been. Just as bold as Cam and just as much out of her league. As she stared at him, she felt the past wash over her. The face that stared at her was the right one, but the man wasn't.

"Fancy meeting you here." She let a smile curve at her lips before raising her champagne glass and sipping at the sparkling liquid. She should have felt uncomfortable, hesitant, but she didn't. She was more intrigued than she should be.

"Hmm. Providence perhaps?" He lifted a dark brow and leaned against the wall beside her, one hand pushing into the pockets of his dress slacks while the other held his champagne glass negligently. "Should I rescue you from this one, as Cam did the last one?"

The mention of that last party, the cool autumn night, the hot male body, and everything she had walked away from when she walked away from him and Cam, flashed through her. Heat whispered over her skin but it wasn't embarassment.

"Courtney might kill us both," she whispered as though they dare not let their hostess hear those words. "I had to promise her I'd mingle, under the threat of dire consequences."

Courtney was her dearest friend. She, along with Sebastian De Lorents, had saved Jaci's life on a dark street in England, years before, when a mugger decided to get ugly.

Courtney and Sebastian were both here now, in Squire Point, Virginia. Courtney had married an American businessman, and Sebastian was working for him. Just as Jaci would be doing soon.

"I'm sure Courtney would understand," he offered suggestively. "And if she doesn't, then I'll have Ian explain it to her. He seems to have some small measure of control over her."

There was a hint of laughter in his voice. Sexy, certain of himself. Confident.

"Chase Falladay." She shook her head, still bemused to be standing there, talking to him as though the years had never separated them. "What are you doing here?"

He leaned forward several inches. "You wouldn't believe me if I told you."

He was close now. So close that all it would take was the smallest movement from her to touch him.

She shook her head, forcing herself to smile as she stared out over the crowd once more.

Fate was definitely being fickle at the moment. Not only were her two biggest headaches at this party, but also the identical twin of her greatest torment. Now, how was that for her life? She dreamed of Cam, but here was Chase. And perhaps, as he suggested, it was providence—a sign, Fate laughing its silly ass off and showing Jaci how fickle its favor could be.

"I don't know," she finally answered as she turned back to him. "I've been known to be pretty gullible at times. Tell me your tale, and then I'll decide if I believe it."

She liked to believe she was much less gullible than she had once been. She had seen the world; at times, she had seen more of it than she wanted to. And she had learned lessons she never imagined she would be faced with.

His eyes gleamed with laughter. "I wouldn't want to make you blush. I hear it's impolite."

Sexy, charming. He was devilishly amusing, and the laughter was just as hard to contain as it had been seven years ago.

Chase had always been the joker, Cam the more serious

one. Cam's dark wit and almost dangerous sexuality had drawn women to him like flies to honey, just as it had drawn Jaci.

"As though that would stop you." She had to force back the laughter, but it was hard. Chase had always had a way of making her laugh. "You delighted in it once. You made everyone laugh, while Cam made certain he made everyone angry." She looked around again, her heart thumping hard in anticipation. "Where is Cam?"

Shockingly, she felt the remembered heat of that night so long ago. Cam's kiss stealing her mind, and then later, his voice breaking her heart with the knowledge that he wouldn't be her lover alone.

For so many years she had wondered if she had made a mistake in running from him that night. If she had stayed, so many things would have changed. And perhaps she wouldn't have spent seven years wondering.

"Cam's around." His voice softened, the dark cadence gentling as she turned back to him. "He'll enjoy seeing you again. It's been a long time."

It had been. It had been too long. And yet, not long enough. Because she still felt that warmth low in her stomach as it threatened to turn into a burn. A reaction only Cam, or the thought of Cam, could cause to build inside her.

And regret. There was always regret.

Bolder than brass, strong, muscled, larger than life. That was what Cam had always been to her. Until the night she realized exactly how bold he could be.

Chase had been her friend, though. Even later, during her odd visits home, he had been there. Flirtatious, yet knowing. He had teased her and laughed at her when they met up; but that spark, that hidden flame had never been the same with Chase.

"It has been a long time," she nodded.

She felt uncertain now. She could feel the nervous tension rising inside her.

Cam was here, and so was Chase. And so much had changed, and yet so much hadn't. But she remembered Cam's warning clearly. He would kill over her. He wasn't a man that made false declarations. And he never forgot a promise. That was a dangerous thing for a woman who knew her past was about to catch up with her.

Now she was going to have to find a way to hold her own fantasies, as well as the men, at arm's length, because the promise Cam made her still had the power to terrify her. God help her, the Robertses, and Cam, if he ever learned what truly happened that night. Blood would spill, and the mere thought of that gave her nightmares. He had sworn he would kill any man that hurt her, and he kept his promises.

It had kept her from contacting Cam, from running to him, for years. The knowledge that she knew he would kill because of her, the look in his eyes that night, the primal intensity, the dark power, assured her he wasn't joking.

She had known him and Chase for too many years even before that night. She knew they were both men that other men knew to be wary of.

She swallowed nervously and felt the flutter of panic in her stomach as her gaze moved around the room. She hid in the shadows of the room throughout the evening, hoping to avoid the Robertses. Now she knew she was going to have to get the hell out of there.

"I can't believe you're this nervous around me, Jaci." Chase's head tilted a fraction as he stared back at her knowingly.

"Who says I'm nervous?" She was. She accepted it. But not because of the past.

Those sexy lips quirked again. "Courtney has an exceptional garden outside." He extended his hand toward the doors that opened out between the two sprawling wings of the house. "Would you like to walk out with me?"

"Courtney will miss me." She gave him a polite smile as she tried to plan the best route out of the ballroom to where she could call a cab and return to her hotel. "She threatened me, Chase. I'm to mingle."

"She'll survive, and so will you."

She inhaled roughly as he caught her free hand and tugged her from the side of the ballroom toward those open doors.

Ian Sinclair and his wife, Courtney, had an exceptional home. The main mansion, built over a hundred years ago, was huge. Later additions included the two wings that sloped back to each side of the main house, creating a hidden, private garden inside.

Dusk was falling as Chase drew her outside, where the music was more muted, more romantic. The haunting strains of the piano whispered through the air as Chase drew her farther into the shadowed, dimly lit garden.

She hadn't expected to see him here. She knew he and Cameron lived in Alexandria, of which Squire Point was a suburb, but she hadn't thought she would see him here, at the Sinclairs'.

She had thought she could take this job, do the work it entailed, and maybe, before she left, she would give an old friend a call.

Her lips quirked at the thought. She was lying to herself then and she was lying to herself now. She was dying to see Cam again. Dying for one more chance to taste his kiss, to feel his touch. To see if anything had changed, if he had grown possessive, if perhaps he had grown out of that need to share with his twin. And if he hadn't, she wondered if perhaps she had grown out of her fear of it. Because the fantasies that had haunted her over the years had nearly driven her insane. Dark dreams and wicked desires had been instilled in her that night. Escaping them wasn't an option.

Knowing she was going to have to avoid the Falladay twins until the job was over, and that the Robertses would surely interfere in any relationship she developed, was quickly changing her plans. If Cam and Chase were close friends with the Sinclairs, then the potential for disaster had just grown exponentially.

She would kill Courtney for not warning her they would be so close.

As they moved onto the wide, flagstone path that weaved and branched off into hidden grottos, Chase drew her alongside him, his hand settling against the small of her back as they walked deeper into the shadows.

The other guests hadn't wandered this far yet. There was a faint tinkle of a fountain nearby. Night birds sang their songs and crickets chirped happily. If she closed her eyes she could almost feel that hot summer night seven years earlier, and she could almost pretend Chase was Cam.

"Are you bringing me out to the gardens in an attempt to seduce me, Chase?" she drawled with a smile, the seriousness of her question hidden beneath the subtle laughter in her tone.

She had forgotten how much fun it could be to flirt with and tease Chase, what it felt like to be with a man that a part of her instinctively trusted, rather than distrusted.

She had learned over the years not to trust anyone, especially good-looking men. And that, she often thought, was an incredible shame. A woman her age should have had more adventures than she'd had so far.

His chuckle stroked her senses.

"I want to catch up with an old friend, nothing more," he promised her. "Damn, Jaci, when did you become so suspicious?"

"When it comes to you and your brother? Seven years

ago." She glanced up at him, amused at the accusation. "You're not old enough to have forgotten, surely?"

She hadn't forgotten a moment of it, and she knew Chase—he would never let her hide from it if he thought for a minute that she was trying to. Better to get it out in the open now. And she couldn't resist it anyway. Seeing him, knowing Cam was close, the needs were rising inside her with all the dark promise of the dreams that had haunted her.

"Now you're just being mean." He gave her a mock glare before pulling her to a vine-covered swing that sat beneath a wide arbor. "Here we go. We can just sit here and visit."

Jaci sat down, carefully smoothing the material of her black evening gown down her thighs as Chase sat down beside her.

The gown, which had felt so alluring when she put it on, now seemed too sexy, too revealing. It made her feel too feminine. The thin straps held the draped bodice over her breasts. Maybe she should have worn a bra. The side slit ran to her thigh. It showed an indecent amount of leg.

Chase chuckled again.

She lifted her gaze and felt the grin that tugged at her lips, as he watched her knowingly.

"You and Cam always made me too nervous," she admitted with a soft laugh. "Sometimes I've missed that."

She had missed the twins after she left town within weeks of the night of the party. She had snapped up an offer to attend a design school in California and headed out as fast as she could. And every day she planned the trip, she'd had to fight herself to keep from going to Cam, to keep from accepting an offer she knew she couldn't handle. Just to be in his arms. To feel his kiss again. To see what she was missing.

"We've missed you." His arm stretched behind her, his

fingers playing with the strands of hair that escaped the decorative clip that held it in the back.

We've missed you. Not *I.* Jaci caught that one quickly.

She ducked her head, hoping to hide her response to that statement as she inhaled with a slow, deep breath.

"You ran out on us, Jaci."

Jaci swallowed tightly, her head jerking up as his tone hardened.

"There was nothing to run out on." She kept her voice firm, steady.

The shadowed landscape lighting gave his expression a darker, more dangerous cast. His eyes gleamed in the low light, piercing into hers.

His fingers paused at the nape of her neck where they had been playing with the hair that drifted down from the clip. His expression became intent, determined.

He nodded slowly. "I guess you're right. There was nothing to run out on." His lips quirked humorlessly. "We still missed you like hell, though. Life wasn't the same without your laughter."

It hadn't been the same without them, either. She had been their friend, when other women were no more than novelties—she knew that. Until one night destroyed that friendship. She had never looked at Chase the same after that, and she had never seen Cam again.

The thought of Cam had her insides burning, rioting with fear and with need. She kept checking the shadows for him, kept expecting him to step into view. And the hunger to see him was growing within her in burning waves.

"I need to get back inside." She rose to her feet, her fingers tightening on the small purse that hung from her shoulder. "It's almost the witching hour for me. I have to get up early in the morning."

She needed to get away from him, to think. It had been too damned long since she had seen Chase or Cam, too long since she had allowed herself to think about the Falladay twins, either separately or apart.

"Let me take you back to your hotel, or are you staying here?" He nodded to the mansion.

"I'm at a hotel. But I'll be fine."

"We could talk—just talk, Jaci, I promise." He smiled. The charm and sensuality that was so much a part of him wrapped around her, encouraged her to join in, to let herself be seduced.

"I don't know."

"Just the two of us."

He said it so easily, with just a hint of amusement, a promise of sensuality. There was a shade of mockery in his tone, an acknowledgement of her hesitancy and the reasons why.

Jaci looked around the thick foliage of the grotto, the scent of summer, of sultry heat wrapping around her, the scent of the man sinking into her. And she weakened. He wasn't Cam, but he knew her. He wouldn't betray her or deliberately hurt her. And she was tired—tired of being alone and wishing for things she couldn't have. Tired of dreaming of one man and regretting one night.

Finally, she nodded. A slow, hesitant movement, a part of her holding back, the other part reaching out for him.

His smile was slow, confident, and for a moment Jaci wondered if she had somehow just stepped into something she didn't have a chance of handling.

"You can't change your mind." He caught her hand and drew her back along the path.

Rather than heading back into the ballroom, he drew her instead to a glass door that opened into the private wing of the house.

"I need to let Courtney know I'm leaving," she said as they moved through the short hall and into the kitchen and formal dining room, before turning into the foyer.

"Matthew will let her know." He drew her to the front door where the butler stepped from the small room that connected to the private wing as well as the main mansion.

"Mr. Falladay. Miss Wright." Matthew nodded his head politely.

"Matthew, please let Mr. and Mrs. Sinclair know we've left. Tell Ian I'll contact him tomorrow about those files."

"Of course, Mr. Falladay," Matthew acknowledged impassively. "I'll inform them immediately."

He stepped forward and opened the door for them, his brown eyes flickering with curiosity as they passed him.

Matthew was the scourge of Courtney's life, and the bastion of the male-only club Ian Sinclair owned—the one Courtney wasn't allowed in. The one Jaci had been hired to redesign, along with the private wing and main mansion. The Sinclair home was being turned over to the club itself, while Ian and Courtney would be moving into the new home they were building out of sight of the club, on the other side of the estate.

"Courtney's going to skin us both," she warned him as she lifted her dress and moved down the stone steps to the driveway beyond.

"I promise to protect you." He flashed a smile over his shoulder, his gaze wicked.

"Who will protect you, though?" She laughed, allowing him to pull her to the curb of the circular driveway as a vehicle's lights moved around the drive.

"Quick service," she murmured, as the Jaguar pulled to a stop in front of them and the valet driver jumped from the car.

"Matthew's a very efficient man."

He opened the door and helped her into the passenger seat before moving around the front of the car.

Jaci watched him move. He didn't hurry. He strode with determined steps, with powerful coordination. A wolf in elegant sheep's wool, she thought with a smile. And he did look elegant.

A second later he was moving into the driver's seat, pulling the door closed, and accelerating away from the brightly lit mansion.

"Where was Cam tonight?" She turned to stare at his profile, unable to forget that Cam was back at that party. She could have seen him. At least from a distance. Perhaps spoken to him.

He turned and flashed her a quick look. "He was looking for Ian when I caught sight of you. By now, they're likely deeply involved in a business discussion."

Had they changed that much over the past seven years? Despite Chase's words, perhaps Cam had forgotten about the immature little virgin who had dared to tease him, then ran away from the truth she didn't want to face.

"He didn't even want to stop and say hello to me?" She didn't want to admit that it hurt, that he had known she was there and hadn't stopped to speak.

"I slipped away with you." There was no smile this time.

His jaw seemed to tighten, a fine sense of tension invading the interior of the car.

Jaci turned her head and stared through the windshield again. There were so many questions raging inside her, so many emotions.

She felt off balance, meeting Chase like this, unprepared for it, not expecting him.

"Courtney's been excited over the design project Ian approved," he spoke into the silence. "I bet it took her two months to talk him into those plans. He wanted to give the mansion over to the club, but I don't think he was certain about allowing a woman to do the designing."

She smiled at that. Ian had questioned her extensively, on not just her credentials, which she knew he had checked out, but also her ideas about a male-dominant domain.

"So you and Cam knew I was arriving?" She turned back to him as that thought hit her.

"We did the investigative check on you before Courtney was given the go-ahead to contact you."

Jaci's lips parted in surprise before she tightened them with irritation. "I'm surprised Ian approved me, then." And now she wasn't surprised Cam hadn't wanted to see her.

Chase was quiet for long moments after that. "If Cam and I hadn't known you, he probably wouldn't have," he revealed. "We were the deciding factor."

She turned from him then, anger stealing past the shield she had learned to keep between herself and the world.

One accidental misstep, one job she never should have taken, and it had nearly destroyed her career. The repercussions were like echoes, they never went away, even five years later.

"Do you want to tell me what happened between you and Congressman Roberts?" he asked, his tone harder now, slipping from curiosity to demand.

She hated being ambushed, and suddenly that was how she felt.

"No, I don't. And if this is why you insisted on returning me to my hotel, then you should have stayed where you were. Perhaps you should have allowed Ian Sinclair to make up his own mind about me while you were at it. I don't need your help."

"You're just as damned stubborn as you ever were," he growled. "It was a logical question, Jaci. Something happened, or they wouldn't have targeted you so heavily."

"So tell me, Mr. Investigator," she snapped, "what answers did you come up with? Why don't *you* tell *me* what happened with Congressman Roberts?"

She knew what rumors the Robertses had spread.

"Wait." She held up her hand before he could speak. "On second thought, let me guess. I was caught attempting to steal a large amount of cash that Congressman Roberts kept in the desk in his private office. When they caught me, out of the kindness of their hearts, they just fired me from the job they hired me for and sent me on my way, rather than calling the police. Did I get it right?"

He shot her a short glance. "There were rumors of an affair with the congressman, as well," he stated.

Oh yeah, she hadn't forgotten about that one.

Jaci propped her elbow on the door ledge, pressed her fingers to the bridge of her nose and breathed in deeply. For five years she had been dealing with this.

It had taken her years to save up the money to finance her dream of settling in one city and opening her own design shop, all because of one malicious, corrupt couple that didn't know how to keep their dirty laundry hidden.

"So, why did you vouch for me? So you could interrogate me?" She turned to him with a glare.

"You're no thief."

"But I could very well be a home-wrecking little tramp out to snag a congressman?" she sneered.

"Or Annalee Roberts could be staying true to form, and attempting to destroy someone who has managed to get in her way, or who knows something she's terrified of others knowing," he suggested. "What happened, Jaci?"

"I breathed," she gritted out as he pulled beneath the entrance to the hotel Ian Sinclair had placed her in. "And now I'm going to my room, alone. Thank you for the ride."

The door opened smoothly, the doorman extending his hand to her as she stepped from the vehicle and headed for the entrance.

She was furious and she knew she had no right to be. She had known in coming here that this would come up, that there was no escaping the past, once she stepped into the Robertses' territory.

Congressman Roberts was rumored to be making a bid to replace his father-in-law in the Senate. He had a lot to lose, and as far as she knew, only one person knew their dirty little secrets. Secrets she wished she didn't know.

"Dammit, Jaci. Hold up." Chase caught up with her in the lobby, his fingers wrapping around her arm, pulling her to a stop as she headed for the elevators. "Talk to me."

"I'm done talking to you," she bit out. "You're as over-bearing as Cam ever was, and I'm not in the mood to deal with it. Go back home, Chase. Find a nice little woman who can put up with you and your brother, and leave me the hell alone."

"Dammit, you don't want Cam asking these questions," he warned her, his voice dark. "And he will ask them, Jaci. He's not the man you left behind in Oklahoma. And trust me, he hasn't forgotten that promise he made to you the night he took you home. Do you remember it?"

His voice roughened, as Jaci became aware of the odd looks they were getting from the hotel staff and the guests that loitered in the lobby.

"I don't know . . ."

"He said he would kill any man who dared to hurt you." His voice was soft, warning. "Did you think he was joking? Do you think for a moment he forgot that promise? Tell me, Jaci, do you want to be the cause of Congressman Roberts's death?"

CHAPTER TWO

Cameron Falladay stood on the stone patio outside the ballroom, his body braced against the brick wall, a drink in hand, head lowered. His head filled with a woman's face and the memory of a kiss that had burned through his soul.

Her. Jaci.

He ground his teeth together and fought against the need to leave the party, to race to her hotel room before Chase could touch her, before his brother could take the woman who had tormented Cam for so long.

He wanted to sink inside her with a hunger that had tightened his muscles to the point that they ached. His cock was iron hard, throbbing brutally with that need.

What had possessed him to refuse to go to her? He had known if he didn't, Chase would, and at that time, that seemed the better solution. It had been seven long years since he had touched the woman that tormented damned near every dream he'd had since she left the small Oklahoma town they lived in.

The first punch of clawing need that had struck him the second he'd seen her tonight had almost stolen his breath. He had stood there, staring at her, the way that dress draped down, baring her back, swishing sexily above her rounded ass.

It was enough to make a grown man go to his knees and worship that rounded flesh and everything above and below it.

Instead of going to her, he had left Chase to go after her instead, because he didn't trust his control. He didn't trust his ability not to demand things he knew she couldn't give.

But letting her go, risking his brother, even the brother he shared his women with, touching her, was fraying his control.

No one had ever tempted his control as Jaci did. Even seven years ago, a tender twenty-one-year-old virgin with stars in her eyes, she had tempted it. She made him want to forget the rules that had defined his life. Made him wish he was someone or something other than who he was.

"Hey, Cam, where's that brother of yours?" The false joviality in Congressman Roberts's voice had Cam tensing, his head lifting as he stared back at the smaller man with barely restrained violence in his heart.

Where he stood was shadowed, darker than the area around it, hiding the anger he had promised himself and Ian he would keep carefully restrained.

But it wasn't easy. Roberts was a maggot, and he was the maggot that had tormented Jaci for five years.

The investigative report they had pulled together on her over the past months had enraged him and Chase. Chase was more subtle; Roberts's financials would be an open book to them eventually—to them, as well as to the Feds. Cam wasn't much into subtlety, though. He wanted to ram his fist into the bastard's face.

"Congressman," he drawled softly, "I'm sure Chase is around somewhere."

Dark brown hair was layered to frame the congressman's face and lend it an "honest" appearance. The false sincerity in his brown gaze had always sickened Cam, but now it made him almost violent.

"I saw him with Ms. Wright earlier." Those eyes flickered with concern. "I was hoping to catch him before he left with her."

"Did he leave with her?" Cam drawled, his hand tightening on his drink glass as he thought of all the reasons why it was a very bad idea to rearrange this man's face.

"I hope not." Roberts sighed. "Ms. Wright is a perfectly acceptable interior designer, but a man in Chase's position should be careful of his reputation."

"And she can harm that how?" If he killed Roberts, he could hide the body really well. The Special Forces had taught him how. But he'd never be able to hide the fact that he'd done it from Chase. And Chase would just give him hell over it.

"Certain women always manage to do so," the congressman sighed. "Ah well, I'm certain he's well aware of her past. Being an investigator comes in handy," he joked, his laughter as false as the concern had been.

"It does indeed."

Roberts cleared his throat. "It's regrettable that Ms. Wright sometimes allows herself to forget her place. Some women"— he shrugged philosophically, with no idea how close to death he was stepping—"some women aren't always willing to work properly for what they want."

Cam felt his hand curl into a fist.

"How *did* she work for what she wanted, then?"

If the bastard said the words, he was dead. As cold and dead as any enemy Cam had taken out in the military. All he had to do was say the words, and Cam promised himself, the bastard's death would be brutal. Bloody.

Roberts shook his head and sighed almost pityingly. Almost.

"I'm not a man to tell tales," he finally said. "Just tell Chase to be careful. I'd hate to see a friend hurt."

Richard Roberts turned on his heel and shoved his

hands in the pockets of his slacks and moved away, his head down, as though he felt sorry for Chase.

The lying, corrupt son of a bitch. That bastard and his wife had made Jaci's life a living hell for five years, and not even once, not once, had she asked anyone for help. Not once had she complained or attempted to defend herself. She had held her silence and tried to deflect their viciousness as much as possible.

Alone.

He pushed the fingers of one hand through his hair and blew out a hard, control-fortifying breath. He was not going to follow Congressman Roberts and beat his brains into a bloody pulp. Cam would not tell that viperous woman Roberts had married what a lousy excuse for a human she was.

And he would not, by God, destroy the hard work Jaci had put into keeping her reputation intact. But she would belong to him. To him, as well as to Chase. She had run for seven years, and now, by God, the running was over.

He had no idea what had actually happened between the congressman, his wife, and Jaci. Even Courtney Sinclair, Jaci's friend, had no clue what had caused the Robertses to target her. Jaci simply hadn't talked. The Robertses had, though.

He remembered that about her. Jaci wasn't into gossip or telling tales. Tell her something, it stayed with her. And she never had been the sort of female to run to others for protection. Whatever the Robertses had done to her, it had caused her to retreat inside herself, to restrain the fiery nature that he had always been drawn to.

He glanced toward the doorway Roberts had used to reenter the house. It was one of the side doors. The congressman was known for retreating to Ian's private study and his better booze, rather than joining the Sinclair parties for long.

Ian allowed it, though Cam knew he didn't particularly like it.

Cam thought of all the ways he could hurt the other man without leaving a mark. How easily he could warn him that Jaci was off-limits. That her name would never pass his lips again.

He took a step toward the doorway, when Ian Sinclair stepped out on the patio. The other man watched him suspiciously, his dark green eyes glowed with knowledge as he slid a cigar from inside his jacket and smiled back at Cam.

"These parties suck," Ian said as Cam retreated, leaned against the wall once again, and cocked his brow mockingly.

"I wouldn't have hurt him too bad," he murmured with a tight smile.

Ian snorted at that before extending an extra cigar toward Cam. Cam took it as Ian lit up his own. Seconds later, the sweet scent of imported tobacco filled the air, and Ian leaned against the stone balustrade of the patio.

"A woman can mess up a man's mind sometimes, Cam." He sighed. "Make him rethink things."

"Don't start on me, Ian."

Ian had been full of wise little comments since he learned Cam had a weakness, and that weakness was a woman. For some reason, the other man had seemed surprised that Cam could care either way.

"Ms. Wright left the party with Chase awhile ago," Ian stated. "Did you know about that?"

"I knew." Cam shrugged. Chase knew the limits, he had always known them, where Jaci was concerned.

Ian watched him for another long moment before staring out at the garden. "Sometimes a man can accept the need to share his woman's pleasure. Sharing her heart is another thing. They can be separate."

"Let's cut the shit," he told his employer coolly. "I don't tell you how to conduct your marriage, or your business. Refrain from giving me advice here, if you don't mind."

He didn't need it. Jaci belonged to him and Chase would know it. But his fist curled at his side and the need to leave the party, to rush to her hotel, was nearly eating him alive.

"Agreed." Ian sighed. "But stay away from Roberts, Cam, until you have proof of whatever you think he may have done. I can handle violence if there's reason for it. Otherwise, stay back."

"I'm well back," Cam mocked.

Cam didn't need proof, no more than he needed proof of Jaci's innocence or her guilt. He understood the world. Sometimes a woman stepped into things she shouldn't— that was always possible. But Roberts had threatened her, and that wasn't acceptable.

He stared into the night once again, a frown brewing at his eyes. The investigation they had done on her had been too damned sketchy for seven years of a woman's life.

There were rumors, here and there, of lovers, but none of those rumors had panned out. For seven years, Jaci had worked her ass off at her career, but she hadn't put much into making friends or developing relationships.

Whatever had happened with Roberts had happened five years ago. After that, even less effort had gone into filling her life with anything other than work.

She didn't party, except for business occasions. She was known for her restraint and cool purpose, her stubbornness and determination. She was outspoken in her design work, but rarely discussed personal issues with her clients. She had only a few friends, and pulling information from two of them had been like pulling teeth.

Courtney Sinclair and the manager of Ian's men's club, Sebastian De Lorents, had been less than forthcoming about anything they might know about her. Such loyalty wasn't common, especially within the society they moved in.

"What are you going to do?" Ian finally asked.

"About what?" Cam turned back to him.

Ian shook his head. "If she's going to design the club, then she's going to have to understand the rules she's working under. I expect you to take care of that."

"It's your club," Cam growled.

"And your woman. See it's done before she leaves tomorrow. Then we'll decide if this job is truly hers or not. I'd rather lose the deposit I paid her than the reputation my wife is building in this community, Cam. You understand the rules and you know the woman. Take care of it. And make damned sure you and Chase know this woman you vouched so strongly for. I'd hate for either of you to be wrong."

Jaci allowed the hotel room door to close heavily behind her before tossing her evening bag to the couch in the sitting room and reaching back to tear the silver clip from the back of her hair.

As the long, thick strands fell down her back, a surge of anger tore through her. A second later the hair clip was arching through the air to smack into the thick curtains covering the balcony doors.

"Damn him!" The vicious snarl that left her lips surprised her, as did the tears that she was forced to blink back.

He couldn't even say hello. Couldn't tear himself from his "business" discussion to even let her know he was there. No, he had sent Chase instead.

Cam couldn't have meant the threat he had made so long ago. She drew in a hard, controlling breath. It was seven years ago, and when it came to women they wanted sexually, men could say a lot of things. She knew that. And

Chase's warning had been just that. The warning of a man who wanted her sexually, and who wanted answers to his questions, nothing more.

But he had acted as though he believed in her, a little voice inside her head whispered. He had asked her what Richard and Annalee had done to her, not what had she done. No one else had ever asked that.

She shook her head, kicking off the high heels and reaching behind her to release the zipper at the back of her evening gown as she moved into the bedroom.

She pulled the straps over her shoulders and let the silk slither down her body, leaving her clad in nothing but her thong and the thigh-high, black silk stockings.

Laying the dress over a chair, she grabbed her robe and wrapped it around her.

She didn't need this headache. It was going to be all she could manage to keep her wits about her and keep the congressman and his wife from attacking her openly.

They were terrified of her. Even five years later, they were so frightened of the truth that it rolled off them in sickening waves every time they saw her. It would have been amusing if it didn't continually destroy parts of her life along with it.

She stared around the hotel suite.

She was alone. She shouldn't have been. Over the past few years, the ache inside her had grown to such proportions that it was nearly physical. She ached to be touched, to close her eyes as a lover touched her, even if she had to pretend it was Cameron Falladay.

It should have been so easy to accept the invitation in Chase's eyes tonight. He could have come up here—she could have touched him, been touched, and pretended it was Cam.

She shook her head. She was losing her sanity, evidently. Chase would have never allowed her to get away with it, and she knew it. Just as she had known it before she left town seven years ago.

She pushed her fingers through her hair again, then let her hand trail down her neck, almost shivering at the memory of Cam's fingers there.

Other men had touched her over the years. Superficially. They had kissed her, held her; but that ache that gnawed at her insides had never gone away. No more than the distrust had.

She was willing to lay her life savings on the fact that she was quite possibly the only twenty-eight-year-old virgin in existence, in the nation.

She stopped at the full-length mirror in the corner of the room and stared at herself. Her nose was straight, eyebrows arched. Her eyes faintly tilted, her lips just a little bit too lush. Her breasts weren't small, but they weren't overly large. They fit her body. She was slender; she stayed in shape. Her shoulder-length auburn hair was a nice contrast to her brown-and-blue-flecked green eyes.

She wasn't ugly. She didn't consider herself beautiful, rather average. There was no reason for her to be spending her life alone.

Other than her own fears. And the simple fact that she was still, even now, waiting on Cam.

CHAPTER THREE

Chase was waiting in the lobby of the hotel when Cam strode through the entrance. The black suit his brother wore did nothing to alleviate the aura of power and danger that surrounded him. The wicked scar that slashed down the left side of his cheek definitely helped the impression, but it was the icy green eyes, the unsmiling lips, the expression that seemed carved from experiences that suggested hell, made him appear even more dangerous, that did it.

Cam was his brother, his twin. And sometimes Chase wondered if he even knew who or what his brother was. He definitely didn't know what had created the dark visage that strode toward him.

"She's not going to appreciate a late-night visit," he told his brother as they headed toward the elevator.

"Too bad," Cam growled. "Roberts waylaid me at the party. The slick bastard. He should be in film rather than congress. His acting ability beats the shit out of his ability to help run this fucking country."

Chase winced. Cam was cussing. That was never a good thing.

"Blindsiding Jaci like this isn't going to help," he advised him as the elevator doors slid closed behind them. "She is a little demon when that temper of hers is roused, you know that as well as I do."

And she was liquid fire when other parts of her were aroused. Chase could still taste the sweet syrup that had flowed from her body, even seven years later. And he knew Cam had never forgotten.

"I want eyes on her twenty-four seven," Cam ordered. "If Roberts even thinks about contacting her, I want to know about it."

"Cam, you can't control her life here." The elevator doors slid open.

As they stepped out, his brother turned to him. The green ice in his gaze flickered with a hidden flame. The intensity of the color was no longer flat with whatever emotions or memories he fought. The color was wild, vivid, shocking Chase with the emotions that seemed to swirl just under the surface.

"I have no intention of controlling her life," Cam stated. "I'm going to *become* her life, Chase. There's a difference."

For a second, Chase stood in shock, staring at his brother's back as he strode quickly down the hall to the suite Ian had reserved for the interior designer.

Cameron had never claimed anything or anyone as his. Not since they had lost their parents, since their lives had gone to hell beneath the less-than-gentle care of their maternal aunt at the tender age of thirteen. But now, he was claiming Jaci?

Hearing him claim something, someone now, was enough to almost cause him to miss that twisted expression of need on Cam's face as he turned away.

Hell, Jaci didn't need to see Cam like this. Chase didn't need to see Cam like this. Brimming with fire and lust and a need Chase had never imagined filled his brother.

"Cam, dammit," he muttered, moving quickly behind him. "Do you think this is a wise move right now?"

Cam stopped in front of the hotel room door and glanced at his brother impatiently.

"What's so unwise about it?" He'd waited seven years for her to grow up, to find them, and now Chase wanted to wait?

"She's not exactly extending an invitation for us together," his brother snorted. "She actually stated we should find someone else to play our games with."

"You pissed her off." He lifted his hand to knock on the door.

"And you're not going to piss her off more?" Chase asked, his voice filled with a hint of disbelief that didn't make sense to Cam.

He turned back to his brother, glaring at him. "Look, I let you talk to her first, I let you bring her home, and look where it got us. You never did know how to handle her, and don't pretend you did. She walks all over you."

It was true. Chase had never been able to tell her no. Cam, on the other hand, could and would, if it meant protecting her.

"Yeah, but it feels damned good when Jaci walks on you, man." He grinned, amusement transforming his expression and filling his eyes with a joy that often made Cam look like more of an outsider than ever.

His brother had kept that sense of fun and prankish delights, while that sense had been carved out of Cam, stripped from him like flesh from the bone.

Cam ignored the protests and the laughter, turned back to the door, and rapped his knuckles against it imperiously.

Staying away from her at the party had been an act of superhuman effort. He still couldn't believe he'd managed it. That witch's black dress, slit to the thigh, the banked fire in her auburn hair, the searching expression on her elfin features as she stared around the room, as though looking for someone. He wanted to think she was looking for him, because he'd be damned if he had eyes for anyone but her.

A second later the door opened. His eyes met hers, and he knew in that moment that the past had dissolved between them—seven years never existed, and it was the night he had brought her home from that party. Her eyes staring at him in those final moments of knowledge, confusion, passion, and lust—and a young woman's fear.

There was no fear in her eyes now. There was excitement. He could see it in her. In the way she leaned against the door, stared at the two of them, and shook her head as though uncertain—now that the moment was here—what she was supposed to do.

Cam crossed his arms over his chest, aware of Chase rocking back on his heels beside him, a grin of deviltry on his face when Jaci glanced over at him.

"And to what do I owe the honor of this little visit?" Husky and sweet, her voice promised delights that tortured his most vivid fantasies, awake and sleeping.

She was dressed in nothing but a long, silky robe. He had to curl his fingers into a fist to keep from stripping it from her body and baring her to his gaze, right there in the open doorway.

"Do you really want to talk about it in the hallway?" he asked.

She looked from him to Chase again. Whatever Chase did, the damned maniac, had her lips twitching with amusement.

He turned in time to catch his brother ducking his head and rubbing his hand around the back of his neck. Chase didn't need to make her fucking laugh. All he had to do was his part. Be here, help Cam maintain his emotional distance while they drove her crazy with pleasure.

"Fine." She breathed out slowly before moving back and opening the door fully. "Come on in. I was just having a glass of wine and thinking about jerks. You'll fit right in, Cam."

Damn, she hadn't changed as much as he had feared she had.

They stepped into the roomy sitting room, as she strolled—glided—all those graceful moves women made when they walked across the floor. But she did it better than any other woman he had ever known.

"The suite's nice," Chase commented, clearing his throat as he glanced between Cam and Jaci. "You should know I picked it out."

She lifted her brows in mock surprise. "You have very good taste, Chase. I've always said that about you."

"Most women do." His cockiness was going to get on Cam's nerves any minute.

Cam threw his brother a hard, warning glare and only received a chuckle in return.

Jaci picked up her wine as she curled herself into the corner of the couch and stared back at them. She knew. He stared into her eyes, watched her gaze flicker, and he knew that she knew exactly why he was there.

It was eating him alive. For years, the memory of that one night had been like a slow, eating cancer, destroying his mind. He had fucked other women. He had taken them, he had danced with them, he had made small talk with them. But Jaci had always been there. Her laughter, her smile, the heat of her kiss, the shock in her eyes when she realized Chase was the man between her thighs, licking with greedy abandon as Cam filled her mouth with his cock.

That memory had the power to destroy his self-control at any given time.

"And what do you say about me?" Cam couldn't hold the question back. For a moment, just a moment, jealousy ate into him. He didn't need Chase flirting with her, showing her everything Cam wasn't.

She turned to him, and what flashed in her eyes stilled the jealousy, the brewing anger.

"That you're the jerk," she stated with mocking conviction.

And for the first time, Cam almost smiled. Because she didn't mean it. He could see the fine tremor in her hands as she brought the wineglass to her lips. The throb of her pulse beating out of control against her neck. And that flush. The light stroke of color on her face that indicated arousal, anticipation, curiosity.

"I've always said that about him, too," Chase assured her as he moved across the room to the bar and poured himself a whisky. "I knew you were a smart girl, Jaci."

Cam shrugged his jacket from his shoulders and tore at the tie around his throat. And her eyes never left him. Her fingers tightened around the wineglass and her tongue stroked over her lips nervously.

"What happened to seduction?" she finally asked, as she heard Chase's muttered curse from across the room.

"Did you know we were here in Alexandria?" Cam asked her then.

"I knew."

"Did you know we worked for Ian?"

She inhaled roughly. "Not until tonight."

"Do you have any idea how much I want you, Jaci?"

He was burning alive for her. His cock was so hard, he wondered if he would survive without fucking her this time—or if he could live through another night of jacking off and needing the touch of her body so much that the need was nearly violent.

"Like I said, what happened to seduction?"

"Was it something he was ever good at?" Chase asked

her then. "If I remember correctly, I'm the nice guy, he's the sidekick."

She glanced at Chase before bringing her gaze back to Cam slowly. "He was never the sidekick."

Satisfaction surged inside him. Everyone knew Chase was the one with the smooth lines and the charm. He convinced the women they needed both brothers at once, while Cam watched, waited, and added to their pleasure—then left them to Chase's smooth maneuvers, once the bed play was finished.

"So, you just show up at my hotel room and expect me to spread myself open to your combined lusts?" She arched her brow mockingly, but her eyes, green and brown with hints of blue, darkened at the thought.

"Chase seduces, if that's what you need first." He had to clench his teeth at the thought of waiting. He needed to be inside her. Now. Fuck charm and seduction.

"And what will you do while he seduces me?"

Her nipples were hard. They pressed against the silken material of the robe, tight and budded with arousal.

"I'll watch." His voice sounded harder, more guttural then he had ever heard it himself. "And go crazy for you. I'll remember the sight of the head of my cock buried between your sweet lips, and the pleasure on your face as my brother licked at the sweetest cream in the world. And go crazy, because right now, nothing in the world is as important as burying myself inside you."

Her face flushed brighter as he talked. The pulse at the side of her throat picked up its pace and her eyes grew wide, almost dazed, almost seduced.

"But it has to be both of you?"

It had to be. He couldn't accept it any other way. Any other woman, he'd be damned if it mattered; however he fucked her was fine. But with this woman? This woman had the power to destroy him, and he knew it. It had to be both of them, because it was the only way to claim her and still retain a hold on himself.

"Jaci." There was no way to explain, but so many ways he wished he could. "It will give you more pleasure than you can imagine. I swear that to you."

It wasn't enough. It wasn't enough for any woman, and he knew it. Chase had warned him for months that it wouldn't be enough for her now, any more than it would have been before.

"It's been seven years since I've seen you, Cam," she whispered then, rising to her feet as her expression suddenly turned somber. "We're not the same people we were then. You can't just expect me to jump into bed with you."

He had expected that. He had known she wasn't that easy, wasn't the sort of woman who just took sex in stride. But he wasn't just any other man, either. And seven years was seven years too long, with this need raging inside him.

"I let what belonged to me slip through my fingers then," he stated as he moved toward her, watching her stiffen, watching her eyes dilate and darken. "You were mine, Jaci. Look at you. You still want me, just as damned badly as I want you. And this time I won't let you slip away from me."

"Cam." Chase's voice was a distant protest.

"All you have to do is say no," he told her, his hands framing her face, feeling the heat and the silk of her flesh as he let his body brush against hers. "Just say no, and it stops."

Her lips parted and his covered them. He pretended she was parting them for his kiss, rather than to whisper that hated word, and for the moment, she went along with him.

Cam felt lust flay his balls as her lips parted. She trembled, and like the virgin she had been seven years before, stood in anticipation as he stared into her eyes and pressed her lips with the kiss.

He didn't devour her, though God knew he wanted to. He needed to. He let his tongue lick over her lips as his arms went around her, drawing her against him. Then he slanted his lips over hers and took what he needed.

Nothing had ever compared to Jaci's lips. She kissed like a wanton. Like she was addicted to his kiss, the stroke of his tongue. She took his tongue like a woman on the edge of coming. And he loved it.

Once she came alive beneath his lips, it was like tasting fire and rain. Her arms lifted to his shoulders, her little nails pressed into the fabric of his shirt, and she trembled in his arms.

She had trembled just like that the last time. Part fear and part excited arousal. Wicked intensity burned inside her as she rose against him, straining for more. Knowing he had more to give her.

And he had so much more. His hands moved down her back, gripped her sweet ass, and lifted her to the cradle of his thighs.

He'd be damned if he would give her a chance to say no. Already the sweet taste of her was penetrating his senses, firing through his nervous system. He was burning for her, awake now to every nuance of the moans leaving her lips. To the feel of the curve of her butt, the touch of her thigh against his.

And Chase moving in behind her.

He could feel his brother coming to her as he relished her taste, her touch.

And he could feel his brother's uncertainty. The twin bond they had once shared had been absent for over twenty years. And that was his fault. But he could still sense Chase's uncertainty, and at times his nightmares.

There were no nightmares now. He wasn't going to allow them for either of them.

Now, there was only pleasure.

"Don't say no." His lips lifted from hers, then he skimmed them over her jaw. Her head tilted back as he moved down her neck. "Just feel. We'll seduce you together. Seven years. Seven fucking years, Jaci, and I'm dying for you now."

It was a craving. An addiction. As though his mind and his body had finally recognized a missing component to his life. Jaci was missing. And he needed her now, ached with a junkie's desperation.

Behind her, Chase pressed closer, his hands sliding to the belt of the robe, undoing the loose knot and slipping it free.

"No means no," Chase whispered at her ear, and Cam hated him for encouraging her to even consider saying that hated word.

"What does no get me?" Her head tipped back until it rested on Chase's shoulder and Cam watched, his body strung tight, his cock throbbing in agony as the silk of the robe parted, revealing perfect breasts, sweet dark nipples, and lower, between slender luscious thighs, a neat little triangle of fiery curls.

Before his brother could convince her to say no, Cam was tasting her. He was licking her.

He was bending, spreading kisses along her torso, her little belly, going to his knees as one hand cupped her inner thigh and he lifted her leg to curl over his shoulder.

Cam's hands were shaking. Hell, his hands hadn't shook since he was fifteen years old. But they were shaking now, as he parted the dewy, syrup-laden folds hiding the sweetest flesh in the world.

"Cam." Her voice was uncertain, just a little dazed.

He glanced up from the sweet treasure to see her braced

against Chase's chest, his brother's hands cupping her breasts and his lips at her shoulder.

"It's so easy," he whispered. "To just feel the pleasure. That's all, Jaci. Let me love you. Let me love you the only way I can."

How much he revealed in those simple words. Jaci felt a sob lodge in her throat, felt the sudden aching need to know Cam, exactly how he was right now. To take what he wanted to give her.

"It's okay," Chase whispered in her ear, a soft caress of breath barely heard. "It's just Cam, Jaci. I promise you. It's just Cam loving you."

She trembled and closed her eyes, hearing in his voice something she needed to know. Her heart had always belonged to Cam, she couldn't share it. Couldn't imagine opening part of it for another man.

Then she couldn't imagine ever thinking a sane thought again. She flinched as sensation drove her breath from her lungs and pleasure began a lash of intensity that threatened to break her.

She felt Cam lick her. His tongue pressed into the narrow slit of her pussy, licked up and around her clit, and had her crying out with the tidal wave force of sensations tearing through her.

She remembered Chase licking her there. Remembered his tongue, gentle and savoring. Cam savored, but he took and gave with a force that left her shuddering. He devoured her like a man starving for the taste. And in turn, he drove hesitancy and doubt from her mind.

She had always wondered what she had walked away from. Now she was finding out. This. Cam's hungry mouth delving into her pussy, his body bending until he could work his tongue into the narrow opening of her pussy, driving into it in a hard, destructive thrust.

"Oh God!" Her hands were threaded in his hair, her

head pressing into Chase's shoulder as Chase's fingers pulled at her nipples. Blistering streaks of pleasure and gentle pain raced from the hard tips to her womb, mixing with the fiery fingers of white-hot sensation tearing from her vagina.

She lifted herself against them, her hips writhing against the hold Cam had on them, trying to work more of that stroking, heated flesh deeper inside her.

He was licking her inside.

He was licking her. And Chase—diabolical, wicked Chase—with slickened fingers was probing at her rear, one finger entering, penetrating her easily as she strained to come. He thrusted with such gentleness that the movements were nearly lost amid the violent pleasure of Cam's fucking tongue.

"I can't . . ." Her head thrashed on Chase's shoulder.

"So easy, sweetheart," Chase whispered, his voice rough and filled with hunger. "Just take the pleasure."

His finger slid free, pulled back, then slowly pressed in again. But this time, it was wilder, hotter. Not one finger but two, pressing inside her, easing into the untried channel as Cam licked and devoured.

She felt pleasure and streaks of pleasure-pain. She felt fiery fingers of sensation racing over her body, and lost her breath as Chase's fingers spread inside her slowly, easily.

"Cam. Oh God. It's too much." She was fighting to hold on to her sanity. Just a little sanity was all she was asking them to leave her. Just a tiny bit.

But it wasn't happening. His tongue pushed hard and deep, retreated then pushed forcefully inside her once again, and nearly had her orgasming as he licked. Chase's fingers slid free, pressed forward, the width thicker, her hold on him tighter; they worked inside her rear with the gentlest movements—experienced, knowing.

He knew how to do this. This wasn't a man just along

for the ride. He knew what the hell he was doing and
how to do it. How to counter each touch, each stroke
Cam gave, how to blend pleasure and pain until there
was no thought, not so much as one thought of hesitation
inside her.

"I have you. I'll hold you, Jaci." Chase bit at her shoulder, his voice thick now, the feel of his bared cock at her
lower back.

They were undressed? She blinked down at Cam to
see his shirt gone, his pants undone. One hand held her
hip, the other his cock. And it was too wicked. The sight
of it was too much to bear. In that moment, she admitted,
sanity was long long gone.

CHAPTER FOUR

She came on his tongue. Cam felt her pussy twitch, convulse, then sweeter than sweet, soft, heated cream slid over his tongue and gave him another addiction. Something else about her to crave. The taste of her release, like nectar, subtle and creamy, destroying his senses.

He'd be damned if he was going to come in his own hand this time. Nor was he going to take her standing up, as though this were all he needed from her. It wasn't. Not in any way.

He lifted her leg from his shoulder, aware of Chase slowly easing his fingers from that sweet ass.

She was weak between them, staring back at him with something resembling shock.

"Come here, baby." She was his.

He picked her up in his arms and moved to the open doorway of the bedroom.

The bed was pulled back, but Chase moved ahead of him, stripped the bed, and laid the tube of lubrication Cam had handed him earlier on the table by the bed.

Hell, yes, he had come prepared. He wanted all of her. Tonight, she would be taken in ways she couldn't have imagined.

Laying her on the bed, Cam came down over her, taking another of those hot, destructive kisses of hers. The feel of it sank into him. Her arms wrapping around his neck as he moved until they were lying on their sides, one leg lying atop his, opening her, revealing her to the man behind her.

He wanted this to be so easy for her. This first time, like this, with both of them. He wanted the full extent of pleasure for her.

Jaci felt them, almost as though Chase were an extension of Cam, moving around her. Cam's chest against her hand as he kissed her, his hair in her fingers as she fought for something to hold onto.

And behind her was Chase.

She whimpered against Cam's kiss as she felt hard, calloused hands part the cheeks of her rear and a second later, Chase's tongue.

He licked her from her pussy to her rear entrance. Flickered his tongue over the tightly clenched entrance there, then pressed against it.

Her leg was lifted against Cam's thigh, his cock pressed into her stomach as he held her to him.

She screamed into his kiss. She bit at his lips. Wild, furious pleasure tore through her and she drove herself back on the invasive tongue.

She needed. Oh God, she couldn't believe she needed this. Not this. Not something wild and deep inside that narrow channel that should never know touch. That could never take the thick width of a man's cock.

"Easy," Cam groaned against her lips. "Look at me, Jaci. Just look at me, baby."

She forced her eyes open.

"Cam." She was frightened, exhilarated. She was burning inside and didn't know how to pull back, how to control the intensity of pleasure.

Behind her, Chase drove his tongue inside that rear opening as Cam had driven his fingers into her slick pussy. Her nails bit into Cam's shoulder and she couldn't help pressing back, lifting her leg higher along Cam's, opening herself farther.

"Don't stop." He was stopping. Chase was pulling away as Cam held her head in place rather than allowing her to turn to Chase. "Don't let him stop."

He was laying down behind her, spooning around her as they moved her legs, pressing her back, and she felt the head of Chase's sheathed cock against that tiny opening.

She fought to swallow, to think. She had to think about this, didn't she?

"Oh God. Oh God, Cam," she cried out for him as she felt the slow, so tender penetration. "Cam help me."

His lips covered hers again. His fingers slid into the drenched folds of her pussy, and a hard hand, whose she didn't know, lifted her leg higher.

Chase worked his erection inside her slowly. Pressing, penetrating then retreating, taking her in slow measured strokes until she was screaming in abandon against Cam's lips and she felt that final, firm push that lodged the thick, heavy length of flesh inside her.

"Fucking perfect," Chase groaned. "So sweet and tight. Tight as a dream."

Cam's lips lifted from hers. Behind her, lodged to the hilt inside the too snug depths of her rear, Chase shifted, dragging a moan from her as she was turned slightly, her leg lifted farther, leaving the aching flesh of her pussy vulnerable.

"Hold onto me, baby." Cam moved beside her, pressed closer, and tucked the head of his cock into her pussy.

Jaci stared at him in shock. She didn't know what she had expected, but not this, not yet. She should tell him she hadn't taken another man. Did toys count? They had counted when she took her virginity with them, she supposed.

Then she couldn't think anymore. He was pressing in, burning, stretching her, making her fit around Chase's cock tighter, almost painfully tighter.

"Jaci, fucking paradise," he groaned, staring into her eyes, holding her gaze as she watched his eyes dilate and darken as he took her. "So sweet."

He grimaced, his hips shifting, pulling back before pressing forward again.

It seemed to go on forever. Taking him in slow increments, hearing Chase's moans at her ear as Cam would stroke inside her, retreat, stroke a little deeper.

Each measured increase intensified the pleasure-pain and threw her higher into the maelstrom of agony-ecstasy. There was no clear boundary between the sensations. No way to differentiate.

He surged in halfway and she felt herself unravel. Clenching spasms rippled through her body as she came, her nails digging into his shoulders as she heard them both curse.

Chase jerked behind her, driving his cock deeper inside her ass. Cam jerked in front of her, his cock driving against the spasming flesh of her pussy and pushing him deeper. Throwing her higher.

"Stay still." Cam's hand tightened on her hip as she realized she was writhing, jerking, trying to force him to take her.

"No." She panted with the force of pleasure driving into her now. "Now. Do it. Take me now."

"Jaci, please God," he groaned, his hips stilling as she undulated against them. "Just a minute baby. Easy. Let me take you easy."

Her eyes flared open. Sweat ran in rivulets down his face. She could feel the perspiration on her own body, on Chase's as he bit her shoulder again and groaned roughly.

"Now."

His eyes narrowed.

"Fuck me now, or so help me, I'll make you pay for it. I swear. Damn you. You always do this. You always make me wait—"

She screamed. Her eyes widened, sparks erupted in front of her eyes and she heard a ragged male cry. Chase's or Cam's—she wasn't certain.

"More." She was crying, begging. She didn't have all of him yet. She wasn't burning enough yet.

They shifted again, pushing her closer to Chase's chest as he turned more. Chase was nearly on his back now, beneath her, her leg lying over his thigh as Cam came over her, braced his elbow on the bed, held her hip and moved. Hard. Fast.

Her eyes flew open, staring into his. They were alive now, wild, burning and intent.

"Good?" His voice was rough, demanding.

"More." She was begging, pleading, staring into the well of vivid green, drawn into them, imagining she felt him in her soul even as she felt him in her body.

He drove against her. A wail passed her lips as he pressed deeper, thrusting and working his hips until, with a strangled cry and one hard thrust, she felt him. Felt all of him, stretching her, burning her.

And she was coming again. She was only distantly aware of the hard, coordinated, driving strokes inside her body now. Chase and Cam moved as a unit, one taking as the other retreated, one giving as the other fell back. In and out, stroking and thrusting, burning and stretching as her orgasm melted her mind.

Her eyes locked with Cam. She watched his expression twist, heard Chase shout out his release behind her. But inside her vagina she *felt* Cam's release. Felt the heated spurts of semen, the throb of his cock, the flesh jerking within her as she dissolved again, and again, watching him, feeling him, and wondering just how much of her he possessed now.

Cam took what had previously been Chase's responsiblity with their lovers, and cleaned the perspiration and sex from Jaci's relaxed body.

She muttered grumpily a few times, but settled back into sleep, as he tucked the blankets around her and stared down at her silently.

"You didn't wear a condom." Chase's voice was disapproving and threaded with anger. "What the hell happened to you Cam, to forget something that damned important?"

His nostrils flared as he excused torment for anger and let the anger reign.

"I'm clean, Chase. We both know it. And she is, too." She was protected. The investigation they had run on her for the club had pulled up all sorts of interesting information. There were still too many questions and not enough answers, but there was no question of any risk, to either of them. She was taking a birth control shot, there were no reports of recent lovers. The risk was minimal.

"That's not the fucking point," Chase growled. "Son of a bitch, sometimes I think you've lost your damned mind."

He pushed his fingers through his hair, satisfaction pulling at the edges of exhaustion and making him more tired than he had been in the past nights. "Maybe I have." He finally shrugged. "Take care of her tonight. Tell her I'll see her when she gets to the Sinclairs' in the morning."

Chase stared back at him in complete disbelief. "You're kidding me? Damn you, Cam, you can't just walk away from her like that. She's not one of the little toys you up and leave laying. She's going to kick your ass."

Yeah, she would. She was going to be madder than hell.

"Cam, this will hurt her. Is that what you really want?"

Chase asked, as Cam turned to head back to the living room.

He paused, his teeth clenching. He couldn't hurt her. Pissing her off, he could deal with that.

"I'll sleep on the couch." He shook his head, but he didn't turn back to his brother or the sight of the woman who haunted his heart.

For once, the thought of Chase cuddling and comforting their lover after the sex bothered him. Just as the thought of him cleaning Jaci's sweet body afterward had bothered him.

And he couldn't help it. He moved into the living room and pulled his slacks back on before sitting down on the couch and leaning his head against the back cushion.

There, he stared at the ceiling; but he saw the shadows of the past and he couldn't make himself return to that bedroom.

The light from the other room flicked off and he heard the muted sound of Chase's voice comforting her as he lay in that big bed with her.

He had never regretted not sharing a bed with a lover, until tonight.

He stared at the couch and breathed out tiredly before stretching out on it. At least it was long enough, comfortable enough. For the amount of money Ian was paying for this suite, it sure as hell should have been.

But, of all the years stretching out behind him, of all the lovers he'd ever known, none had compared to Jaci or the intensity of pleasure and satisfaction he felt now.

He'd forgotten the damned condom. He hadn't meant to, and he'd have to rectify that. But, God, it had been good. So hot and tight, her pussy flexing and milking his cock until he spilled himself inside her.

He'd never done that. Ever. Even with the first woman he'd fucked, he'd refused to do so without protection. And now, with Jaci, he hadn't had enough sense to remember to sheath his erection—because he hadn't wanted that between them.

As he stared at the ceiling, he admitted to himself that there were already so many barriers that he placed between them that he couldn't tolerate that one.

That one pleasure, unlike anything he had known in his life, was one he never wanted to give up.

CHAPTER FIVE

Jaci arrived at the Sinclair mansion the next morning at exactly ten, as per Courtney's demands, so furious with Chase and Cam that she could barely stand to breathe. Cam had been noticeably absent when she had awakened. She may as well have been alone in the bed, because Chase was on one side while she slept on the other. And Cam? The bastard. He had been asleep on the couch. As though sleeping with her were somehow dirty.

She should have known better. Seven years separated them, and Cam hadn't exactly stayed the same. The scar on his face, though not disfiguring, had been the result of something violent and painful. He had changed. He was harder—more demanding. And unfortunately, that didn't do a damned thing to turn her off.

So now, the morning after was like a bad taste in her mouth and the memory of both men, leaving as she had ordered them to do before she showered, only pissed her off more. The fact that she had left the hotel without coffee only compounded her early morning snit.

Coffee was waiting in the solarium, as were delicate breakfast pastries.

Courtney was sitting at the round table, sunlight falling around her long brown hair, no makeup—not that she needed any—and she was still wrapped in a robe. She

looked like a sleepy, lazy kitten contemplating a long nap.
Which wouldn't surprise Jaci. Courtney had been known
for her afternoon naps before she married Ian Sinclair.

"Coffee's caffeinated and the pastries are to die for."
The other woman smothered a yawn and blinked back at
Jaci. "I hate you for looking so beautiful at this ungodly
hour."

Yeah, real beautiful, Jaci thought with an inner snort.
Covering the shadows under her eyes and her pale features while attempting to look natural hadn't been that
easy. Especially trying to do it while she cursed the Falladay twins.

"Courtney, the sun has been up forever," Jaci finally
pointed out as she sat across from the other woman and
sipped at the delicious brew a young servant poured
for her.

"Hmm. Well this is true. But I didn't get to sleep until
well after it had risen." A curl of her lips, satisfied and
filled with feminine pleasure, was all the clue Jaci needed.

"Party lasted that long, did it?" She pretended to misunderstand, because she really didn't want to blush and
give Courtney a reason to suspect Jaci had had her own
late-night party, one she promised herself would not be
repeated.

"Well, Ian had much to make up for," Courtney informed her. "I get rewarded for behaving politely at these
functions. You know, the ones where I have to allow pira-
nhas like the Robertses under my roof."

Courtney's voice vibrated with disgust. She had learned
of the problems Jaci had with the Robertses several years
before, during their friendship in England. Courtney's
parents had hired Jaci after meeting her, to redesign a
guest house, and they, too, had been informed of the rumors after hiring her.

Marguerite and Dane Mattlaw had brushed aside the

gossip and welcomed Jaci into their family, though. Their acceptance and friendship meant more to Jaci than she had ever been able to express. But now, just as Jaci had feared, that friendship would cause Courtney several problems.

"I warned you." Jaci tightened her lips at the reminder of the trouble the Robertses could cause, and shifted her attention from her fury at Cam. "It won't stop until I'm gone."

"Why don't you kick her ass?" Courtney suggested with a clearly bloodthirsty smile. "Pull her hair out and make her orthodontist another fortune by knocking those overly bright teeth down her throat. I'll cheer you on. I'm certain I can find the proper outfit for the occasion."

Jaci had to smother her laughter. She was afraid Courtney was much too serious. This was, after all, the woman who had sucker-punched the mugger she and Sebastian had saved Jaci from in England. They hadn't known her. They had heard her cries as they left the club they had been to, and raced to her rescue.

"Be good, Courtney."

Courtney frowned. "That only works with Ian, my dear. He has the proper reward for such restraint. You do not."

Jaci shook her head. "This is my battle, my friend. What did they do after I left?"

Courtney's lips thinned.

"You may as well tell me." Jaci could feel her stomach sinking. They always did something.

"No more than they ever do whenever they manage to insinuate themselves into whichever party you're attending. Made their nasty little innuendoes and smiled those superior smiles of theirs. Ian should have let Cameron dust the floor with that bastard Richard, like he wanted to do."

Jaci breathed in roughly. "What are you talking about?"

"Ian stepped outside just as his investigator Cameron was getting ready to follow Congressman Roberts to the study." Courtney smiled. "He distracted Cameron, of course." She pouted. "I wouldn't have minded a bit helping that luscious investigator hide the body after he killed him and I informed Ian of that quite clearly."

"And in those exact words." Ian stepped into the room as he gave his wife a mock glare. "Sweetheart, luscious isn't a word you should be attaching to my investigator, you know."

Courtney smiled sweetly, her brown eyes twinkling with love. "I'm not blind."

"I'm sorry, Ian," Jaci breathed out roughly. "I did warn Courtney when she offered the job what was coming."

"Yet you didn't refuse the job," he pointed out.

"If I refused every job that could cause me problems, I'd be out of work." She stared back at him coolly. "I gave her more than the standard warning that I give anyone else, once I know they're associated with the Robertses."

Ian poured his own coffee, then moved to the table and sat close to his wife, staring back at Jaci, his gaze brooding, watchful.

Dressed in black pants and a white silk shirt, his dark hair pulled back from his face to the nape of his neck, Ian Sinclair looked like the finely honed dominant force she knew he was.

"A bit more of an explanation would have been nice," he suggested. "It's hard to deflect the problems they could cause without information, Jaci."

Well, that was one of the more unique attempts to get an explanation from her.

"I don't need anyone to deflect problems for me." She pushed the cup back and stared him in the eye.

It wasn't always easy. Ian's gaze could be brutally piercing.

"It seems to me that you do," he stated. "How many jobs have you lost this year because of them?"

"That's why your deposit is nonrefundable." Her smile was all teeth. It wasn't the first time she had been in this position. It wouldn't be the last. "Would you like me to leave, Mr. Sinclair?"

He merely stared back at her silently as Courtney glared at him. Rather than causing her friend further problems Jaci decided, in that moment, that leaving this job might not be a bad idea.

And after the night before, she doubted Chase or Cam cared where the hell she went.

Jaci rose slowly to her feet, regret laying heavy on her chest, though she made certain it didn't show on her face. Whatever had happened the night before, it must not have been pleasant. The Robertses usually engaged in guerilla tactics, but if Cam had confronted Richard . . . her heart gave a hard, brutal thump. If Cam had confronted him, it might have been worse than she could imagine. No wonder he had been so pissed when he arrived at the hotel, or that he hadn't been able to bring himself to sleep with her.

The pain it caused was brutal, stomping on her soul with steel-spiked talons.

"Ian." There was a thread of steel in Courtney's voice, though her husband only glanced at her broodingly.

"Courtney, your husband has a business to consider," Jaci pointed out softly. "I promise, it's not a problem."

It might very well bankrupt her.

"I can leave now, Mr. Sinclair. As I said, I do understand your position."

"Did I ask you to leave, Ms. Wright?" he demanded arrogantly. "I believe I asked for an explanation instead."

"And I'll give you the same answer I've given everyone else who's demanded that explanation. What happened does not affect how I do my job. I don't owe you explanations. All I owe you is the option of letting you out of the contract."

"Without the deposit?" he answered coolly.

"Ian, stop," Courtney muttered.

Jaci shook her head. What the hell did it matter? As large as the deposit was, in the long run, it wouldn't do a damned thing to halt the slide of her career. Once knowledge that Ian Sinclair had released her got around, she would never get another job that paid well.

"You'll have your deposit back within the week, minus my traveling expenses." She lifted her leather briefcase from the floor and turned, moving quickly for the doorway.

She had to blink back her tears, her rage. It was burning in her now.

"Jaci, wait," Courtney called softly, but without conviction, as though she were hesitating. Everyone hesitated.

With her head down, she strode to the door, then slammed into a completely immoveable, impossibly hard form.

Hard hands steadied her, gripped her upper arms, holding her closer rather than pushing her away, as her head jerked up and her lips parted on a gasp of anger, maybe of hope. Until she glimpsed the ice in his eyes, the hard expression, the fact that the Cameron she had known was here in body only. The man inside had changed.

"Sorry about that." She attempted to pull back, to drag herself away from his body, the temptation, the regret. "I wasn't watching where I was going."

"I was." He didn't let her go.

He had allowed her to plow into him. Just as he had allowed her to climax over and over, before he turned tail and ran. Well, now he could watch while she walked away. Turnabout, and all that bullshit.

"Well, aren't you just the watchful one." Her voice was

shaking as she jerked out of his grip. "If you'll excuse me, I was just leaving."

"No, she wasn't."

Her head jerked back to Ian in shock, even as she was aware of Cam's fingers curling around her arm once again.

"Whatever games you're playing, I'm not involved," she said, her voice cold. "I don't need this job bad enough to play them."

"Jaci, please." Courtney rose to her feet, her expression concerned, as her gaze shot to Cameron. "There are things involved that you're perhaps not aware of."

"Then I'll stay unaware of them." She pulled at her arm, then turned on Cam when he refused to release her. "Let my arm go, Cameron Falladay. I refuse to play your games, either."

His lips quirked. The scar at the side of his face, slashing over his cheek, whitened as he stared down at her.

"You've already lost that option, so let's play the one facing you instead," he suggested.

He released her when she jerked at her arm. She barely glimpsed the surprise on his face, as she brushed past him and stalked through the formal dining room to the foyer beyond.

Screw this job. Between the Robertses and her own weakness where Cam was concerned, the potential for destruction was much higher than the effects of bankruptcy.

"Ms. Wright." The butler, Matthew, moved from the small office between the main mansion and the residential wing, his expression questioning. "May I help you?"

"I need a cab." A polite smile, a gnashing of teeth. "I'll be waiting outside for it."

His gaze glanced over her shoulder, then back to her. "It may take more than half an hour for one to arrive," he warned her. "Perhaps you could wait inside?"

"I'll wait outside."

She moved for the doors, only to come to a rather abrupt stop as a strong arm hooked around her waist, lifted her from the floor, and began to carry her toward the stairs.

"Forget the cab, Matthew," Cam ordered, his voice cold.

"Let me go, or I'll have you arrested for assault."

"Stop threatening me, or I'll turn you over my knee and paddle your bottom," he grunted, as he moved past the staircase toward the back hall. "We're going to talk."

"I don't want to talk to you." Her voice was shaking with anger and pain. "And you and Ian Sinclair can shove this job right up your . . . omph." His arm tightened around her just enough to shut her up and leave her fuming.

"Let's not get naughty, Jaci," he drawled as he moved through the hall.

"How about homicidal instead?" She kicked at his legs, only to hear his chuckle when her slender heels connected with a pair of tough boots.

It was almost laughable. She had awakened with an enthusiasm she hadn't had in years, and now here she was, on the verge of bankruptcy and being toted through the Sinclair mansion like a misbehaving puppy by a man who couldn't even be bothered to stick around in her bed after fucking her half to death.

His arm flexed beneath her hands and the controlled motion against her back assured her that her weight was barely noticed and her struggles didn't effect him in the least.

"Here we go." He stepped into a sunlit office, closed and locked the door behind them, then sat her on her feet. "Don't bother trying to run out. The door won't unlock without the proper code."

Her gaze flew to the door. There, on the side panel,

was a security lock. She hated him. She hated herself because she wanted to stay, even as she wanted to run.

"This is so juvenile," she informed him, as she straightened the thin summer knit shirt she wore over the band of her skirt. "Hauling me around like a damned sack of potatoes. Where the hell do you get your nerve?"

"From a Cracker Jack box." He moved across the room. He was dressed in jeans and a white cotton shirt, his black hair lying loose around his face, brushing his collar and framing his dark face as he glanced back at her.

"Now, why do I believe that?"

Jaci crossed her arms over her breasts and glared back at him as he hooked a leg over the corner of the desk, perched on the edge, and watched her coolly.

"So. Roberts?" He arched a brow.

She rolled her eyes and shook her head. "I'm going to start making people pay me every time they ask me that question," she snarled. "I wouldn't need to work."

His expression didn't change.

There was none of the lover that had taken her the night before in his face. This man was different—as though the passion and lust they had shared had never happened. And she wondered if her heart could have broken worse seven years ago?

"According to the congressman, you attempted to steal fifty thousand from the desk in his home office. When you were caught, you attempted to seduce him. His wife walked in and threw you out of the house."

In reality, she had walked in on the congressman, his wife, and their secretary while the three were involved in some very nasty sex games. Black leather and attachments, and Rick Roberts in a very compromising position.

And they had believed she would join in! No, they hadn't just believed, they had attempted to force her to join in.

Jaci remained silent, staring back at him, refusing to say a damned word. She didn't dare. She could feel the fury pulsing inside her, anger burning through her system as the feminine core of her shuddered in trepidation, because the look in Cam's eyes was deadly.

Courtney had warned her that Cam was after Richard Roberts's blood. He couldn't sleep with her, but he could use her as an excuse to bloody someone he didn't like to begin with. Only a male could understand that one, she decided.

"I'm asking for your side of the story, Jaci," he said.

She had walked in on the sexual drama and had nearly been raped. For years after that, the Robertses had lied, schemed, and connived to destroy her because of it.

"There is no 'my side of the story,'" she finally answered. She had learned that early on. The Robertses had struck first, and they had struck hard. Anything she had said or done would have lashed back at her as a lie.

"Do you remember the night I told you I would kill over you?" he asked her, his voice so dangerously soft that it was almost terrifying.

"He hasn't hurt me," she said stiffly. "And after last night, you have no right to these questions."

"Then what do you call it, if destroying your reputation isn't hurting you?" His head tilted to the side, the sunlight falling through the windows behind him caressing the raven black hair that framed his savage features. "And, sweetheart, I hate to tell you, but last night only made certain that that bastard has to deal with me. No one strikes out at what belongs to me."

"He's an irritant. Nothing more. Now, I really need to leave, before I have to swallow any more of this 'belonging to you' crap. Because, trust me, belonging to you would really make me homicidal now."

The look he gave her was rife with irritation. "You're as stubborn as you ever were."

"And you're just as arrogant."

He grunted at that. "Ian didn't fire you."

"Sounded to me like an invitation to walk." She cocked her hip and glared back at him.

"It was an invitation to accept a helping hand." He sighed. "We can help you with the Robertses, if you can explain the situation."

She stared back at him silently. Oh yeah, she was just going to "explain" the whole sordid episode and watch him gut the congressman. Sorry, but the thought of blood spilling just made her ill. It might have been seven years, but Cam was the type of man who never forgot a promise. Or a warning.

He shook his head at her continued silence. "This job entails quite a few secrets that you'll be privy to," he finally stated. "It's yours if you want it, but only after you understand exactly what goes on here." He rose from the desk and moved behind it.

Lifting a folder, he slid it across the desk. "Read these, sign them, then we'll talk."

She stared back at him silently, aching. Where was the man who had kissed her? Who had knelt in front of her and given her the greatest pleasure she had ever known in her life?

She moved slowly to the desk, picked up the folder, and opened it. As she read, she frowned in confusion.

"A confidentiality agreement?"

Of sorts.

Cameron nodded. "Before you sign, know this: What you're facing if you talk isn't a court battle or a prison sentence. It's hell, like the Robertses could never imagine visiting on you. You, your family, every friend you have or could make in your lifetime, will be subject to the same hell. The people you're facing are lawyers, doctors, senators, and military personnel. They're members of organizations that run everything from NASA to the welfare system and beyond, in every nation of the world."

She raised her gaze slowly. "Is that a threat of some sort, Cam?"

"It's a promise." He inclined his head coolly. "There are no state secrets, no national threats involved, but members of the club are from all sections of state and federal, and private enterprise. There are approximately five hundred members to date, though only a small percentage are here at any one time. You may at any time see those members. It's our job to ensure their privacy, as well as their security here within the mansion."

Her brows lifted. The agreement was that she understood the repercussions of divulging any information learned about the club and its membership, and that the repercussions would be harsh.

Her understanding was that she had the option of leaving, or accepting the position, with a full comprehension of those repercussions. In the statement, she would sign that she understood that the information wasn't illegal, nor involved any information of state or national concern.

"If it's not illegal, then what is it?"

"Sign the papers." He nodded to the file. "You can still walk out once you sign, but the job isn't yours until you have a complete understanding of the confidentiality required, and the punishment inherent in breaking it."

It was simple enough. Clearly stated. She laid the file on the desk, accepted the pen, and signed it quickly, before pushing it back to him.

"Now, what's so damned important about your precious club?"

"It's a club for men who share their women. Their wives and lovers. A safe, protected group of men from which to

choose the third in their bed and to ensure the secrecy of
it. The club is a ménage club, Jaci, and it's existed for two
centuries without detection. Now, are you taking the job
or walking out?"

She stared back at him in disbelief.

"You're lying." She couldn't come up with any other response. The idea that any such club could exist without the
newspapers and gossip rags getting hold of it was ludicrous.

Senators and NASA? Lawyers and doctors and military
personnel? More than five hundred members, and no one
leaked this information? Their wives especially. Women
talked; she knew they talked. They gossiped like hell, and
for some of them, their favorite topics of gossip was their
sex lives—married or single.

"You'll find out soon enough." He shrugged as he took
the file and shoved it in his desk. "There are no sexual
games played out in the club itself. It's just that, a club, a
meeting place, and for many of the members abroad, much
more convenient than a hotel—and much more secure.
Within your position, you'll come in contact with those
members in and out of the club. We do nothing to risk
knowledge of the membership, as many hold sensitive
positions. They've been made aware of the job you'll be
doing, and should you see any of them here, you're not to
mention it outside the club. Period. Not to other members
or anyone else. If you talk, I can't protect you, nor can Ian
and Courtney Sinclair."

It was a good thing she knew how to keep her mouth
shut.

"As long as they don't bother me, I won't bother them."
She shrugged. "But if I were you, I'd start steering a very
wide path around me, because you and I, Cam, are going
to come to blows."

He stared back at her, dark, dangerous. His expression
was hungry, intense.

"I'd never harm a hair on your head," he said. "And there's no turning back, Jaci. Last night ensured that."

"You couldn't even *sleep* with me," she hissed furiously. "I woke up alone, Cam, without you, while you slept on the damned couch. Not happening again." Her hand sliced angrily through the air.

He leaned back in his chair and watched as she stood before him. The feel of his eyes stroking over her sent her blood racing through her veins, and not just in anger.

The effect he had on her hadn't dimmed. Maybe it had grown stronger, because she could feel the intent behind that look, could almost feel his possession from the night before, even now.

"I'm still so hard for you, I can barely walk."

The words stole the strength from her legs. She gripped the edge of the desk and stared back at him as she fought to regulate her breathing.

There was no regulating it. She could feel her breasts heaving, and she knew he could see his effect on her.

"Well, isn't that too bad?" she spat bitterly. "See, I don't believe in three strikes. As far as I'm concerned, strike one and you're gone. Too bad so sad, hate it for you, Cam."

His lips parted, his lashes lowered as he stared back at her. She could feel the intent behind the look, and the reminder of the effect those lips had on her. And then he smiled.

"I'm going to spank you until you come. Then, sweet Jaci, I'm going to kiss it all better," he promised, and the promise sent a shower of heat exploding through the tender flesh between her legs.

She felt the dampness growing, her clit swelling, even her nipples were so sensitive she could barely stand the lace bra that covered them.

"Don't do this to me," she finally whispered, releasing her hold on the desk and backing up. "You can't even tolerate sharing a bed with me, and I can't deal with that. If you ever cared anything for me, stay away from me before you really hurt me. Now, unlock that damned door and let me out of here."

He reached beneath the desk, and a second later, the sound of the lock releasing echoed through the room. His expression hadn't changed; if anything, his gaze was darker, hotter. There was nothing cold in his face now. It was heated with sensual promise and male demand.

She jerked her briefcase from where it had fallen to the floor and strode quickly to the door on shaking legs.

"Tell Courtney I'll be back in the morning." She didn't turn as she jerked the door open. "Good-bye Cam."

She left the office, and seconds later she left the house. Ian's limo was waiting outside the door, the driver opening the door for her with instructions that he was to take her to her hotel. It beat a cab.

She stepped into the luxurious vehicle and breathed out a trembling sigh of relief as the door closed behind her. Seconds later, she was heading to her hotel, alone.

As alone as she had ever been, and hating it more than she ever had.

CHAPTER SIX

"Ya know, you're the dumbest bastard I think I've ever seen." Chase stepped out from behind Cam, watching the limo, as it drove through the gates, leaving the Sinclair estate and taking beautiful Jaci Wright away.

Chase had heard their conversation. It was his job to tape it and to secure the disc the recording was on. He doubted either of them were aware of what the disc revealed, though. A male and female, each eating the other with their eyes, hunger and torment reflected in their gazes.

Their expressions had shown a variety of emotions. Cool hauteur, cold arrogance, irritation, mockery, and pure anger. It was amusing to watch, but the eyes hadn't changed.

"I didn't ask for your opinion," Cam muttered, and Chase almost laughed at the irritation in his brother's voice. There were few things that could piss Cam off anymore, but from the moment they had first begun Jaci's file, Cam had seethed with possessive male fury.

"The worst thing we can do is leave her alone." Chase rocked back on his heels and watched as the limo drove out of sight. "Since you're determined to hold back as you always do, though, maybe I could just continue the seduction myself. You obviously have no clue."

Cam felt his teeth grit at the thought. Jaci's expression

when she realized she had slammed into him had pierced his soul like an arrow. Her wide eyes as innocent, as filled with pain, as they had been seven years ago, had stared back at him for one, unguarded moment. Arousal and pain and the memory of the pleasure that had bound them the night before reflected from them.

"Let her go for tonight," he ordered his brother, an unfamiliar spike of possessiveness resounding through him.

"Women like Jaci shouldn't be given too much time to think," Chase told him. "They get odd ideas, start thinking about protecting their hearts, and off they run. She's ready to run."

"She's not going anywhere." He would see to it.

"I don't know, Cam . . ."

"I'll take care of it." He didn't need Chase for this. Jaci was his fight and his alone.

"Like you did in Oklahoma? Like you did last night and this morning?" Chase questioned with amused condescension in his voice.

"I said I'll take care of it." Cam turned on him, barely restraining the anger burning inside him.

Chase smiled back at him. Cam could see his amusement, the fact that his anger didn't faze him. Not a lot fazed Chase. He rolled with whatever life threw at him, and he did it with the flash of that knowing smile—the same one he was flashing Cam now.

"Maybe that's what I'm scared of, baby brother, the way you take care of things." Chase chuckled. "But I'll let you fuck up first. Piss her off real good, okay? Maybe she'll be receptive to me the next time I offer to take her home."

That really shouldn't have angered him, but it did. Cam turned quickly, his eyes narrowing on the driveway as Chase headed back into the mansion. His brother was

perfectly serious, and Cam knew it. Seven years ago, he
had wanted Jaci with the same hunger that Cam had. But
Chase hadn't known the same emotions, emotions Cam
still tried to hide.

It was Cam *she* had wanted, though. And Cam had
wanted her with a force that he hadn't known before or
since—a force that unleashed all the possessive and
dominant traits he'd never had a problem holding back
before.

"Matthew?"

"Yes, Mr. Falladay?" Matthew stepped from inside the
house.

"Have one of the boys bring the Harley around. And
please inform Mr. Sinclair I'll be back in the morning."

"Yes, Mr. Falladay."

Long minutes later, one of the houseboys Ian employed
to keep the grounds cleared and under control rode the
Harley out of the back garage with a wide grin.

"Here you go, sir." He pushed the kickstand down with
reverence and swung off the cycle. "She's all gassed up
and everything. I took care of her this morning when you
came in."

The wicked, black, customized Harley was the pride
and joy of every maintenance worker on the estate. Ian
really needed to get his own for his employees to lust
over.

"Thanks, Danny." Cam straddled the seat, raised the
kickstand, and engaged the powerful motor. Seconds later,
he was speeding toward Alexandria and the woman that
thought she had gotten away.

Jaci entered her suite with a sigh of relief, kicked off her
pumps, and stared around the elegantly appointed hotel
sitting room.

The ever-present vase of flowers were on the desk. Fresh,

of course. The minibar was fully stocked, the refrigerator filled with a variety of goodies, all at Ian Sinclair's expense—part of her fee for the interior design of the mansion that he would no longer be calling home, but would instead be turning over to his club.

Good Lord, she hadn't heard even a breath of rumor attached to him. Well, perhaps a breath—several years ago, by a wife involved in a very nasty divorce—but it had been quickly silenced. Now she knew why. If it carried half the power Cam had warned her it did, then it was legion. Legendary. Probably dangerous.

She should call Ian Sinclair right now and say thanks but no thanks, return his deposit, and return to Oklahoma to lick her wounds and find another career.

She moved across the room to the bar. It was only a little after noon, but the glass of wine was much needed. Something to settle her nerves and give her a chance to think. She really needed a chance to consider this.

No wonder Cam and Chase were here. Considering their sexual tastes, there was probably no keeping them away. She sipped at the wine before curling into the corner of the fluffy, comfortable couch, where she tried to consider her options. But all she could see was Cam's face. His eyes. The vicious scar that marred one side of his face.

What had happened to him? She knew they occasionally kept in touch with her parents, surely they would have told her if they had known Cam had been hurt.

Or would they have? Her father had been waiting up when Cam brought her home that night, seven years before. He had taken one look at her face and the man's shirt she wore, and had known. He hadn't said a word. He had wrapped his arms around her, patted her back, and then let her escape, as she had needed to.

Perhaps they wouldn't have told her if Cam had been hurt, because she would have gone to him if she had known.

She covered her face with one hand and breathed out wearily. She wouldn't have been able to stop herself. No matter where he was, she would have tried to get to him.

She was just as weak where he was concerned now as she had been seven years ago. He made her want things she knew she couldn't have or accept.

The ring of her cell phone drew her from her thoughts. Pulling it from the band of her skirt, she looked at the display, sighed again, and brought it to her ear as she connected the call.

"Yes, Courtney?" She should have known the other woman would call. Jaci was just grateful Courtney hadn't made a trip to the hotel instead.

"Are you upset?" Courtney asked carefully.

Was she upset?

"Not with you." And did Ian share his wife? If he owned the club, then wouldn't he share those same dark desires? How did Courtney handle that?

"Cam said you didn't quit. Does that mean you'll be back in the morning?"

"I'll be there." She hadn't known until that second that she would be. Hadn't known how crazy she was, until those words slipped past her lips.

"We'll take coffee in my sitting room," Courtney said softly. "We can talk."

"Do we need to talk, Courtney?" Jaci asked her. At this point, she didn't want to talk about it. If she talked about it, then she had to acknowledge it.

"Only about subjects you wish to discuss," Courtney said, but Jaci could hear the question in her voice.

"That works for me, then," she told her friend brightly. "I'll see you around ten."

"Jaci, don't judge things you don't understand too harshly," Courtney warned her softly. "Please."

Jaci shook her head. "I don't judge at all, Courtney. You

know better than that. Except overbearing, superior men," she said as an afterthought. "But I've found I've not judged them harshly enough."

Courtney gave a light, relieved laugh. "Excellent. I'll have coffee waiting and I'll make certain the cook prepares us a nice little snack."

They disconnected the call, and Jaci rose to her feet, finished the wine, and moved to enter the bedroom. As she reached the doorway, she heard the door open.

Turning, she stepped back into the sitting room then stared in surprise at the man that closed the door behind him, his gaze leveled back at her, his expression hard, cool.

Cam.

"Why am I not surprised?" She wasn't. Somehow, she had known he would follow her.

She stared at his scarred visage, the icy green eyes, and felt the same tightness in her chest that she had felt earlier. The thin white scar looked painful, haunting.

"We need to talk."

"You didn't come here to talk, Cam." A bitter laugh left her lips. "I'm just surprised you didn't bring Chase with you."

His lips flattened, his eyes losing their icy cast long enough to flicker with a surge of anger. Fine, let him be angry. She was angry as well. She hadn't asked him about his damned club, she hadn't wanted to know. And if they hadn't intended to pull her into their dirty little games, then they could have made certain she knew no more than she had when she was first hired for the job.

"Chase is on his way." He shrugged, watching her closely.

"You conceited jackass," she snarled. "You make me just want to hit you."

"You really shouldn't hold back, Jaci, just say what's

on your mind," he said mockingly as he moved farther into the room.

"Oh, just go away," she muttered. "I'm not in the mood to spar with you today."

"Because I shocked you?" He stopped in front of her, staring down at her intently, as she refused to retreat. "Or because I hurt you this morning? I didn't mean to."

And he even managed to say that sincerely.

"Because you pissed me off," she told him. "And it has nothing to do with last night. Last night was just a mistake, and I don't repeat mistakes. You talked to me as though you had pulled me off the streets and had to threaten me to gain my silence." She shook her head in disgust. "You should have let me walk out. It would have been easier on both of us."

"Seven years is a long time," he told her as she turned and plopped back on the couch, curling her legs beneath her. "Too long to want a woman the way I've craved you, sweetheart. I didn't say this would be easy. But we'll work it out."

"There is nothing to work out." She glared back at him.

"Isn't there?" he asked, taking the chair beside the couch and staring back at her intently. "You don't trust me, Jaci, or you would have told me what I needed to know about Roberts."

Her lips twisted mockingly. "So it has to come down to what you want, versus my privacy? If you'd done your job right you'd know I don't carry tales, Cam. So, why don't we discuss you for a while? Do you slight every woman you fuck the way you slighted me last night, or am I just an anomaly?"

"If I'd done my job right, I would have managed to identify any old lovers as well," he stated. "But those didn't turn up, either. And I didn't slight you."

It would be damned hard to identify a vibrator. She kept

her lips firmly closed, her gaze locked with his. Would he be shocked to know she had never had sex with a man or a woman? Had that little issue of trust, and the awareness of how easily she could feel betrayed, reared its ugly head too often?

He nodded slowly. "We'll do it your way for now, but my time will come."

Why that statement sent a jagged pulse of heat racing through her, she wasn't certain.

"You've changed," she finally said. "You're harder, Cam. Colder."

"I'm still the man who would kill for you," he stated matter-of-factly.

Jaci swallowed tightly. He was completely serious.

"Fine. I'll make a list for you." She finally shrugged, opting not to believe that declaration. "Give me a few days. It may take awhile to remember every son of a bitch who ever pissed me off. But what will you do when you find your name on the list?"

She should have felt stalked. Instead, she knew instinctively what he meant. Realizing how certain she was of that knowledge was almost frightening. Cam would protect her, and, in his way, he was assuring her of that. Even now, so many years after he had made the promise, he still stood by it. And she had no doubt he meant it.

"I won't find my name on that list." His lips quirked in a cool smile. "And I'm afraid if I did, I'd have to ignore it. I would do nothing to hurt you, Jaci. You know that. I might paddle your behind for being so stubborn, but I wouldn't hurt you."

"Is this a new seduction technique? You keep threatening to hit me Cam, and I'm going to get worried."

He snorted at that before leaning forward, his elbows resting on his knees while he clasped his hands.

"We need to talk about this thing between us." His gaze was intent, somber.

"No we don't." She was perfectly content to just stay furious with him for a little while longer. "Unless you're going to explain why you couldn't sleep with me."

He stared at her from between thick, lush black lashes, his tanned face seemingly wicked, with that scar running down it. As she stared at him, that ache inside her expanded, filled her chest, and then went deeper. What had happened to her dark knight that had scarred his body and made him unwilling to share something as simple as a bed with a woman?

That was such a small intimacy, really, in the total scheme of things. But as she watched him, she could feel a knowledge, a certainty that the Cam she knew was still there somewhere. And she wondered why in the hell she felt so compelled to reach out to him.

"What happened?" she finally whispered. "How were you hurt?"

She needed to know.

"Does the scar affect what's between us?" he asked, watching her closely.

"There is no 'us'," she reminded him, ignoring the clenching of her heart. "You don't sleep with me, you don't do anything else with me. Period."

His lips quirked mockingly as his hand lifted, two fingers thoughtfully running down the scar. "My last mission in the service went bad," he finally stated. "We were ambushed in Afghanistan and taken prisoner for a few days before we escaped. My chest is pretty messed up, too, as well as my back. It's not a pretty sight."

Her breath caught. "You were hurt that bad?" Terror snaked through her.

"I nearly died." He shrugged as though it didn't matter. "The doctors were frankly surprised that I survived."

She had almost lost him. She stared back at him, her breathing harsh, the certainty that he had nearly been taken out of this world slamming inside her.

"I'm fine, Jaci." He was watching her too closely, his eyes no longer icy, but thoughtful instead, as she reached for the wine, finished it, and then smacked the glass back to the table.

"You are now." She hadn't known. She had been focused on her own life all those years, refusing to contact him, to even check on him. He was in the military and she had known it, the chance of danger in his particular field had been high. Why hadn't it occurred to her that Cam could be hurt?

"I am now." He was still watching her with that quizzical expression of a male pondering a puzzle. "Why does it matter?"

She glanced back at him in surprise. "I didn't know." She finally shook her head as she felt the pain of not knowing, of not being there if or when he had needed her. He had promised to protect her seven years before, and she knew that if he knew the truth about the Robertses, he would make certain neither Richard nor Annalee darkened her life again. Yet, she hadn't been able to even contact him, to make certain he was alright.

"Would knowing have mattered?" His expression turned cynical, cool. "Chase was there. I was in Germany for several months recuperating. I wasn't alone."

"But I didn't know," she said again. "I would have been there."

His eyes narrowed. "I don't need pretty words, sweetheart. I survived. That was all that mattered."

Yes he had, and he had somehow, somewhere, turned cold and hard, so that she wondered if the Cam she had been so fascinated with even existed anymore.

And whether he did or not, she needed to know the

damage done. She needed to know what had happened to the man she had idolized, the extent of his pain, and how bad the enemy had scarred his precious body.

It wasn't the scarring that bothered her so much, it was the pain. The scar across his cheek made him appear more wicked—rakish and dangerous. But the thought of the pain he must have felt traveled through her mind and pushed her, tormented her, drove her to see how much worse it had been.

"I want to see." She moved from the couch as he watched her, surprised when she pushed his knees apart and knelt between them, her fingers going to the buttons of his shirt.

The icy expression he had come in with was gone, at least. But she didn't know what to think about the faintly quizzical expression of male confusion in his eyes as he watched her.

"You want to see *what*?"

"How bad they hurt you," she whispered. "I need to see, Cam."

Cameron watched, his head slightly tilted, his arms resting carefully on the sides of the chair, as Jaci's slender, graceful fingers trembled over the buttons of his shirt and began to slip them free.

With any other woman, he would have pushed her from him and walked away. He couldn't tolerate pity, or the horrified distaste that often filled their eyes. But this wasn't any other woman, this was Jaci. And he knew from past experience how she had worried when she was younger, feared for him when she knew he was on a mission.

And he needed to know now, if the scars, the superficial damage done to his body, was going to disgust her. There had been no chance for her to pay attention the night before. He and Chase had overwhelmed her before they even got their shirts off. And she had been exhausted, curled up in sleep by the time he moved from the bed.

"Taking my shirt off could have other consequences, sweetheart," he warned her, as her fingers moved down the shirt, the material parting as she moved lower.

Her gaze lifted to his as the last button released and her shaking hands moved to part the edges of the shirt. Then her eyes lowered and he watched her grow pale. He saw the tears that filled her unusual eyes, the trembling of her lips as her fingers whispered over the worst of the scarring.

He'd taken two bullets, and the bastard that wielded the knife as he was bleeding to death on the ground had sliced not just his face, but his chest and upper arms as well, before Cam could use the sidearm he'd had in his hand.

That night had been hell on earth. Half his team had been lost in the ambush. Cam had been certain he would die before the extraction team made it in.

Silken-soft hands smoothing the material of the shirt back from his shoulders drew him from his thoughts. The fine cotton slid over his muscles, clearly revealing the damage, as the auburn-haired little sprite let a single tear fall.

"Hey, no tears." He frowned, reaching out to wipe the tear from her face. "It was a long time ago, baby. Barely remembered."

She shook her head, the soft fall of dark fire whispering across her cheek as her lips trembled again and her fingertips, like a breath of fiery sensation, eased over the slashed scars.

They weren't as bad as they had been, but they were still pretty horrific. Deep slashes had forever marked his flesh. He'd been damned lucky the enemy had poor aim that night. The one bullet had done the worse damage, so close to his heart that just a breath closer and there would have been no saving him. Angels must have been watching over him, because the bullet had nicked a lung, missed everything else vital, and tore through his back. But he'd lived.

"I would have come if I had known." Another tear fell as Cam watched her in confusion.

Chase had come to him, but there had been no one else to call, no one else to care that he existed for weeks within the shadow land of his own mind.

"Why?" He watched her expression carefully.

He had wanted her then. He barely remembered anything from those pain-ridden months, except the pain and his need for Jaci. And later, he struggled with his fear that the scarring would disgust her. Women were strange creatures at times, he had learned. The brutal slashes along his chest and back weren't a pretty sight. And women did like their pretty things.

There was no disgust in Jaci's eyes, though. The only horror was for what pain he may have felt, not the physical imperfection he now carried.

"Why?" Disbelief filled her eyes as they lifted to him. "Because I cared, Cam. I wouldn't have left you alone."

"Chase was there." Who else was supposed to be there?

She shook her head, her lips pressing together to still their trembling. He wanted to lower his head and kiss them, to steal the saddened curve of them and fill her with hunger, instead of with pain.

"I would have been there, too. For as long as I could have been."

For some reason, he believed her. Or maybe he just wanted to believe her.

"You would have been there for that, but you couldn't stay, the night I brought you home from that party?"

Fire flashed in her eyes for a second. "One has nothing to do with the other," she snapped. "Don't be a moron."

Now, *there* was his Jaci. Fiery, confrontational, speaking her mind, as she should be.

"It's a logical question. Why would you have flown half a world away to be with me while I was dying, but refuse to share my bed?"

"Yours and Chase's? I was only twenty-one, Cam." She sniffed in distain. "Oh, shut up. I was just starting to like you again."

She was kneeling between his thighs, her generous breasts brushing against his lower stomach as she berated him, and Cam couldn't help but smile. How long had it been since a woman had done more than close her eyes in distaste at those scars and whisper platitudes he didn't want to hear?

"Did you stop liking me, Jaci?" he asked her then, lifting his hand again to brush the hair back from her cheek, as her fingers felt the ridged scars that covered his chest.

Her pert little nose twitched in irritation as her brown-and-blue-flecked green eyes, darker than his own, glared back at him.

"You're pissing me off."

He laughed at that. The sting of accusation was absent, but instead, he heard that hint of fondness he needed to hear. "How am I pissing you off? Because I want to surround you in pleasure, but I can't tolerate a bed? Then, yeah, I have to concede defeat there. I guess I'm probably going to have to keep pissing you off."

Her lips almost twitched. He caught the betraying tug at the corners of those luscious curves before she firmly steadied them.

"Why can't you tolerate a bed?" she finally asked softly. "You want all my secrets Cam, but you're giving me so little to hold on to you with."

"I'm giving you everything I can right now," he said. "And that, Jaci, is more than I've ever been able to give anyone else in my life."

Could she go a step at a time? Could she accept being pulled closer to him, while he remained forever distant, and still keep her soul from being scarred?

The sound of a knock at the door caused her head to jerk up.

"It's Chase," he said, his fingers touching her hair.

"We don't need Chase," she whispered. "Why is he here, Cam?"

A second later the door opened and Chase stepped inside the room, his gaze instantly finding them, his expression sober, concerned, as he stared back at Jaci.

Whatever the reason why, it wasn't the first time, and it was a need, at least for Cam. She stared up at him once again, feeling his fingers caress her jawline as his gaze darkened painfully.

It wasn't something he just wanted. He wouldn't take her without it. She could see it in his face, in his eyes, and she needed him. She needed him until she couldn't breathe because of the need. And she couldn't deny the heat Chase stoked in her as well.

Cam watched as she lowered her head, and her lips pressed against his chest. There, where the bullet had entered his body, her soft lips burning his flesh and sending hard, driving spikes of pure heated lust straight to his already tight testicles.

He stared down at her bent head, feeling her lips on his skin, and he wanted nothing more than to bury himself so deep inside her that he would become lost in her. And for a heartbeat, one pain-filled second, he wished he hadn't called Chase. He could feel Chase in the room now, his worry competing with his own arousal. Cam pushed back the need for possessiveness. He could't afford it now. Cam could have done without knowing his brother worried for him, about him, or the needs that whipped around them at the moment. But Cam couldn't do without the balance, not now. The knowledge that as long as he shared her, she wasn't totally his. And if she wasn't totally his, then she could never be taken totally away from him. He had to have that, just for now.

He couldn't force his hands to stay on the arms of the chair, no matter how hard he clenched his fingers into them.

He had to touch her hair. Had to bury his fingers into that heated mass and make certain she didn't stop, because those sweet lips were washing away the torment from those scars, that were caused by the memories of the night they had been inflicted.

She was touching him without coercion, without seduction. Loving him with her lips and her soft breath. And he realized in a single moment of insight that he knew he couldn't have survived much longer without her.

CHAPTER SEVEN

His flesh beneath her lips was like satin stretched over iron. His chest was hard, muscled, flexing beneath her lips as she felt his hands bury themselves into her hair.

And, oh! He tasted so delicious. Like the sun, heat pouring into her, the fresh masculine scent overwhelming her. She couldn't stop tasting. Like an addict, she couldn't force her lips back from her drug of choice. She needed more.

And Cam was in complete agreement with her need to dine on him, if the feel of his hands in her hair and the hard rise and fall of his chest was any indication. He was offering himself as her banquet, and was evidently quite pleased with each bite she took of his hard muscles.

Her hands pressed against his lower chest, her lips ran over each and every scar, and when she reached the most wicked of those thick, silvery lines, she had to taste him.

Her tongue peeked from her lips and she licked him. And she couldn't stop licking him. The taste of his flesh against her tongue was even richer, hotter than it had been against her lips.

His fingers tightened in her hair. A burning pleasure to add to the burning pleasure of his taste. His hard body flexed, one hand left her hair to lift her closer, the other forced her head back, and his lips swallowed her protesting moan, until the taste of his kiss sank into her senses. The feel of it washed through her mind. His lips were like rough velvet, heated and exciting. They rasped over hers, caressed and sent shards of hunger spiking inside her.

When she thought she could stand the gentle rubbing of his lips against hers no longer, that she would die from the need for more, deeper and harder, he gave it to her.

His hand clasped the back of her head as he pulled her to his lap, lifted her into his embrace, and devoured her. With lips, teeth, and tongue, he nipped, licked, then slanted his lips over hers and buried his kiss into her.

Sensations—pleasure, hunger, and need—whipped through her system, attacked nerve endings, drawing them too close to the skin, making them too sensitive. She could feel every breath of air against her flesh, every touch of his hands, every separate sensation of his kiss. His tongue stroking her, his lips moving over hers, his groan meeting the mewling whisper of desire that fell from her lips.

Her hands were in his hair, fisted in it, holding him to her. If she could just keep his lips on hers, hold back reality for just a little longer, then she could find a way to be strong again.

Because she was definitely weak right now. Lost in his touch, melting against his chest and arching closer to him. Nothing mattered but this. His kiss feeding the hunger inside her.

"God! Jaci!" He moved his lips from hers.

She was outraged that he had stopped. Desperate, blinding need filled her, overwhelmed her.

"Don't stop." She fisted her hands harder in his hair, dragging his lips back to hers. "Just for a few minutes. Let me feel you for just a few more minutes."

He muttered a male groan and he was kissing her again. Blissful kisses. Kisses that let her sink into that world of pleasure once again—a world where Cam's strong arms tightened around her, lifted her—where security enfolded her.

She was only distantly aware of her back meeting the couch and Cam looming over her. He was surrounding her. His powerful arms were sheltering her, his kisses dragging her past fear and distrust, and filling her with his hunger, his need.

She let her hands slide from his hair to his shoulders, pushing frantically at the shirt in her quest to touch his flesh.

His knee slid between her thighs, pressed into the sensitive flesh of her silk-covered pussy, and sent talons of desire digging into her womb.

"Slow down, Jaci." He forced his lips away from hers once more, trailed them over her jaw, and ignored her cry of loss. "Easy. Let me touch you, sweetheart."

Jaci arched toward his lips, her head turning as they slid to her neck, her hips lifting against the pressure of his thigh, as his teeth scraped down her neck.

"I love your taste," he groaned as he pulled at her shirt, baring the upper orbs of her breasts for his lips.

He feasted on the rapidly rising and falling mounds, his lips and tongue playing against them as she tried to get closer, tried to force his head lower.

"Sweet Jaci."

She didn't know where Chase was. She thought she felt him at the end of the couch behind her head, but she couldn't drag her senses away from Cam long enough to be certain.

Buttons released from the blouse as he pulled at the edges, popping them loose, and she didn't give a damn. He could shred the blouse if he wanted to.

He bared her bra, delicate creamy lace, to his gaze, and within seconds released the front clasp that held it secure, then lowered his head.

"Cam!" she cried out.

His lips covered the hard, sensitive peak of her nipple and drew it into his mouth. There, he sucked and laved the peak, his tongue flicked over it, his teeth rasped against it.

Liquid pleasure burned beneath her flesh, as her head thrashed against the cushions of the couch. She needed more of him. More of his touch.

"I can't breathe," she panted, yet she arched closer.

"Me neither." He groaned, moving to the other peak. "I don't give a damn."

Another cry tore from her lips as he took the other nipple into his mouth and gave it the same rough loving. He sucked on her with driven hunger. He laved the tip with his tongue, then caught it between his strong teeth, worried it with exciting roughness, then suckled it again until she was writhing beneath him.

Her skirt was past her thighs, pushed to her hips by hard calloused hands, as her blouse fanned out around her.

"I want all of you." He nipped at the curve of her breast. "I want it all now, Jaci."

God yes. She needed it all. She needed him until she felt as though she were unraveling at the seams with the strength of that need.

"Yes." She tried to drag his lips closer. "Don't stop. Not yet. Please Cam, not yet."

He was torn. Cam could feel every cell in his body screaming at him to take her. Nothing mattered but sinking inside her.

He glanced behind her to see Chase loosening his shirt, then his slacks. Sometimes, Chase just watched, and that was okay because Cam couldn't drag his attention off the woman in his arms, and he would be damned if he could pull back from so much as a moment of this pleasure. Right now, while she was in his arms, he needed to know *he* held her. Completely. All of her.

God, he didn't want to lose her again. And he knew he wouldn't be able to deny the need, eventually, to take her alone.

He wanted her just like this, in his arms. She arched against the knee he had planted between her thighs, rubbing herself against him like a needy little kitten. And for the moment they both ignored Chase.

He had to pull his lips back from her breast and grit his teeth against the hunger burning through him.

His hand slid from her breast down her belly and over the skirt that had bunched at her hips—over it, to her lower stomach, and beneath the lacy elastic band of her panties.

He lifted his head and stared down at her, swallowing tightly as he fought to remember that he was not going to take her without making her realize she belonged to him.

Her face was wild with pleasure. Wild with it. Auburn hair surrounded flushed features. Her eyes had darkened until the green was mossy, the flecks of brown and blue like a hidden fire within it.

"Touch me." She whispered the words as he edged his thigh back just enough to side his fingers into paradise.

He felt perspiration bead along his body as her nails bit into his shoulders and her head tilted back with a surfeit of pleasure. Her thighs parted farther, allowing his fingers greater ease into the dew-dampened folds of flesh between her thighs.

Sweet flesh, tender, it parted for him, the heated moisture of her response spilling to his fingertips. He eased lower, fighting to hold onto his control, until he couldn't help himself. He could not hold back the need. He pierced her with a single finger, amazed at how snug, how tight her heated pussy was for him, and then worked deeper inside her.

She arched against him, the muscles clenching on his

finger, surrounding it with slick, heated syrup and satiny flesh. He pumped into her, watching her take him, the pretty pink flesh and auburn curls parting, wet, welcoming.

Hell, she was hot. Hot and writhing in his arms, reaching up for the fragile penetration, as her cries begged for more. And he was no less desperate. His cock was rigid beneath his pants, fully engorged, and aching for the tight clasp of her pussy.

"Cam." Her voice was rich, husky. "Oh God."

A surge of white-hot lust had one of his hands lowering to the belt cinching his waist, while the other, loath to leave the creamy heat of her body, continued to caress and cajole more of her sweet syrup from her.

He wasn't going to be able to hold onto his control this time. It would be rougher than he had wanted. Harder. And fuck making her face anything except his possession. He had been born for this moment. Born to burn in the fire she ignited inside him.

She stretched beneath him, her arms reaching above her, hands gripping the armrest behind her head as she thrust against him. His finger slid deeper, retreated. Pierced her as her hips lowered, slid nearly free as she lifted.

With her body, with each sensuous movement, she was taking him into her, riding his finger with such voluptuous pleasure that his cock threatened to explode before he ever entered her with it.

He tore the belt buckle free, slid his finger from her, despite her husky, protesting cry, and was working to release his erection, when the shrill demand of his cell phone filled the room.

"No." Jaci reached for him, her eyes burning into his with the same need tearing through him. "Don't answer it."

It rang again, the imperious summons causing him to snarl with impatience as he jerked it from the holder on the band of his pants.

"What?"

Jaci watched the grimace that pulled at Cam's expression. Blood thundered through her body, the blistering need burned her from the inside out. But the reprieve was a lucky one, she realized suddenly.

She had lost her mind. She had to have. The careful control she had adapted over the years, the firm rein she had placed on her sensuality and her need to be held had slipped with Cam.

It had slipped with the most dangerous man she could have imagined. He wouldn't reveal her secrets, he wouldn't betray her—but he could destroy her.

She moved to pull her body from his, ignoring the tightening of his hand on her hip, pushing away his hold, as he watched her with that hawklike stare.

She rose quickly from the couch, ignoring both men now, pulling her shirt around her and straightening her skirt as she rushed to the bedroom. She closed and locked the door carefully behind her.

Her shirt was ruined. Buttons were missing, there was a tear at the shoulders. She ripped it from her body and tossed it across the room before pulling a soft, comfortable pullover from her closet, along with a pair of jeans.

As she finished dressing, there was a soft knock at the bedroom door.

"Don't make me break the lock, Jaci," Cam warned her.

Don't make him break the lock. He was so arrogant, so self-assured. So certain of himself that it oozed from every pore of his body and made her want to scream in outrage, because she couldn't find that confidence—couldn't seem to fake even a quarter of that self-assurance whenever he was around.

She turned the lock and jerked the door open.

Standing before them, it was all she could do to rein in the shiver that would have trembled through her body at the look Cam gave her. The way his gaze slid over her body, the mocking quirk to his kiss-swollen lips.

Did her lips look like that? Reddened and swollen and hungry?

"We need to go back to the office," he told her. "I'll see you in the morning."

One hand cupped her neck, his hold dominant, daring her to pull away as his head lowered and he delivered a quick, hard kiss to her lips.

"What was that for?" She jerked back, but only after he released her.

"That was one of those little good-bye kisses lovers share," he said sensually. "Surely you recognized it?"

She would have had to have a lover first. "We're not lovers," she told him through gritted teeth.

At that he smiled. A slow, sexy curve of his lips, rife with promise. "Of course we are, sweetheart. I told you, you can't go back now. The only question in this relationship is when we'll go forward."

"There is no going forward." She had made a grave tactical error with him, and she knew it. He had taken control from the first moment, and he wasn't letting it go. "I've decided enough is enough. It's more than obvious I can't handle you, let alone both of you." She waved her hand toward the silent, amused Chase.

Amusement glittered in his eyes. "You already have."

Jaci stared back at him in disbelief, and she had to admit to the temptation rushing through her at the amused passion, the arrogance in his eyes.

"You couldn't handle it seven years ago. You were too young then, and I knew it. You're not too young to understand it now, Jaci."

"No. Now, I'm old enough to know a disaster walking when I see it," she said, her voice scathing. "And that's what you and Chase are to any woman's heart, Cameron Falladay. A disaster walking."

He chuckled, the deep rumble of amusement stroking across her senses, despite her determination to remain resolute.

He leaned closer, and rather than retreating, she felt frozen before him, staring back at him, mesmerized by the fire in those light green eyes.

"So much pleasure," he whispered. "Remember how good it was last night, Jaci. How hot and sweet, and so good you thought you were going to die from it."

She could feel the sizzle in her womb, the need for that pleasure further dampening the flesh between her thighs. Dangerous. The potential for destruction was rising daily.

"You have to leave, remember?" She forced herself back from him, but she couldn't force back the images raging through her mind, or the fire it built low in her belly.

Just the thought of last night. The thought of being wanton, sexual, of taking all the pleasure she had ever dreamed of and knowing she was safe within it, was a temptation she found hard to deny, now that she had experienced it.

"We'll see," he murmured, stepping back to return to the living room.

"You'll see," she informed him, rather pleased by the strength in her voice. She didn't sound as though she were ready to submit and lay prone before the Falladay brothers, as they covered her in nothing but lust.

He smiled at her declaration. That sexy smile. The way his slightly fuller lower lip tempted her to taste it, and the way his eyes encouraged her to be bad, was a potent combination.

"I'll see you in the morning." He turned on his heel and headed for the door. "I'll pick you up on my way into the office and take you home tomorrow evening. If you need anything or need to go into town at any time, Chase or I will take you."

"Why?" Stunned, she followed after him. "I can rent a car." She *would* rent a car. She didn't need to spend any more time with the Falladay twins than she absolutely had to. That was a recipe guaranteed to wear away at her resistance.

"Why rent a car? I pass by here daily on my way into Ian's home office. The hotel charges an outrageous price for parking, and it would be inconvenient."

"Then I'll get a cab."

He was silent for long moments, just watching her, those eyes piercing inside her.

"Don't push me," he finally said softly. "I'm walking away now because I understand that pushing you too fast right now isn't a good idea. But I won't give up the few chances I'll have to get to know you again. And I won't let you throw them away."

"You would have to invest yourself first, Cam, and we both know you can't do that," she accused, hearing the roughness in her own voice, the fear in it.

She was weak, too weak to spend any more time in his company than she absolutely had to.

"However you want to see it." Powerful shoulders lifted in a careless shrug. "But you don't want to fight me too hard right now. My self-control isn't at its best when you're around. It never has been. And if push comes to shove, we both know, the lust is going to win. So let's not tempt that beast today."

For a second, the savagery of his determination held her speechless. And it wasn't fear that caused it. It was the incredible need to do just as he had warned her not to. To tempt the lust raging in his expression.

"I'll see you at nine in the morning." His fingers grazed

her cheek, the incredible gentleness in that touch at odds with the battle she saw raging in his eyes. Because he wanted to tempt it as well. He wanted to push it and see how hot they would both burn, and she knew it.

Unfortunately, the fallout was going to be destructive.

Before she could argue, he unlocked the door and jerked it open, and as she stood there watching, he and Chase left the suite, closing the door behind them and blocking the sight of the worst temptation she had ever known in her life.

Cameron Falladay had the power to make her forget who she was and the lessons she had learned over the years. That was dangerous. He was dangerous to her heart and to her soul, and she had to force herself to remember that.

Nine o'clock the next morning came way too soon, as far as Jaci was concerned. The night before had been spent tossing and turning, visions of Cam and Chase moving through her dreams. Both twins filled with hunger, touching her, easing her into an embrace that sent fear roiling through her—because behind them, she could sense Richard and Annalee watching, waiting.

Not that she gave a damn what the two knew, she told herself repeatedly after she awoke. Unfortunately for them, a promiscuous reputation wouldn't destroy her career. It could hamper it mildly at this point, because she was finally establishing herself. She didn't give a damn about gossip; she had learned early not to. But they were a threat.

She could feel it in her dreams. They were waiting, watching, determined to destroy her. She had no idea how a relationship with Cam and Chase could affect the congressman and his wife. According to Courtney, Ian detested the congressman, though he had a mildly friendly relationship with Richard's father-in-law, the senator.

Dreams were just that, she finally told herself, as she

put the last touches to her makeup and hair before finishing the last cup of coffee from the pot she had ordered from room service along with her breakfast.

At nine o'clock on the dot a knock sounded on the door to her hotel suite.

She breathed in quickly, ran her fingers through her loose hair, pushed it back from her face, then strode to the door and checked to be certain it was Cam before opening it.

She had dressed in a slim black skirt that ended just above her knees. The black tailored suit conformed to her figure and gave her a strictly business look that was slightly softened by a silky knit dove gray pullover she wore with it.

The pumps gave her an added height, putting her head at his throat rather than his chest. But he still towered over her, still surrounded her.

"I just need to get my purse and case." She turned to do just that, when she found herself swung around, pressed against the wall, as he kicked the door closed and his lips covered hers.

Oh, man. This was the way a girl needed to wake up in the morning. It had coffee beat all to hell.

His lips parted hers swiftly, his tongue licking over them before touching her tongue and jerking her into the maelstrom of sensation she had sworn she would avoid.

Her arms were around his neck, her fingers spearing into his thick black hair to hold him closer to her, to retain the heat of his kiss and the luscious, wild hunger of it, for just another second. Just another second, then she would force herself to pull back from him.

"Damn." He pulled back, staring down at her, his gaze hooded, as she forced her eyes open. "That's better than coffee, first thing in the morning."

He mirrored her own thoughts.

His hands moved from the hold he had on her head, smoothed down her back to her hips, as a slow, lazy grin pulled at his lips.

That knowing smile snapped strength back into her spine. She stiffened and pulled quickly away from him.

"That was completely unfair," she informed him as she jerked her purse and leather case from the table just inside the room.

"What was unfair about it?" Laughter lingered in his voice. "I thought it was pretty damned hot myself."

"Guerilla warfare," she muttered. "That's what it is."

He snorted at that as she turned around. "Sweetheart, guerilla warfare is getting you in the bed, stripped and fucked blind again before you know what's hit you. I'm giving you fair warning."

Was that what he called it? Fair warning? In her opinion, he should rethink that description. It was guerilla warfare. The only difference was, she recognized the subtle war being played out between them.

"I'm giving *you* fair warning, you're picking on the wrong girl," she informed him as she stepped out into the hall.

"Hmm." He hummed his disagreement, rather than arguing with her, as they moved to the elevators.

Once inside, after the doors closed, the hand laying low on her waist moved lower.

Jaci's eyes widened.

"Stop that," she hissed at him, then hissed it to herself mentally as she felt her rear clench in pleasure.

She was aware of the cameras in the elevator. The all-seeing eye behind the lens couldn't detect that his fingers had moved to the crevice between her thighs, where they played with destructive strokes.

She was getting incredibly wet. Wetter than she had been when he released her from the wall moments ago.

"Do you think they can see that flush of arousal on your face?" He bent close, his lips at her ear, as she stood stiffly beside him. "And your nipples are hard, Jaci. I wonder if the security personnel watching this are getting as turned on as I am."

She was saved from having to form a reply by the light ping of warning that the elevator was drawing to a stop. A second later, Cam's hand was once more at her lower back.

He escorted her from the elevator, and Jaci fought to restrain her breathing, to keep from panting. He'd always had the ability to do that to her, to make her breathing too hard, her imagination too intense. Especially after last night's dreams and the night before in his and Chase's arms.

"You haven't had any questions about the club," he stated as they were driving from the hotel long minutes later, heading back to the Sinclair mansion. "Most women would be full of questions."

"It's a men's club, and it's full of perverts. What more is there to know?" she asked mockingly, knowing how judgmental she sounded and at this point not really caring.

She was too damned curious about the club though, and she didn't want to be. She had learned a long time ago that her curiosity could be dangerous. It had been her curiosity that had gotten her into the trouble at the Robertses' mansion. She wasn't going to make that mistake anywhere else.

Cam chuckled at her response. "How do you define a pervert, Jaci? Anyone who doesn't do it straight missionary, or are there other allowances?"

"Acceptable sex is allowable," she said carefully, staring straight ahead as Cam drove.

"Acceptable sex? What the hell is acceptable sex?" He shifted gears, and his body tensed and moved as he worked the clutch and the gear shift, and maneuvered the Jaguar through the heavy city traffic.

"Stop lusting after me while I drive," he drawled. "Answer me, Jaci, what's acceptable sex?"

"I am not lusting after you while you drive. And you're a man. Men know what acceptable sex is."

"But you just called me a pervert," he pointed out, his voice vibrating with laughter. "How would I know what acceptable sex is?"

"Have you ever had sex without Chase?" She turned to look at him, brushing her hair from her face, as he shifted gears again and accelerated through the thinning traffic.

"Often." The grin that tugged at his lips infuriated her.

"Do you have sex with Chase?" She snapped out. She was sick of the questions raging inside her, the need to know, just to *understand.*

He glared at her, offended male sensibilities filling his expression.

"Damn, Jaci, are you trying to make me lose my breakfast here?"

"It's a reasonable question, Cam," she pointed out heatedly. "Give me one reason, just one reason why you would have even considered wanting another man to have sex with your lover, in any way, let alone while you're there? How can you justify that to yourself, let alone to your lovers? How can you justify that to any woman who would care for you?"

Silence filled the vehicle. There was only the powerful hum of the motor, the sound of the gears shifting.

"Does there have to be a reason why?" he finally asked, his voice dark, dangerous. "Don't deny you enjoyed it. You were screaming for more, Jaci."

"That's not the point. There's always a reason why."

With Cam and Chase, there was no other option. Everything they did had a reason. They were controlled, determined, exacting. They wouldn't do something so dark as sharing their lovers without a reason.

"And how do you figure there has to be a reason why?"

"Because, from the time I was sixteen until I turned twenty-one, you and Chase made certain I was protected. One way or the other. You pulled me out of parties, the bad-asses in town stayed well away from me, and no matter what I did, I was aware one of you had been there before me. You were possessive, Cam. If you didn't care who touched me, then you wouldn't have been."

"I'm still possessive of you." He surprised her with the statement. "I'd want to kill any man I didn't choose to touch you."

Her lips parted in shock. Jaci could do nothing but stare at him in disbelief as they made the turn into Squire Point.

"You did not say what I just thought you said."

He was silent for long moments, his jaw clenched tight, his nostrils flaring.

"I said it." The gears shifted smooth and easy, but she could feel the restraint in each move he made. It pulsed in the interior of the vehicle, surrounded them like a smothering blanket.

Jaci inhaled slowly, deeply. A fine thread of tension began to tighten through her body, race through her veins. Turning, she stared through the windshield once again, her hands clutching the purse in her lap tightly.

"You're not serious," she finally whispered, as they drew to a stop in the front of the Sinclair mansion.

"Look at me, Jaci."

She shook her head.

"Look at me, dammit." His voice throbbed with command.

She turned her head slowly, seeing his eyes, darker, brighter than before.

"When you were twenty-one, I wanted you until it was a fire in my gut. Waiting until you were old enough to understand what I wanted from you was hell. Seven years has only made that burn worse, and one night sharing it hasn't eased the fire. You know what I want from you. You know what I need, Jaci. It's your choice. But if you don't want it, then stay the hell away from me. Stay far, far away from me. And make damned sure you stay away from Chase."

Her heart jumped to her throat.

"It's an either/or?" She felt strangled by the knowledge.

"I can't change who I am." His hand jerked out, cupped her neck, held her still. "And I can't let you go now. Not on my own."

"I won't change who I am."

"Then stay clear of me. Walk away when you see me coming. Turn and run if Chase comes your way. Listen to me." His voice turned hard, brutal, as her lips parted and anger fired inside her. "I can seduce you. You know I can. I know I can. If you don't want the man I've become, then stay the hell fucking clear of me."

"Have the control not to come near me, then," she snapped out, trying to jerk from his grip.

"Didn't we figure out a long time ago that control doesn't exist?" He pulled her to him, his lips almost touching hers, almost tasting her. "We both know there's not a chance in hell of that."

CHAPTER EIGHT

Stay the hell away from him. Run if she saw him. Run if she saw Chase. She was supposed to take responsibility for all this? When the hell had that happened? Somewhere, somehow, Cam had come under the illusion that she was a wimp, and she wasn't enjoying the consequences.

It was all the running she had done for the past seven years, she told herself. That little investigation he had done on her had evidently led him to believe she ran from her problems rather than deal with them. And hadn't Chase accused her of it as well? She was tired of it.

Jaci stalked into the Sinclair mansion, casting Cam a glare as he sat in the car watching her, his gaze stroking her even across the distance.

"I hate men," she muttered, before turning and coming face-to-face with a grinning Chase.

Charm oozed from him. Wicked, wild, amusement gleamed in his gaze and in his too handsome face, as he leaned against a door frame, watching her.

"Excuse me while I walk instead of run," she stated with completely false sweetness, her hand clutched around the handle of her briefcase in a death grip.

That was what she got for trying to figure out men, or these particular men. Warnings and dark rumblings, and a complete inability to give her a single straight answer.

Chase's brow lifted, though he didn't lose his smile. If she remembered Chase correctly, it took a lot to make him lose his smile.

"When have I ever wanted to see you run, pretty thing?" He straightened from the frame and dropped his arms from his chest, watching her with that ever-present amusement. "You look pretty as hell when you're pissed off at Cam, but I'd rather see a smile on your face."

"Bite me," she muttered.

White teeth flashed in a wolf's smile. "I thought I did that the other night."

The contrast between Cam and Chase would end up making her crazy. It was like dealing with the opposites of a coin. Night and day. Cam was dark, forbidding, the dominance that was so much a part of him flashing in his eyes and in his expression. Jaci had a feeling that when it came to Chase, a woman would be left reeling, when finally shown that dark, inner core that he kept hidden.

"It's a good thing I'm a reasonable, patient woman," she told him as she headed up the stairs. "Otherwise, I might have to kill both of you."

She heard his chuckle behind her before he moved away, and though his presence was gone, she could still feel the effect of him. Or was it the effect Cam had left her with?

Damn those two. She didn't need this in her life right now. Two men to deal with instead of one? Most women were lucky and just didn't know it. They only had to deal with one man at a time; but no, Jaci Wright just couldn't do it the easy way, could she? She had to go out and get herself tangled up with a man who thought he should be able to share everything, things about her that he should want to keep for himself.

Moving along the hallway, she turned the corner to the residential wing of the house and moved toward Courtney and Ian's suite. As she neared the door, it opened and a stranger stepped from inside.

Smiling, tall, seriously handsome, and as dark as sin. She'd seen his picture a thousand times in the gossip magazines, and had had the pleasure of meeting his sister the year before in London.

Khalid el Hamid Mustafa. The bastard son of a Middle Eastern prince.

As he turned from the door he came to a stop, his gaze going over her slowly, dark black eyes rich with wicked, carnal lights slid over her body before coming to a stop at her eyes.

"Ah, such beauty and fire." He smiled. A devastating curve to his lips, she was certain. Unfortunately, it left her cold and had little effect on the mesmerizing magic Cam had left pulsing inside her body.

Thick black hair was pulled back to the nape of his neck and tied there. It appeared long enough to fall well below his shoulders. He was dressed in dark gray slacks and a white silk shirt unbuttoned at the throat. His eyes gleamed with wicked, sinful charm, and with delights that a woman could only imagine.

Jaci paused several feet from him, her lips twitching as she saw the faint resemblance between him and the young woman she had grown so fond of last year.

"Mr. Mustafa," she greeted him, restraining her grin.

He blinked back at her in surprise. "Have we met? Funny, I would have thought I would remember meeting such exquisite beauty."

"I met your sister, Paige," she informed him. "She warned me to steer a wide path around you."

His expression flickered with fondness and amusement. "Brave women rarely take such warnings to heart," he told her, the faint foreign flavor of his voice as sexy as his eyes. And it pissed her off, because she should have been

swooning at his feet, just as Paige had warned her not to
do. Unfortunately, there wasn't a single swoon inside her,
because he couldn't compare to Cam.

"Bravery doesn't necessarily entail sampling forbidden
fruits, either," she warned him, amused by him, rather than
offended or outraged.

"Paige enjoys warning all the beautiful women against
me." He grinned again, his sensual lips curving back to
flash strong, white teeth. "But I promise you, I am not in
the least forbidden. You may sample me all you choose."

There was an irrepressible delight in his eyes, the look
of a man who enjoyed the chase just as much as he enjoyed
the capture.

"I think I'll pass." She declined his very charming offer
with a wide smile. "As lovely as the offer sounds, I'm really pretty busy these days, and I'd hate to be unable to
give you all the attention I'm certain you deserve."

He laughed at that, then tilted his head and watched her
for a long, assessing moment.

"You must be the lovely interior designer, Ms. Wright,
that Courtney has been telling me so much about. She said
you had a beautiful, fearsome wit. I see she was correct."

"I don't know how fearsome it is, but it's wit anyway."
She extended her hand. "It's been interesting to meet you.
Though I'll have to be certain to tell Paige you no longer
ravish women at first sight."

His hand enfolded hers before he pulled her to him.
Off balance, she landed against his chest to find herself
the recipient of a quick, laughing kiss to the corner of her
lips, before she was carefully set away from him.

"There, my reputation is now once again intact; you
may inform Paige you were ravished after all."

"You are a rogue." She laughed.

"He's also endangered if he doesn't take his fucking
hands off you."

Jaci whirled around, shock, anger, a mix of emotions bombarding her head at the sight of Cam standing at the entrance to the hall, his expression savage, eyes narrowed and dangerous.

Behind him, Chase was watching curiously, his gaze more interested than angry. Cam, on the other hand, was way past angry.

He strode down the hall just as the door to Courtney and Ian's suite opened and Ian stepped outside.

The tension tightened around her, trapped between the four men, aware of Courtney watching from the doorway, all eyes on her.

Suddenly she decided she'd rather face the Robertses on a bad day than the mess she could feel brewing in the hallway.

"Courtney, tell me you have coffee." She turned to her friend desperately.

Courtney took one look at Cam as he stopped behind Jaci, lifted her brows and drawled. "Jaci, I can go you one better. I have whisky. And from the looks of things out here, we're probably going to need it."

She stepped outside the door, snagged Jaci's wrist, and pulled her inside before slamming the door behind her.

Both women leaned their backs against the panel and blew out hard breaths.

"Life getting interesting?" Courtney asked her as Jaci stared straight ahead into the elegantly appointed sitting room.

"Oh yeah." She nodded, feeling the trembling in her legs, the heat in her lower stomach. "Is it like this around here very often?"

"Not since Ian and I were sniping and snarling through our courtship," Courtney responded, before turning to stare at her.

Jaci could feel her friend's look and grimaced at the question she knew was coming.

"You know," Courtney finally drawled, "Cameron Falladay is positively delicious when he's being possessive."

Delicious wasn't the word she would use to describe him. But there was no doubt those few seconds had been filled with such heightened lust that it left Jaci shaking.

"He's going to drive me to drink," she muttered.

"No doubt, he probably will," Courtney agreed.

They both listened expectantly, but could hear little more than the murmur of voices outside.

"Ian will referee," Courtney promised, but there wasn't a lot of conviction in her voice.

Jaci turned to her slowly, turning her wrath from Cam to the other woman. "I blame you for this," she stated. "You didn't even warn me they were here."

To which Courtney grinned. "I didn't, did I? I'll have Ian spank me for that later. But admit it, Jaci, your life was horribly boring. You aren't bored any longer."

She was beginning to wonder, though, if bored wouldn't be better.

Cam slammed the door to his office with a vicious flick of his wrist and grinded his teeth in fury.

Five minutes. She had been out of his sight five fucking minutes, and what had happened? There was that bastard Khalid, his hands on her, his lips on her.

His fists clenched, the need to punch something nearly overriding his self-control. The need to punch that half-Middle-Eastern son of a bitch touching his woman was what crazed him.

"You hit the wall again, and Ian's going to make us pay for the repairs ourselves," Chase warned him as Cam felt his fingers curling into a fist.

He'd already put a hole in the wall once this year. The day after the final report on Jaci was compiled, and he'd had time to think about it, time to let the fury stew inside him.

"Get out of here, Chase." He could not deal with his twin's amused condescension today. He'd end up hitting Chase, and the problem with Chase was that he invariably hit back. They hadn't had a brawl in years, and his ribs were thanking him for it.

"Come on, Cam, she's a beautiful, vibrant woman. Every man she meets is going to wonder if she's as hot in bed as she looks, and a few are going to try to find out. Nothin' you can do about it."

His fingers curled into a fist again. Fury pumped in him; he was hot, blistering with jealousy. He had never been jealous over another woman. He had never ached to punch any man that dared to so much as look at anyone but Jaci.

She had no idea how possessive he was over her. She had no clue how the thought of her with other men had tortured him over the years. And God forbid he should ever meet up with an old lover, because Cam wasn't certain if he could hold onto his control if he did.

"Come on, Cam, Khalid's flirty with all the women, you know that. The son of a bitch lives and breathes his playboy lifestyle just to piss his daddy off. You can't take him seriously."

"He touches her again, and I'll take his hand off," he snarled, whirling around to face the amusement in his brother's eyes.

But he didn't see amusement. He saw the same darkness in his brother that rode his own soul. They were like mirror images of each other in so many ways.

"God, this is a mess," he bit out, turning away again.

Why do you do it, Cam? A man as possessive as you would never share your lover without a reason. Jaci's question ripped through his mind with the force of a dull blade, tearing at his conscience. And still, he hadn't been able to explain. He hadn't been able to put into words that overwhelming, dark need that continually drove him and his brother.

The men of the Sinclair men's club all had varied reasons why they shared. Some for pleasure, some for excitement, some for protection of themselves or others. Some simply because they enjoyed it.

For Cam and Chase, why they shared was mired in so many different, impossible reasons. The bond of twins, of knowing each other's strengths, each other's weaknesses; of understanding the pleasure they could give—and the pleasure they received from it.

They could take women to places together that they couldn't take them alone. Give them a pleasure that drove them to the point where they couldn't find the breath to scream, and could only beg for more.

Cam could hold back, glory in the power of the pleasure they drew from a woman. Watch her eyes glaze over, feel more than his own pleasure. He could feel her pleasure. And he could maintain his distance, he could maintain his control and the ability to hold back the pain. And the nightmares.

And he wanted that pleasure for Jaci, often. He wanted her dazed, wet, and shaking between them, twisting in the midst of a hunger so intense she didn't know who she was, or where she was, only that she needed more. Just as she had the other night. The addictive need to have her like that again was growing, building in his gut, until he wondered how long he could maintain his control.

He *needed* to give her that. It crawled beneath his flesh, drove talons of agonizing arousal through his testicles, and made his cock harder than it had ever been in his life.

"You're going to have to explain things to her," Chase said behind him. "You won't hold her heart if you don't give her yours in return, man."

He shook his head. "How do you explain the impossible, Chase? Hell, sometimes even I can't explain it to myself."

He took his lovers alone often. He didn't require Chase's presence all the time, but sometimes, sometimes the darkness of the sexual needs inside him demanded it. As though there were a core inside himself, livid with a hunger, a need that became sated only in certain ways. And with Jaci, he didn't dare take her alone. There would be no chance of maintaining even a semblance of distance from her otherwise.

"It would help her understand," Chase said. "You can't hide from her and expect her to give you everything. Hell, it's bad enough that you hide from me."

"Explaining it wouldn't help." He clenched his hands, fought to work through the surging fury. "It's like a drug now. You know it as well as I do. Seeing the pleasure, feeling it." He shook his head at the hopelessness of it.

"So, you're going to lose her to the likes of Khalid instead?" Chase drawled. "Smart, Cam."

"I'll talk to Khalid." He breathed in roughly. "He'll stay away from her."

He was aware of the disbelief in Chase's expression. "Are we talking about the same Khalid?" his brother asked. "The same one undressing her with his eyes in the hallway, Cam?"

"Don't push this, Chase," he growled.

Chase held his hands up placatingly. "Fine. I'm out of it. Just consider the I-told-you-sos said when you find out he's moved in for the kill."

"She's too smart to fall for him." Cam shook his head. He had to believe that.

"She's alone," Chase said then, his voice soft, warning. "Remember that, Cam. She's alone and losing the same man for the second time for the same reason. She's been alone for a very long time now. She's not going to stay alone."

No, and she had every right not to have to be alone.

Cam shook his head, fighting his desires, fighting himself. She deserved the love she thought so highly of. Monogamous, possessive, pure love. She didn't deserve the exact opposite of the ideal that she prized so highly.

"You know, Cam, I'm not in love with her," Chase said then. "I won't love her, not like you do."

Cam rubbed at the back of his neck, feeling a relief so intense it was almost weakness. He could share her body with Chase, but the thought of sharing her emotions, her heart, the tender touches and the smoky looks . . .

"Cam, is it worth losing her?"

He paced across the room, his hand dropping from his neck as he moved to the window and stared into the bright morning sunlight.

Seven years. He'd waited, fantasized. He'd dreamt of her.

"I'll figure something out." And he would. Right now, he was allowing them both the distance they needed, but it wouldn't last much longer.

"Evidently, you warned her to run when she saw either of us coming," Chase said. "Why do that? Why not show her the man you are, rather than demanding she give into you without understanding what makes you like that? Damn, bro, you expect a lot from a woman, don't you?"

"From her?" he whispered, watching through the tall windows as Courtney and Jaci moved into the gardens between the two wings of the house. "From her, I expect it all. And I think that terrifies both of us."

CHAPTER NINE

Cam found her in the garden an hour later, a frown on her face as she sketched on the electronic pad she used for drawing and notes. She nibbled absently on her lip, and it made his lips tingle at the thought of having her little teeth nip at him.

He stood and watched her for long moments, aware of the growing hunger building inside him. Pretty soon, it wasn't going to matter if Chase was around or not, he was going to take her every chance he had.

He was burning for her. That addiction thing again. Hell if he knew how to break this addiction, though. He didn't want to break it.

"Got a minute?"

"Probably." She tapped a few commands on the pad, and he watched it darken and shut down, then she tucked it into the carrier bag she wore on her shoulder.

"Come up to the office." He held his hand out to her in invitation. "You can see the equipment we have there, and help me decide which room to try to convince Ian we need for a new office."

"You need a new office?" Jaci took his hand and let him draw her along the stone path.

"Bigger office, anyway." He smiled down at her. The hell if he cared if he had another office. He needed some time with her. He needed to smell the scent of her, feel her warmth, and he needed to do it without distractions. The office was his only chance, unless he wanted to slip into her hotel room again.

He wanted her until his back teeth ached with it. But he was finding he wanted more than just the sex with her. He wanted to laugh with her. He wanted to talk with her. He wanted her in his life and in his home, because he was damned if he was satisfied with the arrangement as it was.

She was continually running from him, and he'd had enough of it.

"So Ian doesn't want you to have a bigger office?" There was a hint of knowing heat in her voice, remnants of her earlier wariness.

"I doubt he really gives a damn." He felt like smiling. "I just want an excuse to spend some time with you."

He glanced at her, and saw the almost-shy surprise in her expression as she looked up at him. That look had his cock hardening to the point of pain.

"You didn't need an excuse." She cleared her throat as they entered the house, and headed through the back hall toward the offices. "All you had to do was let me know."

"You keep running, Jaci," he said softly.

"You told me to run." Her voice was reflective now. "What's the point in running, Cam? I never could stay away from you."

He pulled her into his office, slammed the door behind them, locked it, and pushed her against the wall. His hands framed her face, as though her admission had broken some thread of control holding him back and his lips slammed down on hers.

He drew back at the last second, softened the possession in the kiss, and groaned at the heated welcome of her lips. Wanton. That was what she was. Her tongue met his, and her hands were pulling at his shirt, dragging it out of his jeans to allow her nails to rasp against the mat of hair that grew over his chest.

"You're killing me," he groaned against her lips. "I'm dying for you, Jaci."

His hands were pulling at her skirt. He wanted to touch her. He wanted to feel the sweet warmth between her thighs, slick and wet, beckoning him.

"You wanted to talk." She was panting. She was sweet and hot, and he could feel the need in her body, just as clearly as he heard it in her voice.

"I am talking." He was nipping at her lips, loving the feel of them.

"You are?"

"I'm telling you how hot you are." His lips slid to her neck and he didn't even pause to wonder why the hell he was talking. "Telling you how badly I want to spank you."

"There you go, threats again." She moaned, a rich, soft sound that had his dick jerking in anticipation.

"A promise." The thought of spanking her. God, his hand itched to feel the softly rounded globes of her ass beneath his hand as he laid the heavy caresses against her flesh. Watching them blush, feeling her burn.

And she would burn. The pleasure-pain of him and Chase both taking her the other night had driven her crazy for more. Her eyes had been wild for it, her voice aching with the hunger for it. And when he had plunged into the ultra-tight, heated grip of her pussy, he had nearly come with her.

He nipped at her lips again, then stroked them with his tongue, as she lifted herself against him, trying to capture his lips for the kiss he knew they both needed. As he teased the lush curves of her lips he slid his hands over her ass, pushing her skirt higher to reach the delicate globes.

He moaned at the feel of bare skin. She wore a thong,

and he knew that that scrap of material did nothing to hide the sight of her silken flesh.

Lifting his head, he breathed in roughly, squeezed her ass, and fought to hold on. He couldn't take her here, couldn't take her alone. Not yet. Not until he got a handle on these damned emotions threatening to break free.

Where the fuck was Chase when a person needed him?

"Cam . . ." Jaci's voice was hungry now, her eyes brightening, growing hot with need. "What are you waiting for?"

She pulled at the buttons on his shirt, managing not to rip them from their moorings, but slipping them from their holes quickly, carefully. Her lips were against his neck, hot, demanding.

There had to be a way—a way to take her alone, to slide into the silken grip of her pussy and find the pleasure that awaited him there.

"Damn, you burn me alive." He lowered his head and let his tongue taste her collarbone, as he relished the feel of her butt in his hands.

"That's good." She moaned. "You burn me, too."

He clenched his teeth as he fought to hold back now. He was not going to take her against the wall.

"Come here." Before she could protest, he swung her up in his arms and carried her to the couch across the room.

The office was large, with his and Chase's work centers separated by a seating and meeting center in the middle. And that was where he took her. With his lips buried against hers, his tongue stroking, licking, twining around hers, he sat back on the couch before lifting his head.

"Come here." He lifted her until her back was to him, then, with his hand against her back, he pushed her shoulders to the cushions.

"What are you doing?" There was a hint of something

in her voice now—uncertainty, and a hesitant fear of the unknown.

"I told you I was going to spank you." He grinned as she tried to raise from the couch. "Stay still, sweetheart. I promise it will hurt so good."

"Hurt so good? Are you crazy?" There was a hint of laughter now. He liked that laughter in her voice, that bit of playfulness that indicated her sense of adventure.

But he'd be damned if he could answer her. She was on her knees before him as he knelt behind her, the creamy cheeks of her ass displayed by the bunched material of her dark skirt. And it was a fine ass.

He ran his hand over the curves, grimacing with the need to feel her locked around his cock, milking him, pulling him inside her.

"I didn't wear a condom last time," he told her, his voice roughening.

She didn't stiffen, but she stilled. "I knew that. Good thing I'm protected." There was the lightest snap in her voice.

"I knew you were protected." He lowered his head and laid his lips at the small of her back, feeling the little shudder that moved through her. "Medical records were part of the investigation. You use it for menstrual regulation."

He was taunting her with his knowledge of her. Needing answers.

"Invasion of privacy." She jerked as he cupped the heated flesh between her thighs with his hand.

She would get pissed later, he guessed, but for now . . . for now, the effect she had on him was the same for her. She needed the pleasure. Ached for it.

"You aren't concerned about anything but birth control?" He nipped at the rounded cheek of her ass as he massaged the silken folds of her pussy with his palm.

"With you?" She moaned as he found her swollen clit

and rubbed it slowly. "God, Cam, don't you think I know you would never do anything to risk hurting me?"

Now, Cam stilled. His eyes focused on the little scrap of material that bisected her rear, but something in his chest exploded out of control.

Trust. He heard it in her voice, felt it now in her body, just as he had felt it the other night. She trusted him—even now, seven years later—to protect her.

He smoothed his hand over her rear, taking in her position, her rear slightly raised, her head turned to where he could see her profile. Her face was damp with perspiration, her eyes closed, her expression twisted with pleasure, as he continued to rub against the silken vee of her thong.

He lifted his hand and lowered it against her ass. The heavy caress had her jerking, her head attempting to lift.

"Don't move." He pressed his hand between her shoulder blades, holding her down, pressing her to the couch.

"God, Cam." Her voice was more moan than protest, as his hand landed again and he watched the creamy flesh blush.

It was beautiful. She was beautiful, lifting to him, her legs spreading farther, her clothing in disarray.

"I'm going to make you burn, baby," he promised her, shifting, arranging her legs until they rested between his thighs while he knelt behind her.

He braced his foot on the floor, his knee on the other side of her legs, and lifted her hips farther, before delivering another heated caress.

It wasn't really a slap. Rather, it was a series of heated caresses against tender flesh, over and over, warming her skin, awakening nerve endings and sensitizing them to a point that pleasure and pain combined and turned to ecstasy.

With each caress his own arousal grew. He could

feel her twisting against the hand cupping her pussy, grinding her clit against his palm, the vee of her thong dampening.

He wanted to watch her eyes, but he didn't dare. Not like this, not alone. He could not stare into her soul without the buffer of a third person to ground him, to distance himself from giving her his own soul.

No matter how much he needed to. There were too many secrets. Too much darkness inside him.

"Let go, Jaci," he crooned, leaning down to caress the blushing flesh with his lips, to lick over it with the warmth of his tongue. "Relax for me."

"Relax?" She was panting, pushing against his hand, her juices saturating the thong crotch. "You're killing me, and you want me to relax?"

"But it feels good." He grinned, knowing she was loving it. Jaci was adventurous. She was greedy for the wicked loving, no matter how much she might deny it.

"It doesn't feel good," she said, moaning.

"Are you sure?" He lifted his head and let his hand lower again. "Are you sure you don't like it, baby?"

"Didn't say I didn't like it," she said between panting breaths. "Oh God, Cam. It's killing me."

He caressed her again. The heavy caresses burning through his soul as they burned through her flesh. Because she was giving to him. No questions asked. No demands. Surrendering herself, when he wanted nothing more than to do the same and give everything he was to her.

His head jerked up as the lock on the door activated, and he felt like thanking God as Chase stepped into the room. His expression was heavy, somber, but his eyes were bright with lust as his gaze took in the scene in the middle of the office.

Jaci's head raised then and he felt her grow still. Her breathing got heavier, and he swore her pussy grew wetter against her thong as Chase began to work loose the buttons of his shirt.

"Hell of a time for you to kick in with that twin bond thing," his brother growled, surprising him. "We're going to have to discuss this, Cam."

Discuss what? There was no twin bond. He had destroyed it too long ago to even consider it now.

"Cam," Jaci's voice was thready, uneven.

"Do you remember how sweet and hot it was the other night?" He pushed the thong aside and pressed two fingers inside her, working inside the clenching heat, refusing to give her a chance to deny what he knew they both wanted. What he needed.

He caressed the delicate tissue as he eased her over onto her back, lifting her legs and arranging them, allowing himself to stare into her eyes. Finally, to let himself sink inside her.

Turning his hand, he then speared his fingers into her pussy, cupping her as he worked inside her, caressing her, rubbing at the little pleasure spots until she was twisting beneath the caresses, eager for whatever he would give her.

Chase moved to the couch, naked now, and began undressing her. The blouse was removed quickly, the skirt undone, but Cam couldn't bring himself to move his fingers from the clenching depths of her pussy.

He watched, though. Watched her face as Chase's head lowered, held her eyes as his brother's lips covered the engorged peak of her breast.

Her eyes glazed over. Dazed as she was, her eyes remained locked on his. She was shuddering beneath him, so close. He could feel how close she was.

Pulling back, he quickly pulled the skirt and panties from her, and then almost tore his own clothing in his haste to have her.

He watched Chase lick at Jaci's perfect red nipples before moving down her body, sipping at her flesh, causing her to jerk, to tremble with pleasure.

Yet her eyes stayed on Cam. What did she see, he wondered, when she stared at him like that? And did he want to know?

She had to watch his eyes. They were wild and fierce, and only when he touched her and only when his passion raged out of control did she see what she needed to see.

That Cam belonged to her. In his eyes, she saw it. When he watched her and touched her, she felt it. She could feel Cam. She always had. She could stare into his eyes and see the bleak pain, the regret, the hunger and a man fighting to hold onto whatever secrets he hid. And it all touched her. She saw the shadows in his eyes brewing, saw the need growing.

He hid from her, until these times. Until she let herself fly beneath his touch and the pleasure he wanted to give her, needed to give her, for whatever reason.

She watched as she arched her hips to Chase's mouth, feeling his lips, his tongue, bury between her thighs, and responded with a growl of lust.

Cam's eyes flared as his gaze flickered to the sight, his fingers stroking his bare cock.

Kneeling beside her, he touched her face, her lips, his fingertips a gentle, tender caress.

"Feel good?"

"No." She panted, shaking her head. "It's killing me."

Killing her with pleasure. She felt like a flame inside, a twisting, desperate wildfire with no hope of being extinguished.

He smiled with a hard, tight curl of his lips as he fought to hold back. She didn't want him holding back. Pushing at his chest she drove him back and leaned forward, suddenly swiping her tongue over his cock head.

Touching him was imperative. She stared up at him while she took the engorged crest into her mouth and lost herself in him. When the pleasure burned this hot, this bright, she didn't know whose hands were doing what, just the sensations tearing through her.

She felt fingers stroking inside her pussy, pressing into her rear. Always gentle, easing inside her, preparing her and stretching her. Each penetration into her ass was another layer of lubrication, making her slick, making her want, ache.

She transferred the ache, that need to Cam. She wrapped her mouth around the crest of his cock, drew it deep inside her mouth and sucked with greedy abandon. Drawing on the stiff flesh, hearing his moans, seeing the wildness intensify in his eyes.

"I can't wait any longer." His voice was ragged with desperation as he pulled back, ignoring her protesting cry.

Then Chase was pulling back. Deserting her. Freeing her from the wicked touch of his lips and tongue around her swollen clit.

She couldn't face the desertion. She *needed*—now. She needed to feel Cam, needed the wicked, wild desperation that filled each touch he gave her.

Then he was touching her, pulling her to him, as he stretched out on the couch and dragged her over him. A second later, she was filled with him.

Keeping her eyes open was nearly impossible. Holding his gaze, seeing the bleak pain, the need that never seemed to die, tore her apart, as the pleasure he gave her threatened to explode through her.

Buried full-length inside her, he held her still. Hard hands on her hips, holding her to him, as Chase pressed her down to Cam's chest, forcing her to break eye contact.

"Talk to me." She moaned, needing a connection to

him, a center, as pleasure tore through her and whipped through her mind.

"Tell you how sexy you are? How much you please me?" He groaned, as Chase moved in behind her.

She whimpered at the feel of the wide crest of his cock tucking against her.

"It's going to burn," he whispered. "But you like the burn, don't you, baby?"

She liked the burn; she loved it. She trembled as she felt it building, felt Chase working his erection slowly inside her, burning her, as Cam filled the clenching depths of her pussy.

She was burning inside. Burning outside.

"I love hearing those cries." Cam held her head to his shoulder with one hand, as Chase's hands gripped her hips now. "Feeling your body tighten and grow hotter. It's like a drug, Jaci. I can't get enough of it."

She was almost screaming now. The intensity of the sensation tearing through her was killing her. How was she supposed to survive this?

Heat flared along every nerve ending Chase abraded and those that tightened around Cam's erection. With every inch that fed into her body, she went wilder.

Cam's voice at her ear grew rougher.

"So tight . . . sweet . . . ah, Jaci, that's my baby. Take all of it."

And then he got naughty. "Chase looks like he's dying for you," he whispered in her ear. "You're so tight, Jaci, so hot, it burns us, too." He moaned and the flesh inside her pussy trembled as Chase went deeper. "Fuck, yeah, grip me like that, baby."

Jaci screamed and the male cries joined her as Chase surged inside her, his hands tightening on her hips, taking her fully as she began to shudder, to jerk with the ecstasy, the agony.

"Damn you. Stay still." Chase's hand landed on her ass, but the slight burn wasn't enough. She needed it all. Cam was whispering in her ear, broken phrases, emotion filling his voice. The higher her pleasure went, the more she felt him, inside her soul. She ground herself on Cam's cock, then pushed back against Chase and cried out as his hand landed on her ass again and again, and the pleasure tore through her.

And it tore through them. They were thrusting inside her now, hard and deep, ragged curses tearing from Chase's lips.

"I love you, Jaci." Cam's voice was rich with despair, with pleasure, with pain. "God, yes. Fuck me. Take me sweetheart. All of me."

All of him. She exploded around him, gripping him, dissolving, her teeth biting into the hard muscle of his chest as she felt him jerk, crying out her name before the hard spurts of semen blasted into her and pushed her further into the dizzying vortex.

Pleasure, pain, ecstasy, and agony; and Cam whispering, always whispering.

"God, yes, love me, sweetheart. Love me."

Behind her, Chase jerked and shuddered. His sheathed cock throbbed inside her as he drove deep, stilled, and pumped his release into the condom he wore.

Jaci collapsed beneath them, her breathing ragged, her mind mush while her body continued to jerk, tiny aftershocks of pleasure still pumping through her.

She was barely aware of Chase moving. Cam didn't move. He stayed beneath her, his arms locked tight around her, his head buried against her neck, as he held her.

She needed him to hold her. Right now. This time, he couldn't let her go. If he let her go too soon, she would shatter. And if she shattered, God help her heart.

* * *

Chase cleaned up in the attached bathroom, and dressed before bracing his hands on the sink and lowering his head, gazing unseeingly into the sink.

He could still feel it. Whatever "that" was that had compelled him to find Cam. He couldn't figure it out. The echoes of the twin bond they had formed from the womb reverberated inside him—the bond that had been broken around their fifteenth birthday.

He still didn't know what had nearly broken his brother back then. Sometimes, he wondered if he ever would. But if what he felt now was any indication, God help him, he would have torn apart whoever caused it.

The bleak, dark pain that throbbed inside his mind didn't have a reason. It was Cam's pain; he had known it the instant he had felt it swirling through him. Like the nightmares they had had a habit of sharing as boys. It was like that. They wouldn't know the nightmare, just the fear. That was their bond. They always knew when the other was in danger, when the other feared. And Cam's fear now was like a dark, razor-sharp dagger tearing at his soul.

Jaci wasn't the cause, but she and whatever it was that Cam felt for her was the catalyst. Whatever emotions he fought to keep inside himself, she was drawing free.

But he feared what that would do to her now.

Shaking his head, he moved back into the other room, leaning against the wall as he watched his brother whisper to her.

Jaci was smiling now. A soft little smile, her eyes closed, as Cam sat naked on the couch, stroking her back.

"Better get her dressed. Courtney is waiting on her," Chase announced. "She's wanting to talk about that party she's wrangled us all into."

"No parties." Jaci covered a yawn before glancing over her shoulder at him.

Cam kissed the top of her head as Chase tossed him a damp cloth, then a dry towel.

The fact that her entire body flushed with embarrassment as Cam cleaned her wasn't commented on. The fact that she allowed it was a testament to the fact that, like Chase, she had an instinct about Cam. He needed to do that for her. Just as he needed to help her dress before he dressed himself.

"Invitations have already gone out," Cam told her as he drew his jeans over his legs and let Jaci fuss with her hair. "The Brockheim Ball is important to Courtney. She wants you there."

"Too bad." Jaci frowned at the announcement. "I know the Brockheims. Their events are too damned rich for my bank account to afford the dresses. I'll work on the house plans."

"Taken care of."

She turned to Cam as he drew his shirt on, buttoned it, and tucked it back into his jeans.

"Excuse me?" she asked him, holding onto her temper now.

This wasn't fair. First they drove her crazy, taking her in the middle of the day, and now they were driving her crazy another way. The Falladay twins were going to cause her to lose hair.

"The dress is being delivered to your room. You'll be the belle of the ball. And you're going."

"Not on your life." She stood toe-to-toe with Cam, trying to ignore Chase's amusement.

Cam's brow lifted, amusement sparkling in his eyes. He was loving her anger, and that just pissed her off more.

"You can walk into the ball or I can carry you in." He shrugged. "Your choice."

"I really don't like you," she ground out, knowing it

wasn't true, just as she knew it made no sense whatsoever for her to attend that damned ball.

He grinned back at her. "No, you just don't want me to kill Richard Roberts when he strikes out at you at that party." He tilted his head, and his eyes grew hard. "He's going to learn, Jaci, no matter where, he doesn't touch what belongs to me, either physically or verbally. You can't stop that."

Her lips parted as she fought to pull in air.

"I can take care of the Robertses. I don't need you fighting this battle."

"Then you should have taken care of them before now," he told her firmly. "Now it is my battle."

"By what right?" She felt like screaming. She would have screamed, if her voice wasn't already hoarse from her earlier screaming.

"By the fact that you're mine." He didn't yell, his voice wasn't cold. A simple statement, as he touched her face gently with calloused fingertips. "All mine."

"And you think that's reason enough to order me to this damned party?"

"No. To tell you. You're going to this damned party with me. After that ball, no one will doubt who stands in front of you. Not the Robertses, or anyone else."

Her eyes narrowed. "We'll see about that." She turned and strode to the door, jerked a few times on the knob, then turned back to him furiously.

She caught the glare he shot his brother, as Chase hit the electronic control and unlocked the door.

She snarled at both of them, then yanked the door open and stalked through the house to where she suspected Courtney would be. And of course, Cam was following her. That only irked her further.

The solarium was a small breakfast room set to the side of the dining room. Sunlight streamed through the glass-

enclosed room, gilding Courtney in warmth and light. Jaci
had to smile. That was Courtney. She made an impression
no matter where she was.

She was with her husband, laughing up at him, in the
corner of the room. Her expression was filled with love,
with teasing, sensual knowledge, while Ian's was dark
with desire.

Jaci came to a full stop, ducking her head as the knowledge that Ian was a part of that club slid through her mind
again. That he obviously shared his wife with other men.
That he was there—he watched, and he allowed her to be
touched by another man.

Jaci was suddenly more confused than she ever had
been, because she knew Courtney, she knew the other
woman's possessive tendencies. Courtney did not share
well. How in the hell had Ian convinced her that it was
okay for him to share another man's woman?

"There you are." Flavored with her native Spanish,
Courtney's voice was smooth, exotic. "I swear, if you don't
stop wearing those business suits, I'm going to scream,
Jaci. Wear jeans for a change." She laughed, then paused as
she surveyed Jaci's expression. "I gather Cam has informed
you of the party tonight?"

Jaci's chin snapped up, Courtney's words ignored, as
another thought hit her mind. Had Cam been in Courtney's bed? Had Ian shared the other woman with Cam and
Chase? She had to suddenly force her anger back, because
Courtney knew, she had known Cam's name for years,
knew what he meant to Jaci. Surely, she wouldn't have
thought it was okay to take him into her bed with her husband.

She couldn't handle this. She could feel her heart racing, feel the perspiration gathering along her back and the
sudden force of the anger building inside her, as she
stared back at Courtney.

Then Jaci glared back at her. She felt like declaring ownership, or something, just as Cam had.

She had no right to care. But she did. And the thought that Courtney would touch Cam for any reason, at any time, in a sexual nature, had her seeing red.

"Ian, Cam, I think Jaci and I will retire to the suite for a while. A few drinks and a little girl talk, you know?" She moved from her husband, her long hair rippling around her, snug jeans and a silk T-shirt hugging her body.

Courtney was beautiful, sexy, alluring, and she knew it. She held her husband in the palm of her hand, if the look on his face was any indication. Had she held Cam as easily?

Jaci turned and looked up at him, seeing only amusement, fondness—but none of the heated lust she saw in his gaze when he looked at her. When he looked at her, there was concern, a hint of male confusion. Men were always confused when they didn't get their way.

"Come along, my friend." Courtney patted her shoulder as she turned back to her. "I have wine and sweets. They go great together."

"They go straight to our hips," Jaci muttered, as she pulled away from Cam and shot him a hard look. She had better not learn he had slept with Courtney.

He smiled in return, a male acknowledgment of her ire, but with a total lack of concern.

She was definitely going to stop liking him.

Cam turned and watched as Jaci and Courtney left the room. He waited until they disappeared from sight before wincing, or allowing a measure of worry to show in his expression.

Ian was watching the door thoughtfully.

"Tell me, Cam, did you explain any of the concepts of the club to our lovely designer?" he asked with the air of a man who already knew the answer.

"I kept it simple." Perhaps too simple, because it was evident by the look on her face that Jaci was suspicious that maybe Cam had shared Courtney and Ian's bed as well.

Ian shook his head. "You know Courtney's going to tell her everything."

"Better Courtney than me." He grunted. "Have you ever tried to explain anything to a woman that she just wasn't willing to accept?"

Cam had a feeling that Jaci wouldn't completely understand the concepts of the club. It wasn't what she expected, and it sure as hell wasn't what she wanted to believe.

Ian laughed at his question. "Only every time I try to explain to Courtney why she isn't allowed to enter the club. Let's hope her friend isn't nearly so stubborn." Ian clapped him on the shoulder as he moved through the doorway. "Come into the office, there's a few things I need you to look over."

They moved from the solarium dining room before heading up the hall to Ian's office. The offices were located farther along the residential wing, making them less accessible to guests or members—especially nosy members, such as Richard Roberts.

Congressman Roberts was a thorn in Ian's side, and that was becoming more irritating over the past year. His wife had caught wind of the past gossip of the so-called "Trojans" club and had expended a great deal of effort in attempting to locate the club and the members. Evidently, she considered it her civic duty to reveal such depravity.

So far, any suspicion toward Ian and the little-known Sinclair club had been diverted, but several times Ian's security had caught the congressman attempting to slip into the area with one excuse or another. Just as Annalee Roberts had attempted to subtly question Courtney and several other wives of suspected members. Thankfully, the gossip that had bloomed several years before had been downplayed and eventually drowned out. The wife of the member who had revealed the knowledge of it had learned exactly what she stood to lose, and rather than risking her place in society, she had simply divorced her husband.

Once Cam and Chase had completed the investigation into the incident, the person's membership in the club had been revoked and his yearly security deposit forfeited. He was lucky he still had his job and his good name. The man had been a bastard.

"Roberts is making waves again," Ian announced, as he closed the office door behind them. "Several club members have contacted me this morning with the information that he's attempting to have Ms. Wright ostracized from the parties Courtney's had her invited to. Are you any closer to finding out what the hell is going on there?"

Irritation echoed in Ian's voice, glittered in his eyes.

Cam grimaced at the question. "She's not talking, but I warned you she wouldn't. No one else is talking, either. Evidently, she's chosen her friends very wisely, or, as I suspect, she's not told anyone what happened."

"Why? Her silence indicates guilt, Cam. She has an excellent reputation from that job on, but the rumor of attempted theft and an adulterous affair is making a few members rather nervous."

Cam shrugged. "They signed off on the project as well as the designer. They aren't allowed to bitch. They had all the information, innuendoes, and accusations at that time. Getting nervous now isn't acceptable."

Ian arched his brow. "We're talking about the same members here, right? Just because they signed off on it doesn't mean they aren't going to bitch. Some of those men worry worse than women."

Cam's lips quirked at the accusation.

"Has Roberts managed to have any of the invitations canceled?" Cam asked.

"Not yet." Ian moved across the room, his leanly muscled body tense with irritation. He moved behind his desk and threw himself into the expensive leather chair behind it, glowering back at Cam. "Roberts is pissing me off, Cam. I want to know why Ms. Wright has been targeted, so we can make moves to defend her position. Courtney's worried, and when she's worried she doesn't sleep well."

Which meant Ian didn't sleep well. Cam restrained his smile.

"I'm working on it, Ian. Getting information without her help isn't easy, though. The congressman and his wife protect their own privacy just as rigorously. So far, all we have are a few innuendoes of dirty games, but no definite reports."

Ian slouched back thoughtfully, an elbow resting on the arm of his chair as he scratched at his cheek.

"What kind of dirty games?"

Cam shook his head. "We're working on it, Ian."

They needed that information. Congressman Roberts had targeted Ian nearly a year before, when his application into the Sinclair men's club had been rejected.

The club was known in a very small circle of men. It wasn't hidden, they didn't try for complete secrecy of anything except the reason for it. Which meant there were a lot of applications rejected for one reason or the other. And a lot of resentment.

"We could put his name before the judiciary committee," Cam suggested, not for the first time.

The judiciary committee of the club was a twelve-member table that decided if anyone inside or outside the club required punitive measures. Those punitive measures could destroy a business, an individual, or a group. The combined force of the club members almost always followed the committee's decisions.

"Not yet." Ian shook his head. "I prefer we only use the

committee when the secrecy of the membership or our
charters are in jeopardy, Cam, you know that."

"They could become jeopardized if Roberts and his
wife continue this," Cam pointed out.

Ian straightened and leaned forward in his chair. "I
want proof," he stated. "I want to know why they've targeted Ms. Wright. Then I can go to the committee. She's
your woman; you've already stated that in the proposal for
her work here, in defense of the accusations made against
her. You took responsibility for her. Find out why her reputation is being targeted, and we can take that to the committee. Otherwise, we're S-O-L."

Shit out of luck. That just about described it.

"Ever try to make Courtney tell you something she
doesn't want you to know?" Cam asked him.

At that, Ian smiled. "I have my ways of learning her
secrets, Cam. Find out what works with Ms. Wright. If she
belongs to you, then we can defend her and take care of
the threat Roberts represents at the same time. The club
has its rules, its checks and balances, for a reason. Find
out what he did to her, then we can neutralize his threat to
the club before it becomes valid."

And that was imperative. Part of Cam and Chase's job
was identifying threats before they became a problem,
and finding ways to neutralize them before the committee
became involved; because, if they became involved, then
the punitive measures could affect more than the person
threatening the club. As Cam had told Jaci, it could affect
every relation, every friend, every area of a person's life.
The committee didn't always show mercy.

"It's an issue of trust, Cam," Ian finally said, his expression lightening as he leaned back in his chair. "She doesn't
trust you."

Cam stared back at him for long, silent moments.

"What the hell do you mean, she doesn't trust me? I'd kill for her, and she knows it."

That made zero sense. Jaci knew he would protect her against anything, didn't she?

"You said it yourself. It's been seven years since you've seen her. Seven years is a long time. A lot of hurt and sometimes a lot of pain. She's not going to give you what we need without trust."

Cam rubbed at the back of his neck, grimacing heavily. "There's no reason for her not to trust me, and she knows it."

Ian shook his head, a smile quirking his lips. "Let me guess, you've gone after her the same way you go after everything. Direct. To the point. Stating your demands and expecting her to fall in with them."

"I'm not that bad."

"Worse." Ian laughed. "Talk to your brother, Cam, he knows how to make a woman give what he needs. Maybe you should learn."

"I haven't had any trouble getting Jaci," he growled in disgust. "What the hell are you getting at?"

At that, Ian shook his head slowly. "Getting a woman's body and getting her heart are two different things. And gaining her trust is another problem entirely. You, my friend, are about to learn that the hard way."

And if Ian's expression was any indication, he was going to enjoy the hell out of watching it.

CHAPTER TEN

"You're angry." Courtney led the way into the large sitting room of her suite and glanced at Jaci over her shoulder as Jaci was closing the door carefully behind them.

Jaci turned and watched as Courtney drew a bottle of wine from the minifridge and gathered two glasses.

"Has Ian shared you with Cam?"

The words were out of her mouth before she could stop them. Jaci clenched her teeth and stood by them, though. She wasn't going to apologize for the question. So she crossed her arms over her breasts and stared firmly back at her friend.

Courtney rolled her eyes. "Really, Jaci, do you think I'd allow something such as that? I've known from the beginning what Cam was to you. I would never overstep those bounds. No matter how luscious he is." She winked shamelessly.

And Courtney wouldn't lie to her about it. Jaci knew that her friend, despite her often careless attitude, had a streak of honesty within her a mile wide. She might talk around a subject, she might lie shamelessly to her enemies, but with a friend, she was scrupulously honest.

"Come on, let's relax a bit," Courtney ordered, her voice firm as she plopped down on the couch, glasses and wine in hand. "I'll explain all the complex little rules of the world you've suddenly found yourself in. It's really quite unique and interesting."

Jaci sat down, accepted the wine, and watched Courtney warily. "Do I really want to hear this?"

"Of course you do." Courtney laughed. "Just imagine, Jaci, a group of men whose main focus, whose only thoughts are not just the pleasure but the protection of their women. In exchange for the greatest pleasure a woman can ever receive, by allowing their husbands, their lovers, a single sexual desire, whether they know it or not, they've gained the protection of hundreds. It's really pretty amazing, wouldn't you think?"

"It's really pretty far-fetched."

"But it isn't, Jaci. They have rules. Clear rules. And breaking those rules comes with quick, decisive punitive actions. Complete faithfulness, just to begin with. The men share their women, but those women never have to fear sharing their lovers or husbands, as long as they're with them. Spousal abuse is not allowed, and God forbid if one of those members should abuse his child. They protect their own and they punish their own, and the main reason for the club's existence is that protection. To provide a base of trustworthy men, single men who share the same needs, who understand the code the club was formed upon. A base of protection for themselves and their women. A place to come together with those who understand, and who can be trusted. The club has existed without detection for two hundred years because of that code, and because of the security they enact themselves. For our sakes. It really isn't so bad, being claimed by a member of the club."

"I won't be claimed."

"But my dear, Cam has already taken care of that. Already, members are contacting Ian, the whispers of the Robertses' campaign is drawing concern from them. They're ready to act in your favor, to protect you and to protect Cameron. It's too late to worry about being claimed, Jaci. That claiming is what allowed Ian to make certain you did get the job, despite the accusations the Robertses have spread against you."

Jaci lifted the wineglass to her lips and drained it before extending it for a refill. She didn't bother to reply until she had drained that one as well.

Maybe she needed something stronger than wine.

"Courtney, have you considered that perhaps this code you think the club runs by is no more than a thinly veiled illusion? Where's the honor, when a man expects his wife to take another man to their bed?" But she knew better, *she knew Cam's hunger*—trying to understand what drove it was making her insane, though.

Courtney eased herself deeper into the corner of the couch and drew her legs beneath her.

"There's honor in a pleasure so extreme, so all-consuming that a woman is left so completely sated she can barely move. Ian chose our third very carefully, Jaci. A man he knew was no risk to the emotional bond we share, one he knew would protect me, should anything happen when he wasn't around."

"And when that third decides to find his own lover or wife?" Jaci asked in disbelief. "What then, Courtney?"

"Then Ian and I will decide if another third is required or not." Courtney sipped at her wine. Jaci downed another half glass.

"Does he . . ." She waved her hand as she flushed in embarrassment. "Is he bisexual?"

Courtney's eyes rounded before a burst of laughter escaped her. "Do *you* think Ian's bisexual, Jaci?"

No, she had to admit he didn't.

"God, I'm going to lose my mind on this job." She shook her head and held out the wineglass. "You could have warned me. I hate you for not warning me, Courtney.

I'm going to hate you forever for not warning me." Of course, she really wouldn't . . . maybe.

"Oh, really? Would you have believed me?" Courtney waved the accusation away.

Jaci had to admit, it would have been hard to swallow, but she would have believed it.

"You should have warned me," she said again. "You don't know what I'm facing here, Courtney. Dealing with the Robertses will be bad enough, but now Cam's determined to get answers. Fighting them both is going to be hell."

"Why not just tell Cam the truth? Come on, Jaci, let him protect you. Let the club protect you. This is why it was created, why it still thrives. Your reputation is beyond reproach, as far as they're concerned. But they can't protect you without knowing what they're protecting you from."

Jaci shook her head. She wished she could tell Courtney. Sometimes the need to share the horror of that night was like an acid inside her soul. And the only person who knew couldn't allow herself to be associated with Jaci. If she did, then the plan they had put together would never work.

"Why do you hold their secrets, Jaci?" Courtney asked quietly, referring to the Robertses.

Jaci breathed out roughly. "How far can I trust you, Courtney?"

Courtney watched her, compassion filling her eyes. She sighed heavily.

"Don't tell me what happened, or I'll have to tell Ian. I can't hide that from him, because I'm as bound by the club rules as he is. But anything else, that stays between us."

"Anyone who knows Cam, even years ago, knew he always kept his word. Whether it was a promise or a threat."

"His reputation still stands, then." Courtney nodded.

"He swore he'd kill any man who hurt me," she whispered. "He made it a warning and a vow, Courtney. And there will be nothing I can do to stop him if he decides it's deserved. I won't be responsible for it. This isn't his fight."

"Have you ever told *anyone* what happened?" she asked.

Jaci's laugh was bitter. "The first month, someone I believed was a friend came very close to knowing. I found out he was a very close friend of the Robertses. And he believed everything they said about me." She shrugged. "They beat me to the punch. Their lies came before I could ever tell the truth. Now I would look like a liar, covering my own ass, and Cam would do something incredibly male and incredibly stupid because he made a promise. I won't allow that."

"And his need to share you with Chase?" Courtney asked. "That's not why you're fighting a relationship with him, is it Jaci?"

She shook her head. "I came here determined to do this job, to face the Robertses and win. Then I was going to find Cam. But I can't deal with both issues at once. I *won't* deal with it. After the job is finished, after the Robertses realize that striking out at me is a wasted effort, maybe then I can see where this can go."

Courtney shook her head at that. "Cam won't wait on that, Jaci."

She finished her wine and sat the glass on the table before turning back to her friend. "He doesn't have a choice."

And to that, Courtney smiled. A slow, amused, sympathetic smile. "I think you're going to learn, my friend, that it's you who won't have a choice. Once a club member has chosen his woman, they rarely go back on that vow. Ian knows of only one, in the entire history of the club, to do so, and I promise you, he's regretting it each second of his life. Cam won't wait. And I don't think you want him to."

Her friend's eyes twinkled. "And some men do have

some interesting ways of making certain that the word 'no' never passes a lady's lips again."

She was not going to ask. She was *not* going to ask. She didn't want to know what those ways were, or why Courtney looked so deliciously lost in thought over them.

"How did I know this job was going to make me insane?" She leaned forward, lifted her glass from the table, and held it out to Courtney once again. A refill. Just a little bit more false courage. "Anytime you're near, everything goes crazy."

"I know." Courtney smiled with smug satisfaction. "That's why I'm so much fun to be around."

"We might need another bottle after that comment."

Courtney laughed softly. "So, you'll be at the party tonight?" she asked, pouring Jaci another small measure of the fruity wine.

At that question, Jaci smiled. This time, it was her smile that caused concern to flicker in Courtney's eyes.

"I'll be there," she drawled.

"With Cam?"

"Only if he arrives at the same time I do." She toasted her friend with her glass. "And I wouldn't bet on that happening, Courtney. I really wouldn't."

She may have no choice but to attend the party, but Cam was going to find out that she didn't do orders very well at all. If he had claimed her, well, he could just learn what claiming her very well meant.

One of her greatest fears was being overwhelmed by his dominance and his sexuality. She had always feared she couldn't stand up to him, couldn't deny him. She was going to have to prove to herself and to him that she could. And she was going to have it do it at the same time that she was battling her nemesis.

Damn, why hadn't she just called Cam to begin with five years ago and let him wipe the floor with Roberts and have it done with? At that time, Cam might have restrained himself to beating the hell out of the other man, rather than killing him.

But she was afraid, very afraid, that after all this time, after all they had done to attempt to destroy her, Cam just might kill him after all.

Getting a woman's body and getting her heart are two different things. And gaining her trust is another problem entirely.

Cam wasn't exactly inept when it came to women, but for years, gaining their trust hadn't been one of his primary concerns. At least, no more than it had taken to get into their beds. That was an entirely different sort of trust, and he knew it.

And he didn't have Jaci's complete trust.

It was a startling realization, the knowledge that the woman he had claimed as his own didn't trust him enough to allow him to protect her.

He snorted at the thought of that one as he pulled the Harley into the underground garage of the converted warehouse he and Chase had bought just after accepting Ian Sinclair's offer five years before.

Two stories, cavernous and open; he and his brother had worked in their spare time for years, turning it into a livable space. The open rooms, tall windows, and spaciousness appealed to his need for freedom. After the ambush in Afghanistan, Cam had needed space, room to roam and to heal, after the military had returned him to the states.

Even worse than the need for space at that time had been the need for touch. It was then that he learned how finicky women could be. He and Chase had always appealed to women; it had been a shock to look in the mirror and realize the damage that had been done to his body, but even more surprising had been others' reactions to it. Everything from fascination to complete disgust. And he'd found, just because a woman wanted to live on the wild side for a little bit, it didn't mean that she had to appreciate the body that pulled her into the dark excesses that inhabited that side of her sexuality.

Yet, Jaci had touched him gently, with sorrow. And as she had, the need to take her without Chase had risen inside him.

His body tightened at the memory of that, as he moved quickly up the stairs to the first level of the "house." There, he strode first to the fridge and the cold beer waiting inside, twisted off the cap, flipped it into the garbage, then tilted the beer to his lips.

A long, cold drink later, he leaned against the counter and stared around the open room. There was an enclosed bathroom, shower, and Jacuzzi garden tub on the other side of the huge room. One side of the wall was thick, shadowed glass.

There was the kitchen and work island where he stood, just inside the doorway, then the room spread out into a living area, with sectional couches, thickly cushioned chairs, and a wide-screen television. There was a pool table and several old pinball machines behind that. Then, enclosed by filmy screens, was Cam's bedroom.

The king-size bed and matching unfinished furniture filled that corner of the room.

Upstairs was the weight room, home office, and Chase's bedroom and bath, as well as a kitchenette. As Chase had explained, sometimes a man just wanted a sandwich without trudging down the stairs.

And sometimes he needed his women alone. Sometimes he craved taking Jaci alone.

Chase didn't suffer from the darkness as often as Cam did. Sometimes Cam wondered if his twin couldn't live happily without ever sharing another woman.

Hell, Cam knew he could live without it. He did. Often. But sometimes, the memories crowded inside him, tore at him, and the need became a wrenching, brutal hunger that only increased the longer he ignored it.

Chase understood that hunger. He may not understand how Cam had come by it, but he knew the hunger.

He rubbed at the scars on his chest. The slashing scars weren't just from the bullets or the knife used during the attack. There were scars he had gained from the three days he'd spent as a prisoner of the small band of terrorists that had captured him and his team.

That agony was a joke, compared to other memories, though. Physical pain was a hell of a lot easier to forget than the broken memories of the three years of living hell after his parents had died and his aunt had been left to care for them.

His fingers tightened around the bottle as he restrained the urge to hurl it across the room. Hell, he'd just have to clean it up. And he'd long since grown tired of cleaning up the messes his rage had induced.

He relaxed his fingers slowly, inhaled deeply, and forced himself to remember the fresh, clean smell of Jaci's body, rather than the smell of fucking rose perfume, stale sex, and liquor.

He finished off the beer, breathed in roughly, then strode to the cordless phone at the center island. Jerking the phone from the base, he made a quick call to the exclusive boutique several streets from the hotel.

Speaking to the owner, he gave her his request—Jaci's size and coloring—and authorized the credit card transaction. Mrs. Lisette Miles, the owner of the boutique, was ecstatic with the sale, and more than happy to make certain the purchase was delivered to Ms. Wright at her hotel.

With that accomplished, he allowed a small, tight smile to touch his lips and moved quickly to the shower. Tonight he would try to seduce her into trusting him. Gaining her trust couldn't be that damned hard. Hell, she knew him, knew he would kill for her, knew he would do whatever it took to protect her. God help anyone who tried to hurt her, because he'd make certain they paid for it.

He'd stayed out of her life for seven years because he'd known she wasn't ready for him. Known he wasn't ready for her. She would come to him when she was ready. That was what he'd told himself over the years. He'd made certain her parents knew where he was, made certain he knew where she was working at any given time, and that she could find him if she needed him.

He wasn't a stalker. He wasn't obsessed. He just knew who his heart belonged to, just as he'd realized he may never have what he needed from her. The hardest part was the fear that he couldn't be what she needed. A part of him realized that, accepted it. He might never be the man she needed, but he couldn't walk away from her now.

He could have lived without her; he *was* living without her—until she arrived here, in his territory. She had come to him.

He shed his clothes and stepped beneath the shower, his teeth clenching as he fought back the dominance that raged inside him.

He had been living fine without her, but he was going to live better with her, and starting tonight she would learn that.

She was going to fight him, he could feel it, and it was more exhilarating than he could describe. She would challenge him, she would meet him head-on and make him work for what he wanted.

When was the last time he'd had to work for a damned thing, other than to get the information he dug up during the investigations he and Chase dove into? Sometimes that was work; but women had never been work. If one wasn't interested, then he could find another that was. No big deal, because none of them was Jaci.

Now, it was Jaci.

He washed his hair quickly before soaping his body, grimacing as he soaped and rinsed the thick length of his cock and thought of Jaci. A hard-on always made him think of Jaci.

Her life had been one of loneliness, he knew that from the investigative report. Her lovers were evidently few and far between, because he couldn't find them. She didn't make friends easily, and those friends she had made were intensely loyal.

A woman as fiery, beautiful, and passionate as Jaci needed more than a few long-distance friends, though. She needed a man. A lover she couldn't walk all over, one that would challenge her, make her blood hot. One that could take all that restless, burning passion inside her and return it to her tenfold.

He was the man to not just tame it, but to sate it. To make her burn over and over again, and to put out the flames with his touch, his kiss. His possession.

Ian was right. Jaci wasn't going to give him everything without more from him. He had hoped she would, had expected her to. He should have known better. Seven years wasn't going to weaken a woman who had been strong even at twenty-one. Strong enough to walk away from something he knew she had wanted down to the soles of her feet.

She was adventurous. She was a woman that would never belong to a weak man. And Cam was anything but weak.

Hell, he had more ghosts inside him than a haunted castle, and he knew damned good and well there were parts of him that might never be whole again. That would be the battle. Getting her to *trust* him, to belong to him, while keeping his secrets to himself.

Because those secrets could destroy him.

The secrets had nothing to do with seduction, though. They had nothing to do with making Jaci his.

Anticipation burned inside him at the thought of her and the seduction to come. He had never had to put himself out to seduce, but Jaci was definitely worthy of the effort. She was worth everything, even his own compulsion to never give a woman his release without a condom.

In his entire sexual life, he had never, not once, taken a woman without a condom. Evidently, Jaci had been just as careful, just as picky. And pickiness wasn't the end of it. It was more than picky, and he knew it. She had taken him, a part of her did trust him, he realized. She would have never allowed him to take her without protection if she didn't. So it wasn't just an issue of trust. Which meant he had to figure out exactly what that issue was.

CHAPTER ELEVEN

Jaci restrained her smile as she entered the Brockheim mansion. She had redesigned a vacation cabin for the Brockheims in Aspen two years before. The Brockheims had decided to leave the job to Jaci alone, rather than oversee it. Margaret Brockheim had worried about having her husband there at the time, after hearing the rumors of Jaci's home-wrecking tendencies. Their daughter, Moriah, had been at the cabin, unknown to her parents, as Jaci worked.

Moriah hadn't known Jaci was due to arrive that weekend. She had been hiding, suffering, and while Jaci had been there, they had found a bond in their hatred of the Robertses. That, and a plan.

The Brockheims were old money, old morals, and old grudges. They were in their seventies, considered themselves hip and modern, and enjoyed their social lives to the utmost.

How Courtney had managed to acquire an invitation for Jaci to this party, Jaci wouldn't know; but as she caught sight of her friends across the ballroom, Jaci had to admit it didn't surprise her.

Courtney was dressed in figure-hugging sapphire silk. Her hair was piled atop her head, long strands falling from the top to flow over one shoulder.

Beside her, Ian and Chase were dressed in tuxedos, looking powerful and decidedly handsome, while Khalid— standing nearby—conversed with another guest.

As Jaci made her way across the ballroom, the dark red evening gown she wore swished over the toes of the expensive shoes that had been delivered with it. She had to admit, Cam had excellent taste in women's clothes. Even the lacy panties and thigh-highs were silk, and fit perfectly. She felt like a carefully banked flame, and she knew that was the impression the evening gown gave.

"Oh, you are in so much trouble." Courtney laughed as Jaci grew close, her brown eyes both wickedly amused and chiding. "Cam has called twice from the hotel. He swears you're hiding in your room."

She was aware of Chase drawing his cell phone from his pocket and putting it to his ear.

"Traitor," she accused him lightly.

He was calling Cam, and she knew he was. Brotherly loyalty, no doubt. As he informed Cam she was now at the party, she had a feeling Chase was eagerly anticipating the fireworks.

"You are a dangerous woman," he told her, his lips quirking at her daring, while he pushed the cell phone back into the inner pocket of his jacket. "He's not happy with you right now."

"I've not been happy with him all day." She shrugged her bare shoulders, aware of Chase's gaze slipping over the rounded tops of her breasts, revealed by the snug design of the dress.

Her back was bare to the top of her hips, where the skirt smoothed over her curves, snug and almost revealing. It was one of the most exquisite dresses she had ever worn. It was definitely one of the most expensive.

"Would you like to dance before he arrives?" Chase invited, glancing to the dance floor where the band had drawn several couples out to enjoy the slow, haunting music.

She smiled as she shook her head. "I think I'll wait."

"You might not get the chance to dance later." Courtney laughed lightly. "Cam is going to be all about asserting that wonderful male dominance I'm certain he possesses."

She kept her voice low enough that her words carried no farther than Jaci, but her laughter drew several admiring male gazes.

"Then I'll just have to be all about asserting my own dominance," Jaci informed her.

She was brave. She was courageous. She could stand against the Robertses and she could stand against Cam. It was all in the proper illusion of strength, she decided. She was all about illusion. She had carried the illusion of unconcern and restraint for almost seven years. Five years definitely, ever since the night the Robertses had nearly destroyed her.

Speaking of the devils—she caught a glimpse of Annalee Roberts from the corner of her eye. The woman's falsely concerned expression as she talked to Margaret Brockheim was a warning in and of itself.

She knew the routine. She'd been asked to leave more than one party because of the Robertses. It was one of the reasons she had resisted attending this party.

"The rest of us should be taking notes," Chase teased, distracting her. "I don't think anyone has ever so blatantly defied Cam. He could be going into shock."

Jaci rolled her eyes. "I think Cam is a bit more resilient than that."

"I don't know," he mused. "That boy's sense of humor hasn't been right for a while now, but it was coming around. You could have caused a setback."

Jaci's lips pursed as she fought a smile. She glanced toward Margaret Brockheim, saw the frown that threat-

ened her brow as Annalee moved away to join another of
her cronies. The older woman's expression was troubled
now, her lined face heavy as she turned to her husband
and daughter.

"Excuse me a moment," Jaci said to Chase as she turned
and moved the short distance to the Brockheims.

She had expected this. She had known Annalee would
be quick to attempt to force the Brockheims to ask her to
leave. And Annalee had complete confidence in her ability
to frighten Moriah and force her to take her side in doing
so. Oh, how the mighty would fall soon, Jaci thought.

"Moriah. Mr. and Mrs. Brockheim. I hope you're still
enjoying the cabin." She extended her hand, seeing the
surprise on their faces, the flicker of indecision before
Margaret Brockheim took her hand, albeit weakly.

Mr. Brockheim's handshake was firmer, and Moriah's
held an edge of anger. Her hazel eyes were blazing with
ire, though her features, her expression, was perfectly
composed.

"We're glad you could make it, Ms. Wright." Harold
Brockheim nodded stiffly, his gaze flicking over her head.
"And the cabin is wonderful, as always. We were just there
last month."

"Daddy loves the deck," Moriah injected softly, her
composure perfect. "Especially the hidden ashtray you in-
corporated for his cigars. Mother doesn't fuss at him nearly
as much now."

Harold Brockheim's enjoyment of his cigars on the
back deck, his daughter had told Jaci, had been the cause
of several disagreements between the couple. Incorporat-
ing the hidden smoker's niche had been easy enough.

"The cabin is lovely, Ms. Wright." Margaret smiled
stiffly.

"You're close friends with the Sinclairs, then? And
the Falladay twins?" Moriah stepped around her parents,

the soft, gold material of her evening gown swishing around her.

Her parents watched her worriedly, meeting each other's gazes, as indecision seemed to shadow their eyes. They didn't want their daughter's perfect reputation smeared. Moriah was their only child, their pride and joy, from what Jaci understood.

"Courtney and I have been friends for years, and I've known Chase and Cam most of my life," Jaci revealed.

Moriah's gaze appeared curious now, her head tilting to the side, as the soft fall of sable hair slid over her pale shoulder. But Jaci could see the anger inside her—a hatred, a gleam of desperation that she knew was caused by the Robertses.

"Chase and Cam are good men," Harold stated, as though daring anyone to refute the statement.

"They're very good men." Jaci smiled in return. "And they were quite determined that I attend your ball. I hope the last-minute invitation didn't cause any problems."

"Oh dear, of course not," Margaret twittered nervously. "Courtney is a lovely young woman, and, why, Ian is almost family. I knew his parents quite well. We were so pleased you could attend."

The social lie was smooth and gracious, but Margaret's gaze was concerned. This was her ball, a social event that could turn around and slap her, if the wrong people were offended.

"Ms. Wright, I was just going to the buffet table for a small snack when you arrived." Moriah smiled. "Would you like to walk over with me?" A graceful wave of her hand toward the connecting buffet room was followed by a nervous smile.

"Of course," Jaci said. "I'd love to."

She could feel Chase's eyes boring into her as they moved off together. But it was the Brockheims who both-

ered her the most. They didn't want their daughter in her
company. They wanted her by their side, not making nice
with the problem of the week, where gossip was concerned.

Unfortunately for them, Moriah had her own agenda.
Especially where the Robertses were concerned.

"Richard is becoming more frightened, and spreading
gossip about you more than ever." Moriah lowered her
head as she spoke, pretending to check her purse for a
second as they moved through the crowd. "They'll strike
soon, Jaci."

"And when they do, we'll be ready for them." Jaci
shrugged.

"Annalee tried to order mother to make you leave." A
flare of anger lit the brown depths of Moriah's gaze. "As
though anyone can order my mother to do anything. But
she upset her, and father isn't pleased over that."

"I'm sorry about that, Moriah," Jaci said softly as they
entered the buffet room. "I hate to be the cause of any
problems for your family."

"As though my parents haven't dealt with their kind before." Moriah's voice took a decided snap as she led Jaci to
a deserted corner of the room. "And I'm tired of waiting.
We should make the first move. This has to end."

"Enough, Moriah." Jaci glanced around, making certain no one could overhear their conversation. "We have
to have the evidence first. Until we acquire that, then we
have nothing to back us up."

Moriah's lips thinned in anger, and she turned her
back to the room to ensure no one could see the emotion
on her face.

Moriah Brockheim was a completely different woman
when there were no social rules in effect. She laughed
and played practical jokes, she was prone to drink a little
too much wine when with friends, and she knew how to
keep their secrets, because she had a few of her own.

"They aren't as careful, nor are they as smart as they used to be," Moriah said as she turned and led Jaci from the buffet room. "Come on, let's find Daddy's office. He has a marvelous brandy in there. I think I could use a shot of it."

The office was secluded, private. Moriah coded in the lock, then opened the door and ushered Jaci inside before locking it behind them.

"I hate these parties," Moriah said, as she turned on a lamp and moved across the room, her dress brushing with a soft sigh against the hardwood floor. "Father always gets worried when I refuse to attend."

She moved to the bar, poured the brandy, and then handed Jaci a glass.

"Annalee's stories have been changing over the years," she said then. "The woman is obviously losing it. Father became enraged tonight while she was demanding that you be ordered from the party. It seems, in addition to attempting to steal the money and seducing her husband, that you attempted to seduce her as well." Moriah's grimace of enraged distaste was painful to see. "As though that slut would need to be seduced."

Moriah was a secret friend, one Jaci had made certain no one suspected she possessed. Moriah's experience with the Robertses went back further than Jaci's, and the scars from it went deeper. Neither of them could risk the Robertses knowing how close their association truly was.

"Moriah, you should have told your parents by now," Jaci said.

Moriah sniffed at that. "Father would kill them. Mother would cry for months, and the scandal would be horrifying. But I want to see them destroyed, Jaci. I want it with a hunger that keeps me awake at night." Her fist clenched at her side before she lifted the brandy glass and choked back the liquor in it.

She coughed after it went down, her face flushed, and a second later she seemed to gain the control she needed to breath out wearily.

"Have you told Cameron what happened?" Moriah asked.

Jaci shook her head. "You'll know when Cam knows—everyone will know."

"You're going to have to do something about that bitch soon," Moriah said. "She won't stop."

"I told you, it ends here."

She and Moriah had talked several times after she had come to Alexandria, though they didn't dare to meet outside the social arena that would bring them together.

"Daddy will of course discuss all this in great detail after the party." Moriah's smile was tight and hard. "Mother is upset at Annalee's demands. You could see Annalee's fear in her eyes tonight. Or perhaps I just wanted to see it. I'll let you know what they say. Daddy won't stand for such behavior in his home."

"Moriah, have they bothered you further?" Jaci asked. She worried about that. They had terrified Moriah years before, left her with scars that Jaci feared might never heal.

"They know better," Moriah snarled, her lips tightening as the rage inside her flared to the surface. "The only thing that keeps me silent is the fact that it would destroy my parents. They would blame themselves for it, and I can't bear that." She shook her head as she sat the brandy glass carefully on the bar.

When she turned back to Jaci, there was a glitter of tears in her eyes. "Do you still have nightmares, Jaci?"

Jaci nodded slowly. "Yes."

"I see them and I become ill." Moriah breathed out roughly. "Sometimes I wonder if I'll ever forget it."

"You won't forget it," Jaci said, "but you're surviving, Moriah. That's all any of us can do."

Moriah breathed in roughly and nodded again. "Very well, we'd better get back. I'll call you tonight and let you know what Father said. Perhaps somehow, together, we can find a way to neutralize those monsters."

Monsters were exactly what they were. As Moriah moved ahead of her to allow them to reenter the party separately, Jaci felt her chest clench at the other girl's pain.

It was one thing to attempt to attack a grown woman and force her into the nasty games the Robertses played. But they also had attempted to force a child into them. Moriah had only been fifteen when her parents sent her to spend the summer with the Robertses while they traveled overseas to attend to business Harold Brockheim had.

During that summer, Annalee Roberts had nearly broken the young girl—terrified her to the point that, once her parents returned, she never spoke of it. And she had never forgotten it.

They hadn't raped her; and to this day, Jaci didn't know what had stopped them. But they had tormented her. Tortured her. They spanked her for the slightest infraction. They humiliated her, broke her confidence down. Threatened her and her parents, allowed her to see things she should never have seen and hear things that marked her, where her own sexuality was concerned.

The weeks she and Jaci had spent in her parent's Colorado cabin had been enlightening for her, as well as for Jaci. She was the only person Jaci had ever revealed the truth to, and Jaci knew Moriah would never reveal those secrets.

Now they were both determined to make their stand. The younger woman was the only true ally Jaci had. She would be the only person who could help her when that particular showdown came.

As she moved back into the ballroom, she came to a slow stop just within the wide double doors that had been thrown back to open the buffet room into the ballroom.

She could feel Cam. He was there, his gaze sliding over her, touching her.

She was wearing the dress he had bought her, the shoes, the panties, and the stockings, and she could feel him claiming ownership of her.

A second later, her gaze was drawn across the room; it locked with his, and she could have sworn the ballroom receded as she stared back at him. There was only the two of them.

How interesting. She had heard of the phenomena, had heard others speak of it. How the world and their vision narrowed down to one person, one event, one moment in time. And that was how it happened.

The scar at the side of his face was wicked white, indicating his anger. His expression was brooding, his thick black hair was pulled back to his nape, and the evening clothes did nothing to hide the powerful frame beneath.

He was a man in his prime—intent, dominant, and ready to take what belonged to him. Tonight, he would take her. She could feel it. The knowledge of it was rushing through her veins, heating her, sensitizing her, making her aware of all the ways she was a woman. And he was the man that would own her.

She had hoped to face this moment later—after she had dealt with the Robertses, after she had proven to herself that she wasn't weak, that she could fight them on their own turf.

The knowledge that she had run from the Robertses, when she was younger, had haunted her for five years. She had been weak, too weak to know what they were before they had struck, too weak to strike back. She wasn't weak anymore, she told herself. She had learned how to face the world.

But she hadn't learned how to handle Cam or the desires he caused to burn inside her. She hadn't learned how to handle the knowledge that, with very little effort on his part, she was going to love him with an intensity that had the power to destroy her. From the moment she had seen him, when she had been no more than a young teen, something within her had known he was important to her. And that hadn't changed.

The Robertses had been an excuse, when it came to her forming no intimate attachments. In a blinding moment of insight, she saw that now. She had refused to go to Cam, so she had needed an excuse, a reason not to allow another man to touch her, to take her. Because she couldn't forget him. She couldn't get him out of her mind or her heart, and every man she had met she compared to him, and they had fallen far short of the mark.

How immature she had been, she thought, as he began to move across the room. How stupid. How much time she had wasted coming to him. Because she was frightened. Because she knew she would have to face parts of herself that she wasn't certain she wanted to face. Parts of herself that she knew Cam would force her to face now.

Dealing with the Robertses, as well as what she knew would develop between her and Cam, was going to require some careful stepping. Cam wasn't the type of man who would let her handle it on her own if he knew what was going on. She would have to watch herself, but even more, she would have to keep a closer eye on what the Robertses were doing.

She had worked for five years to gain the power to face them on their own turf. All she needed now was the setup. Moriah would help provide that, but it would take time. And with Cam around, time wasn't something she would have a lot of.

She stood her ground now, took a slow, deep breath, and let her smile touch her lips as Cam stopped within a breath of her.

His gaze raked over her, the force of it stroking the flames inside her hotter, higher.

"Good evening, Cam," she greeted him softly, aware of those around them watching them curiously.

His gaze slid over her breasts then to her eyes. "Are you having fun?" he asked her, the gentleness of his voice sending a flashpoint of warning up her spine.

"Actually, I am." She tightened her fingers on the small evening clutch she held. Nerves jangled through her system, primitive awareness screamed through her mind. "Are you?"

He leaned closer, a dark smile curling his lips. "Not yet. But I will be before the night's over."

"Ms. Wright. Hello there, Cam. Good to see you here."

The spell that had woven around them dissipated at the sound of the booming voice at their side.

Cam eased back, while Jaci flinched, turning to the couple that stood to their side.

She recognized them: Brian and Lenore Zimmer. Brian was tall and balding, his brown hair cut conservatively at the back and sides, the top shining unashamedly. Brian and his wife were lawyers for one of the larger firms in Alexandria. They were upper crust, blue blood, and Lenore had roomed with Annalee in college.

"Hello Brian, Lenore." Cam moved to her side, his hand landing at her lower back, a move that proclaimed his possessiveness as well as his protectiveness.

"Brian, Lenore." Jaci kept her smile even, polite.

"Moriah says you did a wonderful job with her parent's cabin," Lenore said, her cultured voice smooth and perfectly pitched. "Brian and I were interested in discussing a project with you, once you've completed the Sinclair mansion."

Interesting.

The Zimmers were easily as powerful as the Robertses

within the Alexandria-D.C. area, and if they weren't, then Brian Zimmer's father definitely was.

"I'd be happy to talk to you about it, Lenore," Jaci answered, and she opened her purse and withdrew a business card. "Contact me whenever you have a chance, and we'll set up a time to talk."

Lenore's aristocratic features relaxed marginally and her smile became less polite and a bit warmer.

"Courtney is raving about the designs you've shown her so far for the mansion," she said. "There was talk, though, that you had no intentions of lingering in Alexandria once you were finished with the Sinclair home."

"Really?" Jaci asked. "I haven't made any decisions regarding projects in the area, but I'm a businesswoman, Lenore, as I'm certain you understand. My plans often hinge on the projects available in an area."

She was aware of Cam and Brian Zimmer talking quietly at the side. Lenore's gaze flickered to her husband. She turned slightly, the shimmering blue-and-smoke shade of her evening gown darkening her gray eyes.

"I wanted to be certain to catch you before others could arrange your schedule for you." She lowered her head and glanced back at Jaci through lowered lashes. "I'm sure you're aware there are those who are eager to see you leave town as quickly as possible."

Jaci's brows arched curiously. "Some people will have to live with the inconvenience, then."

Lenore's lips twitched in amusement, before her expression smoothed once again.

"I look forward to discussing the project with you, then." Lenore nodded firmly, the sleek, dark hair feathering around her sharply defined face, as a smile curled at her lips. She turned back to her husband. "Are you ready, Brian?"

He frowned, though his hazel-brown eyes gleamed

with laughter. "But Lenore, she hasn't come on to me yet. Do we have to leave before she has the chance?"

Jaci froze, then blinked at Brian in shock, as Cam seemed to growl at her side.

"Brian, it's the wrong time for your jokes," Cam warned him.

"Hit him, Cam. He's only getting worse." Lenore was obviously hiding her laughter. "I can't take him out in public at all anymore."

"Brian, I catch you in the sparring ring again, and I'm going to hurt you," Cam warned him, though amusement lurked in his voice.

Jaci glanced up at him, saw the laughter lurking in his gaze, despite his cool expression.

"Hell, you two won't let me have any fun anymore." Brian shrugged his shoulders and flashed Jaci a subtle wink. "Maybe you can teach him how to enjoy life some."

"You're looking at the wrong girl," she told him. "I was hoping he could teach *me* how to have fun."

Cam tensed beside her, the obvious sexual vibes rising between them were thick enough to cut with a knife. She couldn't push Cam away, she couldn't push him back; that left distracting him. It wouldn't take long, she assured herself. She and Moriah would have things ready soon. She just had to push Richard and Annalee a little bit further. Just enough to make them stupid enough to contact her, to say the wrong thing. Just enough to set them up and neutralize them.

She glanced around the ballroom as Brian and Cam returned to a business discussion, her gaze meeting Annalee Roberts's.

Shoulder-length black hair framed her porcelain face and long, slender neck. Tonight she was dressed in a soft, cream-colored silk. Hell, she looked almost virginal. Her blue eyes were full of fury, though—narrowed, glittering with rage, as her ruby-red lips thinned in displeasure.

She might be dressed in the color of almost-purity right now, but Jaci knew what she looked like in black leather and with a whip in her hand. The scar across Jaci's hip was evidence that the woman liked to use a whip and loved to leave lasting reminders of her sadism.

Jaci ignored the nerves in her stomach, let a smile touch her lips as she accepted a glass of champagne from the waiter and lifted it in a subtle toast to the other woman.

Then she turned back to Cam, deliberately assuring Annalee how little her anger meant.

Oh yes, she just needed to push her a little bit further.

CHAPTER TWELVE

"Would you like to tell me what the hell you were up to at the Brockheim party?"

Cam all but slammed the hotel room door closed hours later, as Jaci tossed her clutch onto the table just inside the room and turned to face both him and Chase.

Chase had been eerily silent during the drive from the party, his expression dark and closed, his eyes watching, tracking both Jaci and Cam's expressions constantly. He'd made Cam feel like a fucking bug under a microscope.

Until Cam looked at Jaci. When he did, he could see the defiance in her expression, but there was something more in her face that almost terrified him. As though the veil of calm indifference that had been there before had been stripped away by some unknown force. She faced him now, none of the shadows that had once hid her from him in place.

"I wasn't up to anything." She spread her arms out from her body, drawing attention to those luscious curves.

Cam gave her what she was after. He let his gaze flicker over that dark red dress, but he watched those incredible eyes from the corner of his, just as he knew Chase was watching her, lusting for her. That defiance only fueled the desire. The desire was in turn fueled by the knowledge that she was his. His, by God, and she would not continue in whatever was up between her and the Robertses.

"You're up to something, all right," he grunted as he shrugged his jacket from his shoulders and moved into the sitting room, aware of Chase crossing his arms over his chest and watching both of them carefully.

She watched them both warily. He could see her thinking, calculating her odds of blowing off his suspicions.

"You challenged Annalee at that party, Jaci. I'm not a fool. I saw that look you gave her."

And he wasn't the only one. Brian Zimmer had seen it, and he had been concerned. As one of the club's legal advisors, Brian had been keeping up with the investigation into the Robertses' vendetta against Jaci, as well as the reports that were still coming in on Jaci herself.

She had met a lot of people over the years; there had to have been someone she had revealed the truth to. A friend, a lover they hadn't yet found, someone she had talked to in a moment of weakness.

It wasn't Courtney, which surprised Cam. Jaci was closer to Courtney than she had been to her girlhood friends in Oklahoma.

"Annalee was trying to have me thrown out of the party." She kicked her shoes off, revealing the smoky silk hose that covered her toes. "I was merely acknowledging the fact that I had won this round, nothing more. Margaret and Harold Brockheim weren't about to throw me out. It wouldn't be acceptable, after inviting me to begin with."

That was true enough. "Didn't you do some designs for them a few years back?" Chase asked.

She smiled. "A cabin in Colorado. They weren't there. I don't think Margaret trusted me around her husband. I'm a home-wrecker, remember?"

Cam's teeth ground together at the mocking retort. Damn her, he didn't need a reminder of the damage the

Robertses had tried to cause her. He was ready to kill them, as it was.

"You're pushing me. I've never in my life killed a man without reason, Jaci, but if I keep seeing the damage Richard Roberts and his wife have done to you, then I might break that little rule."

An edge of panic flared in her eyes, causing him to watch her suspiciously. Why the hell would she care if his wrath fell on Richard Roberts?

"Annalee is a bitch. That's no reason to kill Richard. Besides, neither of them is worth the effort or the cost of a bullet. And before you start threatening others, consider how you affect me everytime you leave me in my bed, alone."

His eyes narrowed as she turned and moved farther away from him, the silk of her gown rustling against the silk that covered her legs. "That bed doesn't define us," he bit out.

"It will soon." The silk of her stocking rasped against her gown as she turned.

He had ordered smoky thigh-highs. Silk. Smoke and fire was the image he had in his mind, and that was the image that met his eyes when he saw her at the party. Jaci was pure stubborn. He knew it. Chase knew it. And Cam was determined to find a way around it.

Cam had to forcibly restrain himself from following after her, from pushing her against the wall, and thrusting as hard and deep inside her as possible. He had wanted her, until it was like a fire in his balls; but seeing her tonight, seeing the confidence and determination in her eyes when he glimpsed her across the ballroom, the challenge she had silently thrown to Annalee and given him as well, it was as though he had always sensed the woman he was seeing now. The hunger that tore at his guts was nearly painful in its intensity. He looked at Chase and acknowledged the fact she might be strong enough to defy him entirely.

This was the woman he had always sensed inside her. The woman that could walk away from him.

He glanced at Chase again, seeing the lust, the obvious anticipation. His brother would fight or fuck, whichever Cam chose in this battle he and Jaci seemed to be waging now. It was going to have to be the latter, because he'd be damned if he could think with this need clawing at his insides.

He swallowed tightly, his fingers going to the buttons of his shirt as he watched her nimble little fingers grip the tab of the zipper at her lower back.

The snug material parted, revealing the silken line of the thong he had bought for her.

He felt his mouth go dry, then water, as she turned to him, gave her shoulders a little shrug, and let the dress slip down her body until it pooled at her feet.

He tore the shirt from his shoulders even as he moved, striding across the room and jerking her into his arms. He heard her gasp as his lips covered hers, and he barely restrained his own primal growl.

She met him hunger for hunger, need for need. Her lips parted, her tongue mingled with his. Slender, silken fingers dove into his hair and pulled, jerking free the dark band that held it back.

His hands were on her ass, gripping the rounded globes and lifting her to him. Long legs wrapped around his hips, the heated folds of her pussy heated his cock, even through the layers of clothing, as he stumbled backward from the pleasure. He kept her in his grip, held her lips with his, and caught himself with his shoulder against the wall.

"Dammit, don't fall," Chase growled. Somehow his brother had actually managed to get in front of them.

Shit. Control. Where the hell was his control? He was

going to spank that pretty ass for being so daring. He was going to teach her to follow his lead. But hell, he'd have to release her lips to do that. He'd have to unwrap those gorgeous legs from around his waist, and he just wasn't willing to do that.

He could barely stand to pull his lips away long enough to taste her jaw, her neck, as he struggled to get to the bedroom. He was not going to take her on the fucking couch.

Then she moved. Her legs tightened around his waist, shifted, heat raked across his dick, and he found himself flat on his ass on the couch.

Okay, he could do this here.

He gripped her ass, moved her against his cock, and ran his lips over the upper swells of her breasts. She tasted like the finest sugar, sweet and lickable. Fucking addictive.

When she lifted against him, her legs drawing from behind his back to kneel astride him, her sweet nipples were just below his lips.

Berry ripe. They were tight and hard, tempting him to taste, to savor. How the hell was a man supposed to resist that temptation? A temptation he had denied himself for— how long now?

More than seven years. Long before she had turned twenty-one. He had noticed her when she was a sweet, tender sixteen, and he had known she was going to be his. He hadn't been more than twenty-one or twenty-two himself. He'd been a man for years by then. A soldier moving into the Special Forces. He'd thought he knew what he wanted, thought he knew what life was.

How damned wrong he had been.

This was what life was all about. This woman in his arms, this fire burning inside him, unlike any fire he had ever known in his life.

"In the bed," he groaned, though he couldn't resist those

nipples. He licked them, sucked them into his mouth, and made no move to leave the couch.

Behind her, Chase turned her head to the side and lowered his lips to hers as Cam devoured her breasts. They were going to take her. Right here. Right now. They would still that defiant fire raging inside her, then attempt to reason the truth out of her. Maybe.

She was a fire burning through him, and he knew he was lost. This time. This time was going to be hard and fast, he knew it, knew there was no fighting it. He had waited too long this time. This time . . . this time, they'd take her on the damned couch.

He lifted her and bore her back onto the couch as Chase released her, watching as she stretched out beneath Cam, her witchy eyes glittering with passion, with lust, her face flushed with it, her breasts swollen, rising and falling with her quick, hard breaths. Beside the couch, Chase was undressing quickly, his expression a mask of desire and interest, as he watched the battle raging between Cam and Jaci.

Cam tore at his belt, the fastening of his slacks.

He rose long enough, just enough to shed his slacks and underwear and to notice that Chase had done the same, then, kneeling by the couch, he spread Jaci's legs, spread them wide, and ran his fingers over the damp silk, the wet silk that covered the soft swell of her pussy.

He was going to take her hard and deep. But first he was going to taste her one more time. He was going to grow drunk on the passion that flowed from her, from the sweetness and wild tang of her lust.

Jaci stared down her body, seeing the sheen of perspiration over her breasts, her stomach, on Cam's forehead as he touched the panel of silk that covered the aching flesh of her sex.

Where had she gotten the sheer bravado that had overtaken her when she entered the hotel room with Cam and Chase, the wild domination and lust clearly apparent in their gazes? It was as though her common sense had decided to go on vacation and leave only her hormones to guard the bastions of self-preservation. And they weren't the best guards. Hell no, they were jumping up and down, burning inside her veins and begging for more.

"I used to dream of this," she whispered. That seductive siren's voice couldn't be hers. "With nothing but a vibrator or my own fingers for pleasure, I thought of this."

Lassitude swept over her, a weakening sexual intensity that melted inside her pussy, prepared her, and left her shaking in need.

Her breath caught as his gaze lifted to hers. Green fire blazed in his eyes, lust and male force, sending a surge of trepidation tripping through her.

"You're not dreaming now," he assured her.

His fingers gripped the band of the thong and pulled. Just that easily, the thin silk was torn from her body, to be dropped carelessly to the floor.

Jaci arched involuntarily, a cry leaving her throat as he pressed her legs farther apart and his head lowered to the dark auburn curls below.

"You ripped my panties," she breathed out roughly.

"You still have the stockings." His hands smoothed down the silk encasing her legs, as his breath whispered over her damp curls—just as Chase knelt beside the couch, the touch of his lips against her bare shoulder causing her to gasp in pleasure. The sheer sexiness, the eroticism of the moment, was enough to make any woman breathless.

In a burst of courage, hormones, or sheer insanity, she let the fingers of one hand trail from between her breasts to the top of her mound. And they watched. Cam's eyes seemed to glow.

"Touch yourself," he whispered, his voice like black velvet. "Show me how you dreamed of me, sweetheart."

She touched herself, and it was more sexually wicked than it had ever been. She let her fingers part the swollen folds, caress around her engorged clit, and felt fire lance through her womb as they watched.

This was hotter than any fantasy, any dream she could have conjured up.

"You're wet for us, Jaci," he growled, as she parted the folds farther, ran the tip of her finger along the drenched slit. "Sweet and wet. Hold yourself open sweetheart. Let me taste all that sugar."

The sound that slipped past her lips couldn't be her moan. That wild cry of need that echoed in the room as Cam's tongue flickered over her clit, then licked through the shallow valley, couldn't have been hers.

"I need you, Cam." She arched, digging the heel of one foot into the couch, the other into the floor, and lifted herself to his lips, his tongue.

Cam. He was finally here, hotter than her wildest daydream, his lips and tongue taking her, stealing her senses with kiss after kiss, as she dissolved beneath him. And Chase, his lips feathered over a nipple, his tongue licked, and a second later she was crying out in burning need when his lips covered the tip and drew it into his mouth.

With each touch of their tongues, each stroke, each male groan against her flesh, Jaci felt herself flying higher. She forgot to hold herself open, because Cam was doing that for her. One hand slid into his hair to hold her to him while she curled her other arm around Chase's neck to hold him in place as well.

It was exquisite. His lips between her thighs, Chase sucking at her nipple—and still it wasn't enough. Her head tossed, her hips rocked beneath their caresses, and fractured moans tore from her throat.

"More," her weak cry was desperate. "Cam. Please."

Pleasure was tearing through her, raking over her nerve endings, drawing her tight. Lips and tongues spread the fire through her, drew her clit tight and hard, and caused her vagina to pulse, to clench with need.

Every muscle was tight, straining. Oh God, she ached, she needed. She was so close, and yet the pleasure she had always dreamed of was so damned far away.

"Oh, yes." It was closer. Closer in the form of the feel of Cam's finger dipping inside her, pressing into the torturous depths of her pussy, stroking and caressing as his tongue licked at her clit, his lips kissed it with gentle pressure.

As he kissed and stroked, she felt another finger easing lower, teasing, stroking, caressing.

"There you go, sweetheart," he crooned, as she twisted beneath him, the feel of his finger inside her, another pressing, stroking against her rear. Preparing her.

It was so good. she had never felt anything like this, never known such pleasure as she felt with Cam. Then he drew her clit into the heat of his mouth, suckled at it firmly, stroked it with his tongue, and sent her screaming into orgasm.

Jaci lifted into the violence of the pleasure, let it consume her, let the intense burning pleasure tear through her with an ecstatic cry.

It rose and rose inside her, built and raced through her in a succession of bone-jarring explosions that had her crying out his name in desperation. And Cam had no mercy. The second the intensity of the pleasure began to ease, the violence of the shudders began to dim, Cam moved over her.

Jaci forced her eyes open, forced herself to focus on his, as she fought to pull oxygen into her lungs.

"There, sweetheart." His expression was tight, savage

with lust, while beside her, Chase rolled a condom over the impressive length and thickness of his erection.

"Another of those will kill me," she panted, her hands moving to the hard muscles of Cam's abs, feeling them flex and ripple beneath her touch.

"I'll keep you breathing, darlin'." Cam's voice was rough, grating with need, as he came over her, one elbow bracing his weight, while he used the other hand to guide the head of his cock into place. "Just hold onto me, Jaci. Hold onto me tight."

Her fingers clenched on his shoulders, her legs lifted as he shifted her beneath him, then her lashes fluttered in the most exquisite pleasure yet.

"Look at me, Jaci," he ordered roughly. "Look at me, let me see your eyes."

She forced her lashes to lift, met his gaze, and whimpered at the sensations flooding through her.

The feel of his cock working inside her was ecstasy, pleasure and pain combined, as the delicate muscles stretched to accommodate his length.

She had taken nothing larger than her dependable vibrator, and she hadn't anticipated needing a thicker one than the one she had. But Cam was much larger, harder, and so much hotter.

"So good." Her head tossed against the couch cushions. "So good, Cam."

He slid deeper, stretched her, burned her.

"Later. I'll spank you for making me this crazy later," he swore.

For some reason, she wasn't the least bit frightened of that promise.

"Okay. Fine. Later." She lifted her head, kissed his shoulder. "Later." Then she bit him.

The pleasure was burning, ecstatic. She forgot where Chase was. She didn't care. She had Cam now, and it was incredible. It was brutal and overwhelming. As her teeth sank into his shoulder, she heard his ragged cry and felt his muscles bunch. A second later, he moved. He lifted her, pulling her against his chest as he went to his back, drawing her over him as she felt Chase behind her.

Her eyes locked with his. They always did. She needed this connection with him to accept the connection with Chase. She needed to hold onto him, somewhere deep inside his soul, as she felt Chase preparing her. Felt his fingers opening her, stretching her. She felt the slickness of the lubrication, and torturous minutes later, felt the broad head of his cock pressing against her.

She couldn't scream. She cried out Cam's name, she clenched him tighter, bit him again, and felt the final thrust inside her rear bury the full length of Chase's cock inside her.

There was barely enough time to draw in a ragged breath, before they were moving again. Deep, hard strokes buried them inside her over and over again, stroked nerve endings that had only been revealed by their touch, stroked liquid flames inside her, and sent her exploding into a thousand, a million brilliant pinpoints of light.

She felt Cam jerk, shudder, felt his release inside her. She heard him growl her name at her ear, felt his lips, his rough kisses at her shoulder, as Chase jerked and shuddered, his cock throbbing inside her.

Cam possessed her, heart and soul. There was pleasure in the touch of both brothers, but in Cam's touch—in his hands, in his kisses—there was so much more than pleasure. And instinctively she knew, for him it was so much more than just the pleasure of sharing her. For now, it was more than just a need. It was a defense.

In a whisper of insight, she knew that part of Cam, the part he kept so closely guarded, saw this as a defense. If he shared her, if he let his brother have her as well, then in a way, he was holding a part of himself safe. There was no chance of releasing whatever he held so tightly bound. And in that moment, she swore that one day she would find out what he hid, and she would break into that heart. Because he owned her, and by God, she deserved to own him as well.

"Don't leave me, Cam," she whispered. "Not this time."

As soon as he could get his breath back, damn, as soon as he could find his brain rattling around in his head, Cam managed to ease Jaci into Chase's embrace so they could get her into the bedroom.

She whimpered in protest as his cock pulled free of her body, her fingers tightened at his shoulders then slipped and lay against Chase's arms, as Cam rose slowly to his feet and then lifted her from his brother.

"Don't leave her, Cam," Chase ordered. "Don't do that."

She cuddled against him, trusting, exhausted, as a bitter smile pulled at his lips and he carried her to the bedroom.

Pulling the blankets back, he laid her on the bed before carefully removing her stockings and covering her up. He stood there, refusing to crawl into that big bed with her to let her curl against him. It was a risk he couldn't take. Not now, not yet. He heard the door close in the front room as Chase left. He fought it. He had to.

Reaching down, he brushed the hair from her cheek, then whispered a kiss over her brow, before straightening and staring at that big bed once again. He wanted to stay until it ached inside him. But the fear of those emotions slashed too deep.

Shaking his head, he left the room, extinguishing the lights behind him and once again entering the sitting room. Long minutes later, dressed and ready to leave, he sat down on the couch, penned a short note, then collected his jacket and left the hotel room. Hating it, hating himself for his inability to give in to that need.

As he drove away from the hotel he felt the guilt that tugged at his chest, and calculated the risk he had taken in walking away from her. Women liked to be cuddled by their lovers, and he knew she considered him *her* lover; and it pissed them the hell off when a man up and left before they awoke. But he knew Jaci. If he had awakened her, she would have questioned him. Those too perceptive eyes would have seen too much right now, things he couldn't risk. Besides, he had work to do. Preliminary reports had come in from England on the investigation into Jaci's link with the Robertses, and he needed to get on that. He had to find out what the hell had happened, because he had a feeling Jaci was up to much more than just thumbing her nose at the congressman and his wife.

Cam was well aware of the very shadowed rumors that circulated about the congressman and his wife and the games they played with their secretary. There had been no rumors that those games had gone any further, but Jaci had stayed in the Robertses' mansion for a week, after they'd hired her to redesign the layout of the mansion. It was at that time that the Robertses had targeted her.

Something happened during that week. He knew it, could feel it, something that threatened her.

Cam could feel the hairs at the back of his neck prickling whenever he thought of the Robertses and Jaci together in that house for a week. Something primal awakened in him at the thought of that, an anger that threatened to burn into destructive rage.

Richard and Annalee Roberts kept their dirty laundry carefully hidden, but Cam knew what it was. He'd known others like them, had experienced the depravity that was a part of them. And he swore if he found out that depravity had touched Jaci, then Richard Roberts and his wife would burn.

* * *

Jaci heard the hotel room door snick closed, and opened her eyes slowly. She could feel the anger beginning to build inside her. She didn't want to admit that he would leave her like this. That he would just tuck her into the bed and then walk away.

There was a part of herself that reminded her that at least he had taken her to the bed. She'd heard complaints in their hometown that he would just get up, dress, and leave, with no more than laying a blanket over them.

Chase, it had been rumored, was the considerate one. He was the cuddler, the hugger. He was the one that stayed the night and left the next morning with a kiss and sweet words. Tonight, neither of them had stayed.

So why had she fixated on Cam instead?

She rolled over, flipped the blanket off, and left the bed. Padding into the living room, she moved to where she had dropped the evening gown and picked it up, her hand smoothing over the wrinkles as her gaze moved to the coffee table and the small note he had left.

She stopped and just stared at it. He had left her a note? He couldn't wake her up and explain why he was leaving, but he had left her a note.

She moved to the table, picked it up, and read. Her lips tightened and outrage trembled through her body.

You were sleeping so well, I didn't want to awaken you. I returned home to check on a few things and shower and change. Will pick you up at nine. Cam.

Oh. My. God. It was the same as a lie. He had written the note as though leaving at dawn, rather than minutes after the most incredible orgasm of her life.

"Bastard!" She wadded the note up and tossed it to the couch with a furious flick of her wrist.

Then in a burst of anger, she scooped it up, smoothed it out, opened her briefcase, and furiously shoved it inside.

"You're so dead, Cameron Falladay," she snarled, shak-

ing with anger as she stood naked, her body still sensitized
by his touch and sated by his possession of her. "You are so
fricken dead."

Jaci jerked her cell phone from the desk and hit Courtney's number. It was late. Too late to be calling, but she
was burning inside, furious.

"Jaci?" Courtney's tone was concerned, and faintly
drowsy, when she answered. "What's wrong?"

Jaci looked at the clock. It was after one in the morning.

"I'm sorry." She blinked back angry tears. Hurtful tears.
"It's too late to call."

"No, don't hang up. Just a second."

There was murmuring, the sound of Ian's voice in the
background, then silence.

"He left you, didn't he?" Courtney retorted moments
later, her tone irritated now. "I've heard rumors he does
such things, but I never believed he would be so insane as
to do this with you."

Jaci shook her head. She shouldn't have called. She
pushed her fingers through her hair, grimacing at the unfamiliar need to just talk.

"I don't know what to do," she finally whispered, knowing there was no one else she could talk to, no one else
who could come even close to understanding this problem.
"The sharing." She shook her head again. "The pleasure is
incredible, Courtney. But I need more."

"We are women." Courtney sighed. "The need to be
held is as strong as the need to be possessed."

Jaci moved back to the bed, pulled the comforter around
her, and stared into the darkness.

"I shouldn't have come here," she said then. "I should
have learned my lesson when I was twenty-one. Cam
doesn't want to be a lover, Courtney. When am I going to
accept that?"

"Jaci, dear, Cam is your lover already," Courtney stated.

"The possessiveness burns in his eyes. The need for more will resolve this. You have only to press the right buttons within him."

"He has buttons?" She sniffed. "I haven't found them."

And then, she heard the sound of a diabolical little laugh. Grown men were known to flinch at that sound. It was soft and sweet, filled with knowledge and with wicked, certain purpose.

"Ah, my friend," she drawled then. "Shall I tell you about the buttons such men possess?" Her voice lowered. "Take notes now dearest, because trust me, there are buttons and then, there are *buttons*. And for this man, who I know has never looked at a woman as he looks at you, for as long as I have known him, he would have many, many buttons."

Jaci breathed in roughly. "Games," she whispered. "I hate playing games."

"Not games, Jaci." She could almost see Courtney's frown. "This is no game. It is a war, my friend. And you must learn the rules or he will walk over your heart and bleed you to death. You know your lover, you know what you need. Fight for this, Jaci. Fight for his love."

The foreign flavor of her friend's voice soothed, softened.

"Do not worry." Courtney laughed then. "I intend to help you in this."

And this time, it was Jaci that flinched.

CHAPTER THIRTEEN

Here was the problem with becoming involved with a man a woman thought she knew. There were all those tangled memories, times when there was tenderness, times when there was anger. There was the memory of adrenaline coursing in those first stages of attraction. The memory of the man, who had always been dark but who had watched her in a way he hadn't watched other women. Even though she hadn't been fully a woman. And there was the memory of Cam's "buttons."

And there was the memory of the times when she had been so pissed with him that she could have kicked him. Each time he had dragged her from a party, each time she had learned he had warned a particularly wild boy away from her. Damn him, every time he had looked at her with those eyes of his full of the silent promise that one day she would belong to him.

And there was the memory of certain "buttons." Certain ways of ensuring Cam's attention, of pricking at the male instincts she had sensed he had. Ways of making certain he noticed her, that he came to her, that he desired her. When was been twenty-one, at that party he had dragged her from, she had realized then how the presence of other men around her made him nervous.

Defying him made his eyes darken. Challenging him

made his expression flex with what she had then sensed and now knew to be hunger. The little things she had forgotten over the years poured through her memories.

Courtney was right. This was a war. A very subtle war. And if she wanted to tear Cam from whatever demons drove him, then she was going to fight fire with fire.

Instinctive fire. Feminine fire. The kind of fire that she knew made him blaze with possessiveness and with hunger.

As she dressed the next morning, she let the memories of those days wash over her. Laughing with him, teasing him, making a game of drawing a smile from him. It was easy to make Chase smile; he was a prankster and loved laughing. At least, then he had been. He was older now, more mature, but that wicked amusement still lurked in his eyes. Possessiveness could still fill his gaze.

But Cam was darker, even less prone to laugh than he had been seven years before.

As with all small towns, there had been rumors of the Falladay twins even before they had reached maturity. With the death of their parents at a young age, they had been raised by a spinster aunt from out of town.

The day they turned eighteen, the aunt had been escorted out of the house by the local sheriff. There were rumors that she had abused the boys, but no verification of it. Cam had joined the military straight out of high school, and Chase had gone to college.

They had separated, and Jaci had never understood why. As she cinched the bright yellow belt over her jeans and adjusted the black, embroidered T-shirt over her stomach, a frown pulled at her brows.

No one had expected the twins to separate like that, but everyone had agreed there was a darker, more dangerous core to Cam than there had been to Chase—one that they hoped the military would dilute. It seemed, though, that whatever had happened there had only increased that darkness. Not the violence; Jaci didn't think there had ever been true violence inside him. But there was a core of hard cold steel inside him. He could be violent under the right circumstances.

No. Not violent. Violence was uncontrolled. No, Cam would be deadly when provoked. Cold. Hard. Merciless.

Staring into the full-length mirror, Jaci admitted to herself that that core had always drawn her. The steel, the determination, the danger that swirled in his eyes. He was the ultimate bad boy, and he called to her as no other man ever had.

Shaking her head, she strapped a black-and-silver watch to her wrist, smoothed her hands over her black jeans, and smiled with hard determination.

Cam had evidently come to the conclusion, along with others, that she was an easy mark. That her back was made to tromp on. Richard and Annalee had gotten away with it, simply because she hadn't known how to protect herself; and later she hadn't wanted Cam involved, because of the promise he had made to her. God forbid he should kill either of them, because she wanted them to suffer. She wanted them to lie awake at night and wonder, she wanted them to see her and, rather than finding ways to shred her reputation, she wanted them running the other way.

She had worked for this day, let them believe they had won, that she was frightened, that she could be manipulated. She had worked the situation until she knew their guard had dropped just enough—just enough to allow her the opportunity she had found with Moriah.

It was fate, she had decided the night she learned what Moriah had suffered at their hands. Only fate would have brought both of them together, would have given them both the feeling of trust in the other to reveal the secrets they harbored, and only fate would have put them both here in Virginia, together with the Robertses.

Just as fate had placed Cam here at the same time. Nothing could possibly be easy where this situation was concerned.

Breathing out roughly, she sat down on a chair and pulled on the leather ankle boots, lacing them quickly, before standing and checking the time.

Ten minutes.

Oh yes, she would definitely be waiting on him.

She grabbed her purse and leather case, then left her hotel room and entered the elevator. It was a quick trip to the lobby, where she moved to one of the stately columns rising from the floor of the lobby to the second floor. She leaned against one of them, restrained her smile, and watched as Cam pushed through the doors. He wasn't aware of her yet, his expression wasn't as controlled as she was certain he wanted it to be, because she saw the edge of concern pulling at his brows.

His expression fit the stormy, overcast skies outside the hotel.

She tightened her lips and restrained her smile at that expression. Oh, he knew he had messed up. She could see it in his face.

When his gaze finally found her, he paused, almost stopped, his gaze flickering, before it cleared and showed nothing but supreme male confidence and dominant assertion.

Jaci almost laughed. God, he could make her madder than anyone she had ever met in her life. How the hell did he think he was going to get away with sneaking out on her last night?

He moved to her, his arm bracing on the column her shoulder leaned upon and lowered his head. At the last second, he kissed her cheek rather than her lips. Not by

design, but because she had anticipated what was coming,
because she knew Cam. A kiss would weaken her, and he
knew it. She wasn't about to let him weaken her.

"It's rainy today." She looked up at him, keeping her
expression clear, keeping all indications of her anger buried beneath a bright smile. "I bet Courtney is whining
this morning. She hates the rain."

His gaze flickered again as he straightened.

"Are you ready?" He all but growled the words. "I
would have come up to your room. You didn't have to meet
me in the lobby."

Oh, she just bet he would have. And she bet he would
have immediately attempted to seduce her to make certain
she forgot about the night before. There was no forgetting.
The next time he got into her bed, he was going to know
the rules. There was no sneaking out five minutes later.
She hadn't waited all these years for her first lover, just to
have him ruin the experience by acting like an ass.

"I didn't mind meeting you." She smiled at him, giving
the words just enough of an edge to let him know she pre-
ferred it that way.

"What time did you leave?" she asked as they moved
through the doors and beneath the sheltered entrance to
the car that was waiting.

She didn't hear his answer, it was mumbled, muttered,
just as he helped her into the car and closed the door behind her.

She was starting to remember all the little idiosyncra-
sies that men had that made her crazy. She might not have
actually had sex in the past seven years, but she'd had
enough men try to bed her, to actually put time and effort
into it, to figure out some of the worse habits they had.
That mumbled, indistinct attempt at a reply was one of
them. At least he wasn't actually lying to her.

The ride to the mansion wasn't much better. She could

feel him trying to guess at what point she realized he had
left her room. No doubt he had already guessed; Cam
wasn't anyone's dummy. And now he was trying to anticipate just how angry she was and the best way to soothe
that anger.

Keep guessing, baby, she thought with an inward smile.
He might get it right. Eventually.

After pulling up to the Sinclair mansion in a drenching
rain, Cam watched as Matthew strode from the house, a
large umbrella held overhead as he helped Jaci from the
car.

"I'll see you later." She cast him a bright smile that did
nothing to fool him.

He knew women, and he knew she was pissed.

Damn. He pushed the car into gear and pulled around
the house to a covered parking area and came face-to-face
with his brother.

Chase was leaning against the side of his own car,
watching with a smile as Cam exited the Jaguar.

"What's that smug-assed smile for?" Cam grunted. It
was a familiar smile, one that assured him that somewhere,
somehow, Cam had managed to amuse him.

Chase shook his head. "I wonder about you sometimes,
bro. How can you manage to completely fuck up the deal
of a lifetime?"

Cam stopped at the hood of his own car and stared back
at his brother.

"What did I fuck up this time?" He almost smiled. As
far as Chase was concerned, he was invariably fucking up.
That big-brother complex was always in effect.

"Ian just called. He says Courtney is laughing her ass
off, after an early morning call from Jaci. Seems someone
slipped out five minutes after an orgasm that evidently
registered on the Richter scale." Chase was obviously
having trouble controlling his amusement. "Ian's rolling,

too, by the way. He could barely tell me what he heard for all his laughter. What the hell did you do? Leave right after I did?"

"I'm glad you're so fucking amused," Cam snapped, moving from the car and heading to the house. He and Jaci were going to have to have a talk about what she discussed with Courtney. Everything Courtney knew, Ian managed to find out. Of course, it worked in reverse, and that part sucked, too.

"Cam, man, you don't run off after registering on the Richter scale. Don't you know better than that? I thought you'd at least stay when I left."

Cam clenched his teeth and tried to shake off the anger he could feel building inside him. There was silence behind him as he moved toward the back entrance.

"When are you going to tell me what happened, Cam?"

Chase's question drew him to a stop. It wasn't the first time his brother had asked him that question. It wouldn't be the last time.

"Nothing happened." It was his standard answer.

He didn't get the standard response. Before he could anticipate Chase's move, his brother had swung him around to face him, his anger clear on his face now.

There was no amusement, no laughter lurking in his brother's eyes. For the first time since they were boys, Cam could feel his brother's rage directed toward him.

"How stupid do you think I am?" Chase bit out. "Do you think I haven't always known that something happened? Even when we were boys, I knew it. Tell me what the hell it was."

"Nothing happened, Chase." He was lying through his teeth, just as he always had.

Chase was the oldest twin; he had always felt responsible for Cam, always tried to look out for him.

His brother would never forgive himself if he knew.

Even then, all those years ago, it would have destroyed Chase even worse than it had Cam.

Chase's eyes glared into his, his expression furious, his dark face twisted into lines of pain.

"I hate it when you lie to me. I hate it even worse to see you screwing up your fucking life with the only woman that ever meant a damned thing to you. Is it worth losing her, Cam?"

"I won't lose her." No matter what, he would hold onto Jaci. No matter what it took. She didn't have to know the truth.

Chase pushed away from him, dragging the fingers of one hand through his hair as he all but snarled. "Damn you, Cam. What the hell are you doing to yourself?"

Cam could feel the threads of that twin psychic bond tugging between them. He could feel his brother's frustration, his worry, just as he knew Chase couldn't feel those darker emotions that Cam made certain stayed carefully buried.

He had learned over the years, when the darkness was like a bitter acid eating into his soul, he could share a lover with Chase, his or his brother's, and he could release that darkness and still stay grounded. It was the reason he had left Jaci so quickly. He could feel that darkness rising inside him, that need eating at his guts, and he knew he had to get away from her. From the need to give her everything. To explain. To belong.

"Stop worrying, Chase." He shrugged his shoulders, knowing that wasn't enough, knowing it did nothing to ease his brother's concern.

"Yeah, that's what you said when you joined the fucking military," Chase snapped. "Eighteen years old. You couldn't even wait two years, could you Cam? You had to go. What the hell did you get for it? A medical discharge and a thanks, but sorry, we can't pay you for your sacrifice?"

"The military didn't do this to me, Chase," Cam bit out.

"No, it just made it worse," Chase retorted. "Cam, listen to me man, you're fucking up with Jaci. Just like you did in Oklahoma. If you can't tell me what happened, then you damned well better tell her. Because I'm telling you, she's going to walk away again."

"She's not walking away." He would stop her. He didn't have to tell her the truth. He could hold her without it. He would make certain of it.

"If she walks away, that's it," Chase informed him, his voice tight and hard. "Do you understand that, Cam? If you push her away like you've pushed me away, and anyone else that could have cared for you, then I've had enough. If you can't trust me enough with the truth, then fuck it. What the hell are we even brothers for?"

"Blackmail, Chase?" Cam crossed his arms over his chest and glowered back at Chase.

"Fuck you, Cam." Chase's expression was tight, frustrated. Cam could see the conflict raging inside him—hell, he could feel it, and there was no way to help it.

"Chase, bro, you're blowing this all out of proportion," he told him lightly. "Jaci's going to be fine."

"You left her within minutes of taking her last night. Hell, I had barely left," he snapped. "Trust me, she's not fine. And, by God, neither am I. I'm sick of this. You can't even trust her enough to sleep with her. You don't trust me enough to tell me what the fucking problem is, but you expect both of us to just accept it."

"To accept me." The words tore from him.

Cam didn't know who was surprised the most. Chase by the demand, or himself because of the vehemence of it.

"Son of a bitch, do you have to have explanations for every damned thing?" Cam cursed. "What the hell is bothering you so bad? That I didn't stay with her last night? Or that you don't know every fucking area of my life? Do

I question you when you don't share a woman with me? Do I harass and interrogate you when you don't stay all night with one?"

"I'm not the bastard sleeping on the couch after bringing a woman home, either," Chase argued furiously, "but I am the one that can feel whatever it is inside you eating you alive. And whatever it is, Cam, it's going to drive her away. Trust me when I tell you that. If you don't tell her why you need to share her, why that hunger is tearing you apart, then she's going to tell you to get fucked."

"No, actually, she'll tell him he can do without being fucked. At least, by me."

They both swung around. Shock tore through Cam at the sight of Jaci, hip cocked, her arm braced in the open doorway, her expression unwavering.

Cam inhaled slowly, locked his teeth together, and fought the burning hunger inside him. He could see her, dazed, screaming in pleasure, trapped between him and Chase, burning with them as he loosed the gnawing intensity tearing through him.

"Shit, Cam," Chase muttered.

There was enough of that twin bond so that Chase could feel the echo of that need. Cam was amazed the ground wasn't shaking with the vibrations of the hunger. And, son of a bitch, the possessiveness.

"What the hell are you doing out here?" Cam shook his head.

Didn't it just figure? Any other time he would have brushed Chase's demands aside, rather than arguing over them. The one time he let his brother draw him into this argument, Jaci just had to show up.

Dressed in those snug jeans, in that T-shirt that revealed glimpses of her lower stomach between the hem of the shirt and the band of her jeans. The clothes were comfortable, wild, wicked. They weren't the business clothes she had been wearing, that was for damned sure. He was going to kill Courtney for demanding Jaci wear jeans. It should be illegal for her to wear jeans, dammit.

"I forgot my case in the car." She ambled from the doorway, smooth feminine grace and outrage emphasized with each step, as she moved past him. "I'm glad I did. So, tell us Cam, exactly why *was* it so important that you walk out on me last night?"

"I left you a note."

He hit the unlock on his auto key chain as she gripped the door latch, allowing her to open the door.

"Of course you did," she drawled sweetly, dangerously.

She bent to retrieve the case and he felt a fine film of perspiration coat his forehead at the sight of her rounded, taut little ass lifting, before she straightened, case in hand, and slammed the door closed.

She turned to them, and he knew what she saw: him and Chase both watching, their damned tongues hanging out in lust.

"Answers would be nice, Cam," she told him as she moved away, unhurried—that walk sexy as hell and causing his mouth to water at the remembered taste of her flesh.

"Yeah, answers would be really nice," Chase muttered.

"You two are barking up the wrong tree." He snorted with the casual denial he should have used earlier. "The only problem I have is a hard-on and a sexual twist. No big deal."

Jaci and Chase both snorted at that one.

"Let me know when you're ready to talk." She stopped and glanced at them both over her shoulder. "Maybe then I'd be ready to discuss your sexual twists and my own little abnormal desires. You never know what we all might learn that we haven't already."

With that, she turned and moved back into the house,

closing the door behind her and disappearing out of sight.
And Cam found his back slammed against the side of
Ian's Hummer, his brother in his face.

Lust and irritation flared in his brother's eyes. "You
better start talking," he grated. "Because you know what
she just did?"

Oh yeah, he knew, and his dick was hard as stone. It
didn't matter how many times he had her. She could still
do this to him.

"She just dared us, Cam. And I don't know about you,
but the thought of 'abnormal desires' dancing through her
mind is going to drive me fucking crazy. Now, fix it."

With that, Chase, too, stalked away, leaving Cam to
stare at the door, his lips quirking into a little smile of
disbelief. He'd be damned if she didn't stoke that burn inside him higher and hotter.

The need to have her again was already rising inside
him. That dark hunger, that need to push her, as well as
himself, was brewing inside him like a shadowed, furious
blaze. He could feel it building, the need to let loose, to let
all that hunger free that he kept tightly restrained, tearing
at his control.

God, what a mess. He'd latched onto that crutch when
he and Chase had first experimented with sharing a
woman. That darkness in his soul, the brewing bitterness,
was eased in seeing the pleasure, being able to watch as
the woman received pleasure, in building it, in pushing his
own boundaries, as well as hers. And in the distance sharing afforded him.

What it came down to, though, was that the very core
of that need was hidden in the twisted, demented evil of
the woman who had raised them.

They weren't even sexual desires. Not really. He had
known that even then. But the horrifying years he had
spent in silence had created something inside him that

he couldn't explain, and the only time he could release it was in the heated, wild ménages he had grown to depend upon.

As thunder and lightening crashed in the skies above, Cam swore he felt it crashing inside his soul, because Chase was right: She had dared them both, challenged them, made an offer he had no choice but to refuse. He wouldn't weigh down his brother's soul with the truth, and he sure as hell wouldn't burden Jaci's with it. He'd just have to convince her to reveal those "abnormal" desires.

He smiled at the thought, anticipation building inside him. She had thrown out the challenge, now he'd take her up on it. In his way. With all his secrets intact. Because he didn't know if he could survive the revelation of those secrets.

CHAPTER FOURTEEN

Chase stood inside the kitchen, staring out at the parking area, watching as his brother pushed his fingers through his hair, shook his head, and moved into the house.

"What happened to you, Cam?" he asked softly, knowing it would do no good to ask his brother that question. He had been asking that question since the first night Cam had disappeared from their bedroom, just after he turned fifteen.

They had been big for their ages, well developed, almost men, physically, but lost, uncertain, even for their ages. The death of their parents the year before had shaken them. The arrival of the Bitch from Hell, their mother's older sister, Davinda, had nearly destroyed them.

Whatever had happened had revolved around her.

Some nights, it was never predictable; Chase would wake up and go to check on his brother, and Cam would just be gone. Davinda never seemed to have answers to where he was, but she always knew. Chase had seen it in her eyes, she always knew. And as each year passed, the boy that was his brother had changed. The day they turned eighteen, Cam disappeared from school and showed up at the local sheriff's department. Chase never knew what he had told Sheriff Bridges, but that evening the sheriff arrived, took the Bitch into another room, and then waited silently in the hall while she packed and left their lives forever.

He had gone through her luggage before she left. Through her purse. He had made certain she left with nothing but her belongings. When she had left, he clapped Cam on the shoulder, muttered an apology, and left.

Cam had never told Chase what happened. Four months later, he joined the military and just left. Ten years later, he had been captured, then nearly killed during an ambush that had occurred after he and his team escaped their captors. The man that had returned five years ago had changed, to the point that Chase sometimes wondered who Cam even was.

The only times he even felt as though his brother were alive inside were the times they shared their lovers. Cam was different then. That stony, dark control loosened, and the hunger inside him was given freedom, to a small degree.

Well, it used to be a small degree. Since Jaci had walked back into their lives, Chase had come closer than he ever had to learning what had changed the boy so severely that it had created the man Cam had become.

With Jaci, the hunger was closer to the surface, and for the first time since they were fifteen, Chase had begun to glimpse his brother's nightmares.

They'd done that a lot when they were boys—sensed each others nightmares. Not their dreams or fantasies, or even their fears, just their nightmares. And the nightmares Chase had begun sensing was sending chills down his spine.

God help Davinda Morris, because if she was still alive, Chase knew he would have to seek her out and kill her himself. Whatever she had done to Cam had come close to destroying him. And now it was coming close to destroying Cam's last chance with Jaci.

Chase had known, even seven years before, that Jaci was Cam's weakness. He had felt it each time Cam had seen Jaci, talked to her, heard her laughter.

It wasn't a sexual or even an emotional knowledge. Just a sense that the darkness inside his brother had eased, and it had eased because of Jaci.

As he stood there, staring into the gloomy, rain-swept morning, he wondered if his brother would ever release the hold he had on his secrets, because he had a feeling he saw something in Jaci that Cam refused to see. She would never allow what Cam needed for the sake of pleasure alone. For Jaci, it would always be emotional, and it would always be tied to Cam and her trust in him. Without that trust, she would never allow it.

"Have you tried checking into your aunt's past?" Ian stepped into the room, his voice quiet. He knew Chase and Cam well enough, had seen Cam in the throes of that darkness, to know what was going on.

It was a problem that plagued both of them.

"Only about every year." Chase sighed. "He's not talking, and evidently I'm not looking in the right places."

He crossed his arms and leaned against the wall beside the wide, tall window that stared out into the covered parking area.

"I've investigated the sex clubs, both above- and underground. I've had every sexual predator known at the time investigated. I've had investigators working on Davinda's past as well her friends'. Nothing. No records, no hints of abuse. I'm missing something, Ian. I just can't figure out what."

He'd figured it was sexual abuse years before, but in the years since his brother had joined the military, and after, he'd never found proof of it.

Ian moved across the room and pulled a chair from the

table. Lights were out, the room was shadowed, lit occasionally with the hard, jagged flashes of lightning.

Straddling the chair, Ian stared back as Chase turned to watch him.

"If she walks away from him, I'll lose my brother forever," he said. "It's been coming for more than a year. That much I can feel. He'll leave, join a private paramilitary group, and the next thing I know, I'll be burying him. He was talking about it last year. Hints here and there." He shrugged. "The military nearly destroyed what was left of his compassion. The killing. Seeing the hell nations can visit on each other." He shook his head as he breathed out wearily. "He's cold inside, Ian. Almost pure ice."

"A man can't hinge his survival on a woman, Chase," Ian said compassionately. "I think you're wrong about him. He's stronger than that."

"He's too fucking strong." Chase rubbed at his chin wearily. "That's the problem. Too controlled. Too secretive. Too determined to make certain I don't blame myself for whatever happened to him. What makes him think that hiding it changes anything? I still blame myself."

He was the oldest by minutes only, but it was his job to protect his brother.

"He's not a boy anymore, and neither are you," Ian told him. "And Jaci's not his savior. If the ice is starting to crack, then it would have anyway. And I think it has. Cam was restless before Courtney mentioned her name. He needed the sharing more often, he brooded more often. I think Jaci being here will only push him into it faster."

"If he'll let her," Chase said uncertainly. "What if he doesn't?"

"Then there's no way you can fix it," Ian pointed out. "He's a man, Chase, not a boy. You can't make him do anything he refuses to do. All we can do is be here if he needs to discuss it. But my guess is, you might never know. Some things a man just can't share with another man, even his brother. But maybe, if Jaci has to have answers to accept him, then maybe he'll tell her. Maybe he can heal with her. That's all we can ask for."

To that, Chase shook his head. There wasn't much else he could say.

"Sometimes a man takes too much responsibility on his shoulders, Chase." Ian stood up before continuing. He shoved his hands into the pockets of his slacks and watched Chase somberly. "I think you and Cam both do that way too often. Give him a chance to work this out." He smiled then. "He might be better at it than you want to give him credit for."

"He's my brother. I'm supposed to worry." Chase grunted. "Secretive bastard."

"Uh-huh, I guess that's why you told him why you need the sharing as well." Ian asked.

Chase frowned, a sudden suspicion drawing him tight. "What are you talking about?"

Ian chuckled. "Seems Cam's not the only one with secrets, Chase. And maybe he senses that as well."

With that, Ian turned and moved from the room, leaving Chase with his thoughts and his worries.

What could have happened to his brother? There was no evidence of sexual abuse that he could find. The pedophiles in their area at the time had had no knowledge of Cam, outside the fact that they had seen him around town.

Chase frowned at that. He knew, knew in his soul, it was sexual abuse, but the parameters of abuse he knew of weren't exactly right. They were off. Just a little something that wasn't right about it.

And in all these years he had never figured out what that little something was, and he had a feeling he might not ever know. But, as he'd told Ian, it didn't stop the guilt.

Something had nearly destroyed his brother, and Chase hadn't been able to stop it. It was a guilt he would carry for the rest of his life.

"What the hell happened, Cam?" He breathed out again. "Son of a bitch, what did she do to you?"

Chase wasn't going to let it go, and Cam knew it. A part of him had always known that his brother at least suspected part of what happened; but hell, even his brother couldn't have guessed the truth. The truth was so fucking twisted, so incredibly depraved, that sometimes he wondered at the truth of it himself.

Shaking his head hours later, he ignored Chase's grumblings from behind about the lightning and the shitty Internet reception. The rain always seemed to affect both the satellite and cable reception. Neither were perfected yet, even with Ian's top-notch, ex-government computer expert on board. Storm-laden days still had the reception lagging, until it was slow enough to make a saint curse.

Slow enough to leave a man time to think, and Cam was thinking in overdrive. Courtney and Jaci were in the club section of the mansion, under Ian's supervision. Jaci needed sketches, measurements, a feel of the rooms, she had told Ian.

Cam's hands itched to feel her again. He'd like to hide her in one of those rooms, strip those damned jeans off her ass, and bend her over—take her, as he gripped the rounded curves of her rear.

He shook his head and punched in the search command again before sitting back in his chair and waiting. He lifted his gaze to the security monitors lined up over his desk.

Security was wired into his and Chase's office, as well as Ian's and the central security room, to allow for multiple-room surveillance. Ian believed in backup.

As he watched the main room, the double doors opened and Ian stepped inside, followed by Courtney and Jaci. Courtney, as always, was like a little kid at Christmas, every chance she got to enter the club.

She moved immediately to the table where Khalid was finishing his breakfast. He'd spent the night in one of the club's suites, rather than return to the penthouse where his family was visiting.

His smile was easy, familiar, as Courtney chatted away. While Khalid had been Ian's third, he had often been subject to many of Courtney's practical jokes and shenanigans. And he seemed to love every minute of it. Other men might have been jealous, but Ian knew what others only saw: Courtney's complete devotion to her husband.

She was prone to flirt, but lightly. She teased, but only with those she knew were less likely to take her seriously; and she was shamelessly aware of her own power over the opposite sex. But it was a power she never used, except in the most playful of ways. And it was a power she forgot entirely, whenever it came to her husband. The love Courtney felt for Ian lit every part of her.

As Courtney and Khalid joked, Cam watched as Ian indicated the security cameras, which were cleverly hidden along the walls, behind decorative smoked glass.

They turned a few moments later, and a silent whistle pursed his lips at the sight of Jaci's shapely ass.

A second later, he was on his feet, stalking from the office and heading for the club, indignation and anger burning through him. He had caught the looks of the few members in the renovated ballroom. Sons of bitches were all staring at her ass like it was only a matter of time before they would have license to touch.

Wasn't going to happen. Damn their sorry-assed hides, if the need ever arose for a third other than Chase, he could bet it wasn't going to be any of the three devouring the sight of Jaci's backside right now. He doubted he'd be able to let them breathe the same air she breathed, without anger burning inside him for months.

She was his. Until she realized it, until he knew she wasn't going to walk out on him again, then they could just deal with it. Club rules were club rules. They were banned from laying a hand on her after he'd declared her as his woman. He'd make certain that any of them who tried were kicked out of the club so fast it would make their heads spin. Hell, he'd kick their sorry asses himself.

The possessiveness tearing through him had a haze of red edging at his vision. Something primal, so instinctive he couldn't fight it, rising inside him since that first night he and Chase had touched her. A need, a burning hunger to stake a claim on her that he had never staked on another woman. A hunger to have her, to know, she was *his*. Just fucking *his*.

He could share her. He needed that sharing on a level that he knew had nothing to do with the emotions Jaci had always tempted inside him. That temptation to feel was the basis of the sharing. But the need, the hunger, was pushing past every promise he had ever made to himself where she was concerned.

Letting his brother touch her was one thing. But another man? No way in hell, he couldn't imagine it happening. Couldn't imagine ever allowing another man to touch what belonged to him. And Jaci belonged to him.

Minutes later, he strode into the room, throwing a dark frown to the guests there before moving to Ian and Jaci. Ian's smile was almost too smug, and Jaci's surprised look was filled with an edge of remembered anger, and remembered hunger.

"Are you finished in here yet?" If he didn't touch her, didn't remind her who she belonged to, then he was going to explode.

It was building in him. Damn her, he could feel the darkness building, the hunger fraying at his control, and knew it wouldn't be much longer. He'd have to have her.

"Not really," Jaci answered mockingly. "Was there something you needed?"

Oh, she had no idea how much he needed.

"Actually, there is." He gripped her arm, careful to keep his hold light, but firm. "We need to talk."

"Really?" she drawled.

"Cam, she's mine until five o'clock." Courtney was suddenly there beside them, her lips tight, her brown eyes flaring with determination. "Take your hands off my interior designer, until she's finished for the day."

"Courtney, sweetheart, she deserves a break now and then." Ian cleared his throat, which was no more than an attempt to hide his laughter, and Cam knew it.

"Then she can take coffee with me, instead of running off with him," Courtney decided. "Go back to work." She waved her hand at him. "Don't you have investigating stuff to do? I'm certain you do. Ian is always careful to keep you and Chase busy. Now, go be busy."

He released Jaci slowly. "Courtney, it will only take a few minutes," he gritted out.

"Then it can wait until this evening," Courtney decided, before turning back to Jaci. "The testosterone is getting so thick in here. I say we return to my suite. You said you had ideas you wanted to discuss, so the best way to do that is while you're taking a break. Come now. We'll go discuss them." She grabbed Jaci's hand like a worried mother and tugged her through the room. "You can play with Cam later."

"Courtney . . ." he growled.

"Do something with him, Ian," she called over her shoulder, as Jaci kept her head carefully averted and moved to the doorway with Courtney, "he's going to irritate me."

They moved out of the room, turned the corner, and disappeared from sight.

"Whoa! Damn, Cam, I guess you should have warned Jaci about telling on you when you slipped out on her at night." Ian chuckled. "Courtney might be more pissed than Jaci is."

Cam jerked around, his lips tightening at the surprised looks on the faces of the men in the room.

"Thanks, Ian," he ground out, "for informing everyone else of my shortcomings."

Khalid snorted at that. "Ian, my friend, if Courtney knows your weaknesses, you can believe the rest of us will. She believes the only way to dissuade us from acting on our male shortcomings is to be aware that, should she find out, others will know as well. She's worse than my mother."

"Even my mother wasn't as bad as Courtney," another member groaned. "She told that sweet little thing I was talking to at the Brockheim ball that she should consider another escort to the next party, considering my habit of being late to everything except dinner."

"Yeah, and she told my father about the speeding ticket I got last week. Do you have any idea how long it's been since anyone dared to do that?" That member was the son of a high-ranking judge.

Cam winced in sympathy. The only secrets that were safe were those few she learned from the club itself. If she learned anything outside the club, then she considered it fair game.

"You're part of the club, you're part of the pain." Ian sighed. "Look at it this way: if she didn't like you and didn't know you so well, she wouldn't give a damn."

"Yeah, remind me of that the next time His Honor decides to lecture me for a few hours," the judge's son growled, but laughter tinged his voice.

"I'll be sure to remind her again that she shouldn't get

her friends into trouble." Ian grinned. "But I won't promise it will help."

Everyone laughed but Cam. With a tight grimace, he stomped from the room instead, and headed back to his office. No doubt Chase had watched the entire debacle on the security monitors. Just what he needed: a damned conspiracy among his brother and friends. At this rate, he'd be babbling like a moron within a week.

"You do know he's going to get back at us over this," Jaci informed Courtney as they stepped into the sitting room, just as Matthew was arriving with the fresh coffee that he seemed to have known she would be ordering.

Jaci had noticed that things just seemed to happen around Courtney. There were things she didn't have to ask for. They just materialized, as though the very fact that she wanted them was enough.

"Thank you, Matthew." Courtney eyed the tray he sat on the table suspiciously. "It isn't decaffeinated, correct?"

Matthew looked down his imperious nose at her, his expression pinched. "I wouldn't dare serve you anything but real coffee," he informed her, before turning and stalking from the room.

Courtney snorted as she flipped her hair over her shoulder and glared at the tray. "As if. He's always trying to sneak that fake stuff in on me. As though I wouldn't know the difference."

Jaci eyed her friend curiously. "What has you so upset?"

"Cameron Falladay." Courtney bit the words out. "You are aware of why he intended to rush you off the job, are you not?" Her accent thickened with ire. "He had every intention of trying to seduce you, my friend."

Jaci's lips quirked into a grin. " 'Trying' being the operative word here, Courtney. I'm not in the mood to be seduced."

"Who has to be in the mood?" Courtney's brown eyes rolled expressively. "The man is like a volcano ready to explode. Trust me, when Ian's like that, it doesn't matter how irritated I am with him, I am seduced. It's impossible to resist." She waved her hand for emphasis. "So I saved you."

Courtney moved to the tray, poured two cups of coffee, and then took a tentative sip of her own cup.

Jaci accepted her cup before curling into the corner of the couch and watching as Courtney did the same on the other end. Perhaps she really shouldn't have called Courtney last night.

"This is more than Cam," Jaci stated. "What really has you upset? I'm the one that should be upset with Cam."

"As though you aren't?" Courtney sighed. "How could you not be? I heard the pain in your voice on the phone, Jaci. Had Ian done anything so unforgivable to me, I would have had to break one of his bones."

Courtney was always threatening physical harm, though, to Jaci's knowledge, she had never actually attempted to follow through with one of the threats.

But she was right, when she had called Courtney, she'd been hurt and confused. She still was. That didn't mean she was seducible.

"You said he does this often?" She couldn't stop the question. It was tearing at her mind. She was wondering, was it just her? Or was it normal?

Courtney sighed. "Yes, Cam seems to have a habit of annoying his lovers. At least the few I've known of him having. He never spends the night. He always leaves when his part of the fun is over. Though usually, Chase is there to soothe any ruffled feathers."

At least it wasn't just her, though she wasn't certain how much easier it made things, to know that Cam never slept with a lover. It was frightening, knowing it was a habit, rather than just her—that she was no different from any other woman who had gone before her.

"He's a difficult man. Even Chase admits to that." Courtney shrugged.

A difficult man didn't even come close to describing it.

"I shouldn't have called you and upset you, Courtney," Jaci finally said. "I don't even know why I did."

Because she had been furious. She had been hurt.

"Oh, he'll survive my ire." Courtney flashed her a grin. "Perhaps it will even give him something to think about. He's a little too confident at times, wouldn't you agree?"

Jaci could only shake her head. Hell if she knew what he was after last night. She did know she couldn't handle another night of feeling as though she had been cast off.

"And on that note, I'm going to have Matthew bring the limo around and return you to your hotel, while Cam is certainly otherwise occupied," Courtney stated. "You're exhausted. Rest. Don't think about that irritating man. We'll have dinner this evening, if you like. The hotel has a wonderful restaurant."

Lightning flared outside again, and thunder boomed. Jaci could almost feel the rain that fell in a steady downpour, and she wanted nothing more than to curl into bed and sleep for just a few hours.

"Maybe that would be the best idea." She sighed, setting her cup aside and rising to her feet. "I'll see you tonight then."

She collected her case and notes that she had left there earlier, and moved to the door.

"Matthew will have the limo waiting out back," Courtney promised. "He'll meet you downstairs and take you to it."

"Thanks, Courtney." Jaci flashed her friend a tired grin. "And don't be too hard on Cam, I have a feeling there's more to this than just a need to sleep alone."

"Of course there is," Courtney stated. "But trust me, my friend, he's insanely crazy about you. He can fess up to the truth to you, or suffer the consequences." She nodded as though it were entirely her decision.

With a quick wave and a shake of her head, Jaci left the suite and headed downstairs. She didn't run into Cam, and she wasn't certain if she was thankful or sorry that she didn't.

After the night before, her emotions were so torn regarding him that she could barely make sense of them right now. The more she thought about it, the more it hurt. The more it hurt, the more she became angry with herself, as well as with Cam.

As promised, Matthew was waiting for her downstairs. He led her to the back entrance where the limo waited beneath the sheltered parking area.

The chauffeur stood next to it and opened the door as she neared. She was halfway in the car before the fact that Cam was there fully registered. He pulled her the rest of the way in before she could do more than squeak a protest.

"Tsk-tsk. Play nice." He caught her around the waist and pulled her to his lap as she moved to push the door open once again.

"Play nice, my ass." She wiggled against him until he released her, but it was already too late, the limo was pulling out of its parking space and rolling along the driveway.

"I could play real nice with your ass, sweetheart. Just give me the chance." The words were teasing, but his expression, when she glanced at it, was dead serious.

"Oh, I just bet you could." She moved to the seat opposite him and glared back at him. "Too bad it's not going to happen."

He sighed heavily. "I should have awakened you before I left. I apologize."

Jaci eyed him warily. "I don't require an apology."

"Then what do you require, Jaci?" He asked the question so seriously, that for a moment she was taken aback.

"You know, if I have to answer those questions, then we have a serious problem from the get-go. Let's just drop it, Cam. I'm going to return to the hotel and get some sleep. We can discuss this one later."

She stared outside the limo, watching the rain and the wind, feeling the fury of the lightning and the clashing force of the thunder inside her.

She had to curl her fingers into fists to keep from touching him, had to force her muscles to keep her in place and keep her from curling into his lap again.

"I'm not taking you back to your hotel," he finally said.

Jaci stared back at him in disbelief. "Excuse me?"

He frowned back at her. "We're going to discuss this, Jaci. I'm taking you back to my place, where we can do so in some semblance of peace. Courtney wouldn't dare barge in on us there. She wouldn't have a damned problem doing it at the hotel, though."

Arrogance tightened his features as he stared back at her, thinning his lips and turning his eyes to green fire.

"Have you ever heard of the term 'kidnapping'?" she asked sweetly.

He leaned forward slowly. "It's like this. Say 'no.' That's all you have to say—to anything I'm doing at the time—and you'll go back to your hotel and I won't bother you. Just one word: 'No'."

"And if I do?" she asked him. "Tell me, Cam, just how will you play the wounded male, once I do that?"

"No means no," he growled. "No repercussions. I won't bother you again, unless you specifically request something. I'll leave you alone."

"So, if I say no to going to your apartment, then things are just over? I accept it all, or I accept nothing? Now why does that little rule just piss me off further? You know what? Screw it, Cam. Fine—" The word was forming on her lips, ready to pass them, when his fingers touched them, halting the word.

"There are rules," he said softly.

"Rules to what, Cam? To being with you? Sorry, I never was one for all those pesky little details. Shove your rules, too."

"There are rules to the lifestyle I live, not so much for you as for myself," he revealed. "My control is shaky right now, sweetheart. I want you, until it's eating me alive, but I'm trying to do this your way. We'll talk. We'll make this work."

She shook her head slowly. "You think we're going to make this relationship work without trust, Cam?"

She saw the subtle flinch in his expression.

"What trust?" he finally asked. "Look, you can't pay attention to everything Chase rattles on about."

"No, you're right," she whispered. "But I can pay attention to the shadows I see in your eyes. Do you think I'm one of what must be a long line of brainless idiots to inhabit your bed? Do you think I'll ever be satisfied with only half of you?"

"It's more than anyone else has ever had," he told her. "And it may be, Jaci, that that's all I have to give."

CHAPTER FIFTEEN

The rain was still pouring down when the limo pulled into the small lower level garage of the renovated warehouse.

Cam opened the door and stepped out, then turned and extended his hand to her.

"Are you going to run from me again, Jaci?" he asked her.

She should, she knew she should. Instead, she let him grip her fingers and pull her from the car.

"This doesn't mean I'm agreeing to anything," she informed him, as the limo pulled away.

"I understand that." He curled his fingers around hers and led her to the wide staircase that led to the next floor. "You need to rest. We need to talk. You can rest here, and later we can talk."

As if that was really going to happen, she thought with a silent, disbelieving snort. They were both so damned aroused it was a wonder they didn't combust. There wasn't a chance in hell she was going to sleep, with him so close to her. So close, yet so damned far away.

When he told her that half of himself was all he had to give, she hadn't had an answer for him. What the hell was she supposed to say? That it wasn't good enough for her? She had promised herself that if she ever had the chance

again, she would fight for him. That she wouldn't run like
the scared little girl she had been before. She had promised herself she would try not just her way, but his way
as well.

But to realize that the man she had waited for all these
years wasn't willing to give enough to even sleep with
her, left her feeling strangely bereft.

As they stepped into the first floor apartment, Jaci
gazed around at the open, airy layout of the converted
warehouse and felt something clench inside her.

"This is your level?" she asked, looking toward the
stairs. "Chase's is upstairs?"

He stood beside her and stared around the room as
well, before turning back to her with a short nod.

Jaci's throat tightened. It was so deserted. There was
nothing but the most minimal furniture. No pictures or
personal items, no little knickknacks or souvenirs. It was a
place, it wasn't a home, nor did it have a feeling of life.
Dear God, as she stared around she realized that, in some
ways, this was what she had always seen inside Cam.
A man that refused to let himself belong.

He cleared his throat, standing beside her. "It gets a
little dusty sometimes."

Cam stared around the apartment, wondering what
had put that look of abject sorrow on her face. Hell, he
had the place cleaned weekly, it wasn't as though there
could be much wrong with it, except the dusting. Well,
actually, he couldn't see any dust, but he knew his cleaning lady was a little lax where the dusting was concerned.

"A little dusty," she whispered faintly as she sat her
briefcase and purse on the wide table beside her and stared
around again.

This went way beyond a little dusting, Jaci thought sadly.
It was empty. Almost soulless. And Cam wasn't soulless.
She stared up at him as he looked out at the room again,

and she saw that edge of complete aloneness that seemed to surround him.

It had been there seven years before, that distance he forced between himself and the world. It was more apparent here, though, in this place he called home. The complete starkness of it was heartbreaking.

"What's wrong with it?" he suddenly growled. "The place is clean. I'm not exactly a slob."

"No, you're not a slob," she said sadly. "You're very neat, Cam."

"Yeah, well, neatness is a virtue," he continued to grump, as he headed away from her toward the kitchen. "Are you hungry? I can have something ordered in." He pulled the refrigerator door open and glared inside before jerking a beer free, then slammed it closed again.

"I'm going to guess the only thing your refrigerator holds is beer," she ventured. "Do you ever actually live here?" She stared around again.

"Every day," he almost snarled.

"Really? I bet Chase's level looks totally different."

"Chase is a slob." He was glaring at her now. "A damned packrat. He has to have every fricken momento and gift everyone ever gave him. They line the damned walls."

He slapped the beer on the counter and braced his hands flat on the gray marbled top. "Do you have a problem with where I live, Jaci?"

"None whatsoever." She shrugged. "But I think I'd prefer a clinic. It would be less sterile."

Surprise registered on his face as she paced through the large open apartment to a set of tall glass doors that led out to an open balcony. "What the hell does that mean?"

She opened the doors and breathed in the scent of the rain. The thunder and lightning had moved into the distance, but the rain continued to drench the world outside. The clouds were low and heavy, fog rose in misty sheets, giving the grounds an otherworldly appearance and a feeling that they were the only inhabitants in a mystical world.

Jaci usually loved the rain and the fog, but today it seemed to emphasize the complete sterility of Cam's life. Had he done it deliberately? Or was it really just so much a part of him that he didn't even realize it?

"The apartment isn't sterile." He moved behind her, the heat of his body spreading along her back as his hands bracketed her hips with a firm, almost desperate grip.

"Yes it is," she said. "And I wonder if it isn't deliberate."

She glanced over her shoulder at his closed expression, the stark, icy green eyes, before turning back to the rain. Dampness pelted her face—cool, inviting, drawing her into an almost primal awareness of it. Rain cleansed and eased, and it always had been a source of peace for her.

"How long has it been since you played in the rain?" she asked, smiling as the wind drove a sheet of dampness against them.

She mesmerized him. Seeing her there, a teasing imp in her eyes, yet with that glimmer of sadness still shining. How was he supposed to resist her?

Cam was silent for long moments before he finally answered. "Too long to remember."

She didn't look back at his face. She was afraid if she did she would cry. She could hear the loneliness in his tone, sense the male confusion caused by her expression.

She took a deep breath and swallowed tightly before turning her head and staring up at him, seeing all the things she had heard in his voice.

"Let's get wet and wild," she whispered. "Come on, Cam, play in the rain with me."

"You'll catch your death of cold." He eyed the rain skeptically.

"Then you can feed me homemade chicken soup." She grabbed his hand and pulled him out after her.

The rain was drenching, falling down in sheets that soaked them within seconds. It ran over Jaci's hair and face in rivulets. Spreading her arms wide, she lifted her face and turned in a circle, her eyes closing as the summer shower spilled over her.

When her head lowered and she opened her eyes, she saw Cam, his head lifted, eyes closed. His shirt and slacks were drenched and he looked primal. So male. So intense.

When his eyes opened and he stared back at her, she saw a core of need inside him that she wondered if he even knew he possessed.

"Dance with me," she whispered. The need to feel his arms around her was driving her crazy.

"There's no music." He tried to smile, but she could see the edge of dominance burning inside him. He wanted much more than to dance.

"Then we'll make our own music." She moved into his arms, feeling them go around her as he looped her arms around his neck. "Haven't you ever wanted to make your own music, Cam?"

The rain ran down his hair and face in thick rivulets, highlighting the light growth of beard that shadowed his face.

The ice in his eyes was thawing, being replaced by desire, by a hint of emotion that had her heart racing.

"Are we making music yet?" he asked, his voice rough with arousal now.

Within the soaked slacks, his cock throbbed hard and insistent, as his hands slid the hem of her shirt along her midriff so he could touch her bare back. At the same moment, she became aware of Chase watching from the door, his gaze heavy, arousal evident; but he did nothing to join them. She prayed he wouldn't.

"Don't you feel it?" she whispered, her fingers moving to the buttons of his shirt.

She wanted to see his bare chest, the rain running through the mat of dark chest hair, drenching the corded muscles of his upper body.

Within minutes she had the shirt opened and pushed it from his shoulders. Still, Chase watched. It added to the eroticism, made her feel somehow more wicked, sexier.

"Do you know what you're doing?" he questioned her, his voice rough, his expression tightening with lust. "I'm going to end up fucking you on the damned balcony, Jaci."

"Good thing you have lots of trees around here, then." She smiled up at him before glancing out at the grounds around the warehouse. Huge, stately oaks grew high and close, sheltering the open balcony.

One hand lifted from her waist to cup her cheek, and he danced her back to the brick wall, his hard body sheltering her from the force of the rain. She forgot about Chase—forgot about everything but the pleasure burning inside her.

The other hand slid around, flattened against her lower stomach, and pressed demandingly against her, as his head lowered.

The taste of the rain and her kiss was intoxicating. Cam was certain he had never known anything, any woman, that had ever tasted as good as Jaci. His tongue swiped over her lips, drew in the raindrops that clung to them, before he caught the lower curve of her lip between his teeth and nipped at it erotically.

She jerked against him in response, her breath coming hard and fast now, her body heating, despite the water pouring over her.

Her body curved against his, her lower stomach cushioning the erection throbbing beneath his slacks, her breasts pressed into his bare chest.

The cool rain did nothing to tamp the fire burning inside him. She was like a drug in his system now, and he wondered how the hell he would survive if he didn't manage to bind her to him.

"This is so good," she panted, as his lips moved from hers to the curve of her jaw, and lower on her neck. "Feeling you like this, Cam—all over. Like the rain."

He grimaced as he buried his head in her neck. Going slow and easy with her was killing him. His control was so damned frayed, it was all he could do to force himself to hold back.

He slid his palm lower on her stomach, his fingertips pressing against the mound between her thighs, rotating, caressing the flesh just above her clit through the material of her jeans.

He wanted those damned pants off her.

"I have to feel you," he groaned. The words were rasping, his voice guttural, an indication of his loss of control.

Damn, he'd never had trouble controlling himself with a woman. Never known a time that he couldn't draw the pleasure out, make her scream before he reached the point that he had to bury himself inside her. Until now.

He gripped the hem of her shirt and drew it up her body. As he leaned back, he watched as her arms lifted gracefully, the clinging material peeling off her flesh to reveal paradise beneath.

Tossing the shirt aside, he flicked open the clip of her bra and drew it away from the swollen mounds of her breasts.

His mouth watered at the sight of her tight, hard little nipples. They were flushed a ruby red, puckered, and seemed to beg for his kiss.

His head lowered as he felt her hands on his shoulders, her nails raking across his flesh.

He should take her inside. Hell, he knew he should take her inside, out of the rain, but he couldn't seem to force himself to do it. She was made for the caress of the raindrops—water running along her flesh, soaking her as she burned for him.

Pulling back his hands, he attacked the bright yellow belt that had teased him all day. It cinched her slender hips, drew the eye to the sway of her ass. He loosened it quickly, before undoing the metal snap and zipper. Within seconds his fingers were pushing into the sweltering heat of her pussy, penetrating the tight tissue, and drawing a ragged cry from both of them.

"That's not fair," she panted, jerking to her tiptoes, her back arching as her face flushed with pleasure.

He loved watching her face. Watching the pleasure suffuse it as her incredible eyes became dazed from the surfeit of sensations.

He raked his teeth over the upper curve of her breast as he lowered a hand to his slacks.

He released the belt and the closure to the pants quickly, drawing the material aside to release the heavy length of his cock.

He was dying for her.

"Not yet." Her nails skimmed along his shoulders as her lips moved to his neck. "This time I get to have fun."

"Damn, Jaci, my control is shot." He grimaced as her lips moved from his neck to his shoulder, then his chest.

She was going down, that incredible body shifting and flexing in his arms, as her lips followed the trails of water flowing down his chest.

He couldn't feel the rain now. All he felt was the heat, the caress of her fingers and her lips against his chest, his abdomen. Her nimble little tongue dipped into his belly button, then licked and stroked farther down. Slowly, so fucking slowly.

"I've dreamed of this." She was on her knees in front

of him, one hand cupping his balls, the other gripping the hard length of his cock.

"Jaci. Baby, this is dangerous." He tried to keep his voice full of warning, but it was more desperate, harder, hungrier than he could remember it ever being.

Then she leaned forward and licked the dark, engorged crest.

The feel of the cooling rain, her heated tongue, her silken fingers stroking him combined, until he threw his head back and felt the throttled groan that tore from his throat.

As though that sound were all she needed, her liquid, hot mouth enclosed the engorged crest and began suckling at the throbbing heat with soul-destroying pleasure.

Before Cam could halt the impulse, his hands were buried in her saturated hair, clenching in the silken strands, as he pulled, moving her, as his hips followed, fucking her lips as pleasure swamped him.

Hell. He stared down at her, watching the heavily veined flesh as she stroked it, watched as her mouth caressed him, and had to fight back the need to come.

He could feel the wicked trails of sensation tightening his balls and traveling up his spine. The back of his head tingled, and dark, desperate impulses began to fire inside his brain.

He stared down at her, watching her suck him—hell, *love* him with her mouth. He could feel the difference. No other woman had touched him like this. He had never been touched the way Jaci touched him. The expression on her face, the way she touched, there was nothing more inside her but the need to give pleasure. The need to make him feel.

He watched her face, saw the dazed pleasure in it. There was nothing depraved, no ulterior motives, there was nothing in her face but pleasure. Just that. She enjoyed it.

He felt mesmerized by her face, and when her eyes opened, the green-and-brown orbs staring up at him with desperate hunger, he lost it.

In all his life, Cam had never lost control of his orgasms. Control had always been there for one reason or another. But when Jaci stared up at him, her eyes darkening, dilating with hunger, her mouth sucking him with wicked innocence, her expression flushed and filled with need, he couldn't hold back.

He tried to pull back. He jerked a hand from her hair, gripped the rigid, pulsing stalk of his cock and tried to pull it from her mouth.

Her hand tightened on his balls, the other wrapped over his, and her whimper of need rippled over the swollen crest as the first desperate spurt of cum shot from the tip.

A growl tore from his throat as she took him. Her mouth became hotter, snugger, the suckling cavern drawing more and more from him, until he was shuddering in reaction, his knees weakening as he filled her mouth with his release.

And still he needed more of her. He couldn't believe how stiff, how hard he still was. He couldn't believe the hunger flowing into him as he pulled her to her feet and jerked her jeans down her legs, pushing her to the soaked pad of the sun lounge behind her.

He knew Chase was watching. That was enough this time. He was there, centering him, holding him back. He hoped. There were so many emotions tearing through him that, hell, he couldn't tell anymore if it helped or not. All he knew was this time, just him and Jaci. The need for it was killing him.

Unlacing and removing her boots took only seconds. The sodden jeans and panties were stripped from her legs, and he had only a brief moment to thank God that the privacy railing around the deck was high enough to hide what was going on behind it.

He tore his shoes from his feet, peeled his pants off his legs, then knelt at the bottom of the lounge, pushed his hands beneath her ass and pulled her to his mouth.

Her legs curled over his shoulders as he buried his lips in the heated syrup of her pussy. He licked and stroked, pursed his lips and kissed the tender bud of her clit until she writhed in his grip.

Jaci was awash in sensuality, in complete sensual overload. She arched to Cam's devouring mouth, twisted against him, then cried out when she felt his fingers stretching her deliciously.

Turning her face into the saturated pad of the cushion, she fought just to breathe. The pleasure was tearing through her, blazing across her nerve endings. Cool rain and blistering hot sensations, her system was rapidly approaching overload and she knew it. Too much pleasure. Too much hunger.

"You're as sweet as candy," he groaned against her flesh, the words rasping, tormented with male lust.

"I can't stand much more," she panted, pushing against him, straining, desperate for release.

She could feel her pussy flexing, milking his fingers. Involuntary contractions tore through her womb, rippled through her core, and sent her juices spilling onto his fingers. And he used the slickness of her response, the juices that spilled from her, and drew his hand back: Protecting her tender flesh from the rain, he slowly lubricated and eased the entrance to her rear, pierced it with his fingers, stretched it as he had her sex.

Jaci's head thrashed on the cushion as her hands burrowed into his hair and tightened in desperation. His lips caressed, his tongue licked.

She could feel the flames of need burning in her rear

as he eased into the tender flesh there. He penetrated with first one finger, then two, stretched her, and sent her senses careening with the burning pleasure and pain.

She could feel her own response burgeoning inside her, a dark core of agonizing need that she had only felt in Cam's arms.

"You love this." His voice flowed over her like the rain, like her own dark desires. Because she didn't have to ask what he was talking about, she knew. The image had hit her head the moment his fingers had pierced her ass.

"Tell me you love it."

His head jerked up. Green eyes burned with hunger, with dark, wicked desires, with torment. The agony of hunger she had only glimpsed in him before was burning in him now. His expression was savage with the hunger, with a lust he was doing nothing to hide.

The rain had eased, but the water still washed over his head and face in rivulets. The hard contours were savagely defined now, his eyes narrowed and bright with a ravening desire.

"I love it," she said, moaning.

"I need you," he growled, his fingers pushing deeper inside her rear as his thumb pierced her pussy and sent her arching into exquisite pleasure.

She held his gaze, her vision dimming as the sensations began to pile atop each other. Flash points of need ratcheted through her system and left her shaking in his grip.

"What do you need from me, Cam?"

"All of you." His fingers slid free of her, then he was pushing her thighs apart, coming over her, blocking the rain with his broader body, as his erection nudged into the desperate entrance to her pussy.

Jaci slid her hands to his shoulders, caressing, stroking, then gripping in agonized pleasure as he began to work himself inside her.

"Take all of me, then." She arched closer, her legs lifting, wrapping around his waist as he pressed into her.

His eyes narrowed further. "You're mine."

"Then prove it, Cam. Prove it, damn you. Take me."

He wanted so much more than to just take her. She knew it, she could see it building in his expression, in the battle for control in his eyes. And she watched him, felt him, lose that control.

She arched, twisted, felt the hard thrust that burrowed the length of his cock inside her, stretching her, burning her, taking her with a desperation that rocked her soul.

The hard, plunging strokes fired a pleasure and pain that tore past preconceived notions of pleasure. It whipped through her mind and left her reeling, and it tore through her senses and left her fighting for the breath to scream.

She felt the sensations rising, building. Each hard thrust, as he shafted inside her, threw her higher. Her nails bit into his shoulders, her legs tightened around his plunging hips, and a second later she dissolved around him.

"Fuck. Fuck. No." He was shaking above her, spilling into her, and those haunted, beautiful eyes of his blazed. With possession. With love.

CHAPTER SIXTEEN

Cam stomped into the house, pulling Jaci behind him, before releasing her in the living room and heading to the enclosed bathroom for towels. Chase was gone. She didn't know when he had left, or how long he had stayed.

Seconds later Cam was wrapping the thick, thirsty material around her wet body, then drying himself off and wrapping the towel snugly around his waist.

He stared at her, horrified by his loss of control, by the sheer thoughtlessness of what he had done. Or what he had nearly done. What he had wanted to do, with a hunger that even now drove spikes of need straight through his balls.

Hell, he still wanted her. He would always want her.

"At least you didn't wait until I was asleep to pull away from me," she said tightly, as she secured the towel over her naked body.

He shot her a glare before stalking to the fridge and beer. His control was still shot. He clenched his teeth and fought to hold on to what few threads were still left.

"Don't push this, Jaci," he finally told her, twisting the cap off the bottle before turning to face her.

Her arms were crossed over her breasts, her hip cocked, her expression as confrontational as any pissed-off redhead. If he were a smart man, he'd have been terrified instead of turned on.

"Don't push this," she drawled. "Excuse me, Cam, but do you think I can't see what's inside you right now? What's inside you every time the three of us come together?"

Hearing the words pass her lips was enough to make his blood boil with that need. He could see her, flushed, screaming, drowning in pleasure.

"Did you expect something different?" he growled. "You knew what I wanted seven years ago, and you knew what it would come to when you invited me and Chase into your hotel room." He stalked toward her. "You came here, and you came to Alexandria, knowing I was here. You knew what you were walking into. You knew you wouldn't be leaving here without this."

And then she smiled—a slow, knowing smile that made his back teeth grind with desire.

"Oh, I knew." She shrugged, and it infuriated him. "Just as I know that I'll be damned if I'm just one of a long line of little pets you and Chase share."

"Did I ask you to be a pet?" he snarled, continuing to advance on her, watching as she retreated until he had her against the wall, until all he could think about was taking her again—plunging inside her, holding her to him, and feeling her hot and tight around him, bare and so slick, so sweet, as he felt every ripple of that snug little pussy. "I warned you, Jaci." He caught her to him. "I warned you that you're mine."

"And what does being yours mean?" Her voice was tight, angry. "And why the sharing? Why do *you* want it?"

"Why do you want it, Jaci?" he asked.

She froze at the question. Her lips parted, her heart stuttered in her chest as she pulled in a shocked breath.

"You love it." He leaned closer, his voice lowering, his body tightening. "Just as much as I do. Tell me, Jaci, why do I see that same need in your eyes?"

Dominance and arrogance filled his expression and his eyes. He was primal, and he knew it—and she should have known there was so little she could hide from him. He had the experience she didn't have. He knew women, he knew lust, and he knew desire. And he knew her.

"I enjoy it," she admitted. "Sometimes, yes, I would crave it. But for God's sake, Cam, I need more than a threesome when you take me. I need more than that for you, for both of us."

Hurt and need welled inside her, tore at her heart and had her shuddering with the attempt to hold it back. "I need more from a relationship than a man that can't bear to spend more than five damned minutes with me alone. Forget sleeping with me. Damn you Cameron. I need you to hold me. I need you to need me, not me and your brother."

She pushed at his chest, the anger building inside her again. No, it wasn't anger, it was fear. What the hell made her think she could come here and not risk every part of who and what she was?

She had promised herself the last time he left her alone she wouldn't be seduced into what he wanted, without owning his heart as well. And she'd be damned if it was working out that way.

Surprisingly, he let her go. She could feel his eyes on her back as she gripped the front of the towel and paced away from him. But he didn't have an answer for her, and she hadn't really expected one.

"What good does it do me to love you?" she finally asked him when she turned toward him. "You're going to destroy us both. Because you won't be honest with me, and I can't trust everything to you, Cam, without the same in return."

"Fine," he snapped. "Start telling me what happened with the Robertses. You want trust, Jaci. Give it."

She stared back at him, wishing with all her soul that

she could tell him, that she could trust him not to keep his promise to kill any man that hurt her. And perhaps he wouldn't, but she knew Cam, he would spill blood, and it wasn't blood that she needed to neutralize those two.

"Trust you first, huh?" She smiled sadly. "Doesn't work that way."

She moved back to the balcony. The rain had eased to a drizzle, the soft breeze that blew through was almost cooling. She collected her clothes, wrung them out as best she could, then moved back into the apartment. "Where's your dryer?"

His gaze raked over her, then the clothes. "Subject's not changing that easy, sweetheart."

"Conversation is over," she told him.

A second later she was against the wall again, staring at his furious face in shock. The towel was lying on the floor, and Cam was holding her in place. Not painfully, but carefully, as he glowered down at her.

"You're not leaving here," he snapped. "When I said you were mine I wasn't joking. I'll be damned if I'm letting you go again this easily."

"Does that mean you're sleeping with me tonight, Chase?" She pressed her hands flat against his chest, and knew the answer when she felt the flinch that raced through his muscles. "Can't do it, can you? Well, guess what? I can't let you leave me feeling like something you bought for the night, either."

He released her slowly, but she saw the struggle in his eyes, in his expression. Letting her go was just as damned hard for him as it was going to be for her to walk away.

"I need to dry my clothes," she told him, forcing herself to hold back the tears.

How could she have let this happen? Hadn't she hurt enough over the years? Lost enough?

She clenched her teeth and breathed in roughly as she

watched him jerk the wet clothes from the floor and stomp away toward what was obviously an enclosed bathroom on the other end of the cavernous room.

A few minutes later he returned, dressed himself, and brought her a T-shirt.

"Put this on." His voice was still tight, savage.

Jaci stared back at him miserably, aching for things that didn't even have a name. She stared around the open apartment, seeing so much emptiness, and wondered what made her think that Cam would be able to let her fill any part of his life.

God, she wasn't twenty-one any longer. She should have stopped dreaming of fairy tales a long time ago. Cam's heart was as empty as his apartment, and she knew she couldn't survive loving him with nothing in return. She needed his love just as desperately as she needed to love him.

Pressing her lips tightly together to hold back the pain, she finished drying off, then pulled the T-shirt over her head. It was obviously his, or perhaps Chase's. Though she doubted that in his present mood, he would give her one of Chase's shirts to wear.

"I want you to move your things from the hotel to here." His voice was strained, as though he knew the request he was making was ludicrous.

Jaci just stared back at him silently for a long moment before staring around the sterile apartment.

"No."

"Look, you don't like this place? Do whatever the hell you want to it," he said, waving his hand stiffly to indicate the large area. "I don't want you at that hotel. I want you here. With me."

"And where will you sleep?"

He drew in a hard, deep breath. "I don't sleep in the bed. I use the couch, anyway."

"I'm not looking for a roommate, Cam."

She watched his jaw clench spasmodically and felt her heart ache at that sudden flash of pain in his eyes. He stared around the apartment as though searching for answers, searching desperately for the argument that would sway her.

"Look, we could try it for a while." He flexed his shoulders as though shifting a weight he suddenly realized he carried. "What the hell will it hurt, Jaci? You want to be here, you know you do. This isn't something either one of us can walk away from now."

"You appear to be quite good at walking away from it," she argued. "What's going to happen, Cam? You and Chase have me, but it's Chase you would allow to wrap his arms around me and hold me through the night, while you lie in solitary splendor on that big couch?" She waved her hand toward the couch. "Doesn't it ever get lonely? Don't you ever wish you were brave enough to cuddle your lover on your own?"

"Not until you." His voice echoed with despair. "Not until you, Jaci. And you have more of me than any other woman could ever have."

Cam watched the emotions flicker over Jaci's face and felt the fragments of his heart cracking, breaking. She didn't bother to hide her emotions. They were there for him to see, and he hated seeing the pain in her eyes. He hated it even worse, because he had put the pain there.

His gaze flickered to the couch. The wide frame, firm cushions—the piece of furniture had been bought solely because of its sleepability. Because, since his teens, he couldn't fucking bear sleeping in a bed for more than a few hours at a time.

He could still remember the sensation of his flesh crawling, awakening to the feeling of hands touching him, a whining voice demanding him. The last time it had happened, he had nearly killed.

He flexed his hands. He could still remember the feel of her neck in his grip, the soft flesh giving, watery brown eyes wide and filled with horror, as dry, aged flesh clenched beneath his fingers.

God, he hated that bitch. Her and her fucking friends, and the hell he had lived through for five fucking years before he found the guts to get out of it. Until he found a way to get out and still hold on to what little pride he had left.

He had no idea what kept him standing, what kept his shoulders straight. He moved to the only woman who had ever filled more than just a passing urge for sex. The woman who had filled his imagination, the pieces of his heart, and his hunger, for so many years.

He had often asked himself, why this woman? He had tried to make sense of why she drew him to her when others didn't. Why he wanted to be different for her, why he needed to give her parts of himself that he thought were dead long ago.

There she stood, his T-shirt hanging nearly to her knees, her damp hair mussed and feathering around her face and shoulders, naked vulnerability shining in her eyes. And she needed more than he could give. He knew she needed more than he could give, but he couldn't let her go, could no longer risk her finding it somewhere else.

"You've had seven years to find someone else," he told her. "I left you alone. I didn't come looking for you when the need to do just that ate me alive, Jaci. I gave you seven years to find a man that would deserve you, and you didn't. Now you're here, and I won't let you go. If it means destroying what's left of me, I won't let you walk away."

"And if it means destroying what's left of me?" she asked then, her lips trembling as her eyes looked too wide, too filled with sorrow for her pale face.

He cupped his hand around her neck, lifting her face

to his. The pain in her eyes nearly broke him. He couldn't let her know the truth of him, he couldn't let that rage and bitterness spill onto her. God help him, hurting her more just might destroy him.

"I don't want to let you go," he repeated, realizing that if she decided to walk, he could do no more to stop her than he had seven years ago. "I've missed you, Jaci. I've ached for you. We deserve to see where it could go."

"And if I grow to care for Chase the way I care for you? What then? I wait and watch as he goes to another woman? Isn't that just asking for more pain?"

Cam shook his head at that. He knew better. "It won't happen. This is for the pleasure, for both of us. Chase cares for you as a friend, the same as you'll always care for him. But nothing, no other man, is going to fill you like I do."

It had to be that way, because he knew no other woman could fill him as Jaci did. Despite the short time she had been here, she was filling parts of him that he didn't know had been empty, that had just been waiting for her.

"I need more," she whispered as his head lowered, as his lips touched hers, caressed hers. "This isn't going to work the way you need it to."

"We could try." He laid his forehead against hers and stared into her eyes, pushing the pain back.

Jaci closed her eyes and sighed. She was going to do this. Move in with Cam and Chase. She wasn't walking away from Cam again. It had hurt too much the first time, and it had haunted her too damned long.

She was smart enough to realize that some things, no matter how hard you fought them, were meant to be. This feeling, this need that bound them, was too strong, and she was tired of fighting it. Tired of fighting herself over it.

His lips caressed hers, his thick lashes sweeping down as he closed his incredible eyes.

"Let us love you," he said. He nipped at her lips, a little

pleasure-pain that reminded her of the darkness she had glimpsed in his eyes earlier. "Let me have you."

Her hands slid from his T-shirt-clad chest to his shoulders, then to the damp hair that lay along his neck.

"You'll destroy me," she said sighing.

"I'll love you."

And her heart raced. It felt as though a minidetonation had been sent off inside it, flooding her with emotion, sending it pulsing through her veins as her breath caught with the intensity of it.

Oh God, how she needed him to love her. But she was terribly afraid it was the physical, rather than the emotional, that Cam was associating with the word.

Whichever it was, she wasn't strong enough to resist him.

Her arms tightened around his neck as his lips caressed hers, patient now; deep, possessive kisses that had her lifting to her tiptoes and straining against him.

Until they heard the front door slam closed, and Jaci knew who it was. She could feel Chase's gaze traveling over her bare legs as Cam drew back. He stared down at her, and she saw the hunger that only spiked hers.

Damn him. He made her ache for it, made her remember what it was like, and she wanted to cry with the knowledge that as much pleasure as they both gained from it, as much as they were both aroused by it, it was still a way to distance himself from her.

"This is what you want?" she asked softly.

He stared down at her, his gaze searching, darkening, filling with arousal. "I need it almost as much as I need you."

She wondered if he needed it to allow himself to have her. Whichever the case, it was the pleasure, a freedom, a certainty she could be as wild, as tempestuous as she wanted to be, and he would know nothing but pleasure. She would know nothing but pleasure.

As she turned to him, Chase saw the vixen she was and wondered if Cam had a clue how easily she was turning his life upside down. He was there because of what she was doing to Cam. Because he could only feel that psychic twin bond kicking in when Cam's strict control was being tested by this woman.

And he came, even though he knew he shouldn't. If he stayed away, Cam would break faster, that control would fall, and Chase would know the secrets his brother hid. But there was a part of him that knew that now, this time, was the wrong time for that. If he forced Cam into it, he would never forgive himself, and Cam wouldn't forgive him.

"The two of you amaze me," Jaci told them with a very female smile of knowledge and amusement. "So arrogant and stubborn. So secretive and certain of yourselves."

She cast Cam a look from beneath her lashes, and Chase felt his own body tighten. It was a very seductive weapon she was wielding in this little skirmish, and he could feel it. He glanced at Cam and saw the knowing quirk at his brothers lips as he removed his shirt, still watching Jaci.

"And you can fix that for us?" Chase was the one to ask her as he pulled his T-shirt over his head and dropped it to the floor.

"I intend to fix it for one of you at least." She flicked Chase another look, then slowly, sensually, gripped the hem of the shirt she wore and pulled it over her head.

Luscious, sweet. Creamy skin, full high breasts, and nipples that stood out in demand as she moved toward him.

He glanced at Cam, saw his brother watching her as he undressed, desire and hunger heightening his expression as she moved for Chase.

"Has a woman ever had it so good?" she asked as she laid her hand against Chase's bare chest.

The warmth of her palm sliding down his chest, along his tight abs, had his stomach tightening in response as he toed his shoes from his feet and finished shucking his slacks after pulling out the condom he had tucked in them. Damn, he was hard. Cam wasn't in any better shape if his expression was anything to go by.

Tormented need, nightmares. The shadows of it raced across Chase's mind a second before he felt the wild, wet heat of Jaci's mouth surround the head of his cock.

"Hell!" One hand clenched in her hair as he held on to the foil package in his other hand with a desperate grip.

Cameron removed a tube of lubricating jelly from the table by the couch and moved back to them, his eyes on Jaci's, upturned little ass. He leaned back against the kitchen counter, somehow knowing this experience would be different from the others. It was in Cam's face, in his eyes, as he stared at his lover's pert backside.

Chase ground his teeth together as her mouth sucked him, drew on him, creating a friction against the sensitive head that had his balls drawing tight. He tightened his fingers in her hair, tugged her head, forced her to lower and raise her mouth as he fucked those sweet lips.

"You know what he's going to do," he growled. "You let him off too easy, Jaci."

"Shut the fuck up, Chase." Cam's voice was hard, harsh with arousal, his gaze bright as his hand smoothed over her rear, his hand large, dark against Jaci's creamy flesh.

Chase felt her hand cup his balls, her tongue stroking over the sensitive underside of his cock as the heated, erotic sensations began to race up his spine. He let the rest of it slide, because damn if it didn't feel good. And here, in this, he could forget his own demons.

Then the pleasure was gone. Chase opened his eyes, watching as Jaci slid from between them, a teasing smile on her lips as she watched them, backing her way into the living room.

They followed, drawn by the hunger clawing at them. For Cameron, drawn by the witchy, earthy sensuality that filled her eyes. She accepted his needs, his desires. He could see it in her face, in her expression, feel it in the heat of her body as he touched her.

Nearing her, he stopped as she placed her hand against his chest.

"Not yet." Flirty, seductive, her lashes swept over her eyes as Chase came closer.

"Like hell," Cam growled.

"Like hell," she whispered back. "Watch. You want to see the pleasure, Cam. Watch the pleasure I can give him."

"He gives you pleasure." He was straining, dominance and hunger vying inside him.

"This will give me pleasure," she teased him in return before turning to Chase.

Cam watched, enjoying the daring he could see in her eyes, recognizing her need, just this once, to control some part of the love play he demanded from her. He let his lips quirk as she glanced back at him while pushing Chase to the couch.

"She's not exactly submitting, Cam," Chase pointed out, amusement threading through the arousal in his voice.

"Not yet," Cam murmured, watching as Jaci reached out, snagged the tube of lubricating jelly from his hand, and turned back to the lover that watched her with heated lust. Just lust. There was no emotion. Her heart was his, but her body . . . oh, the pleasure he knew she gained from this particular freedom.

He watched as she went down on Chase again, pulling the head of his cock back into her mouth as she laid the tube beside her. She worked her hands over the thick shaft, stroking and pumping as Chase's hips lifted to her. His hands buried in her hair, his head tipped back in pleasure. And Jaci's expression became suffused with her own just. Her freedom.

As she bent over his brother, Cameron moved to her. His hand smoothed over her rear, reached between her thighs, and cupped the hot, wet folds. Her clit was swollen, throbbing against the tip of his finger as he circled it.

She jerked, the dampness between her thighs growing as she moaned around Chase's erection. Cam eased closer, bent, his lips moving over the rounded globes of her ass as he slid the tube of lubricating jelly from the couch and opened it slowly.

Drawing back, he grimaced in sensual hunger. He parted the curves of her ass, glimpsed the tiny entrance and felt his chest tighten as the hunger tightened his muscles and sped up his heart.

He watched as he prepared her, as aroused now as he had been earlier in the rain. Lubricating his fingers he began to work one inside her, taking the entrance easily before pulling back and adding a second finger, a third. He watched the penetration, his cock so hard, so desperate to feel the heat of her that he was close to losing his grip on that last thread of control he possessed.

Pulling his fingers back, he moved to take her, only to stop.

"No." Jaci lifted her head and stared back at him.

Cam paused, his chest rising and falling harshly, black hair falling over his face, the hint of a shadow of beard darkening his savage features.

"How I want it," she whispered.

He grimaced. She watched his jaw bunch as she moved, took the lubrication and squeezed a thick amount into the palm of her hand. Still watching Cam, she stroked her palm down and around Chase's cock. She could feel Chase tighten, the tension in the air around them almost feverish with lust now.

This was what he wanted? She could take her pleasure in it, return it, and enjoy the hell out of it. But he was going to watch her do it. He wasn't hiding from her. He would not take her from behind while his defenses were lower than they ever had been.

"Jaci. That's not as easy as you think it is," he told her as she turned, straddling Chase's hips as he sheathed his erection in a condom, her back to him, one hand holding herself steady on the back of the couch as she lowered herself to it.

"Then help me." She was breathing hard, need was like an inferno burning into her, whipping through her. "I always knew what you wanted Cam. Do you think I didn't play? That me and the vibrators that helped me hold onto my sanity didn't have fun?" She gasped then.

The head of Chase's cock tucked against her rear as his hands moved to her hips as he strained against her. Heat speared through her rear entrance, rocked up her spine.

"Like this, baby." His voice was gentle, hoarse.

His hands gripped her thighs, pulling them forward as Chase's hands eased to her waist, bracing her, pulling her back until his cock was postioned at an angle, pressing into her, the thick crest beginning to force inside her.

She watched Cam as he watched the possession. She felt herself opening, heard her own cries, but she couldn't take her eyes from his face. He loved watching her take his brother. His gaze lifted to her then, his fingers moving to her pussy, parting the folds, stroking around her clit as her hips began to move, to ease Chase deeper inside her.

She moved her hips back and forth, fucking herself onto him as Cam moved until he was between their spread thighs, watching, stroking her pussy until, with a sharp, desperate cry, she felt the entire length of Chase's cock slip inside her.

She writhed now, her head tipping back, watching Cam's face as he moved to her.

"You have all of him," he breathed harshly. "Deep and thick inside you, Jaci. This position makes you tighter, did you know that sweetheart?"

She shook her head. She didn't know. She knew she was dying, fighting to breathe, to make sense of the sensations tearing through her.

Then there were more sensations. More pleasure. More heat. There was Cam's cock pressing inside the saturated, slick depths of her pussy. A little at a time. Working the heavy flesh inside her as his expression tightened, as sweat ran down his temple, his neck.

His hand gripped her hips as Chase's supported her back, holding her in place as she was bent back. She could feel his cock throbbing inside her ass. A thick, iron-hard intruder stretching the sensitive tissue as Cam's cock stretched her pussy.

Heat seared it. Burning, electric ecstasy began to race through her body as she watched Cam give his head a hard shake, fighting to hold onto his control.

"I love you," she whispered, staring back at him. "I love you inside me. I love how you take me."

His hips jerked, hard, burying him tighter inside her. He stared back at her, his eyes locked with hers as she licked her dry lips quickly. A moan escaped her. Pleasure was tearing through her as Cam worked his erection inside her.

"Fuck me hard, Cam."

His head shook. "I'll hurt you." His jaw was bunched with effort. "Stop this, Jaci."

She clenched around the flesh filling her pussy, taking only half of his length and needing more.

"Do it faster, then." She whimpered, feeling the muscles spasming around his flesh. "It's too slow."

She tried to move, to jerk in their grip and force him deeper. But two pairs of hands held her in place, forced her to accept only what they gave. But she could see the thin boundary of Cam's control. It would take very little to break it. And she wanted it broken.

She was breathing so heavily it was hard to talk.

"The first time," she gasped. Cam stilled. "The first time. You were there."

He shook his head.

"You were there, Cam. Me, my vibrator, and you. I cried your name."

"Oh, God." His hips jerked.

"I fucked myself and cried out for you."

"Jaci." He breathed her name harshly.

"And I needed it. I need you now, Cam."

He gave his head another hard shake.

"Do it," she cried out. "Take me, damn you. Stop torturing me. Fuck me."

He pulled back, pressed in, harder, deeper.

She dug her nails into his shoulders and shuddered. Tremors were racing through her, she could feel her orgasm, just there, so close, almost enough.

"Make me burn."

His head shook again.

"Make me scream, Cam. I dare you."

Chase jerked beneath her, driving his cock deeper, retreating precious inches and impaling her with a swift, hard stroke. The pleasure made her vision glaze, her lips part in suspended pleasure.

Cam lost it then. He saw the haze of ecstasy wash over her face as Chase lost patience and began fucking her. Short, tight strokes in her ass that tightened her pussy further. And the extremity of the pleasure on her face broke the last threads of control Cam possessed.

His hands tightened on her hips and he surged inside

her. Quick hard strokes, pumping into her as an agony of pleasure clenched around his cock. He could feel her juices weeping around his cock, slickening his way even as the tender muscles tightened around him.

He buried it to the hilt, again and again. Each desperate lunge inside her shot pleasure to the base of his skull until he wondered if he could survive it. He'd had her once today, and still he was fucking her as though it were the first time. Moving furiously between her thighs, shafting hard and deep and feeling her melt around him as her orgasm began to shatter her.

And it took him. He heard his shout, heard Chase's, and felt the violent, overpowering pleasure of his release spurting inside her, possessing her, marking her. Belonging to her.

Sweet mercy, he was dying inside her. Coming until he was certain the top of his head had exploded along with the seed erupting from his cock. And still he was thrusting, fucking, pouring into her and losing parts of himself to her.

He was lost to her. It was only a matter of time and he knew it. Only a matter of time before she knew everything, every secret, every shame. And he would hold onto her for as long as he could. Because only this, only Jaci, mattered.

CHAPTER
SEVENTEEN

The next evening, Jaci packed her bags at the hotel and waited for Cam and Chase to pick her up to move her into their apartment. She had put off the move to give herself time to think, to get her own priorities straight. She wasn't denying what Cam meant to her any longer or how much she wanted what he wanted, but even after a night and nearly a full day of fruitless soul searching, she still couldn't decide if the risk was worth the memories she would build, if things didn't work out.

And the situation with the Robertses wasn't even close to being resolved. They hadn't contacted her or Moriah, and Jaci was beginning to wonder if that was another plan she was going to watch disintegrate around her. Because she sure hadn't managed to work things out where Cam was concerned.

As she placed her bags next to the doorway, she heard the security lock disengage. Cam had the extra key. The door swung open and he stepped inside, his expression still and satisfied.

Courtney had been surprised to learn she was moving in with Cam and Chase. According to her, they had never invited a woman to stay with them, not even for a weekend. And when Jaci had tried to pin Cam down to a time frame, he refused to discuss it.

"Is this everything?" He picked up one of the suitcases and several dress bags, before handing them to Chase, then collected the other two bags and several more dress bags for himself.

Jaci picked up her purse, a travel bag, and her notebook case, and gave one last look around the sitting room.

"That's it."

"Hell, you don't travel light, do you sweetheart?" Chase grinned as she followed them into the hallway.

"For a several-month stay?" She rolled her eyes. "I like clean clothes, Chase, and the convenience of wearing more than a few outfits. Courtney told me to plan for six months. If the designs for the mansion are accepted, then she wants me to begin on the house as well."

And it appeared she might be picking up a bit more work in the Alexandria area. She'd had several calls from potential clients that she had met at the Brockheim Ball. She was hoping to meet with them soon and discuss details. She wouldn't mind staying around for a while, she thought. Whether things worked out with Cam or not, she had a few friends here. It would be a good place to settle down for a while, perhaps to build enough of a client base to make her dream of her own studio a reality.

They entered the elevator with Cam strangely silent. The ride down to the parking garage was over quickly, and within minutes they were storing her luggage in the back of the Jaguar and Chase's jeep.

Perhaps it was best that she didn't give herself more time to consider this move, she thought. With the weekend beginning, it would give her time to settle into the apartment, perhaps to settle in with Cam. To try to make sense of the fascination he had always been for her.

Always.

"Regretting?" he asked as he closed the door behind him and started the motor.

"I rarely do things that I think I'll regret," she told him as she smoothed her hands down her jean-clad thighs. "Maybe you're the one who's regretting?"

"I learned not to regret what I can't change." He slid the car into gear and drove from the underground garage.

"You're luckier than the rest of us mortals, then," she said.

He shifted the gears, his thigh bunching as he used the clutch, the muscles of his lower arm flexing and tightening as he moved the gearshift. Damn, why did watching him shift gears always make her hot?

"How am I luckier?" he finally asked. "I would have assumed I was smarter. I learned a long time ago how useless regret can be."

There was darkness in his tone, not anger, but a dark realization that made her realize the hunger was growing inside him.

She looked at his face, seeing the hard angles, the tightening of his jaw, and felt that same restraint inside her he had talked about the day before begin to unravel further.

It was as though the wickedness she could see building inside him called to a once-hidden, wicked core inside her. She wanted to get wild with him. Right here, right now. She wanted to be wicked, wet, and seductive, and she wanted to see him lost inside her. Just as he had been the day before on the balcony.

"How long has it been since you've had sex without a condom?" Suspicion was tearing through her, because she knew Cam. She knew his control.

"Until you, I've never forgotten." The tightly leashed hunger throbbed in his voice.

Was this what she really wanted? Jaci stared at him, realizing the anger that pulsed just beneath the surface.

"What about when you and Chase share your women? Are you as particular then, Cam?"

He glanced at her, his pupils flaring, the green of his eyes darkening. "I've always been more particular, until now. With you, I won't be."

Jaci's lips parted in surprise, in shock. "Have you lost your mind?"

"I'm warning you." He stared straight ahead now. "I've never taken a woman without a condom, Jaci. I've never claimed another woman. I'm claiming you."

"And if I hadn't been protected?" she snapped back.

He gave her a mocking look. "I ran the investigation on you, sweetheart. I know better."

Well, that took care of that. "And this is all your decision? I don't think so, Cam." She shook her head furiously. "What the hell gives you the right to think you can make that choice for me?"

"The fact that I lost my fucking mind with you," he stated, obviously not pleased with the fact. "For God's sake, do you think I didn't realize then what the hell was going on? I don't have any control with you alone, Jaci. There's not a chance in hell I'll have any, once things get wilder."

Once things got wilder. Once he and Chase started touching her again, once they were taking her again.

He didn't like admitting it, he didn't like the loss of control. Cam shifted gears with a brutal flick of his wrist, grimacing at the grinding, before pulling back and breathing in roughly.

"I'm sorry," he bit out, shaking his head at the feelings he couldn't make sense of. "I'm just trying to be as honest as I can with you. And I swear to God, that's more than any other woman has ever had."

"So I'm supposed to be thankful?" she retorted brutally, and he really didn't blame her for being pissed. "You know, there's a difference between being curious about this lifestyle you've adopted for yourself, and allowing you and

Chase to take over every part of me. I don't belong to you. Which means you'd better find control, because until we figure out where the hell this relationship is going, you won't be playing without it."

He almost grinned. "No glove, no love?" he snorted.

He caught the little twitch of her lips, the way her delicate nose flared to hold back the sudden spurt of amusement.

"If that's the way you want to look at it." She finally shrugged.

"I want you bare, Jaci," he told her softly. He wanted it with a desperation he could hardly control. It was primal. Overwhelming.

"And I want all of you, Cam." She turned her head, staring back at him with resolve. "Not just your body, not just your possession. I'm risking all I'm willing to risk with you at the moment." She needed him there. If nothing else she needed that.

Cam concentrated on the road as he fought himself. The past was like a broken mirror inside him, reflecting back at him in fractured memories.

The pain, the humiliation, the complete fury that he could be used so easily. The humiliation, he realized, had been the hardest part. How was he supposed to tell his brother, or the woman that held parts of his soul that he hadn't known he possessed, that he'd been a fucking whore for his aunt's aging, depraved friends?

It was sickening. But Davinda had been smart, she had known exactly how to hold him, how to force him into what she wanted him to do.

At fifteen he had been almost man-size. And so easy to work. Uncertain, lost without the parents that had spoiled and protected him and his twin, it had taken very little for his aunt to maneuver him. A little spiked soda and he had been nearly unconscious. Then came the pain.

The photos. Her hole card against a young man whose sense of pride was so easily broken.

He would have done anything to keep Davinda from showing those pictures—from letting Chase or anyone else see them. And he had. He had done things that made his skin crawl, at the thought of them, until he found a way to break the bitch. Until he had what he needed to make certain she was gone—that *he* had the pictures, and that the inheritance she had been so certain she would get when he and Chase turned twenty-one never made it into her hands.

He wiped his hand over his face with a weariness he hadn't known in years. This was one of the reasons he had let her run seven years ago. They had been in their hometown and a part of him had been terrified those who had "bought" him, the few who were still alive, would talk.

He wanted to laugh at the thought now. He was sure a few of those old crones had had strokes from pure fear after Davinda was sent packing. They were afraid he was going to kill them, just as he had threatened he would.

And God help him, sometimes he almost believed he would have. He had nearly strangled the last one to death. Days before he turned eighteen. The malicious bitch had thought she was going to force him to spend the night with her. He would do it, or Davinda would show those pictures to his brother.

Before he'd realized what he was doing he'd had his hands around her throat, his fingers squeezing, and something inside him had gone stone-hard and icy cold. There had been no conscience, only a need to kill. It was a need he had barely walked away from that night. And he remembered it. He remembered that need with such strength that he had never allowed himself to spend the night in any woman's bed.

"Cam?" Jaci's voice drew him back from things he

swore he wouldn't let himself dwell on. As he had told her earlier, regret changed nothing. Regretting the past and what it had created inside him was useless. But he'd lied to her, too, because the more time he spent with her, the more he regretted things he'd never believed he would.

Not the sharing. God, the sharing was pure, fucking pleasure, he couldn't help that. The thought of watching her, seeing her immersed in it, made him harder than hell.

But other things, other parts of himself. Those he regretted.

"Yeah?" he finally answered, realizing his voice was rougher than he liked, harder.

"How did the sharing start?"

He turned and stared back in her surprise. "What?"

"Sharing your women with your brother. How did it start?"

He smiled then. Because that memory was one of the better ones. Chase had thought his eighteen-year-old "virgin" brother needed to experience the birds and the bees. And Chase's then girlfriend, a pretty little coed from out of town, had been as wild as the wind, with a tempting little fantasy of doing it with twins.

"With a dare," he finally said, flashing her a smile, as that memory helped to bury the others. "Chase dared me."

"That doesn't explain why you keep doing it," she pointed out. "What does that have to do with . . ."

As they pulled into the garage beneath his and Chase's apartment he turned and stared back at her.

"Because he saved me that night," he finally answered her. "He saw the animal prowling inside me, the darkness and the inability to control whatever drove me. He saw it, and he showed me the outlet for it. How do you explain why the grass is green or the sky is blue? Just because that's the color it is. The name given to it. It's the color it was created to be. Just as I'm the man I was born to be. No more. No less."

"Or the man something else made you?" she asked softly.

He shrugged then. "Who the hell knows, at this point, Jaci. But you can excuse it any way you want. It's damned powerful and pure fucking pleasure. And we both know it."

"All I know is that I want to own as much of you as you want to own of me." She surprised him with the answer, sent a shaft of pure lust shooting through his balls, and caused him to clench his hands around the steering wheel while she opened the door and stepped out of the car.

"What if I told you you already owned me?" he asked her.

She turned back with a sad little smile. "I'd call you a liar," she said. "I don't have enough of you, Cam. And that might be what breaks this little almost-relationship we have going on here. Because the day will come when what little I have won't be enough. What will you do then?"

"Everything I can to change your mind," he told her, aware of the arrogance that was reflected in his tone.

She could think he was arrogant until hell froze over, but he wasn't going to lose her. Whatever it took, he'd do it. He just couldn't tell her. He wouldn't be able to bear the disgust he would see in her eyes if he did.

He loved her. He wasn't fighting it, he had no idea if what he saw in her eyes was really love or just his own wishful thinking. Hell, he'd loved her seven years ago. It had nearly destroyed him when she turned away from what he was, without so much as considering the needs that drove him. But he had understood. He had let her go. And the hunger for her had only grown.

And Cam knew, it wasn't going to go away.

Chase watched as Cam and Jaci got silently out of the

Jaguar. He could feel the tension as he neared them, Jaci's luggage in his hands, and watched as Cam pulled her bags from the back of the car.

For years he had fought to feel something through that twin bond they had once shared so long ago. Chase remembered when he stopped feeling it. When he started feeling as though the brother he had known since conception had died. Until they had learned Jaci was arriving at the mansion, that lack of a bond had only gotten worse over the years.

Now he wished he could make sense of what he did feel. Cam's guard was dropping; whatever he had done to block his nightmares and the echoes of emotions that went along with that twin bond was weakening.

He could thank Jaci for that, and he knew it. As he watched his brother escort her up the staircase to the lower floor of the converted warehouse, he knew that Cam's feelings for Jaci had started it.

Cam had always had a soft spot for Jaci, even before he had started desiring her. She had been a precocious snot-nosed little kid that trailed after Cam every time she saw him.

Come to think of it, Jaci had started trailing after him about the time Cam had started drawing away from everyone else. Just after he turned fifteen. With her big eyes and her wide smile, she had bounced around Cam every time she saw him. And she had known him even when he was with Chase; Jaci had always been able to tell them apart.

"I can't believe I'm doing this." Jaci was laughing at Cam as they entered the lower apartment. "You are aware aren't you, that bringing me here is like giving an artist a blank canvas, or a writer a blank journal?"

"I told you, do what you want with it." Cam's voice was patient and sincere, surprising Chase. Nothing he had done over the years had ever convinced Cam to put up so much as a picture. Anything Chase had gotten for Cam's apartment always ended up back in his own apartment, slipped back in there by Cam while he wasn't looking.

He shook his head as he moved through the large open room to the screened-off bedroom, and put Jaci's luggage on Cam's bed.

If she thought the apartment was sterile, he could only imagine what she thought of the bedroom. Cam didn't even have a fucking blanket on the bed. There was a sheet and a few pillows thrown on the headboard. Chase knew for a fact his brother slept on the couch with nothing but a light throw blanket for warmth.

The large sectional couch had been bought with sleeping in mind, Cam had told him once. For some reason, his brother hated beds. Another of those anomalies that had begun in his teens.

Jaci stared around the bedroom. The bed was plain. The wood chest and dresser plainer still. There was a closet at the side, open and empty.

She felt like crying. There was nothing in Cam's apartment that proclaimed it as his. And here, in the bedroom, the one room that most people marked as their own more than any other, it was more sterile than the rest of the apartment.

"You can do whatever to it." Cam cleared his throat behind her, staring around the screened-off room and seeing what she saw. Starkness. Brutal emptiness.

Hell, he should have at least bought a comforter for the bed, for appearance's, sake if nothing else.

"You can even do the frills and stuff." He shoved his hands in his pockets and stared at her stiff back.

He glanced at Chase. His brother shook his head and turned on his heel, walking from the partitioned room. Son of a bitch. He grit his teeth and held back the ire building inside him. So he didn't like bedrooms. So the hell what?

"Hell, it's not that big a deal," he finally snapped. "I don't like beds, why would I care about the fucking bedroom?"

"You're right." She swung around to face him, a bright smile curling her lips, though her eyes were shadowed. "It's not that big a deal. Like I said, a blank canvas. I have a free hand through the whole place, right?"

"The whole place." He shrugged easily.

"You're paying for it," she told him as she picked up the first of the dress bags and moved to the open walk-in closet. "I hear Ian pays you a killer wage, so you should be able to afford it."

Of course he could. He didn't have many vices. The Jaguar was his biggest expense. They'd bought the warehouse cheap, using money from the sale of the house in Oklahoma and some savings they had. He didn't care about the damned money, either.

"I'll make sure you have a credit card," he promised.

It might be nice. She would probably pick out rugs and stuff. Frilly bedroom stuff. Maybe stuff some flowers in vases and put them somewhere. He could handle that. It was a woman thing. Women liked their frilly stuff.

She was here, that was what mattered. That was all that mattered. He could handle anything else.

CHAPTER EIGHTEEN

Cam stood in the kitchen, his hands braced on the bar, his head lowered as he fought the need to go to Jaci. He could hear the whisper of her movements through the cavernous apartment. He could smell her. He could almost feel her warmth. And he needed it.

He lifted his head and glanced at Chase where he stood by the balcony doors, staring out into the heavy covering of trees that separated the building from the street.

They could go to her, take her now. Make her scream with pleasure. And that was what he needed to do. Chase was as highly sexed as Cameron; having her now would be pure fucking pleasure.

Except, the sudden need for something more was building inside him like a dark, shadowed wave. It was rife with emotion. It was dangerous. He knew how fucking dangerous it was, because being with Jaci, alone, would open parts of him he hadn't allowed free for twenty years.

That was the reason for sharing her. The need to hold back the emotions that clawed at him, the needs that filled him like demons that refused to rest. He had forced back every emotion he could find within himself for too many years. Jaci threatened that.

And now, an unfamiliar hunger threatened the distance he needed between them. A clawing, desperate need to claim her, to mark her, to show her she was his. He shared her body, her pleasure, because it was so fucking good, so damned hot that he knew letting it go entirely might never happen.

But the moment she stepped into his apartment, as his woman, something had snapped free inside him and he couldn't rein it in.

As he watched Chase, his brother turned to him, his expression somber, thoughtful.

"I'm going upstairs," he suddenly announced.

Cam tensed, hunger tightening through him.

"For how long?" The question slipped free, and Cam grimaced at how revealing it was.

Chase's lips quirked knowingly. "For as long as I need to, Cam," he said, moving through the living room to the stairs. "For as long as I need to."

Cameron stood still, silent, watching until Chase disappeared up the staircase and the upper door closed softly. He breathed in harshly. It was slipping. His careful control over the twin bond they had once shared. Losing control of that was dangerous. Because sometimes, Cam had nightmares, and in those nightmares the past tortured him. It was nightmares he and Chase had once been able to share so easily.

He didn't have to sleep with Jaci to take her alone, he reminded himself. If he slept on the couch, then he didn't normally awake to the nightmares. As long as he didn't sleep in a bed, he didn't dream of his fingers wrapped around an aged neck as murder filled his soul.

If he didn't sleep with Jaci, then there was no risk. She wouldn't know, and Chase wouldn't know.

And he could take her, take the woman his heart claimed as he needed to take her. And that was exactly what he was going to do. He pushed away from the counter and headed through the apartment. To the woman. To his woman.

It didn't take Jaci long to store her clothes in the empty closet, dresser, and chest. There was even plenty of room to spare. None of Cam's clothes were present. The bedroom was as bare as the rest of the apartment, perhaps more so.

There wasn't even a blanket, there were no cases on the pillows, there was just a sheet, white, no frills, and rather cheap.

The bed was just a metal frame. Could any one bedroom be more sterile than this one? Could any one man's life be more sterile than Cam's?

She stored the suitcases in the top of the closet, then turned and rubbed her hands together slowly. This wasn't what she came here for, exactly. At least not yet. She had intended to tackle Cam later, but now would work, too. She had planned this for a while, she knew what to do, she knew how to do it. She would just have to divert Cam a little bit until she neutralized the Robertses. Once she finished with that, then she could concentrate on making Cam's life a little less sterile.

As she moved out of the closet, she came face-to-face with him. More accurately, with his bare chest. Broad and muscular, so horribly scarred, a representation of the scars that were inside his soul as well.

"I need you."

Yes, she could see he needed. She could see the hunger in his eyes, the darkness. She saw things she didn't want to admit to, and suspected worse. What had happened to him when he was in the military? What horrible things had they done to him?

She reached up and touched the scars on his chest, her

fingertips trailing over the raised ridges as she lifted her eyes to his.

That darkness she had always sensed within him was growing. A sexual core perhaps. A hunger and a need that was darker, deeper, than any she had glimpsed inside him before.

"Alone," she whispered, seeing, feeling, that need for more.

His hand cupped her neck, his fingers curling around it, strong and broad, heated.

His head lowered, his strong teeth catching her lower lip, pulling at it as his tongue rasped against it.

"Just us here." His voice was dark, dangerous.

"Where—"

He laid his fingers against her lips as he pulled back.

"He's not here. He can hear nothing upstairs. I promise."

"What would he hear?" she asked as he moved back, catching her hand and drawing her to the bed.

"Take off your clothes, Jaci."

She stood beside the bare bed, staring back at him as his hands moved to his belt.

He wore only his pants, dark jeans that molded his thighs and cupped the erection raging beneath them. He loosened the belt, then tugged at the metal snap.

"You're wasting time," he told her quietly.

Yes, she was.

She gripped the hem of her shirt, and the soft, dusky rose material slid over her head and fell to the floor. Her hands went to her jeans as she toed off the sandals she wore.

"Leave the panties on," he told her, as her fingers hooked in the thin elastic band beneath the jeans and she moved to slide them from her hips.

She left the panties on. The jeans cleared her hips and pushed slowly down her legs, while he removed his own—

until he was naked, and she stood before him in nothing but a red silk thong.

"I knew that was a thong."

She stood still as he began moving around her, gripping his cock with the fingers of one hand, massaging the engorged crest slowly.

"How did you know?" She swallowed tightly as she felt his free hand cup the rounded curve of one cheek.

"Those jeans were nice and snug." He rubbed at the underside of her ass before his fingers moved beneath the thin band between the cheeks. "There were no panty lines."

"Oh." She was breathing roughly, her flesh so sensitized now that she swore she could feel the brush of air from the cooling unit against her, and the feel of Cam's breath on the back of her neck. It was so sensual, so intense, she could feel her body heating, preparing, growing wet and wild for him.

"How did this happen?"

She froze as his fingers caressed a scar of her own. She knew what it looked like, what it was. A perfect curve over her hip, thin and deep.

"Does it matter?" She trembled beneath his fingers, then shook as he knelt behind her. "What are you doing?"

"You kissed my scars, didn't you?"

"Oh, Lord. Cam." His lips feathered over the mark, then his tongue.

"Someone took a whip to you, Jaci." His hands framed her hips, his fingers tightening on them. "You really want to tell me who did this."

She shook her head. "There's nothing to tell."

"Are you telling me this isn't a whip mark?" His teeth raked over it.

She shook her head as she tried to draw air into her lungs. "I'm telling you it doesn't matter."

She nearly collapsed to the floor as she felt his teeth rake across it. The pleasure was simply destructive. It shouldn't have been. It should have killed desire, the thought of that mark, the thought of how she had received it. But it wasn't the scar or the memories that weakened her. It was his touch, the shadows in his voice, the growling, primal pitch of his tone.

"I need more than a few gentle touches tonight." He laid his cheek against her hip, still kneeling, his hands holding her as she fought the tremors racing through her.

"What do you need?"

"I need to make you scream, Jaci."

"I always scream with you." Her voice was trembling now. She could feel an intensity in him, that driving heat and blazing need that he kept so carefully banked.

"But there are other ways to scream, sweetheart." He rose, his hand caressing her rear once again.

A second later a light, burning slap streaked across her rear.

"Cam!" She jerked forward, a soft cry leaving her lips as that heat moved from her rear to her clit.

How strange was that? It shouldn't have been erotic. It shouldn't have been tinged with heat and with pleasure.

"That's a nice start." His voice was harder, bolder. More dominant.

"What are you doing?"

"Letting you get to know me." His lips pressed against her shoulder.

"Really?" She breathed out roughly. "Why do I have a feeling this might not be something either of us are ready for Cam?"

His chuckle was a rough, dark sound against her neck a second before his teeth scraped there.

"There's pleasure. Pleasure that's soft, gentle, erotic." He petted her ass again. A less-than-gentle caress that had her breath catching, a whisper of a moan leaving her throat.

"Then," he continued, "there's pleasure that burns. That rides a line so close to pain that the senses open, nerve endings blaze with sensation, and when you come"—the slap at her ass was harder, hotter, and sent pulses of heated pleasure burning into her pussy—"When you come, Jaci, you're begging for the orgasm. Screaming for it. So desperate for that little death that you're pleading for more and more, until you come so hard, so deep, you swear you've died."

His hand curled around her neck again, turning her head to him as his lips touched hers.

"Tonight, you're going to swear you've died in my arms."

There was something in his gaze that captured her. Something so primitive, so fierce it stole her breath.

"No means no," he told her. "If you say no, I'll stop whatever makes you uncomfortable. But be certain, Jaci, that it makes you uncomfortable. Make certain it's not just fear of the unknown that makes you turn it away. Because if you say no, we don't revisit that again. I won't ask it of you again."

He pushed her to the bed, moving beside her as she stretched out on her stomach, that fear of the unknown already rising inside her.

"Why are we doing this now?" she whispered.

"Because it's the only alternative to the sharing that I have." He bent over her, his lips caressing the shell of her ear as his hand traveled down her back. "Because I'm burning inside, Jaci. Burning to hear you scream for me, to watch your eyes glaze over and your body shudder. Because it's a hunger I can't control."

"What are you going to do?"

His hand slid over her ass again, then lifted.

"Everything."

His hand landed on her ass again, a gentle slap, slightly more than a tap or a heavy pet.

Jaci jerked, her hips arching as she drew in a harsh breath.

"It burns a little more each time." His hand landed again, but added to the burn was the feel of his lips and teeth at her shoulder, in a caress whose pleasure seemed amplified by that slight burn at her rear.

Pleasure and pain.

Her fingers curled into the sheet beneath her as she fought to hold onto her senses. She could feel the anticipation curling inside her now, that dark force of arousal beginning to churn in her womb.

Her thighs parted as his hand slid between them. As he pushed at the back of her knee, she rose slightly until her ass was elevated.

"I want you here." His fingers slid beneath the elastic band that ran between the cheeks of her ass, and the thick pad of his finger pressed against the entrance to her ass. "Right here. I want to feel how hot your ass is, Jaci. I want to feel you taking me, hear you begging for more." His voice was a smooth, controlled demand, as her eyes widened.

She wasn't saying no. She couldn't. She could remember the feel of his fingers inside her, the pleasure and the pain, and she needed more.

"Pain and pleasure." He kissed the back of her neck. "But first things first. Turn over for me baby. Let me get you ready, then we'll fly together."

Fly together?

She turned, already burning as she stretched out on the bed before him, her thighs shifting, parting as his hand caressed down one leg, easing them apart.

Cam knelt on the bed before her, the hard length of his

cock standing out from his body, tempting her. Her mouth watered to taste him again, the desire rose inside her like a conflagration that wiped out her control.

She licked her lips and watched in regret as he came over her, that stiff length of hard flesh disappearing for a second while his lips settled over hers.

That kiss. Cameron's kiss. It burned inside her soul.

Her arms lifted from the bed and wrapped around his shoulders, her palms and her fingertips feeling his flesh, the tough, hard muscles beneath strong skin. Warm and vibrant, and for this moment, hers.

"I love your sweet lips," he murmured against them, before licking over them. "Look at me, Jaci. Let me see your eyes while you burn."

She had to force her lashes open, and when she did, a whimpering sigh tore from her throat.

His expression was filled with tormented need, with a desire, a hunger, a burning flame of desperation that pierced her soul.

"There you go," he crooned. "Just like that, Jaci. Let me see you. Let me see you need me."

He needed to see her eyes. He needed to watch her, needed to watch the fine edge of agonizing pleasure as it began to sweep over her.

Here he could forget what he had once been. In her arms, from the first touch, the first kiss, it was pure pleasure, nothing more. Just Jaci burning with him, needing him, rather than simply wanting him. Pure desperation rather than pure depraved lust. She ached for the pleasure he could give her, and he wanted to give her so much.

Holding her eyes, he let his lips settle over hers, his tongue piercing them, sweeping inside to wrestle with hers in a kiss that had him tightening, forcing back the wild hunger.

She did that to him. She made him crazy. Made him so

desperate to push her, to make her wild, that it ate at him like a sensual disease.

"Come here." He lifted his lips, then pulled her arms from around his neck, stretching them above her head. "Just like that."

"But I want to touch you." Her voice was thick, yearning.

Cam grimaced, hearing the need gathering inside her.

"Later. This time, it's just for you, sweetheart. Just feel. Let me love you, Jaci. Just like this. Watch me, feel me."

She watched him.

His lips settled over hers in a kiss that ate at her sensuality. She stretched beneath him, a ragged moan leaving her lips as her nipples brushed against his chest.

Cam framed her face with his hands, caressed her jaw and down her neck and was kissing her with a fierce driving hunger that reflected in the green fire of his eyes. Lips, teeth, and tongue, he devoured her until she was shaking against him, reaching for more, her body lifting to him as desperate mewls of pleasure echoed in her throat.

When she was certain the need couldn't rise higher, his lips slid from hers, nibbled down her neck, and kissed over her shoulder while her neck arched and her lashes drifted closed.

"Look at me, Jaci. Watch me." The hunger for it was a growl in his voice.

Her lashes lifted, her head lowering again as her panting became low, pleasure-filled cries.

"So beautiful," he whispered, touching her cheek as his lips hovered over a nipple. "Your eyes, Jaci. I can see straight to your soul. See the pleasure building inside you. I want to see that, baby."

She could barely see him. She was dazed from the pleasure to the point that she had to force her gaze to clear, force his face into focus.

That did nothing to help her self-control. His dark face

was flushed, the color of his eyes darkening as his head lowered. His gaze locked to hers as his lips covered her nipple and he drew it into his mouth.

Her cry was ragged, shocking her. She fisted her fingers in the sheet, pulling at it as his hand slid down her stomach, caressing and touching as he suckled at her.

The sensations were building inside her. One atop the other, each touch making each shard of pleasure sharper, deeper. Opening her soul further to his touch, despite her vow to keep him from that deepest part of her.

But he was taking it, overtaking it, overwhelming her. As she stared into his eyes, she could feel him inside her.

His lips moved from one nipple to the other, his palm cupping the mound while his other hand slid between her thighs, his fingers feathering over the curls there.

"I want you bare here," he told her, the words barely registering. "Promise me, Jaci. I want your pretty flesh bare for me. Nothing between you and my touch."

"Yes." She was only barely aware of what she was agreeing to—to the need to feel him, skin on skin, on every part of her body.

His smile was tight, triumphant, as he licked at her nipple, then moved lower.

His kisses were like touches of fire, laser points of exploding, cascading desire that wrapped around her mind and her senses.

"I need to touch you," she cried out as his lips traveled down her stomach, his hands pushing her thighs farther apart.

"Not yet," he breathed against her flesh. "Stay just like that, Jaci."

His breath whispered over the saturated curls between her thighs as she arched and fought to breathe. Oh God, she couldn't handle this. It was too much.

She could feel the perspiration gathering on her body,

heat filling her to the point that she expected to see flames at any second.

"Get ready." His fingers parted the swollen lips between her thighs. "Now it gets hot, Jaci."

It wasn't hot yet? She was dying.

She stared down at him, her eyes widening as he reached to the side of the mattress and lifted several items she hadn't seen him place on the bed.

"Cam." She heard the hesitancy in her own voice.

"No means no," he told her again, pausing. "Be sure before you say no, Jaci."

She licked her lips, catching the lower curve between her teeth as he laid the items between her thighs.

"One step at a time," he promised. "One pleasure at a time. I promise. Slow and easy."

His head lowered and his tongue swiped through the juice-laden slit, flickered around her clit as her senses exploded.

Jaci felt her hips arch involuntarily, felt pleasure wash over her in blinding, heated waves. The sound of his murmur of approval against the swollen bud was nearly too much pleasure. Her lashes fluttered, almost closing before she forced them open once more, locking her gaze with his.

"Good girl," he whispered, and delivered a gentle, sucking kiss to the tormented bud, and she trembled and shook at the sensation.

It was never-ending. The pleasure kept rising and rising inside her. His tongue licked and stroked, two fingers slid inside the weeping entrance of her pussy, where he stretched her, caressed her, and had her arching closer.

Her orgasm was just out of reach. Tormenting, burning. It built inside her with no hope of ease. He slowly pulled back.

"Don't stop." Her voice trembled as hard as her body. "Please, Cam."

"Turn over for me." His hand cupped her hip and lifted.

"Not yet," she cried out. "Don't stop yet, Cam."

He smiled. Warmth, lust, desire, and hunger were reflected in the curve of his lips. Approval glowed in his eyes, but it didn't sway him.

"We're not finished yet, sweetheart. Just a little while longer. Just a little more pleasure."

"You're going to torture me," she moaned, but she couldn't complain too hard—because it was unlike anything she had known before, anything she could have ever imagined.

Sweet heaven, the pleasure was incredible. It was flashing through her, brilliant rays of sensation so hot, so incredibly deep, that she wondered if she would survive it. And he said there was more?

CHAPTER
NINETEEN

Cam watched her eyes for as long as possible. Those brilliant green-and-blue-flecked depths, not really hazel, the colors too intense for that, as they glazed over, grew mesmerized with the pleasure.

She was wanton, adventurous, more so than she even suspected. He saw it in her eyes, and when she settled on her stomach, he saw it in the quivering curves of her ass.

She knew what was coming. She knew what he needed. At least part of it.

There was a point where a woman surrendered everything to her lover—physically, mentally—when she gave up control, trusting the one that held her to protect her pleasure, to draw her into the final sphere of pleasure.

At that point, her body belonged to the hand that brought that pleasure, and her body was willing to give up every measure of sensuality and surrender to the right touch.

He smoothed his hand over her ass. Soft, rounded flesh trembled and tensed, and he smiled tightly. She was almost there—not quite, but getting closer.

He eased the thong from her, watching as her thighs and buttocks tightened, lifted to him, then eased back to the mattress. Once there, she shifted again, pressed deeper, searching for enough friction to ease the ache in her clit.

His hand landed on her ass, the flesh blushing slightly as she gasped and grew still.

"Relax," he murmured.

"Relax?" The moan in her word was filled with need.

"You need to relax for this." His hand lowered again, delivering a burning little caress to her rear, and this time, she lifted to him.

Moving to her side, he let his lips trail down her spine. For every kiss along the silken flesh, his hand landed on her rear. The delicate, burning little slaps had her moaning within seconds, lifting, reaching, the additional sensations whipping inside her as she begged for more.

Her voice was dazed, almost incoherent. Her body shook, trembled, and the muscles of her ass eased; and as his lips reached the dimpled rise, the cleft of her buttocks parted easily beneath his fingers.

He kissed each cheek, then kissed inside the cleft. A second later, his tongue rasped around the puckered entrance as a shuddering cry tore from her lips.

He was burning with her now. He could feel the edge of his control fraying as he lifted her hips, turned, and eased his head beneath her before pulling her to him. He needed this. Needed to show her what she meant to him. The need for it tormented him.

His lips sank into fragrant, sweet juices. Her cry filled his ears. As he licked at the spill of sweetness he lubricated his fingers, then found that tender, tiny entrance once more. The toys. The play. Keeping her sexually off balance aided the slight distance he needed now.

Jaci's eyes flared wide and unseeing, ecstatic, burning pleasure swamping her senses, as she felt the smooth glide of his fingers in her rear, his lips at her sex.

She tried to twist in his hold, to get closer, but his arm tightened around her hips, holding her in place. His finger slid deeper, retreated, then another joined and entered.

She screamed out at the sensations. Surely she couldn't bear it. It was too much. Too much pleasure, too much heat. She could feel tiny explosions whipping through her senses, her mind, her body. Nerve endings were exploding with pleasure, burning.

Her nails dug into the bed, fractured cries tore from her lips as his tongue circled her clit, drew it into his mouth, and brought her close. Oh God, so close. She was so close to exploding, to finding a pleasure she knew for certain would destroy her, tear into her soul, leave her wasted and reaching for more. She would always need more now, would always beg for it.

Just as she was begging now, her voice torn, ragged, as he stretched her where she had never been truly stretched before. Preparing her for a possession of more than just her body.

"Now!" He pulled from between her thighs, ignoring her attempts to scream, to protest the throbbing, aching emptiness inside her pussy, the gnawing agony of her clit.

"Don't stop."

"Never." His voice was ragged as his fingers eased from her, then returned. Eased back, returned again. Lubricating her further, stretching her farther. Creating a need inside her that she suddenly feared would destroy her mind.

"Cam. Please." Her head dug into the mattress, her nails clenched at the sheet, finally tearing it away from the mattress as she felt him move closer, his hard thighs brushing against hers as the head of his cock slid against the prepared entrance.

"Easy," Cam crooned.

She felt the cool edge of the curved vibrator against the entrance of her pussy. It entered slowly, penetrating her as she writhed and tried to take more. She needed this. Needed it so desperately she was dying inside for it.

"Beautiful." He sighed behind her as the vibrator wedged inside her, the curled end pressing against her clit, the soft vibration tearing through her bundle of nerves.

"Hold it for me." He pulled at her arm, caught her hand, then drew it beneath her. "Hold it right there, sweetheart."

Her fingers curled against it, holding it in place. She was past denying him anything at this point.

Then she felt him, hard, thick—so hot. The crest of his cock pressed against the entrance to her ass, parted her, sent flames exploding, burning, tearing through her. It was pleasure and pain, agony and ecstasy, and she was dying for more.

"Cam!" She tried to scream his name, but she couldn't find the breath to scream.

"Should I stop, Jaci?" His voice was ragged, growling.

"No! Don't stop. Please. Oh God, Cam. It's killing me!"

She tried to rear back, tried to take more. A hard chuckle sounded behind her, and he eased farther inside her. Stars exploded behind her clenched eyelids, her body drew tight, juices spilled down her thighs.

"All of me, sweetheart." His rough croon stroked through her as he eased back, then eased farther inside. Retreating, then penetrating farther.

"Mine." The sharp declaration of possession had her womb clenching, more juices spilling around the intrusion of the softly vibrating erotic toy.

Each slow advancement inside her rear tightened her pussy further, filled her more. Nerve endings became more sensitive, electrified, desperate for release.

She was crying now. She could feel the tears as they mixed with the perspiration on her face, need clawing inside her until she was certain she wouldn't survive it.

"Easy, baby. Sweet love. So tight and sweet and hot." His hand landed on her ass again, and she almost exploded. "So beautiful. So giving."

He pulled back, forged inside, deeper, taking all of her as she took all of him. She felt his balls, tight and hot, pressing into her, felt his cock, so thick, scorching, wedged inside her.

He was breathing roughly behind her. His breath sawing in and out of his chest, then his hands suddenly clenched on her hips.

Cam could hear her cries, the broken words, the pleas. He could hear the surrender in each broken cry and feel it as her ass flexed around his cock. He could do this. Take her like this. Find the distance by not staring into her eyes.

The vibration of the curved dildo echoed through the thin tissue that separated her pussy from her rear, the added sensation driving spikes of agonizing hunger through his veins.

God, he wanted to see her face. Her eyes. He wanted to be beneath her, watching her, filling her tight sex as Chase took her from behind. The ultimate surrender, and it was denied to him. He needed to give her this. She needed it or he might lose her forever.

He gritted his teeth and fought to take her easy. He pulled back, then reentered her. He shook his head, felt the sweat roll over his shoulders, chest, and abdomen. He felt her tighten, bearing down on the intrusion as she managed to push back, to force his cock deeper. And he felt his control break. He felt everything inside him flow into her, and thanked God she couldn't see his face.

She writhed beneath him, fucking back with each stroke and demanding more. She was wild in his arms, her auburn hair flaming over her shoulders, her head lifting as she rose before him, moving around him, begging for more.

He pressed her shoulders back to the mattress forcefully with his palm below her neck, gripped her hips with one hand, and began to thrust powerfully inside her.

Her ass rippled and clenched around him. Her cries filled his head. He was seconds—dear God—only seconds away from ecstasy.

Jaci fought the hold Cam had on her, feeling the burning pleasure and pain envelop her as he fucked her with smooth, hard strokes. The vibrator rocked inside her, curled up along her pussy, and pressed into her clit, driving shards of sensation through her womb.

Each strong thrust was agony and ecstasy. Each pushed her higher, burned hotter, deeper. She screamed his name, felt his hand land hard on her ass one last time, and then she exploded.

She couldn't breathe. Her eyes jerked open, dazed, unseeing, her body tensed, tightened, then a ragged scream left her throat as everything unraveled inside her with furious, blazing rapture. Explosions erupted in her clit, her pussy, her womb. Clenching, convulsing, she jerked beneath him then cried out again as he thrust inside her one last time before giving in to his own release.

And that release, buried so deep, sending thick, hot jets of his semen erupting inside her, threw her higher. It was more than the physical pleasure, more than the wicked intensity. It was the possession. A possession that defied the limits of either pleasure or pain finally erupted inside her soul and left her shaking, replete, beneath him.

Jaci collapsed on the bed as Cam shuddered behind her, his chest pressed tight to her back, his lips at her ear, his voice whispering, crooning, approving.

She didn't know what he was saying, couldn't make sense of the fractured words, but it didn't matter. She was drifting on clouds of pure satiation now, dazed, mesmerized by the aftereffects of his possession, as he slowly pulled free of her and collapsed on the bed beside her.

The vibrator eased from the tight clasp she had on it as he slowly pulled it free and silenced it. She heard a thump, a drawer grate closed, then he was pulling her in his arms, surrounding her with his warmth.

She didn't want to move. She wanted to drift here forever, so replete that even her soul dozed, sated with such an excess of pleasure that she didn't want to move. Not forever. Or at least for a few more hours. She wanted to stay wrapped in the intimacy of being alone with him.

She didn't know how long they had lain entwined, exhaustion wrapping them together. But she knew when she felt him move. Cautiously, carefully, he untangled his body from hers, rolled to the side of the bed, and sat up.

She stayed still, praying, hoping against hope that he was going to lie back down beside her, that he was going to hold her for just a little longer—doze with her, let the final remnants of what he had done to her ease inside her before he deserted her.

Finally, long moments later, she heard him breathe out roughly, then felt his weight ease from the bed.

Damn him. Pain poured through her as she felt a sheet settle over her slowly, then listened as he picked up his clothes and left the room.

He would be back, she told herself. He wouldn't leave her alone like this, not after the pleasure he had just given her, the soul-deep possession he had just taken of her. He would not just desert her.

But he had.

She waited, listening carefully, and finally heard the muted drone of the television, the refrigerator door closing in the open kitchen.

Her eyes opened and she rolled over in the bed slowly, suddenly so lonely she could barely stand the feeling that poured through her.

Lifting herself from the bed, she pulled on a robe and then collected a pair of soft, cotton pants and a sleep shirt, before moving from the bedroom.

Standing at the entrance, she stared through the open rooms at the man that had just loved her as no other man had even had a chance to. In the time he had spent with her in that bed, he had marked her body and her spirit, laid claim to her heart, and left her pulsing in bliss. And now he was breaking her heart.

He sat in the recliner, a beer on the table in front of him, the television droning as he sat forward, his elbows braced on his knees, a heavy scowl lining his face.

He looked as lonely as she felt, and just as alone. Like a man who had faced a battle and came out on the losing end.

Moving toward the living area, she watched as his head lifted, his gaze flaring as he stared at her. His eyes were filled with shadows, with torment.

"I'm going to take a shower before I fix dinner. Would you like to join me?"

She took him by surprise. He blinked back at her, his lips parting as though he wanted to say something, before they pressed together firmly, and he gave a sharp nod.

"Cam."

He stopped as he moved to push himself from the chair.

"I can understand that you have an aversion to beds, but the next time you leave me like that without letting me know, without a touch or a word, then I'll walk out of this relationship. Do you understand me?"

His eyes narrowed on her.

"You hurt me," she continued. "Keep hurting me, and whatever's growing between us will turn bitter. That's the only warning you're going to get."

His jaw clenched before he nodded again, dominance and arrogance at war with the challenge she was putting out to him and the demands she was making.

"Hurting you isn't what I want," he finally said.

"Then don't do that to me again," she whispered. "For both our sakes."

She watched his face as he moved to her, the heaviness in his expression, the flash of pain in his eyes. Then his arms were around her, just a little too tight, his body tense as he held her to him.

"Never again," he promised, though his jaw bunched as it pressed against the top of her head, and she could feel the anger—it had to be anger—growing inside him.

She held onto him and closed her eyes tightly, wondering how in hell she was going to survive the pain she was watching brew inside him. Whatever it was, what they had done in that bedroom hadn't eased it. The wildness was still there, the flaring desperation, and the haunting shadows that had no explanation.

She loved him, but she was beginning to wonder if love was going to be enough.

The next night, Jaci tossed in the freshly made bed, uncomfortable, cold, and alone. Silence filled the apartment, except for the soft drone of the television.

Cam had kissed her forehead and told her good night. And then he had left her, moving from the bedroom back to the living room and the cold emptiness of the apartment.

Why? Why couldn't he sleep with her?

She rolled over to her back and stared at the ceiling above her. She hadn't expected this when she moved in with him, this sense of bonding, and still the aloneness. This was the second night he had taken her like a wild man, pushing her, pushing both of them, and leaving them shaking in the aftermath.

And it was the second time he had left her to face the night alone.

Well, too damned bad, because she had faced too many nights alone. Too many nights when she had needed him close to her and refused to allow herself other options. Too many nights when she had wondered what she had allowed to slip from her fingers. So, the fight was going to be harder than she had imagined it would be. She would just have to adapt.

She rose again from the bed, padded to the living area, and stared at Cam as he lay unmoving, silent and awake, on the large sectional couch.

The short curve of the cushioned furniture was empty, so she curled up there, her feet tucking against his as she drew another of the thin throws from the back of the couch and pulled it around her.

His legs parted enough to trap her feet farther within the warmth of them, then the television winked out.

Silence stretched between them, but it was a warm silence, one that felt comfortable, that wrapped around her and sent a surge of relief rocking her.

"Good night, Cam," she whispered.

"Good night, baby."

She turned on her side, tucked her back closer to the couch, and closed her eyes. Within minutes, sleep overcame her as it hadn't in that too-big, too-cold bed.

Cam knew the moment she fell asleep and lay still and silent, waiting for the sense of smothering unease to fill him. He hadn't slept with a woman since he was in his teens, since he was forced to stay in those old bitches' beds until the sun rose. He had rarely slept, certainly, other than once, he had barely dozed. His skin had crawled with the feel of their naked bodies plastered against his back, their hands groping at him, even in their sleep.

Rather than the need to get up and find another place to sleep, a place alone, Cam found, instead, an uncertain peace. Jaci's feet were tucked against his lower legs, fragile, soft, and warm. He could see her face from where he lay, her expression serene now, as it hadn't been when he'd checked on her the night before.

She was comfortable and warm, and close to him.

His lips quirked at the thought of that, and at the fragile enjoyment he was finding in her feet shifting, pressing closer to him.

They had been cold when she first lay down and curled herself on the curved section of the couch. The chill had quickly turned to warmth though, and as she fell asleep, her graceful little toes had curled as though in contentment, before relaxing once again.

And now, rather than wondering how long he'd have to lie there before he could leave her without hurting her, he found drowsiness drifting over him instead.

He hadn't slept worth shit the night before, and he'd feared tonight would be no better. Now he smothered a yawn, let his eyes close, and found himself drifting to sleep with a speed and contentment that he hadn't known since he was a child.

Jaci muttered in her sleep as he felt himself drifting off, and he smiled at the sound. He could get used to that, he thought. He could get very used to it.

CHAPTER TWENTY

"I think it's singularly unfair that you're being given freedom to roam the club, while I have to beg for months just for a drink at the bar," Courtney pouted several days later, as she trailed Jaci through the club.

Jaci snapped another picture with the digital camera she used, before turning to look over her shoulder at her friend.

Courtney's eyes were filled with amusement, though her expression was less than pleased.

"No doubt you cause as much trouble in here as you do anywhere else," Jaci accused her. "Where's the fascination in it?" She let the camera hang by its strap below her breasts, as she made a few notes on the electronic notepad she carried with her.

"Tell me you see the possibilities, Jaci." Courtney's voice was scandalized. "It is an adventure."

"It's a place full of men," Jaci said as she lifted the camera and zoomed in on the molding at the ceiling. "The exercise room is sweaty and smelly. The library is dark and gloomy, and the living area has a bar and a billiards table. Give me a break. It's so male-oriented, you nearly choke on the testosterone."

She could feel Courtney behind her, almost see the outraged expression on her friend's face.

"And they do not want us here." There was a pout in Courtney's voice. "They are determined to close us out of their little conversations and their conniving. It's totally unfair."

"Hmm. Maybe we should invite them to the spa with us," Jaci suggested. "See what they think about estrogen overload."

Unlike Courtney, Jaci had no interest in the club or the men who gathered there. She didn't want to know their identities, and she sure as hell didn't want to be a part of their conversations.

"You're being mean to me today." Courtney sighed, though Jaci heard the amusement in her voice. "Doesn't it make you curious about them? Sometimes, I think if I could be invisible, then I could move about them, perhaps find the answers I seek in what makes these men so different from others. The few I know that are members here are unlike other men. This fascinates me, wondering what has created these men, what makes them as they are."

"Have you asked Ian?" Jaci asked, though the only member that fascinated her was Cam.

"Ian's answers would only infuriate you." She rolled her eyes expressively. "He is a man. I have decided that male language and female language are not always compatible."

God, wasn't that the truth.

"Maybe men are just aliens," Jaci suggested, thinking of Cam.

Over the weekend, being with him had seemed so natural, so easy. She hadn't imagined that living in that huge apartment with him could be anything but taxing. She hadn't lived with anyone since she had moved from her parents' home.

But she had also realized there was so much about him that she didn't know, and that she didn't understand. Chase was easier to read. Cam hid much more of himself. She was learning that there was so much about him that she didn't know.

He was doing just as she had once asked him not to do, though. He was seducing his way not only into her heart, but around it, through it, binding her to him in a way she hadn't imagined she could be bound.

And at the same time, it worried her. The dark sexual core of him was growing. Despite the sexual excess of the weekend, he never seemed to lose that wild, desperate hunger growing inside him. And she was terribly afraid she knew the only thing that would ease it.

After she finished the photos and notes and walking through the club rooms, she returned to the main mansion with Courtney trailing behind her. Jaci couldn't help but wonder at the hunger driving Cam, and if she was making a mistake in pushing for more before giving in to that need that tormented him.

There was something that warned her that whatever drove him, whatever tormented him, wouldn't be revealed easily. It was a part of him that worried her, even before she left Oklahoma.

That thought caused her to pause as she entered the office Ian had assigned her. She had known Cam before he joined the military. Admittedly, she had been too young then to understand much about the unsmiling Falladay twin. He was five years older than her. They hadn't even gone to the same school, but sometimes her father hired the boys to help on his small ranch.

And she had always thought it a game, a challenge, whenever she saw him, to draw a smile to his lips, to his odd light green eyes.

She moved to the desk, downloaded the pictures on auto pilot, and frowned at those memories.

Cam had joined the army when she was still a young

girl, but each time he returned home on leave, he had made it a point to check up on her; he managed to be wherever she was, and she had always dropped whatever she was doing to make Cam smile.

Whatever happened had happened there in Oklahoma.

She licked her lips nervously. Her father's best friend, Sheriff Bridges, had made a point after she turned sixteen to warn her about Cam. It was a warning she had informed him she didn't need.

Sheriff Bridges was retired now, but he was still a close friend—of hers, as well as her father's. But would he tell her what she needed to know?

She pulled her cell phone from the clip at her side and laid it on the desk beside her, staring at it. Did she want to know?

"You look like a woman with a lot on her mind."

She lifted her head and stared back at Chase. He didn't know what had happened to his brother, either. The argument she had glimpsed the week before proved that he was as much in the dark as she was when it came to Cam.

"Quite a bit," she finally admitted, watching as he stepped into the room and closed the door behind him.

He leaned against the heavy wood panel, a scowl working at his face as he watched her. His gaze dropped to the cell phone, then moved back to her face.

"I've run more than a dozen investigations into our past," he said quietly. "I've personally questioned everyone I could think of in that fucking town, had every pedophile and every filthy molesting son of a bitch I can think of questioned, and I don't know any more now than I did when we were kids, when he disappeared from the house."

She stared at the phone again. Did either of them have the right to steal the secrets he was fighting so hard to hide?

"Do you like sleeping on the couch, Jaci?" he asked her

then, his voice hard, filled with anger. "Do you like having nothing but your feet held between his, rather than his arms around you?"

"Stop, Chase!" She jumped from the chair and pushed her fingers through her hair, fighting her own fears and the need to have Cam hold her through the night.

"Do you know why he shares his women?"

She stared back at him, her chest aching as her heart clenched at the pain in his face. She shook her head slowly. She didn't have the right to give Chase answers that Cam wouldn't. But, God, she wanted to. She wanted to know why her lover hurt so desperately that he couldn't even bear to share a bed with her.

"He shares them because he can't hold them. Because he can't bring himself to give them more than the pleasure of his body. It's my job to hold them through the night, while he finds a couch to sleep on," he snapped out. "Is that what you want? Do you want me holding you while he sleeps on that fucking couch?"

"If that was what I wanted, then I would have come to your bed, rather than the damned couch he shares with me," she retorted. "For God's sake, Chase, what do you want from me? He hasn't told me anything, and if he had, do you think I could tell you? Do you think I'd betray him like that?"

She pushed her fingers through her hair again, and this time she clenched the strands furiously as she turned away from him.

He looked so much like Cam. There were no scars, the haunted shadows weren't the same, but in his expression, in his eyes, she could see his pain and his worry.

"When we were fifteen years old, he began disappearing at night," Chase bit out. "Until that summer, I could always feel him, knew when he was hurting, when he had nightmares. We always shared our nightmares, Jaci. After that, it was as though my brother, my twin who I had shared space with since conception, was dead. He walked and he talked, but I couldn't feel him. I couldn't talk to him. By God, I couldn't reach him. Now I'm asking for your help."

Her help? Jaci stared back at him in disbelief, wondering how the hell she was supposed to help him when she couldn't even help herself where Cam was concerned.

"You're asking me to betray him." She dropped her hands from her hair and stared back at him miserably. "Even if I knew anything, Chase, how could you ask me to do that?"

"Because he's my brother and I need to know who to fucking kill for what happened to him."

Her lips parted as she fought to drag in air. He wasn't joking. Just as Cam hadn't been joking seven years before when he threatened to kill for her.

"You and Cam just seem to have this thing about killing people," she exclaimed. "Tell me, Chase, where do you hide all the bodies?"

The grimace of disgust that twisted his face would have been amusing, if the conversation were a different one. He breathed in roughly, obviously gritting his teeth as she crossed her arms over her breasts and stared back at him, sorrow building inside her.

She could see the fear in his brother's eyes, and she hated knowing that fear was for the man she loved.

"Cam's still alive," she finally whispered. "Whatever happened to him, he survived."

"Do you call that surviving?" He straightened from the door and shot her a furious glare, then paced across the room before turning back to her. "Is that what you call it?"

"He walks, he talks, he smiles, and he laughs," she whispered. "He's fighting his demons the only way he knows how. And he's trying to love me. Do I have the right to ask for anything more?"

She had left him. She realized that she walked away from any right she had to call his demons her own, but that didn't stop her from doing it, and it didn't stop her from aching at the loss she sensed inside Cam. And Chase.

"Is that enough for you?" He propped his hands on his hips and stared back at her knowingly.

No, it wasn't enough for her, but it was that or leave. And she wasn't going anywhere. Not yet. Not as long as Cam could tolerate her laying at his feet.

"For now," she finally answered him.

"You're not even going to fight for him, are you?" Chase shook his head as though in disbelief.

"Chase, what do you think I'm doing now?" She held her hands out demandingly, before they dropped to her side. "Do you think I liked having him walk away from me five minutes after he thought I was asleep? Do you think I enjoy seeing the hunger that's building inside him, knowing what he wants and what he needs, and being unable to give it to him? Do you think I enjoy seeing his pain?"

"Then do something, Jaci."

"Like what?" She almost yelled the words back at him. "What the hell do you want me to do? Hurt him worse? Blackmail him? 'Sorry, Cam, but you spill your secrets or do without me'? Damn you, Chase, what the hell do you want from me?"

"I want you to fight for him this time." He was suddenly in front of her, his hands gripping her shoulders as he gave them a little shake, shocking her with the depth of his anger. "Damn you, stop fucking letting him take the easy way out, like you did the last time. If you're going to let him get away with this macho, closed-mouth bullshit, then you may as well just fucking leave the same way you got here."

He pushed her away, stomped across the room, then turned back, his eyes blazing in accusation as the office door slammed open.

Jaci flinched as the panel slammed into the wall and Cam strode in, fury lining every strong, sharp contour in his face as his gaze found and pinned Chase.

"Cam." She moved for him.

"Stay put!" His finger stabbed in her direction, drawing her to an abrupt halt, shock rocking her on her feet as the two brothers faced off.

Both were furious. She watched their bodies tense, watched as they glared back at each other.

"Did you forget about the cameras in the office, Chase?" Cam asked him, his voice silky, dangerous, as he glanced up at the darkened glass of the security monitors.

Chase smiled, all teeth, all fury. "I didn't forget, little brother. Just as I didn't forget that you were supposed to be in a meeting with Ian, not spying on your girlfriend."

"Jaci, are you ready to leave?" Cam didn't turn his gaze from his brother, didn't so much as slide his gaze away as he asked the question.

"The two of you here alone?" She wasn't that stupid. "I don't think so, Cam."

"Get whatever you need and we'll leave together then. Now." His voice grew darker, softer.

Jaci almost shivered at the fury she could feel in the very stillness of the tone.

She wasn't the only one that watched him warily. She watched Chase's expression. He was studying his brother like a scientist would examine a curious specimen. Something unknown. Something potentially fatal. There was almost a calculation in his gaze, as though he had meant to push Cam to this point, and now he was wondering how to push him further.

She was terrified to see if he could actually do it.

She moved quickly back to her desk, shoved her phone into her purse, and grabbed it up. She wasn't permitted to take the design pad or the pictures with her.

"I'm never going to get this job finished, at this rate," she muttered. "I have to work sometime, you two, not just when your testosterone allows it."

She slung her purse over her shoulder and moved from the desk. She strode to Cam, laid her hand on his arm, and stared into his face.

"Are you going to fight, or what? Not that a lot of testosterone and blood would do anything to turn me on right now. It really wouldn't. But all this posturing has to be for something, right?"

His gaze finally slid from Chase's and Jaci found her knees weakening. She wanted to go to the floor and wail, to cry for the bleak sorrow, the agony and rage she saw in his eyes.

She felt her breath catch in her throat, and had to forcibly still her lips from trembling. How did he bear whatever raged inside him? How did he contain the pain, the desperation she could see tearing him apart?

He turned back to Chase. "If I see ever you handle her again like I saw on that monitor, I'll take you apart," he told his brother. "And I'll make certain you never so much as breathe the same air she does."

Chase's lips curled in sarcastic anger. "Will you now? And tell me, brother, who will you share her with?" He glanced at Jaci again. "I don't think she's going to allow just any man to take that beautiful ass of hers, just because it's what you need."

Jaci nearly blanched at the dare in his voice. Fury raced over her.

"Enough!" Her voice cracked into the sudden tense stillness of the room. Her nails dug into Cam's arm as he tensed to pull away from her. "The first one of you to raise your fists to the other will deal with me."

They turned the combined power of their furious gazes on her.

"I mean it, Cameron Falladay." She stared into his eyes, the twisting pain, the rage, the obvious disbelief that she would threaten either one of them. "And you"—she turned to Chase—"if you want to antagonize your brother, I'll be damned if you'll use me to do it."

"And he's not using you?" he growled furiously. "Come on, Jaci, get a grip here. What is it, if he's not using you to forget something he doesn't want to remember? Too bad it's not working, is it, Cam?"

At that, Jaci loosened her hold on Cam. She looked from one brother to the other and realized she was only adding fuel to the fire Chase was attempting to feed.

"When you two are finished acting like children, could you let me know? I'll be upstairs with Courtney and a bottle of wine." She stepped away from Cam.

He caught her arm, halting her before she could move an inch. "No, you'll be with me. Chase can play his games with someone else."

He turned and pulled her from the room.

"Running away, Cam?" Chase snapped. "Why doesn't that surprise me?"

Cam stopped in the doorway as Jaci glanced up in time to see the regret, the loss that flashed across his face.

"It shouldn't surprise you in the least," he finally said, his voice bleak. "After all, I think I've gotten damned good at it in the past years. Almost as good as you have."

CHAPTER
TWENTY-ONE

Jaci managed to hold onto her temper, barely, as Cam drove back to the apartment. She kept her lips pressed tightly together and warned herself repeatedly that this wasn't any of her business. Not yet. Not until her and Cam's relationship was more established. She didn't have the right to make certain demands, she reminded herself. She didn't have the right to tell him what unacceptable assholes both of them were being.

And perhaps that was the point where she lost control of the temper she swore she wouldn't lose. Because it *was* her business.

It seemed as though she had waited all her life to be with one man. She had pushed herself away from him, she had fought her battles on her own, and she was still doing so. And she still managed to find a way to love. Cam refused to risk himself that far, even for his own brother. If he wouldn't risk brotherly love, what the hell made her think he was going to risk loving her?

"This situation between me and Chase has nothing to do with you." Cam finally spoke as he drove, his body rigid and corded with tension. "This won't happen again, I promise."

"Then it's a promise you'll break," she forced out, staring

out the window of the Jaguar. "He's your brother; he'll do whatever it takes to find out what happened."

She could feel the tension thicken in the car.

"Nothing happened." Hard, cold, his voice had the bite of winter, freezing to the bone.

She turned to him then. Slowly. That last thread of anger was fraying, and God knows, she didn't want to lose her grip on it.

"You couldn't convince a five-year-old of that, so don't lie to me."

His hands tightened on the steering wheel and the gear shift, his knuckles turning white from the force.

"This is none of his business," he said quietly when she clamped her lips shut and turned away from him again.

She couldn't stand to see that ragged sorrow on his face. He was hurting inside, and sometimes she wondered if she didn't make the pain worse. Because whatever drove him was eating into him now, tearing at him, and she could see it, feel it.

"I have to disagree with you, Cam. He's your brother, your twin."

"That doesn't make him my keeper," he snapped out. "I've dealt with my life and my own mistakes, and he's going to have to deal with the fact that he doesn't need to know every corner of my life."

She turned back to him, that pain-filled anger building inside her as she watched his jaw tighten in fury. "No, he just has to watch that demon inside you, twisting you in agony, whenever he stares into your eyes. Excuse me, Cam, but it does make it his business. His and mine. Because whatever tears at you is going to rip us apart."

He stared back at her in disbelief before jerking his eyes back to the road, then shifting the gears with a rough hand.

"No one asked him to stick the fuck around," he bit out.

"No, but you asked me to," she reminded him, her voice almost breaking. "I sleep at the bottom of that couch, rather than against you, and I accept it, because at least I'm with you. And I keep praying that need I see and feel burning inside you will ease, but it never does."

"Son of a bitch! I'm not a kid, Jaci." He cast her a confused, incredulous look. "Fine, I hate beds. I know men who are terrified of frogs. What the hell does that matter?"

"If it doesn't matter, then why are you so pissed off?" Jaci shot back. "For God's sake, Cam, something happened! Chase knows it. I know it. Don't you think it hurts us worse to have to continually guess at it?"

"Guessing doesn't hurt you near as bad as knowing the truth would hurt me." The car screamed into the underground garage, tires locked, the vehicle sliding until it rocked to a stop. His fist struck the steering wheel. "Let it fucking go."

Cam slammed out of the vehicle as Jaci followed more slowly, watching as he paced around the car for long minutes before he breathed out roughly and leaned against the side of the car.

"I can't let it go," she finally whispered, moving alongside the car, her hand running over the cooling hood.

Cam wiped his hand over his face and bit back the curses that hovered at his lips. Damn the two of them. Chase for waiting until he was weak, when his need for Jaci was driving him crazy, to start digging. And Jaci . . . He looked at her, her pale face, her worried eyes. Damn her for being the one woman he couldn't walk away from.

"I can't," she whispered.

"Why? For God's sake it doesn't concern or affect you, Jaci."

She smiled, a sad, bittersweet smile that ripped at the

fragments of his heart. A brutal reminder that she could affect him as no other woman could.

"But it does," she said softly. "I love you, Cam. And I can't understand or accept the things you want from me, not like this. Not without the truth between us."

"And you're being so honest with me? What about your honesty Jaci? You and Congressman Roberts?"

She shook her head. "Richard and Annalee have nothing to do with us. I need to stand on my own two feet, Cam, and that's what I'm doing with them. It's that simple. Whatever's going on inside you does affect us, though. It affects us because you hold yourself back; there's always something between us."

"It doesn't affect us, and there's nothing between us but too many clothes."

She stared back at him silently for long moments, forcing him to turn his head to look at her, to hold back the growl of rage at the pain in her eyes.

"You don't even hold me, Cam," she said then. "You leave me as fast as you can, and the closest you come to holding me is keeping my feet warm at night on that damned couch. Do you realize that? Do you realize that unless you're fucking me, your arms aren't around me? You hold yourself so distant from me that it hurts. And I allow it. Because leaving you now would hurt worse."

"I hold you." He knew he did. His arms were always aching to surround her, he was always forcing himself to hold back, to pull back, because he didn't want to smother her with that need, with that overwhelming urge to pull her to him and never let her go. To shelter her. To protect her. To make certain nothing or no one could ever hurt her again.

"When do you hold me?" A sheen of moisture filled her eyes. "Other than during sex, Cam, when do you hold me?"

His head jerked in an instinctively negative movement.

That wasn't true. As bad as he wanted to hold her, as much as he ached to hold her—she was right. He hadn't held her.

"Holding you is all I think about sometimes," he admitted, his voice hoarse. "I hold back Jaci, because I don't want to hold too hard. I don't want to frighten you away before I even have you, sweetheart."

He pushed his fingers through his hair and grimaced at the impossibility of what he was trying to do. The very thin line he was trying to walk.

He turned and moved back to the Jaguar, bracing his hands on the hood before turning back to her. She watched him, as she always did, those eyes breaking his heart, so filled with life, with a purity of spirit, that sometimes she terrified him.

"I love you, too." He watched the shock that filled her face. "I've always loved you, Jaci. And I always let you go when you needed to, because I was always afraid of holding you too tight. If I held you too tight, if I wrapped myself around you the way I wanted to, then you might leave forever. And where would I be if you left forever?"

She took a step forward, then stopped. She stared back at him as a single tear slipped from her eyes, and he ached that he had caused it. He would have killed any other man that made her cry, but how did he punish himself for it?

"Why?" she whispered, her voice low and rough with emotion. "Why would you even think of it like that, Cam? I want to hold you, as often as I can. I want you wrapped around me however you can bear it as I sleep. I want every memory we can fill our lives with so that if you're ever gone, if you ever walk away, or God forbid something should happen to you, then I'll have something of you to hold onto."

He tightened his jaw and turned away from her again. He remembered being a boy, so young, so determined to enjoy every memory he made. Then he remembered the destruction. His parents deaths, the father that had been so strong, so filled with laughter. His petite mother, always hugging and always loving. A woman far different from her sister. Davinda had nearly destroyed him. In a way, she *had* destroyed him.

He inhaled roughly and shook his head. Jaci didn't need to know the horror of what he had endured. Neither did Chase. It was bad enough that he knew, that he remembered.

"I need time." He turned back to her, steeling himself against the need to give her anything, everything she wanted.

"You've had seven years," she stated.

"And if I need seven more?" He glared back at her now. He'd be damned if he was going to spill his shame to her. Enduring it had been bad enough. Going to Sheriff Bridges had torn a part of his soul free of his body. He would always, *always* remember the shame of telling the other man what had happened and why he needed to get that bitch away from him and Chase.

The sheriff, despite his attempts to get Cam to file charges, had seemed to understand that rage and shame, though. He had gotten the pictures, the negatives. He had made certain Davinda didn't leave the house with anything but the clothes on her back, and he had made certain she left town. And he had used his connections to block every investigation Chase had attempted in the past years to find out what had happened to his brother.

Jaci's lips parted, but then the pouty curves pursed in anger and she stared back at him with all the fire and passion he'd always loved about her.

"I can't make you talk," she snapped. "But I'll be damned if I have to like your silence. And I'll warn you right now,

Cam, this macho bullshit you're pulling, on not just me but your brother as well, is going to get really old."

"Bullshit to you," he growled back. "It's not bullshit to me, Jaci. And trust me, what you want to know has nothing to do with what we have together."

"There's where you're wrong," she yelled back, that fury igniting inside her, and though he knew the response was completely incongruous to the situation, it made him as hard as hell. "It has everything to do with us, Cam. And everything to do with a relationship developing between us."

"If that's true, then you can tell me about the Robertses," he demanded. "You can tell me where you got that fucking whip scar from."

Her smile was pure sarcasm. "You're repeating yourself, Cam."

"Fine, then let's repeat this."

The argument, the anger, the pure lust she inspired inside him rolled through him like a tidal wave. He had never felt so hot, so in need of one woman's touch.

Before she could move to evade him, his arm went around her waist and a second later he was laying her over the hood of the Jaguar and bending over her.

God, she was meant to be touched, to be taken with lusty hunger as she took in return. And she was taking. Her hands latched on to his neck, jerked his head to her, and before he could evade her or take her kiss, her teeth nipped, rather hard, at his lower lip.

Cam jerked back, his eyes narrowing on her, his lips pulling back as he fought to breathe through the lust and tasted blood.

"You bit me, Jaci." Blood was suddenly thundering through his veins, filling his cock until he was certain the hard length was going to rip through his jeans.

"Let me kiss it better." Her voice was witchy, husky, threaded with anger and arousal as her fingers threaded through his hair, and she pulled him back to her. "Unless you're scared."

He kicked her legs ruthlessly apart as his lips slanted over hers. Lowering himself against her, he pressed his cock into the notch of her thighs and ground himself against her, feeling her heat even through the layers of clothing between them.

"I'm going to take you. Here. Now." He pulled back, ignoring her hands in his hair long enough to jerk her shirt over her breasts. "Let me take it off, or I tear it from you."

The blood rushing through his veins was like lava, burning him, searing his nerve endings as she narrowed her eyes and her expression became seductive, challenging. And she pulled his lips to her again.

He was barely aware of ripping the delicate cloth. He had no idea how many shreds were left of it, all he knew was that the light cotton no longer covered her, no longer hid her body from him.

He didn't ask the same question of the delicate lace of her bra. He pushed the cups beneath her swollen breasts and palmed the heated flesh. His fingers plucked at her nipples. Sweet, tight little nipples that puckered and hardened further for him as his lips consumed hers.

He was on fire for her, there was no doubt. Hell, he had always been on fire for her. There had always been something about Jaci that defied his determination to remain cold and aloof.

She could break through his defenses like no other woman, leaving him burning and wanting. As he was burning now.

He tore at the fastening and zipper to her jeans, loosening them before pushing his hand beneath the material and finding the sweet, soft silk and wet heat between her thighs.

This is where he longed to be. He needed to be inside her. He needed to lose himself inside her, because it was the only place he had ever been that the tormented memories didn't consume him.

Jaci fought for the same touch, the kiss, the overwhelming pleasure as she felt his fingers spear inside the depths of her body. Two fingers worked inside her, pumped inside her vagina, and left her gasping, reeling from the pleasure as she arched in his arms.

She struggled to loosen his pants, tearing at them, shoving at them until she could grip the thick, hard length of his cock in her hand.

He was hot, throbbing and thick. The heavy veins throbbed against her palm and she could feel the silky dampness at the tip.

"Get these fucking pants off." He pulled back, jerking at her jeans, almost tearing them from her as she pushed her sandals off her feet.

He managed to roll her onto her stomach, his lips curving into a tight, hard grimace of painful lust as she bent over the hood, one hand reaching back for him, gripping his hip and trying to pull him to her.

There was no danger of being seen in the garage, but the wickedness of the act, the sheer desperation of the man behind her, beat through her senses and heightened her pleasure.

God she wanted this. Wanted him so deep inside her that she could never forget what it felt like to be taken by him. She wanted him devouring her, wanted him possessing her. She wanted all that powerful, dark passion centered around her, inside her.

Beneath her the heated warmth of the car hood caressed her nipples; behind her, the thick, heated press of his cock head probed against her.

Jaci caught her breath and arched back to him with a

cry. His hard chest pressed her against the car as his legs pressed hers farther apart, and a second later one hard, fierce thrust sent him spearing into the hungry depths of her body.

He stilled once he was lodged inside her. Hard hands held her in place as he controlled her movements and his teeth raked over her bare shoulder.

She was only barely aware of the fact that, somehow, he had managed to don a condom. Where he had fought the control to do that she couldn't imagine because she could feel the uncontrolled need raging around them.

"You're tight and hot around me," he groaned against her neck. "Being inside you is like being burned alive by pleasure."

Her nails raked against the hood of the car as she fought for something to hold onto. He moved behind her, grinding against her, stroking her internally as a ragged cry left her lips.

There was no pleasure that could compare to this. Nothing, Jaci knew, that could fill her, physically and emotionally, as Cam filled her.

"I'm holding you now." His arms came beneath her, his hands cupped her sensitive breasts, his fingers gripping her nipples and sending arrows of sensation shooting to her womb. "Here's how I want to hold you, Jaci. So close to me, so tight, you're a part of me."

She turned her head until her cheek lay against the hood of the car, panting for breath and fighting to hold on to a semblance of sanity as her body shook beneath him.

"Feel how tight you hold me?" He flexed inside her as his lips moved to her ear. "That's how I want to hold you. Wrap around you until you don't know where you end and I begin."

He was wrapped around her, his arms embracing her,

his powerful thighs and legs outside hers, his head at her neck. Surrounding her with pleasure, filling her with it.

The involuntary flexing of her vagina around the thick intrusion of his cock, and the subtle strokes of his cock deep inside her dragged a groan from his throat.

The throb and caress of the thick cock head deep inside her was driving her insane. She wanted the hard strokes, the furious thrusts. This gentle caress inside her, where she was most sensitive, was making her insane.

"I love how you hold me here." He nipped her ear, drew it into his mouth, and soothed the tiny hurt.

Jaci stared at him in dazed pleasure, her eyes locking with his as his head lay beside hers, his lips touching hers.

"You're torturing me," she cried, breathless, fighting to move, to force him to give her that last stroke of sensation needed to throw her over the edge.

"I'm loving you." He caught her lower lip before she could reply, nipped it, licked it.

The ice green of his eyes was fiery now, burning with pleasure, with hunger.

"Then do it." She whimpered as he released her lip and licked it again. "Take me, Cam."

"Soft and easy?" He shifted, pulled back, then slid into her with such destructive ease that she wanted to scream out with the punch of ecstasy that ricocheted inside her.

"Or hard and fast?"

He held her hips and slammed inside her. Her back arched, bowed, she screamed out his name and a second before the flames consumed her, he stopped.

He stopped. Just stilled inside her and did that stroking thing that made her so crazy. Ah God, if he didn't move, if he didn't pound inside her, she was going to die. She could feel herself shaking from the inside out. Burning, flaming, so desperate to orgasm that she clawed at the hood of the car again.

"Easy sweetheart." His hands trapped hers, holding them still. "Let's just play a little bit. See what you like. See how much you like." He pulled back and slammed inside her. Once. Just once.

"No. Oh God. Damn you, Cam." She fought to push against him, to find the incredible, mindless pleasure of seconds before.

"Ahh, my baby likes it hard and fast," he crooned. "Whatever you want, Jaci. However you want it. All you have to do is tell me."

"Fast. Fast." She wanted to scream the words. "Damn you, Cam, fuck me. Hard. Fast."

He held her hands. His lips touched hers. And his hips moved. Hard. Fast. He pounded inside her, sending pleasure screaming through her nerve endings and the orgasm she fought so desperately for exploding through her senses.

A tidal wave of excruciating pleasure swept through her, tightened her, released and exploded again in a furious sweep of ecstasy.

She was aware of him shuddering behind her. The feel of his erection throbbing, his release sweeping over him. And for a second, she hated that damned condom. She wanted to feel him exploding inside her. Feel him taking her, marking her as he had never taken another woman.

But even more, she needed him to hold her.

CHAPTER
TWENTY-TWO

He carried her to the shower and beneath the warm spray of water he held her, he loved her slow and easy. And he felt something break inside him.

This woman he had dreamed of. She held him through the night the only way he had allowed her to. She touched his body, but more, she touched his soul.

Just as she had so many years ago. She had been no more than a child when she found him, and he had been broken. But there was something about her. *Wait for me, Cameron. I'll grow up and I'll make all the bad things go away.*

He clenched his teeth to hold back the emotion that swept through him. Because she had taken the bad things away enough that he'd found the strength and the courage to do what he had to do.

"You make all the bad things go away," he whispered into her wet hair as he held onto her.

The water sprayed over them, washing over her hair, along his hands as he caressed her naked back, and spilling to the floor below. It embraced them the way he wanted to embrace her, always. All over. Like a protective shield between her and any harm.

He felt her smile against his chest, a bittersweet curve of her lips that had him kissing the top of her head as he clenched his eyes closed in agony.

"The big bad Falladay brother," she whispered against his chest. "Everyone thought they were supposed to be scared of you."

They'd had good reason to be scared of him. He'd lived in hell and he tried to take it out on any willing fist that would face him.

"You weren't scared of me."

"I couldn't stay away from you." She sighed. "You're like a drug. One taste of you, Cam, and all I do is crave more."

"You stayed away for seven years." She had stayed away and he had allowed it. Because he'd needed the distance, needed to hold back the secrets he knew she would demand.

She lifted her head from his chest as her hand touched his cheek. "It was only by monumental effort."

He knew her, knew the varied looks in her eyes, her expressions, her stubbornness and her loyalties.

"You stayed away because you were scared, and you weren't scared of what I wanted from you, either."

They were going to finish this, now. She could protest until hell froze over, but the Robertses were a threat to her and that threat was not going to continue. She didn't have to tell him what they had done to her, his imagination was good enough. That was all he needed.

She pulled away from him and stepped out of the water. Jerking a towel from the rack on the wall she dried off quickly, refusing to look at him.

The deliberate challenge was like a match to tinder. He could feel the surge of dominance that burned inside him now. He had lost control of this situation and this relationship, and it was time to draw it back. If he didn't, then all control was going to be lost, and he'd be damned if he would allow that to happen.

"How do you know I'm not scared of what you want?"

She shrugged as she dried her hair, hiding her expression from him. "You know, it's not every day a man wants to share you with his brother."

Just hearing the words out of her mouth had his dick twitching in anticipation.

He hadn't forgotten that need; to the contrary, he knew it was the reason the memories were tearing into him with such brutal precision lately. The dreams, the needs, they frayed his control and weakened the barriers he had between himself and the world.

"It's not every day you have a twin for a lover, either," he told her.

She snorted at that, as he knew she would. Cam felt a smile tilt at his lips, felt a part of his heart lighten at the sound.

"I've known plenty of twins, Cam," she informed him. "You and Chase are the only ones that share your lovers. It's not exactly natural."

He pulled the towel from her hair and tilted his head to steal a kiss before using it to dry himself and grinning back at her unrepentantly.

"Maybe we're just special." He chuckled.

"Maybe you're just too determined to have your own way." She moved away from him, running her fingers through her wet hair until it lay around her head in soft, damp waves.

"Determination is my middle name."

"No its not. It's James." She laughed from the doorway. "I know, because I asked Chase years ago."

She sprinted from the door with a little laugh as he pulled the towel back as though to snap it at her. That laughter raced through his bloodstream nearly as hot and arousing as her touch could.

He closed his eyes and treasured it. She was here with him. Things might not be as smooth as he would have liked, as she would have liked, but it was going to work. He'd make sure it worked because as far as he was concerned, he wasn't returning to the bleak, empty days he had known before she had come back into his life.

As he moved into the connecting walk-in closet that held his clothes he heard her call out that Chase was there. He smiled at the ire in her voice. Evidently, Chase had come in as she was running naked from him.

Dressing quickly, he left the bathroom and glanced in the bedroom where the light remained on in the closet on the other side of the screened-in bedroom. How long did it take a woman to pick out an outfit to wear at the house?

"Ian called as I was on my way home." Chase was pulling a beer from the refrigerator as Cam neared him.

He caught the bottle his brother tossed to him and twisted the cap off. Lifting it to his lips, Cam watched him, seeing the careful restraint, the banked anger Chase didn't bother to hide.

He was still pissed over the argument in the office, and Cam knew it. Chase didn't let things go easily, and he had been probing Cam for more than a year now, determined to learn what had happened in their youth.

"What did Ian want?"

"He had a visitor after we left." Chase shrugged his shoulders before lifting his own beer and taking a long drink.

"Who was the visitor, Chase?" Cam finally asked, patiently. Chase could be a bastard when he was pissed.

Chase's lips flattened as he glanced to the bedroom.

"It was Roberts. Seems the bastard thinks Ian should fire Jaci in return for the change in that zoning law Ian petitioned for on one of his properties. His wife seems to have some influence on one of the members of the zoning board."

Cam finished his beer before tossing it into the garbage can beside the kitchen island.

"What did Ian tell him?"

"Told him to get fucked," Chase grunted. "But the bastard made the mistake of upsetting Courtney before Matthew could let Ian know he was there. Evidently, Courtney was cursing in Spanish when Ian made it to the foyer."

Cam grimaced. "This could get ugly."

"Sebastian was there during the meeting with Ian. Roberts ran a background check on him, and he's made some very subtle threats, evidently where De Lorents is concerned. Did you know Spain has a mafia? Seems Sebastian thinks Roberts would fit right in with them."

"Every country has a mafia," Cam said, as he pushed his fingers through his hair in frustration. "So, what's Ian's take on this?"

"The Robertses are scared," Chase bit out. "They can't use gossip to get rid of her, because evidently, no one gives a fuck about old trash talk this month."

Cam glanced back at the screened-off bedroom.

"Have the final reports come in on the Robertses yet?" he asked Chase.

Chase shook his head. "All but a few. We don't have any proof of the rumors we've heard about some of their games. Their secretary isn't talking, but she's a little arrogant, for her position. The servants aren't full-time at the mansion or their penthouse, so we haven't been able to pull out any information there."

Cam scratched at his jaw, his eyes narrowing as he let the problem roll through his mind. Anyone driven by fear had a weakness, he knew that well. There was no way to keep everything quiet, unless you spilled blood. And even then there were risks involved.

"Go back further," he finally said, quietly. "They've had overnight guests before; check their backgrounds further, see if they have any ghosts in their closets. If we can't get dirt on the Robertses with the check we've done on them, then we'll find it there."

Chase shook his head. "I've done that. A few house parties, a few close friends who have come out squeaky clean. The Robertses are so damned clean its making me sick. They even keep friends' teenagers through the summer or on vacations, to allow them to apprentice with Richard. The whole 'see what the congressman does' routine."

Cam felt a chill run up his spine. He grew still, his head lowered, his eyes burning into the tile on the floor. That was it. That was where they were missing it.

"Moriah Brockheim stayed several weeks with them, didn't she?" he mused, as he turned away from his brother, as though thinking.

"Yeah? Moriah's clean, Cam. I ran her check myself."

He turned back to Chase, and his eyes narrowed on his brother. "Run it again. When I went looking for Jaci at the party she was sneaking into Brockheim's private study, and Moriah wasn't in the buffet or ballroom."

He rubbed the back of his neck and glanced back at the bedroom again. "They're up to something."

This was what he was good at. Unfortunately his head had been so filled with hunger and memories and a red-headed, stubborn woman, that he'd let that slip.

"Moriah's clean, Cam," Chase argued again, his voice impatient. "Hell, she's so damned stiff, she'll barely nod at the two of us, because of our reputations."

"Then why was she meeting with Jaci secretly?" Cam asked him. "And why didn't Moriah turn up as a contact to Jaci? Jaci spent a month in their cabin, supposedly alone, and had no other contact with the Brockheims. Yet, her familiarity with Moriah is close enough that the girl let her into her father's private study? That doesn't add up for me."

Chase's lips pursed thoughtfully as his eyes narrowed, then he nodded slowly. "I'll handle that myself," he told him. "Until then, we need to come up with a way to counter Richard and Annalee."

Cam shook his head again. "They're scared, and they got nowhere with Ian and Courtney. They'll come after Jaci now."

The minute he said the words, other details shifted together, slid into place, and he felt himself tighten with nearly violent rage.

The accidents: a mugging in England, faulty brakes in Italy, an attempted break-in of a hotel room in New York City. Too many coincidences and supposed accidents.

"I need the reports on those accidents again," he bit out, causing Chase to stare back at him with dawning comprehension. "Full reports, including eyewitness accounts. Talk to Sebastian and Courtney about the mugging. They were there."

"You think they're trying to kill her?" Chase asked carefully. "Hell, they'd do a better job of it than this, Cam. They have the money and most likely the connections."

"There's also knowledge that there's bad blood between them," Cam reminded him. "Jaci's played it cool. Her reputation is one of pure, honest, and restrained elegance. There aren't even rumors of a lover, until me. She's bested them with her silence, and she knows something. I'm betting its something big. But something she has no proof of. They couldn't destroy her reputation, so they're trying to take her out instead."

"They would be using someone they know and trust," Chase said. "Someone trying to be careful, to make certain they aren't caught and that the Robertses aren't implicated."

Cam nodded slowly, but the rage was building inside him. He was tense, tight with the need to kill. He'd tried to leave the killer behind when he left Special Forces. He'd promised himself he wouldn't give that darkness inside him an avenue like that ever again.

"We need cover on her, then." Chase's voice was tight, his expression savage. "She's not exactly predictable when she decides she wants to do something."

She had a bad habit of borrowing a car from Courtney or Ian and heading to the shops in town, or to other studios to consult with business associates on specific design areas. Keeping up with her was chancy at best.

"I'll update Ian."

Chase was the one to first glance toward the bedroom.

"Keep Courtney in the dark," Cam warned, carefully unclenching his fists as he heard Jaci moving around in the bedroom. "Keep this quiet until we can get something. And get on the Brockheim girl. There's something there, I just don't know what yet."

He could feel it now. As the pieces began to shift into focus and Jaci's life began to form before his inner eye, he realized he didn't want to know that she had been in trouble and hadn't come to him.

Damn her, she knew he would protect her. She knew he would die before he would let anyone hurt her. And she hadn't come to him, she hadn't asked for his help. That wouldn't happen again. He was going to tie her so close, so tight to his side, that she wouldn't want to breathe without his help.

"You two look way too serious." Jaci moved into the open rooms with a deliberately provocative sway, her tone amused, her eyes filled with warmth as she moved to Cam. "What are we doing for dinner? I'm starved."

She reached up and kissed Cam quickly on the cheek, before looking between him and Chase with a frown. "No fighting tonight, either. One a day is enough."

"He starts them," Cam reminded her, more to distract her too-perceptive little mind than for any other reason.

"Don't let him fool you," Chase said. "You picked the wrong brother, Jaci. He's like a bear with a sore paw, trying to hide the bruise."

It was no more than the truth; but this time it wasn't important.

"How about dinner at Carlyle's?" Cam suggested. "Me, you, and Chase. Neither of us cook much more than TV dinners or cereal. We do great delivery, though."

She sniffed at that as she pulled a bottle of water from the fridge and turned back to them.

Jaci saw the surprise that Chase barely hid, and imagined that perhaps this wasn't the reaction he had expected out of Cam after his deliberate prod about the sore paw. It was a bit of a surprise to Jaci as well. Cam was usually more confrontational, less willing to allow his brother to get the last word in on any argument.

"Carlyle's sounds good." She nodded. "Do you think Ian and Courtney would want to join us? I have a few ideas I came up with while I was dressing. I'd like to discuss them with her."

"I'm scared of you two in the same place. That's like putting in an order for trouble, rather than just wishing for it," Chase admitted, his voice amused, though Cam saw the cold, hard purpose in his brother's eyes when he glanced at him.

Jaci was a piece of their past, their shared past. Chase cared for her, wanted her; but they both knew who she belonged to. In that one moment, one shared look, Cam could feel his brother's determination to protect her as well.

"Scaredy cats," she accused them with a laugh, as Chase turned back to her. "We're just women. What could happen?"

"Mass confusion and heartbreak?" Chase suggested lightly as he pulled her against his side for a quick kiss to her forehead. "That's okay though, we're real men. We love danger. Don't we, Cam?"

Cam felt more than rage burning in him now. Jaci wasn't aware of it, but the moment Chase had pulled her into his arms she had softened, conformed to him for a just a second, before tensing and pushing out of his arms.

"Of course Cam loves danger," she informed them both, her smile slightly nervous now. "He's always trying to piss me off. That proves it."

She wasn't pissed off, she was aroused. Cam watched her carefully, aware of the knowledge in her eyes, knowledge of her own arousal, as well as his.

Chase chuckled at the statement. "I'll call for the reservation, and let Ian and Courtney know before I shower. I'll catch you both down here in an hour."

Before moving around her to the stairs, Chase let his gaze linger on her. A heated, intense look that assured her exactly what his mind was lingering on.

Then she surprised both of them. Deliberately provocative, amused, and just a little playful, she pursed her lips in a silent kiss, before turning and moving quickly away from Cam with a laugh.

"If I'm going to Carlyle's, then I need a dress and makeup," she informed them both. "Hurry up, Chase, time's awasting. I'll be ready in an hour." She turned back, glanced at both of them, and said, "And, boys, I am hungry."

Chase knew exactly why Cam had chosen Carlyle's. Invariably, if the Robertses were in town and there were no parties pending, they held court at Annalee's maternal uncle's restaurant.

He held back his concern after discussing it with Ian,

but he had to admit that the return of Cam's recklessness was starting to worry him.

He hadn't been like this in years. Not since his return from the military, and when they started sharing their lovers. As though he needed an outlet, something to pour all that darkness into. And the wicked games they played with their women had provided that outlet.

Jaci, sweet, innocent Jaci, was holding out on the game, and it was pushing Cam. Chase could feel it. But he couldn't blame Jaci, either. She wasn't a woman who went to bed with one man that easily, so giving in to Cam's more extreme desires would be harder for her.

She was fighting her curiosity, too. He and Cam could both see it, feel it. She was fighting for Cam, and though Chase gave her an A for effort, he didn't hold out a lot of hope that his brother would ever willingly tell either of them what had happened all those years ago. As they moved through Carlyle's—Chase moving ahead of them, with Jaci in the middle and Cam at her back—he noticed the knowing looks they received.

Ian's club was safe, but there were a few of the members who were known for their sharing. Not a lot of them, but a few—those who willingly fronted for the club and drew attention away from the married members.

Ian's ancestors had known gossip and society. They had learned the most effective way of hiding was in clear view. Give the greedy piranha's something to latch onto and the others could slip by undetected.

Cam and Chase had no problems with others knowing who and what they were, to a point. They were members of Ian's club, but they were also members of several other men's clubs that were as staid and uptight as any ever created. Clubs based on wealth or position, and a clientele that benefited from the particular arena they fed off of.

None of those clubs were based on sexuality. He and Cam avoided the sex-based clubs like a plague. They were counterproductive and just too much damned work.

"Ian, Courtney." Chase nodded to them as the waiter showed them to the private table Chase had requested.

"And here I thought the night would be boring." Courtney's smile was all teeth as she glanced across the room to where Richard and Annalee Roberts were currently holding court at a long center table.

"You promised to be good, Courtney." Ian glanced at her from the corner of his eyes, but Chase saw the carefully banked anger there.

He hadn't been pleased with the information Chase had relayed to him, and Chase knew he would now be working to make certain that, no matter how Jaci's relationship with Cam fared, the Robertses would never touch her again.

Ian didn't need proof, all he needed was his own certainty with which to go to the punitive committee. He and Cam needed more, though. Protecting Jaci from not just the Robertses, but from herself. Because he was damned certain Cam was right: Jaci was trying to take care of this all on her own.

He glanced at Cam, then to Ian. That shared look assured him they were in agreement. It was time to neutralize the bastards. No one, but no one, attacked one of Ian's employees, and especially a female employee. They were family. They were under his care. Under all their care.

Jaci watched the shared look between the three men, and glanced at Courtney. She was glaring at the Robertses, her gaze flickering back to them every few seconds before she would murmur a Spanish curse beneath her breath.

"What's going on?" Jaci kept her voice low, but she felt Cam tense in the chair beside her, just as Chase did on the other side.

She watched Courtney's gaze flicker over the two as Ian watched in amusement.

Courtney's lips pressed together as the waiter placed the water before her and Ian ordered wine. As he retreated, she leaned closer to Jaci and hissed, "Whose idea was Carlyle's?"

Jaci pointed to Cam with a subtle shift of her finger.

"Remind me to make you pay for this." Courtney glared at him.

"Undercurrents, undercurrents." Jaci smiled. "What the hell is going on?"

"The bastard dared to threaten Sebastian and Ian," Courtney huffed, ignoring Ian's warning look. "Chase should have told you. I am certain Ian informed him of it."

Her accent was thicker and her eyes glittered with ire.

"Sometimes they neglect to tell me things," Jaci told her calmly. "I'll discuss that with them later."

Courtney smiled at that, the gleam in her eyes turning to one of immense satisfaction as she glanced at the twins. "I gather they haven't exactly met the wrong side of your shoe, as of yet?"

Jaci only smiled, carefully keeping her gaze from turning to Chase and Cam as the waiter returned with the wine.

She stewed over their obvious machinations. The pure arrogance in bringing her here just pissed her the hell off and, she admitted, deeply worried her. Cam had been willing to let the subject of the Robertses slide earlier, just as she had wanted him to. Needed him to. And Richard had destroyed that.

Threatening Sebastian wasn't a good idea, and it was obvious he had pissed off the wrong woman when he made Courtney angry. Jaci knew Courtney. The fiery temperament could turn brutally cold and vengeful.

It was Cam and Chase who worried her now. They were . . . stealthy. Dangerous. She could see it and feel it in them now, where she hadn't earlier in the evening. She hadn't been looking for it. Cam especially had a way of hiding his anger when he needed to. It made him more dangerous, and she had a feeling it could make him more merciless.

Just what she needed, Cam in a merciless mood while Richard and Annalee were in the same room.

She sipped at her wine as they waited on the meal, chatting with Courtney and Ian, and doing her best to ignore Cam and Chase. It was hard, because both of them insisted on flirting with her.

After the meal was finished, the dance floor on the other side of the room darkened and the haunting strains of the band whispered around them.

Chase leaned close. "Dance with me?" he asked.

She sniffed at the thought. She had no desire to dance with either of them. She wanted out of here as quickly as possible, before years of planning were destroyed.

She had known what she had to do to declaw the Robertses, and it was just her misfortune that Cam and Chase had to be right here in Virginia at the same time. She could have used just a few weeks advance notice, she thought furiously.

"You can dance with me or you can dance with Cam," he said then. "And we both know how Cam gets when he has questions, don't we sweetheart? You'll fare a hell of a lot better with me."

She stared back at him mutinously, only to have him grip her hand and pull her from the table. Short of causing a public scene, she had no choice but to follow behind him.

"This is called force," she pointed out, careful to keep her voice low, as he pulled her against his chest and gripped her hand in his.

He grunted at the accusation. "It's called the better part of valor," he argued. "Cam's getting tenser by the moment.

Better to give him something to focus on for a while, other than Richard Roberts."

And he was focused on *her*. She could feel his eyes stroking over her, and when she caught a glimpse of them, it was to see his expression flicker with a subtle sensuality. He had no problem seeing her in his brother's arms, that was a certainty. And it turned her on. Turned her on enough that she let her body relax, let herself give in to him.

She felt his erection pressing against the soft silk covering her lower stomach.

They moved around the floor and she glanced over at Cam. He stared back at her, shadows moving around him, intensifying the hunger in his eyes.

"He watches you like a wolf watches his mate," Chase murmured in her ear. "He always has, Jaci. Since you were sixteen years old and he dragged your ass out of that first party. Do you know, each time his leave was up he would make me swear to watch after you?"

She shook her head. She couldn't tear her eyes away from Cam's. She didn't want to. Right here, she could feel Chase's hard body against hers, his arousal heating the air around her, and Cam's need reaching out to them.

As Cam watched, the music changed. The soft, slow tune became faster, almost Latin, a sexual mix of music filling the air.

And he knew what was coming. His teeth clenched, his body tensed as Chase pulled Jaci into his arms and swung her into a sensual, hip-rubbing rhythm. A simple routine, but sexual, sexy. He turned her to him, turned her against him. Her hips swung, brushed Chase's and Cam felt his dick harden in his pants.

Chase loved dancing to the Latin beats, and Cam knew Jaci loved to dance. Her expression became sensually distant. Her gaze stayed locked with his whenever possible, her body moved and she teased. She teased Chase. And she was teasing him.

Jaci felt the blood pounding in her veins as Chase's hands slid down her sides then up. His fingertips brushed the rounded curves of her breasts, then slid to her hips, turned her, caught her. He pulled her to one side, to the other, her lower stomach brushing his erection with each swing of her hips as he lifted her arms with his, turned her again, brought her back to his chest and she made certain she teased.

She rubbed her ass against him, watched Cam, and let him see, know her pleasure. With each look, with each move of her hips she gave him a sensual view into the pleasures they shared, letting him see her pleasure, letting him experience it.

His gaze never left hers; his expression never wavered in its sensual, sexual demand.

As Chase turned her again, twined her arms around his neck, the music shifted once more, slower, a whisper of sex and a throb of lust. She moved against him, forward, backward. When she stared into his eyes, she saw Cam's. As she buried her hands in his soft black hair, it was Cam's. She touched Cam, and she desired this too sexy, too dark brother of his.

"You know what we're doing?" His lips quirked as he watched her. "Cam's going to be insane for you, Jaci."

"That's what we're doing," she admitted, staring over his shoulder, seeing Cam's shadowed face, his eyes, bright, lit with wicked hunger.

"Not the way to gain what you're looking for." Her lashes fluttered as his lips touched her neck. Pleasure was a cascade of color behind her closed lashes, it was an ache, a need, it was the thought of one man and his touch, and the knowledge that another man could spur her pleasure as well.

When she looked at Cam again, it was to see him moving, striding to them, his expression dark, forbidding, laced with lust and with need.

Chase stepped back, gave her a mocking grin, and Cam took her in his arms. His hands gripped her hips as the beat of the music grew slower, even more sensual. It was like making love in public. It was like touching and being touched, finally having a part of him, just to herself.

He stared into her eyes, he held her to him, and they swayed, rocking to the music, and Jaci felt herself coming alive for him.

"I love you, Cam."

His expression tightened, his eyes darkened. "I love you, Jaci." He pulled her closer, tucking her head to his chest, holding her, moving with her. "I love you."

CHAPTER
TWENTY-THREE

Once they returned to the table, Jaci and Courtney escaped to the ladies' room. She wasn't unaware of the fact that Cam followed behind them until they entered the inner sanctum. He was watching her, protecting her. He was blowing all her plans to hell, and she knew it.

Making use of the facilities, Jaci and Courtney repaired makeup, waited, and watched until one of the few lulls in occupation in the room came.

"What the hell is going on, Courtney?" Jaci hissed as the last woman pushed through the heavy oak door.

"I don't know, Ian won't tell me everything." She grimaced. "All I know is that Chase called, and then Ian retreated to his office without me. He refuses to tell me what was said, but he's very concerned. I assume it has something to do with those detestable Robertses."

Courtney leaned her hip against the counter. The radiant, deep red, silk-and-lace dress she wore complemented her dark skin and long hair. She looked as wicked and wild as she was, until Jaci looked into her eyes again.

"Jaci, something's not right with this whole situation," Courtney whispered. "Whatever you're doing, you can't do it alone. Cam simply isn't going to allow it."

She didn't have a *choice* but to do it alone.

Shaking her head, she checked her appearance once

again, smoothed her hands down the little black dress she wore, and thought of the man waiting outside for her.

"They were acting strange after Chase arrived at the house," she admitted. "I thought they were getting ready to fight again."

"They always fight." Courtney waved that away with a flick of her fingers. "Chase always pushes Cam for answers and Cam always pisses him off by refusing. This is normal, from what Ian says. But there's something added now, Jaci. Especially tonight. Cam's attitude makes me remember the stories Ian told me, that Chase related to him, of when Cam was in the military. He was merciless. He has that look in his eyes tonight."

Yes he did. Along with the hunger was the sheer anger that she had glimpsed only once or twice, and twice was enough. It was savage, and always directed toward the Robertses' table.

He couldn't have found out the truth of that night. The Robertses and their primping, sluttish secretary certainly wasn't telling, and she knew Moriah would never tell. There was no one else who knew, no other avenues for Cam and Chase to learn the truth. And if they did know, they wouldn't be watching her like junkyard dogs, they would have already taken the Robertses apart.

"Dammit, Courtney, I need to know what's going on!" she whispered fiercely. "I have my own plans, my own way of dealing with this. But I have to do it right."

"Good luck," Courtney said, with a moue of irritation. "Those men, once they band together, they tell me nothing. And Ian is the worst. He is worse than the clam. Refuses to open his mouth and tell me things I wish to know."

Jaci almost laughed at that—almost, because right now, Ian's silence was making it harder to take care of things herself. She needed to know what Cam could know.

"If you hear anything, will you let me know?" Jaci asked her.

"Of course, no matter Ian's wishes," Courtney agreed. "But heed me well, my friend, he'll say nothing."

"But anything I tell you is fair game?" Jaci sighed.

Courtney bit her lip in indecision, then breathed out roughly. "Your pain would upset me greatly, Jaci. Because of this, I would share whatever you told me with Ian. And we both know, if it's bad enough, he will tell Cam and Chase, no matter my wishes. They are men." She shrugged as though that explained everything. "And he believes this situation is dangerous to you. You are a friend, but even more, you are like family, because of Cam. Ian feels it is his duty to be protective."

"Being men is not a good enough excuse."

As the words slipped past her lips the door opened and several women filed in, laughing, chatting about the food and the band.

Biting off a curse, Jaci checked her makeup quickly, then she and Courtney moved back into the wide hall.

Cam, Chase, and Ian. All three waited stoically, their expressions as patient as only men who were waiting on women could be.

"Now, why would men who have so much in common to discuss wait for two women outside the ladies' room?" Courtney smiled at her husband, shaking her head in exasperation. "You are being bad with these boys, Ian."

Cam's hand settled at Jaci's lower back as he moved to her, leading her through the restaurant and to the exit. They passed the Robertses' table. Catching Annalee's glare, Jaci took the only opportunity she was going to find to tighten the noose around her nemesis's neck.

She smiled a smug, satisfied smile that assured Annalee that she'd found a way to beat her. She made certain the smile was completely confident and edged with knowledge.

And Annalee read it exactly as she was meant to. As they passed, she watched the little flicker of fear in the other woman's face and steeled herself not to turn and give her anything more.

She had to be subtle. She had to play the few chances she had just right. She and Moriah had it planned; they would bring Annalee down.

The scar at her hip seemed to smart as they left the restaurant; the whip mark had cut deep into her flesh and nearly allowed Richard to catch her that night. Annalee knew what she was doing with that particular weapon. The sound of the whip cracking in her nightmares never failed to bring Jaci awake in a surge of fear and sweat.

They had been so confident she would fall right into their little games, Jaci remembered, as Cam helped her into the Sinclair limo and got in behind her. What in the world had made Annalee think for a second that Jaci would accept a role in their dirty games? It still didn't make sense, even years later.

For five years, Jaci had tried to figure out why Richard and Annalee would ever conceive of the idea that she would join in. And they had been confident, so certain that she was theirs for the taking.

She let the conversation between the men drift around her, but she was very aware the moment Cam's arm slid around her and he pulled her closer to him. He did it comfortably, easily, almost as though he wasn't thinking about it as he listened to whatever Ian was telling him. Something about zoning laws and checking out problems with them.

She had to admit, she was paying even less attention now than she had been earlier. As he talked, his hand played at her hip, stroking it through her dress, the pads of his fingers moving in little circular motions that were destructive to her thought processes.

There *were* no thought processes when Cam was touching her. It was like autopilot hit the brain, and her hormones took control of her body.

She wanted to lean into him, feel him against her and over her. She couldn't get enough of him. No matter how often he took her, or how sated he left her. She always wanted more.

The limo pulled into the underground parking garage beneath Cam and Chase's home. After he parked the car, the chauffer jumped out and opened the back door.

Jaci said her good nights to Courtney and Ian, then, once again walking between Chase and Cam, moved away from the vehicle.

That was odd. They had done that all night long, keeping her securely between them.

"You two want to tell me what's going on?" she asked as Chase locked the door behind them and set the security.

"With what?" Cam asked innocently.

"With the whole keep-Jaci-between-you thing." She waved toward them to emphasize exactly how they had done that throughout the evening.

A smile curled at his lips—sexy, and diabolically sensual.

"I can't believe you had to ask that question," Chase injected with a chuckle.

A flush washed beneath her cheeks, heating her face.

"Chase, you're a pain," she told him, moving through the house.

"Duly noted," Cam replied. "Why don't you go on to bed, Jaci. Chase and I have a few things we have to take of for Ian tonight, so I might be a little late."

She stopped on her way to the bedroom. She had visions of comfortable clothes in her mind, and maybe a few hours in front of the television with Cam. She enjoyed those hours they spent together and she would miss it tonight. There was something in his voice that warned her, though, a vague suspicion that he wasn't being totally honest with her.

She turned and stared back at him silently, letting her gaze take in both men, comparing their expressions. She had to restrain the shiver that would have rippled over her. They looked dangerous. And they looked like men eager to ditch the little woman, to do whatever it was they had to do.

She wanted to roll her eyes at them. "Go play." She waved her hand over her shoulder as she headed for the bedroom. "I'll have fun here all by my lonesome. I'm good at that."

They watched her until she disappeared into the bedroom; she could feel their eyes on her, caressing her, intensity and male impatience swirling through the air to wrap around her.

"She's going to drive me to drink," Cam murmured, once Jaci disappeared around the heavy screen that surrounded the bedroom.

"She's chilling you out." Chase clapped him on the shoulder as he headed for the stairs. "Come on, let's see if any of my contacts have made any progress in the past few hours. I'm sick of dealing with those two."

Those two. The Robertses. If Chase thought he was sick of dealing with this shit, then he should be sitting in Cam's place, waiting for the other shoe to drop. There were times when he could stare at Jaci and see her mind working. He could almost feel her gearing herself up to face the congressman and his wife, and that he couldn't allow. There was something about the Robertses that set off every warning instinct he possessed. He just couldn't figure out what it was.

Rumors were they were into BDSM with their little secretary. But those rumors were unsubstantiated, and no more than giggling little tales told by a few women during their little ladies'-only cocktail parties.

As he followed Chase up the stairs to their office, he had to fight back the impulse to return downstairs and demand answers from her. Not that demanding jack shit worked with Jaci. She stared back at him with that red-head temper in her eyes and that stubborn chin of hers lifted. And then she would drive him crazy with her smart-assed little comments and her declarations that he give as good as he demanded.

He couldn't frighten her into telling him the truth, and he damned sure couldn't seduce it out of her. For some reason, those games just smacked of foul play with him. He didn't want games between them, he wanted trust. And he knew that was the crux of the entire matter. Because Jaci wanted the same thing from him.

"I put the files together before we left earlier," Chase said, as they sat down at their separate computers. "England, Italy, and New York. I also found another reference in Cancún. She was there on vacation. Left early when her dad got sick about a year and a half ago. The night she left, there was a hit-and-run on another guest of the resort. Auburn hair, about Jaci's build." He pulled up the picture of the tourist. She would have resembled Jaci in the dark. "We missed this in the first investigation. We were just looking at her, rather than at any strange occurrences revolving around her."

"Have you managed to pinpoint a suspect?" Cam stared at the picture of the tourist that had nearly died during her vacation, simply because she looked like Jaci.

"Nothing and no one." Chase shook his head at the question. "If you're right about her having a connection to Moriah, then the only time it could have occurred was the time she was at the Brockheim cabin. Moriah was supposedly on vacation in the south of France, but there are no records of her, there or anywhere else."

Cam breathed in deeply. "What does Moriah have to do with this?"

Chase snorted. "Coconspirator. Whatever Jaci is up to, Moriah is most likely right there beside her."

Cam had no doubt.

"The woman needs to be locked up for her own safety," Cam growled. "Son of a bitch, she knows they've targeted her and she still won't let me help her. Stubborn-assed woman."

"You sound surprised." The mockery in Chase's voice had him wincing. "Hell, Cam, you knew how stubborn she was when she was no more than a girl. What would make her any less so now?"

"Common sense?"

"Oh. She had some of that, then? When?"

Cam had to chuckle. When it came to him, she had never shown good sense. From the time she was thirteen to now, they had gravitated to each other like bees to honey. And he had to admit, she had the sweetest honey he had ever tasted.

"She was a virgin," he told his brother. The truth of that still filled him with a warmth that made no sense at all.

Silence met his statement. When he turned to look at his brother, it was to see the same primal arousal on his face that had filled Cam at the time.

"Damn," he finally blew out roughly. "Damn."

Chase rubbed the back of his neck and turned away, shaking his head. Cam knew what his brother was feeling. That sense of male fascination, the knowledge that her sensuality was theirs to mold and teach. It was a heady feeling for a man to have a woman as passionate as Jaci, one whose sensual pleasures were awakening beneath his touch.

He loved it. The pleasure it brought him to see the fascination on her face, the dazed pleasure in her eyes, the shock and surprise, the adventure it brought to each touch, each kiss. It made him ache to show her more, to teach her all the ways of sensuality and desire that he knew.

"We have to get the Robertses taken care of." Chase's voice was rough with arousal. "Getting her to trust us while you hide all those pesky secrets of yours isn't going to be easy." There was an edge of disgust to his brother's tone.

Cam had a feeling it wasn't going to be possible at all. As he pulled up the files he'd transferred to the home computer throughout the investigation process, he concentrated on finding a weakness to exploit in the Robertses.

This situation had to be taken care of, had to be resolved *now*. He was tired of waiting, and by God, he was sick of that flicker of fear he caught in her eyes every now and then.

Jaci had to be safe. No matter what. He just prayed it didn't mean revealing everything about himself to force her to reveal her truth.

A glass of wine and an old movie. Jaci sipped at the wine as she let the movie drone in the background. She was curled up on what she had claimed as her end of the long sectional couch, a frown pulling at her brow as she glanced again at the stairs leading to Chase's apartment.

What the hell were they doing up there?

Cam didn't bring work home in the evenings since she had moved in. And she'd gotten the impression it wasn't something that was normal, either.

She swirled the wine in the glass, staring into the clear liquid as she tried to make sense of this relationship. The relationship and the man.

Cam had held her heart for so long, sometimes she wondered if there had ever been a time when he wasn't a part of it.

Wait on me, Cam. I'll grow up and I'll take all the bad things away.

She had told him that the day she found him alone in the pickup, and something in his face had warned her that she was about to lose him forever. Even then, at thirteen, she had recognized that soul-deep sorrow inside him. A shame, a fury that devoured his soul.

Stay away from those Falladay boys, Jaci, her father had warned her as she grew up. *The games they play aren't for the likes of a decent girl. And that Cameron, he's a danger to himself, let alone a little girl like you.*

How many times had her father given her similar warnings? And then there had been Tim Bridges, the sheriff, a close friend of her father's. She sipped at the wine, remembering the night the sheriff had come to her dad and they disappeared into her father's workshop to talk. Jaci had heard Cam's name mentioned and had been terrified. His name, and something else that hadn't made sense to her at the time. Something about drugs and Cam's pride.

Sheriff Bridges had mentioned Davinda Morris, Cam's aunt, and his tone had been filled with disgust and anger toward the woman, but not toward Cam.

What had happened to him? She knew what she was beginning to suspect terrified her. Cam was a man with a mile-long streak of pride. Even then, so many years ago, he would have fought at the slightest slur to that pride.

Had Davinda abused him? How else would a woman like Davinda have been able to abuse or molest him, unless she drugged him? And that would have destroyed Cam. He would have never wanted anyone to know.

At fifteen, a young man's pride was so fragile anyway, just being defined. He had just lost his parents, Chase was as wild as the wind and grieving in other ways, and Davinda Morris could have easily exploited his developing sexuality.

Why hadn't she realized before now? She had suspected the darkness inside him had developed in the military; now she suspected it had developed long before that.

No, she knew it had. It had called to her as a young woman, drew her, made him more dangerous, more exciting than a boy her own age. Cam was the dark prince, the sensualist, the dangerous bad boy, and the wildness she kept locked inside her had always known that.

Chills were sweeping over her body, premonitions of knowledge racing through her, as she jerked to her feet, ignoring the wine that sloshed over her hand. She finished the last quarter glass in one drink and fought back a scream of rage.

She knew that was what happened. Cam was so totally certain of himself, so dominant and fierce, and he had been so when he was younger as well.

Oh, God, the hell he would have gone through.

The wineglass clattered on the table as she tried to set it down, while fighting to hold back her tears. If he came downstairs and saw her upset, he would demand to know why. And she couldn't let him know what she suspected. He had fought so hard to hide it, to preserve his own sense of strength.

She covered her lips with shaking fingers and inhaled roughly. She could be wrong, but she knew she wasn't. And she knew the only way to find out for certain was to call Tim Bridges or her father and demand to know.

She couldn't call from here. There was too great a chance of Cam coming in during the conversation. She would call tomorrow, while she was locked in her office, and she would find out what her father had hidden from her.

And there was no doubt he'd hidden it. He had warned

her away from Cam every time he so much as suspected she was watching him, or had been in contact with him. He had been firm, demanding. She was to stay away from Cameron Falladay, because men like that could only destroy a woman.

Learning a truth her father knew, that Cam would never want her to know, would destroy Cam. It would have back then, and she was terrified it would now. Some scars never healed, and she knew scars that went as deep as something like that would always strip a man to the bone.

She was so immersed in her thoughts, so torn by the pain roiling inside her at that moment, that the sound of her cell phone ringing nearly had her jumping out of her skin.

Jerking it from the coffee table, she flipped it open quickly and brought it to her ear.

"Jaci Wright." She inhaled slowly as she answered.

"Jaci, it's Moriah." The other girl sounded panicked, terrified. "Annalee called."

Jaci grew still, her eyes going quickly to the stairs.

"What does she want?"

"She saw us talking at the party," Moriah whispered fearfully.

"We knew she would." Jaci kept her voice low, calm. "Has she threatened you?"

"She wants me to have you meet me tomorrow evening at a hotel downtown. I'm to tell you that there are some clients that will only be in for a few hours and that you have to be there. She and Richard will be there instead."

Jaci inhaled deeply. There wasn't a chance in hell.

"Call her back, Moriah. Tell them I don't meet potential clients like that. I'll meet with them at your apartment instead. We need control. You know how to set up the video equipment, and you can do that in advance. They know you're scared, they won't suspect we're doing this."

"What if they refuse?" Moriah's voice shook with fear.

"Then there will be no meeting," Jaci told her patiently. "Settle down, Moriah. It's coming together. Tell them I'm paranoid, they'll believe that. Everyone knows I always meet potential clients in safe atmospheres. Now, call them back and tell them I've agreed to meet them at a restaurant or other public area. When they refuse, you suggest your apartment. Act as though you're trying to be helpful." Jaci could feel her palms sweating now. "Let's get them where we need them and then I'll take care of the rest of it."

Moriah knew electronics. She knew how to set up the video camera they had bought and how to make certain both sound and video covered the right room when Jaci met with Richard and Annalee.

She could hear the other girl breathing harshly, thinking, trying to calm herself. The Robertses had the power to make Moriah lose all sense of calm or confidence.

"We can do this," Moriah finally said. "This will work, won't it, Jaci?"

"It's going to work perfectly," Jaci promised her. "We'll record them admitting to what they've done. People like Richard and Annalee love to brag when they have the upper hand. Look how smart we are. Look how good we were. Richard especially. He can't resist it. We'll use that against them now."

It was coming together. She would take care of the Robertses, then she could concentrate on Cam and this relationship. She knew what he needed, and in a way, now she understood why he needed it. Once she talked to her father, she would have the details she needed, and then she could make this relationship work.

"What about the twins?" Moriah asked. "How will you get away from them?"

"I'll just borrow Courtney's car for a meeting. Tell the Robertses that I said I'll be bringing a friend if it's an evening appointment." There wasn't a chance Cam would let her out alone in the evening if he so much as had an itch of suspicion. And he would have. "Tell them the best time is an afternoon meeting. Three would be perfect. Play them, Moriah. Tell them you can't make me suspicious, and that demanding anything more would do so. Play on their paranoia."

"Jaci, what if they don't believe me?" Moriah's breathing was fast and hard, her voice just a shade whining, when Jaci wouldn't have expected that from her.

They had planned for this day for too long.

"They'll believe you if you do as I told you to," Jaci told her firmly. "We're not going to balk now, Moriah. If we're going to stop their threats and lies, then we're going to stop them here, or it will never be over. Is that what you want?"

"I'll go insane if it doesn't stop," she whispered tearfully. "They're evil, Jaci."

"Just remember that while you're talking to them. Tell them I can only meet them at three and only in a safe location. You'll suggest your apartment, and tonight you'll set up the video camera."

"Okay." Moriah breathed out roughly. "Okay, I can do that. You'll take care of the rest, right?"

"I'll take care of the rest, Moriah. Everything will work out. You'll see. Call me back and let me know what they say."

She disconnected moments later. It had taken a few more very firm reminders to Moriah to breathe and stop panicking. Jaci stared at the phone as she lowered it back to the table.

Moriah had rarely shown Jaci this side of her. Confidence normally oozed from the girl's pores—until Annalee had demanded her help.

But Moriah had been damaged by the Robertses, while

Jaci hadn't been. Jaci had been terrified, her reputation damaged for a while, but other than pissing her off and shadowing the relationships Jaci had tried to make, they hadn't really scarred her mentally.

Just physically.

She rubbed that scar at her hip and sighed heavily at the memory of that night. Annalee dressed in leather, a strap-on penis waving in front of her body while her secretary and Roberts knelt at her feet.

It would be amusing if it hadn't been so damned terrifying.

One thing was for certain, she couldn't live here in Alexandria, she couldn't protect Cam, if she didn't do something about the Robertses. And the time was now.

CHAPTER
TWENTY-FOUR

She was curled up on her end of the couch, a frown on her face as she watched the news channel. Only Jaci would watch the news to go to sleep, Cam thought with a silent laugh.

Then he saw her lower lip trembling. He saw the shimmer of tears on her lashes. Then, he noticed other things: The tip of her nose was red, her face pale. He had seen her cry only once, long ago. If he remembered, Charlie Mack had tried to run Chase down on the street. Cam had beat the hell out of him but Charlie had laid in some hard punches. When Jaci saw the blood on Cam's face, she had cried. And her dad had dragged her away, scowling, furious.

"Jaci." He knelt beside the couch and touched her face as she tried to duck away.

The shimmer of tears were tracks on her face and he felt his heart stutter to a stop within his chest.

Jaci couldn't cry. God help him, he couldn't stand this.

"Sweetheart?" He fought to keep his voice low, comforting, when all he wanted to do was howl in rage at the pain on her face. "Baby, what's wrong?"

"I'm okay." Her voice was more angry than hurt. "I'm just a foolish woman. PMS. Moodiness. Whatever."

She wiped at her face and stared at his chest as he stared

down at her, trying to figure this one out. Jaci didn't just cry. And he had a feeling that if the effects of PMS were going to show themselves, then he would be in no doubt when they hit or exactly what they were.

"I don't like it when you lie to me," he told her gently, pushing her hair back from her face to reveal her profile. "Why don't you tell me why you're crying?"

He couldn't stand this. He would fix it. No matter what it took, he would take the pain away and make it better if he could. If he couldn't, well, he'd just have to kill anyone who had done this to her.

"You don't have to be honest with me. Why do I have to be honest with you?" Her words seemed to echo through his head. He knew what she was talking about, and he couldn't face it. Not yet. Not right now.

"I haven't lied to you." He watched her carefully. "Come on, baby, this isn't over us. You'd just kick my ass and have it done with, if it was. Tell me why you're crying."

She was crying because the longer she had lain there without him the more she had realized how strong her lover was. He didn't make excuses for mistakes, hell, he never admitted to any mistakes, that she knew of. He had been so strong. Somehow he had managed to stop Davinda from destroying him, and he had kept his honor and his strength. As much as he wanted to share her with Chase, as much as he needed to, he still held back, he still gave her the room she needed to make the decision herself.

He was a good man, though his childhood must have been a nightmare.

"I need to make you stop hurting, Cam." She straightened until she could rest against the back of the couch, until she could stare into his shadowed green eyes.

"Jaci." His lips quirked sadly. "I'm not hurting, baby. Unless you count the hard-on I can't seem to control around you. And I'd just as soon deal with that."

She shook her head at that, reached out and touched the stubbly cheek. The dark shadow of a beard gave him a rakish appearance and emphasized his eyes. So light a green, she could get lost in them, become mesmerized by them.

"Can I have you on the couch, Cam?" She slid her legs around until they lay outside his powerful thighs as he faced her. Her hands went to the snap of his jeans, the zipper. "Right here, where you sleep?"

Surprise reflected in his gaze as a sexy grin curved his lips. "Sweetheart, you can have me wherever you want me. However you want me."

Arousal sliced through the pain. Cam's eyes lightened, turned playful, as his expression became heavier with sensuality and the shadows dissipated.

After loosening his pants, she moved her hands to the buttons on his shirt. "You're wearing too many clothes, Cam."

The clothes were disposed of quickly. Cam leaned forward and took her lips in a hard, passion-fierce kiss as he shed his own. Then his lips lifted and her arms raised so he could dispose of her T-shirt, leaving her almost nude before him.

A second later she was naked, the light cotton sleep pants puddled on the floor as he spread her legs farther, then gripped her rear and dragged her to the edge of the couch.

She expected him to take her. To spear inside her, wild and deep; instead, he lowered himself farther, bent his head, and let his tongue circle the engorged nubbin of her clit.

Jaci's head fell back against the couch, her hands tangling in his hair as pleasure began to suffuse her. She loved this. Loved the feel of his lips and tongue caressing her there. The way he licked and hummed his approval

against the sensitive flesh. The way his head went lower
and his tongue flickered around the clenching opening of
her sex.

She couldn't stop her moans. They filtered through the
room, echoed around her. She spread her thighs farther
and lifted herself to him, whimpering as two fingers
worked inside her.

"Cam," she whispered his name, staring down at him,
dazed by the enjoyment of the act that she saw in his eyes.
"It's so good. I love your mouth. Your hands." His touch.
She loved him. Loved him until her heart broke for his
pain and for the scars he carried.

He let her watch as his tongue licked over her clit
again. His fingers were moving inside her, thrusting slow
and easy, stretching her as her juices coated them, making
the entrance slick and hot.

His lips pursed then, and he kissed the little bud, throwing her higher.

"Touch me more." She lifted closer, feeling a need
growing inside her that she couldn't make sense of. It was
burning in her, locked inside a part of her soul she didn't
know existed. She needed him harder, deeper, stronger
than she had ever needed him before. She needed him to
sink inside her, needed to sink inside him.

He kissed her clit again, drawing it into his mouth as
another cry tore from her lips and she tried to pull him
closer, tried to force his fingers deeper.

He was being too slow, too easy. She needed more sensation, and he was deliberately withholding it.

"You're going about it the wrong way, Jaci."

She froze as Chase's voice sounded at her ear. Her eyes
jerked open to stare into Cam's, to see the arousal burning so hot, so deep, she wondered flames weren't covering
them.

And she nearly orgasmed. Her womb spasmed and she felt the muscles clenching around Cam's fingers.

Her lashes drifted closed, and Cam chose that moment to flick her clit with his tongue again, to flex his fingers inside her. Need, brutal and sharp, tore through her, and she whimpered with the force of it. Did she want him to leave? Did she want to step across a line she knew she could never return from?

"There's no pressure," Chase whispered as Cam sucked at her clit now, flicking with his tongue, his fingers moving deeper, stronger inside her. "No need to worry, baby. It's all about you." His lips slid over her neck. "Just you, Jaci. Your pleasure. Your need."

Just her pleasure. Her need. It was about so much more, and she knew it, sensed it.

She forced her eyes open, forced herself to stare back at Cam as he watched her.

The pleasure was intensifying in his expression, in his eyes. As though seeing her pleasure only amplified his. Seeing his brother touching her, his teeth raking over her neck, pushed his own arousal higher.

His fingers retreated from her vagina, then a second later pushed forward, forcibly opening her, shocking tender nerve endings with a pleasure that nearly sent her screaming into orgasm.

Chase's hands moved along her side and curved beneath her arms, cupping her breasts in his large palms, his fingers gripping her nipples and working them roughly.

Oh, she needed that. That edge of pain just shy of agony. Pleasure intensified inside her, burned so bright that perspiration began to slicken her skin.

"Cam, please," she cried out breathlessly, feeling release just a breath away.

His gaze was filled with nothing but hunger now,

nothing but pleasure. There were no shadows, there was no pain.

Jaci twisted in his hold, arched her breasts into Chase's hands. She kept the fingers of one of her hands locked in his hair, while she curled her other arm behind her and gripped Chase's hair.

His was coarser than Cam's, just a little. He nipped her ear as she pulled his head to her and pressed closer to Cam's mouth.

They were destroying her. This was beyond pleasure, beyond ecstasy. It was wicked and daring, and she couldn't help but abandon herself to them.

"No. No, Cam." She tried to jerk her hand back from Chase, only to have him catch it, hold it above her head while Cam drew back from the moist, slick flesh of her pussy. "Don't stop."

He ignored her cry. Instead, he lifted her—they lifted her—until she was stretched out on her back on the couch and Chase was moving closer.

He wasn't naked. He wore only a pair of hastily donned jeans, the snap undone, his erection pressing tight and hard against the zipper.

"Watch." Now Cam held her, his arm beneath her shoulders, his lips moving to hers as they parted to protest. "Watch me. Feel what he's doing. Watch me, Jaci. Feel him."

She watched him. She forced her eyes to stay open, to stay on his, as his lips settled over hers and Chase's tongue suddenly delved into the wet depths of her sex.

She screamed into Cam's mouth. It was too erotic, too sensual. The feel of Cam's lips taking her, his brother's tongue fucking her.

Her nails bit into Cam's shoulders as his lips slid from hers. His teeth nipped at her jaw, her neck. As she writhed beneath Chase's ministrations between her thighs, her back arched, lifting her breasts, as she screamed out from Cam's possession of a tight, violently sensitive nipple.

As Cam drew her nipple into his mouth, raked it with his teeth, and then sucked it hard and deep inside his mouth, she felt herself explode.

Chase's lips and tongue pushed her further over the edge. Hands roved over her body, rough and dominant, stroking and caressing, as she felt herself melt from the inside out.

It was like unraveling. Like coming apart at the seams, with no hope of ever coming together the same again.

Then, Chase was at her side, his lips lowering to her breasts, his cock free of his pants as he stroked himself.

Oh, God, it was so sexy. So hot. Watching his large, tanned hand, his fingers curling over his erection, stroking the glistening flesh.

"I'm dying." She stared back at Cam as he lifted her until her rear rested on his thighs and his cock nudged into her pussy. "You're killing me." Her head tipped back as the words became a scream.

Cam pushed inside, thrusting hard and deep before he bent over her, pushing his arms beneath her shoulders and lifting her against his chest before straightening and laying back, pulling her over him.

Her thighs gripped his hips as his cock surged inside her. Behind her, she felt Chase preparing her. Felt the lubrication, the touch of his hands, and then the slow, easy entrance into her rear.

It was just as hot, just as brutally sexy as before. But staring into Cam's eyes, she knew it was more. This time, as hot as it was, as much pleasure as it was, it was only Cam's touch, his need and his hunger that her body was responding to.

His hands gripped her hips as he moved beneath her, and Chase moved over her. Hard and deep, thrusting inside her with swift, hard strokes, taking her.

A throttled scream filled her throat. She felt them thrusting harder, stroking, caressing her on a level of pleasure that sent her spiraling into ecstasy. She heard a male growl of pleasure, Chase's or Cam's, she wasn't certain. She didn't know. She didn't care.

"Jaci. Baby." Cam. His voice was charged with lust and pleasure. "There you go, sweetheart. So fucking sexy. So hot and sweet."

He was pounding inside her, his voice tight and groaning. There was no doubt that he wanted it. No doubt that he needed it. But there was no doubt in her mind now, either. She was as wild and as wicked as she had always feared she would be in his arms.

She felt the hot, driving jets of Cam's release spilling inside her, though she was only barely aware of Chase releasing as well behind her.

"Ah, damn." Cam held her, jerking against her as he shuddered against her. "God, Jaci. Ah, fuck." He jerked again, harder, spilled inside her again, then trembled against her. "Ah, baby. My wicked, wild little Jaci."

She was lost in the pleasure. There was no other way to describe it. Lost and drifting—and serene. Cam held her to him as he rolled to his side, his breathing hard, ragged gasps against her neck, his arms tight around her, holding her secure.

Cam was almost asleep before he realized it. Drifting in drowsy contentment, his arms locked around Jaci's sleeping form, his legs encasing hers, holding her close and tight against him.

Hell, he didn't want to wake up, he thought drowsily. It was nice right here. Damned nice. She was warm and sweet against his chest, her soft little hand beneath her cheek, curled against him like a little cat.

He stroked her hair, albeit weakly, because he swore she had milked the strength from him with the same force she had milked his seed from him.

His release had nearly destroyed him. He wouldn't be surprised to realize he had sprained muscles with that one, because every muscle in his body had tightened to the breaking point.

He wanted to lie here just a little longer. He'd never done this, he realized—curled a woman into his arms and just lay with her. He had never held a woman. He had been held by them, by monsters who didn't care what they were doing to him, but he had never held.

He held now, and realized he was holding her as though he were terrified someone would try to take her from him.

The information he had found earlier drew a frown at his brow. It terrified him, the thought that some idiot was out there trying to kill her. Because only an idiot would have bungled it this long. And there was the terror part. He was thanking God it was an idiot. But even idiots got lucky eventually.

He pulled the throw over them as he let the information sift through his mind, let himself drift in the curious contentment he found here. With her.

Maybe it was just the bed, he thought. Because right here, on this couch, a little wider than most, it just felt right.

One thing was for sure, he was going to have to do something about Richard Roberts. There was a senator on the punitive committee of the club. Roberts was a threat to Jaci, and Jaci belonged to him. He could petition Ian to have the committee brought together to take action against the Robertses. That would be easier than killing the bastard.

Not that Cam cared if he did kill him, but he knew

Jaci. She would just get pissed off over the blood, and she might not let him hold her like this again.

And he did like holding her just like this.

He smiled, curious at the feelings that swept over him, that made him question the long, lonely nights he had allowed her to sleep on the end of the sectional, rather than right here in his arms. Because this was where she belonged.

He kissed her brow, the top of her head, and closed his eyes. He'd try it, just for a little while. Sort through his emotions and his little phobia while he drifted in this lazy contentment.

One thing was damned certain: He wasn't letting her go. And he wasn't going to let her cry over him ever again. He'd make something up if he had to. Hell, he could come up with something that would explain this darkness, while holding the truth back. He just had to think about it, that was all. Then Jaci and Chase would be reasonably satisfied and he could keep the shameful truth to himself. As far as he was concerned, all that mattered was comforting her. He couldn't have her crying for him, not ever again. Hell, he'd survived. He had a few inconsequential issues, but he hadn't turned out too damned bad. He'd turned out good enough for Jaci to love, and that was all that mattered to him.

And she did love him.

He smiled at the thought of that, tucked her closer, and slipped deeper into the warm darkness surrounding him.

"I love you," he murmured against her hair.

Damn, though, the sight of Chase touching her, the pleasure burning inside her. Sanity had flown the hell out the window and there had been nothing left but hunger. A hunger that went deeper, further than mere lust.

Tomorrow night, he told himself, he would have roses and candlelight, candles everywhere. He'd get rid of Chase if he had to knock him out and lock him in the trunk of his car, and he'd tell her then. While he stared in her eyes, while he touched her lips. He'd tell her. He loved her.

Chase stared at the entwined pair and breathed out silently from where he stood just below the entrance to his apartment. He could see them, curled together like two halves to a puzzle, and Cam was drifting off to sleep.

For the first time Chase could remember, there was contentment on his brother's face. For so long, even in sleep, Cam scowled or frowned. He didn't rest easy most nights, and he had never, ever, slept with a woman alone that Chase knew of.

He had known Jaci would affect Cam, had known having her here would break down some of the defenses Chase had erected and strengthened over the years.

His lips quirked as he now felt an echo of the twin bond. The peace that flowed along that bond brought his heart ease. There was no other word for it. He had worried about Cam for so damned long. Seeing him like this, seeing him wrapped around Jaci, it eased him.

Relief began to unfold inside him. Each night he had checked on them, each time he had seen them sleeping on opposite ends of that fucking couch, he'd wanted to break something. Foremost, Davinda Morris's neck, because he knew she was involved in whatever had nearly broken Cam. It was too damned bad the fucking bitch was dead.

Shaking his head, he turned and moved back up the stairs and into his office. He still had information to dig up on the Robertses and, unlike his brother, his lust was nowhere near exhausted for the night. But then, his never was. Sometimes he wondered if it ever would be.

He pulled a beer from the fridge and went back to work, if not content, at least breathing easier. Cam might not be sleeping in a bed, but he was sleeping with Jaci. It was a major step, and Chase knew it. Now he just had to figure out the rest of that little mystery.

First things first.

"Come on, now," he whispered, as he began searching through the files he had dug up. "Show me what you've been up to. Just a little bit more here . . ."

CHAPTER
TWENTY-FIVE

It was almost over. Jaci could feel the anticipation, the sense of excitement, and the edge of satisfaction churning inside her the next day. The clock seemed to move at a snail's pace, ticking off the seconds before the meeting with the Robertses.

Moriah had called at least a half dozen times. Though the other girl wasn't half-hysterical anymore, she was still off balance and frightened.

Jaci was feeling a lot of emotions herself, but there was no fear. Maybe that was why the odd feeling of disquiet nudged at her brain. Should she know fear?

She shook her head at the thought as she pretended to work. The only fear she had was the fear of failure, and at this point, failure wasn't an option for her. She couldn't fail, because she had too much riding on it. She had to clear the Robertses out of her life and then she could look forward to a life with Cam.

The thought of that brought the beginnings of a smile to her lips as she checked her watch again. She needed this chance with Cam. Especially after last night.

He had slept with her. For the first time, he had slept with her. Okay, it might have been on the couch rather than in a bed, but she could live with that. Because the feeling of contentment, of complete satisfaction that filled her when she awoke, his arms snug and secure around her as he *slept,* had brought tears to her eyes.

She couldn't lose that. She couldn't let Richard and Annalee destroy it.

But would Cam really kill Richard? The question skittered through her mind as she moved from the desk and paced to the high window behind it.

Five years ago, that question would have resulted in a resounding *yes.* At that time, Cam would have easily killed Richard Roberts for the terror she had experienced from that night. At the very least, she thought now, he would have made Richard wish he was dead.

Wishing he was dead was okay.

She crossed her arms over her breasts and glared into the sunlit beauty of Courtney's gardens. Jaci had spent so many years locked into the Cam that she had known seven years ago that she hadn't made allowances for the man he was now.

He was controlled, sometimes more so. He was restrained and quiet. She had no doubt he would kill if he had to, but she was starting to realize that he wouldn't kill on a whim, otherwise Richard would already be dead.

She pushed her fingers through her hair and breathed out roughly. God, she had been such a fool, and she hadn't realized it. Because, as she grew closer to him, as the man he was now became apparent, she knew Cam would never lose himself to that extent.

She had told herself all these years that she was protecting him, when the truth was she had been protecting herself. Because she knew her own independence was too fragile, too shaky at the time. It would have been so easy to lean on him, to depend on him, and she couldn't let herself do that then. He would have overwhelmed her at the time.

He didn't overwhelm her now. Now, he made her want

to curl up in his arms, made her want to be wrapped by him, held by him.

She would tell him the truth after this meeting. She still needed to do this herself. She needed to know she could take care of herself, that she could defend herself. Otherwise, she would never be certain that she could stand beside him rather than behind him.

Cam was a strong man. Not just physically, but psychologically. He was enduring, and he was a damned good man.

Good men were few and far between, and the best of them had held her through the night as he had never held another woman.

She licked her lips nervously, praying her luck held out for the rest of the afternoon. Cam and Chase were usually busy through the first part of the day investigating potential club members, and meeting with Ian and the head of security.

She had the keys to one of the estate cars, a sporty little BMW waiting beneath the parking awning. And the meeting was set and firm.

Five years. It had taken her five years to get here, to vindicate herself for one night of bad judgment, and maybe to find out why. Why her?

That question plagued her. The Robertses were exactingly particular about who they played their games with. They weren't so stupid as to allow their dirty laundry wave in the public winds. So why decide to take a chance on an interior designer they barely knew?

That question kept her up at night, because it simply did not make sense.

She pushed her fingers through her hair, then rubbed at her arms, trying to chase the chills from her body. It was the normal reaction. A warning, or a premonition? There had always been a feeling that the unanswered questions were the most dangerous ones, where the Robertses were concerned.

Her cell phone chimed, drawing her out of her thoughts, and she pulled it from the clip at her side and checked the number.

"Is everything okay?" she asked.

Moriah was becoming more nervous by the hour.

"Everything's set."

Jaci's brows lifted at the quiet tone. Moriah had been freaking out since the night before; now, other than a slight nervous quiver to her voice, she was calm, steady.

"Have they called?"

"Annalee just called to make certain you're going to be here. I'm to leave the apartment after you arrive. I'll slip back in the back door and make certain everything's going smoothly."

Jaci nodded slowly, checked her watch again. "I'm leaving early. I don't want to give Cam a chance to get out of his meetings early."

"You can't show up early," Moriah hissed. "They'll be suspicious."

Jaci nodded at that. "I'll drive around for a while. I'll be right on time, Moriah. Make sure everything's ready on your end, and I'll do my part."

"Yes, you will." Moriah seemed to breathe in harshly. "I'll call Annalee and let her know everything's ready to go. She and Robert will be here a little early. I know them." Silence filled the line.

"It's almost over, Moriah," she promised.

"Yes, it is." Satisfaction filled Moriah's voice now. "It's finally almost over."

Jaci disconnected, gathered up her purse and the keys, and moved quickly from her office to the residential wing and out the door to the back parking area.

The BMW was sitting right where Matthew had promised it would be, waiting for her.

Five years of dodging the Robertses' threats, their destructive stories, and the frustration of being unable to
fight back, was over. Within a few hours, she and Moriah
both would have what they needed to force the Robertses
back, to end the subtle, destructive war they were waging.

And she would have done it on her own, without help.
She would have protected herself, secured herself. That
was important to her, to know she could do what she had
to do alone, if necessary.

No doubt, Cam would have a fit when he found out
what had been going on, what had happened, and what
she had done to stop it. He would rage and probably end
up hitting Richard next time he saw him.

Jaci could tolerate him hitting Richard, she decided
with a smile. She'd cheer him on. Hell, she'd help him.

As she pulled out of the Sinclair estate, she breathed a
heavy sigh of relief and headed to Moriah's apartment on
the other side of the city.

It was almost over. She should be relieved. Instead, she
couldn't seem to stamp back the heavy feeling of dread
growing inside her gut. She had been poised on the edge
of this for too long. She had fought for it for too long. Now
that the end was so near, she couldn't seem to convince
herself it was going to work.

She had planned it meticulously. She had laid all the
groundwork, she had made herself hold back, kept her
silence when she wanted nothing more than to inform
the world of the depravity of those two, each time they or
one of their friends sliced at her.

She wasn't a woman to sit back and take everything
someone wanted to dish out to her. Doing so had torn at
her pride more than once. But she'd had a plan. A plan

that had formed the moment she realized the Robertses had managed to nearly destroy her reputation.

She could have told Cam. She probably should have told Cam. But she knew him. He would have insisted on handling it his way and taking over. He would have beat the hell out of Richard and probably terrified Annalee. He would have had the satisfaction, Jaci wouldn't have. And she needed it.

She pulled her cell phone from the clip on her jeans and turned it off before placing it in her purse. Before she entered Moriah's apartment, she'd set it to record. A backup. Insurance, just in case.

She trusted Moriah implicitly, but the other girl was too nervous, too shaky. There was always the chance that she could have miscued the video recorder, or that the Robertses were smart enough to find it.

Backup was always a good plan, her father had told her once. And on her desk was the letter she had left for Cam just before she left. Why the hell she had written it she couldn't figure out. She had been compelled to leave something, though. To prove she trusted him? She wasn't certain.

She gripped the steering wheel, breathed in slowly, and forced back that edge of panic. This was going to work. She had no choice but to make it work.

Cam charged into his office and faced his brother with an edge of irritation. Chase had demanded he drop the scheduled interview he and Ian had with the first line of the punitive committee for the club.

Even Ian was unaware of who the exact members of that committee were. Every three years the membership elected a prosecutor to the committee, as well as a defender. Those two would investigate the charges and take their findings to the committee.

He was neutralizing the Robertses one way or the

other. He'd be damned, after last night, if he would allow anything else to hinder his and Jaci's life. He'd take care of the Robertses' threats to her reputation, then he would try, God help him, he would try to be honest with her. As much as he could be.

Losing her wasn't an option. Something inside him unclenched a little more every day that she was back in his life. There was a sense of newness, of life now, and he wasn't losing that.

And if that meant involving the club, then that was what the hell he would do. He couldn't kill a congressman, no matter how much he wanted to; besides, that was guaranteed to piss Jaci off.

"What the hell is going on? We've been working for hours to get this meeting with Obermeyer, and you cancel at the last minute?"

"This is what the hell is going on."

Papers spilled from the printer as Chase jerked a small stack from the tray and slapped them on the table.

"I was looking in the wrong fucking place, Cam. Son of a bitch, I fucked up."

Cam took the sheaf of papers, gave his brother a long, hard look, and began to scan them. As he read, he felt his blood chill in his veins.

England, Italy, New York, and Cancun. All four locations, and one person had been there each time. Someone Jaci shouldn't have even known at the time.

"Why?" he asked.

"That was the hard part." Chase shook his head wearily. "I've spent last night and most of the day today trying to figure that one out. I finally found a source, though. An ex-lover. It's all because of Annalee. A love for Annalee. And Jaci somehow had threatened the Robertses enough that she triggered a psychotic need to defend the congressman's wife."

Cam stared at the information, laid it on the desk, and braced his hand beside it as he used the other to go through each page.

This explained the bungled attempts to hurt Jaci, to kill her. There was no strength here, no experience; there was only emotion and fear.

"I missed it." Chase's voice was filled with disgust. "I looked right the fuck over it."

"You're not the only one." Cam could feel rage icing inside of him now. "I went over the same information, Chase. I missed it, too."

This particular area had been Chase's. The division of the investigation, the years they required to go back on anyone, required that they divide certain portions. This one hadn't been Cam's responsibility, but he had still gone over it, checked it. Hell, he had double-checked it. And he had missed this.

"What now?" Chase moved behind him, his voice hard, furious.

Chase was burning with the anger, Cam was icy with it. He couldn't allow himself to burn right now. He would burn after he talked to Jaci, after he figured out the best course of action to take to protect her. Because there was no doubt there were going to be problems here.

"The psychiatrist's report is in there, too," Chase revealed. "I might have had to do a little hacking to get that. It's not pretty, Cam."

No, it wasn't. He found it even as Chase spoke, and the records of the meetings sent a chill racing down Cam's spine. He was certain the psychiatrist had felt that same chill, if her comments were any indication.

It wasn't pretty at all. It was a life of petty hatreds, of uncertainties and fears and paranoia. It was a mind that had somehow lost its grasp on reality, until one person had found a way to reach inside the fears and connect with it.

A gentle hand. A woman who had shown compassion, sympathy, and—strangely enough—affection. Though it was incredibly hard for Cam to find proof of affection inside Annalee Roberts, still, by all accounts it had been her efforts that had soothed the increasing erratic psychotic impulses that had been showing themselves.

He turned and stared back at Chase, seeing the heavy regret in his expression, the pain that the knowledge brought.

"The committee has to know about this," he stated. "It's a risk to the club, Chase. We can't allow it."

Chase's gaze flickered with demons. They weren't as shadowed as Cam knew his own often were. Chase had demons that walked with him, he had for years, and they burned in his eyes now.

"At least it won't be the punitive committee." Chase sighed. "Do you think there's even enough sanity there to understand punishment?" His hand waved to the report. "God, Cam. How does someone like that move in the world without giving themselves away? Without at least arousing suspicion?"

Cam shook his head. He couldn't imagine it. A combination of drugs and fear, he knew, could do amazing things. And come to think of it, the public appearances were few. And, he guessed, only during the more lucid moments.

"Jaci didn't know," he finally said. "She has no idea anyone has been trying to kill her."

"No fucking wonder," Chase snarled. "With those bungling attempts, they looked like nothing but accidents."

"She's stubborn, not stupid." Cam shook his head sadly, knowing how this was going to hurt Jaci. "If she thought her life was in danger, she would have come to me."

He knew that now. She had waited until she thought she was strong enough to stand with him, to stand on her own two feet. But she was smart enough to know she was in no position to protect herself against a psychotic killer.

"Annalee's reputation means everything to her." Chase sighed. "Nothing else matters. Being believed to be a bitch is a strength to her. No one sees the other side. She strikes out at potential enemies first. She's protecting that reputation. Protecting her public life."

Cam shook his head at that. "Jaci's going to have to see this." And he hated that. Taking this to her, seeing the hurt, the disillusionment in her eyes, was going to kill him.

"Courtney as well," Chase warned him. "They're both in danger here, Cam. Courtney's loyalty is as fierce as Jaci's. She'll have to see the proof of this."

"It's a hell of a mess, Cam," he said. "I'm not looking forward to taking this to Jaci. Or Courtney. It's going to break their hearts."

"But it'll save their lives." Cam turned back to him, that ice hardening inside him. "Take this to Ian. I'm going to find Jaci and get her ready to go home. I don't want to tell her this here."

Home. It was home now. It wasn't just the house or the apartment. It was a home with Jaci there.

Hell, he'd had plans tonight. Candlelight and soft music. A bed of roses and Jaci sweet and hot. He hadn't figured betrayal and tears into the equation.

He moved from the office, rubbing at his jaw as he tried to fight back the rage. He would kill for her, but he'd sure as hell prefer not to have to deal with the mess in this situation. Killing someone could barely distinguish fantasy from reality, even with the aid of drugs, wouldn't be a pleasant experience.

Richard Roberts, well, he had a beating coming. There was no doubt of it. Cam had had the chance to read the account in the psychiatrist's report of what had supposedly happened the night Jaci had left the Robertses' mansion, that night years before.

The Robertses' certainty that she would enjoy being a plaything. What was the comment? *They were only trying to love her. They wanted to love her and she just wanted to run and hurt them.* Like a child. Hell.

He moved downstairs before turning and heading to the back hall and the offices there. As he turned into the well-lit hall, he met Matthew coming out of his own office.

"Hello, Cameron," Matthew greeted him in his precise, formal tone. "I gather you're not joining Miss Wright for lunch?"

Cam paused. "I'm heading to her office now."

Matthew paused. "Miss Wright has already left for her engagement. She left in the BMW approximately thirty minutes ago."

Cam didn't wait to question him. He moved quickly to the door of her office and jerked it open, striding inside, his gaze moving around the room. She wouldn't have left without telling him. She knew they had plans tonight. She wouldn't have gone out this late in the day without telling him when she would return.

His gaze swept over the desk, his eyes catching the note laying there. He moved to it, jerked the paper up, and read it as pure terror began to race through him.

No. Ah, fuck. No. He wouldn't lose her like this. He couldn't.

"Chase!" He raced into the hall, aware of his raised voice, the pure shaking terror in it, and the sound of feet racing from upstairs.

He slid into the foyer as Chase and Ian rushed down the stairs and Courtney paused at the door to the formal living room.

"She's gone!"

"She had a lunch date," Matthew objected.

"She's meeting with Moriah and the Robertses." His gaze connected with Chase's as he handed him the paper.

I'm taking care of this situation with the Robertses today, Cam. I'll be at Moriah Brockheim's, meeting with them. Don't worry. We both know they're not dangerous, just irritating. I'll explain everything tonight.

The note had pure terror and rage burning through the ice now.

"Moriah will be there. What's the big deal, Cam?" Courtney snapped. "Jaci's a big girl. Let her deal with this."

Cam stared at her in disbelief before he and Chase both tore back upstairs. They raced to their office. Weapons. They needed weapons.

Shoulder holsters were strapped quickly around their torsos, Glocks shoved into the holsters beneath their arms. Backup at their ankles was strapped on.

"Matthew, call Detective Allen at the Alexandria PD, and have him meet us at Moriah Brockheim's apartment in Alexandria. Tell him to come in quietly, we have a potential situation."

"Cam, dammit," Ian cursed as he weaponed up as well. "What the hell is going on?"

"We'll explain on the way." They headed out of the office at a run and Cam began to pray. Pray that he got there in time. That Jaci was safe. That he could hold back the rage building inside him enough to pull her out, to protect her, without shedding unnecessary blood.

She was his. And no one, but no one, threatened what was his. Not man, woman, or lunatic.

CHAPTER
TWENTY-SIX

Jaci smoothed her hands down the snug jeans she wore as she reached Moriah's apartment door and roughly blew out a breath, telling herself once again that it was nearly over. She would finish this here, tape the Robertses' admission of what had happened the night she ran from their mansion, and use it to make certain neither of them harassed her again.

She didn't need her relationship with Cam overshadowed by this, and she wasn't going to have it overshadowed. She would stand on her own two feet, take care of herself, and end this now.

With a sharp nod at the thought, she lifted her hand and pressed the buzzer with the tip of her finger. Moriah's upperclass, second-story, corner apartment overlooked a small flower-adorned park.

A second later the inside latch could be heard sliding free and the deadbolts releasing as Moriah opened the door. Jaci stared back at her somberly. Dressed in a pretty white-and-gold sundress, she looked young and sweet, with her shoulder-length hair framing her face.

Jaci stepped into Moriah's apartment, staring into the other girl's eyes and seeing the cold, hard resolve there.

"They're in the study." Her voice was faint, husky, as though with emotion.

There was something off with her demeanor, though—a cold, hard light was in her eyes that Jaci hadn't expected.

Jaci nodded, gripped her purse, and followed Moriah through the apartment to the study. There was a back door just through the hall in the kitchen. It led to an iron balcony and a fire escape to the alley. Just in case Annalee had brought her handy dandy little whip with her.

Jaci breathed in deeply as Moriah headed to the kitchen and she stepped into the study.

Annalee was as beautiful as ever. Long black hair that flowed to the middle of her back, gracefully arched brows and blue eyes. She was slender but not skinny. The soft, pale peach silk dress she wore emphasized the golden hue of her flesh. It also made her appear almost innocent. A far cry from the black leather, stilettos, and whip she had worn that night so long ago.

In contrast, Richard appeared confident, aloof. Almost aristocratic. The aristocracy was spoiled by the hint of nervousness in his eyes and the sheen of sweat on his brow.

"Margie isn't here?" Jaci looked around, wondering where their secretary was lurking. The one who had been sheened with sweat and sex that night, her dark eyes wild with lust.

"Margie isn't needed here." Annalee leaned against the desk at the side of the room, her hands braced on the walnut top behind her. "There was no sense in upsetting her. Margie can be delicate sometimes."

Margie was as delicate as a barracuda, but Jaci understood the other woman's hardness as she thought about Moriah's experience with the Robertses.

"Yeah, that happens when you mess with a kid's head," Jaci snapped. "Tell me, Annalee, did you choose Margie when she was a teenager, too?"

Annalee blinked at her in surprise. "Sorry, Jaci, but I

don't do teenagers," she sneered. "Strange, I didn't expect you to resort to lies after all these years."

Jaci snorted at that. "I wouldn't dare try to fight you on those grounds, Annalee. I can accede to the fact that you're by far the best liar here. So I *will* stick to the truth. And if teenagers aren't your style, then how do you explain Moriah?"

Annalee looked to Richard with an expression of confusion. That look sent her stomach sinking. Something was off, either it was genuine confusion, or they had to know they were being taped. Had Moriah given the game away somehow?

"Moriah is an adult, Jaci, and a very good friend of Annalee's. There's a difference between a friend and a lover," Richard finally said. "And we're not here to discuss the whys and wherefores of our personal lives. If that's why you called this meeting, then we're all wasting our time."

Why *she* had called the meeting?

"What?" She stared at both of them in confusion. "I didn't call a damned thing."

"Look, Jaci," Annalee's delicate voice flowed over her protestation. "I regret we had to take the steps necessary to ensure that nothing you said against us was ever believed. I can understand it's been frustrating to you over the years. But we've always made certain to compliment your design abilities, to send clients your way. There are rules to the little skirmish we're involved in. Rules we've all had to abide by."

That flash of regret had to be a lie, Jaci thought as she watched the emotion wash through Annalee's eyes. Who the hell were these people, and what happened to Richard and Annalee Roberts?

"You two are certifiable." She shook her head at the sight before her. "Excuse me, Annalee, you've told everyone for years that I tried to steal from you, that I was a home wrecker, but you say you regret it? Why don't I believe that?"

Richard breathed out heavily. "Because you don't understand the world you're stepping into," he told her impatiently. "We accept responsibility for the situation."

Well now, wasn't that just big of him?

"You tried to rape me, Richard. You, your wife, and your demented little secretary," Jaci snapped, her voice full of fury. "Excuse me, but that's a little more serious than you obviously want to accept."

She felt as though she had dropped into the twilight zone, and she didn't like it. She had come here with several certainties—one being that it was time for this "skirmish," as they called it, to end.

Richard grimaced heavily at her declaration. "You misunderstood that night."

"I didn't misunderstand that damned scar on my hip from your wife's whip," she bit out. "For God's sake, what the hell is this?"

"Look." Annalee raised her hand to still the animosity rising between them all now. But there was no stilling it. Jaci had spent years being angry, years fighting their lies. "We're aware your association with Cameron Falladay and his employer Ian Sinclair halts anything we could do to still your retaliation against us. We've already received our first warnings. I assumed you wanted to discuss the parameters of the truce that would evolve now."

Jaci stared back at them in silence. She scratched at the back of her head, wondering at the niggling warning there, as she gave her head a quick shake.

Something wasn't right here, and it didn't make sense. She had never imagined, not in all these years, that this meeting would be conducted with such civility and rationality. Hell, she wanted to scream and yell and throw things. And they were being nice?

She stared around the room before shaking her head and turning back to the conversation.

"What warnings?" she finally asked.

Annalee smiled then. A soft curve of her lips, not a smirk or a sneer, merely an acknowledgment of Jaci's disbelief.

"As I said, there are certain rules as you move up in society. One of those rules, once your relationship with Cam is cemented, is that your power here has the potential to match our own. There's no hiding that from you, you'll learn it in time. Courtney Sinclair's power already outdistances my own. Richard's position as congressman gives us only a slight edge. Because of this, we're now willing to listen to your demands and put an end to our mutual vendettas. The gossip could hurt both of us if it continues, Jaci, and it could hurt the Falladay twins as well. So let's end this now."

"My demands? Fine. Why? Why did you do it to begin with? What the hell made you think I'd play those games with you?"

Forget the confusion, she'd get the answers first. She wanted to know why she'd had to battle this couple for so many years, and then they'd move on to a few other questions.

Annalee sighed and stared at the floor for a moment before lifting her head and staring back at her. "That, my dear, was your own fault. If you hadn't belonged to a gigolo and a man known for his ménage lifestyle, then I would have never considered it."

Jaci froze. She could feel her heart beating sluggishly, fear slamming inside her mind. She felt weak, torn, she didn't want to hear what she feared was coming.

"You're lying!" She threw the accusation back at them. "And you have no idea the hell he'll bring down on the two of you for it."

"Cameron Falladay, for all his power in this town, is still a product of his unsavory roots." Richard sighed regretfully. "We do have proof, Jaci. Being a man-whore at age fifteen isn't something to be proud of, but he did rise above it. His sharing with his brother, and your nearly lifelong association with them, led us to an erroneous conclusion that you would be agreeable to our lifestyle as well. We apologize for that."

Chase stood still outside the study, every bone, every muscle in his body tightening as he heard Richard Roberts' statement. He felt a howl of rage, felt agony sear through his body as that twin bond opened just enough for a glimpse into his brother's soul.

It only added to his own rage, to the pain that sliced through his guts and opened his soul to reveal the raw, aching center of agony.

His gaze jerked to Cam's, where he stood on the other side of the doorway. His brother was staring into the study, his expression frozen, but his eyes enraged. Chase could see the rage, and he could see the grief.

How had he allowed that to happen to his baby brother? Cam had been his responsibility, his brother, all he had left to hold onto in the world at that time. And he had allowed that to happen.

He saw Cam shake his head. A quick little jerk as he flinched, a betraying flicker of raw agony as the truth was revealed to the woman his brother loved more than life.

"You're lying." Jaci wanted to scream the words, but could barely manage a whisper as she forced the words past her lips. "Cam never sold himself. He would never do anything like that. Not then and not now." For a moment, something like compassion flickered in Richard's eyes, and he turned to his wife.

This wasn't the couple she knew. Cold, hard, all icy distain and superior disgust. They had to be monsters. Pure evil. Only monsters could stand and lie like this with such convincing compassion. They couldn't be real. This had to be a game being played out for the camera.

"No, actually, his aunt was the pimp." Annalee shrugged, sympathy flickering in her eyes as she continued for her husband. "I have it all in the investigative report we had made when you came to work for us. Richard, Margie, and I were very attracted to you, Jaci. We felt you would have fit in with our circle of friends because of the information we found on you, Cameron, and Chase. But once the mistake had been made, we were forced to control any damage it could have caused to Richard's political career and my own place in society."

Jaci needed to sit down, but there was no place to sit, no way she could sit and still stay strong before them. But grief was tearing through her. Cam had fought to hide his past, and these two had known all along. They had known and they had used it to hurt her.

"Jaci." Annalee shook her head gently. "Were we the monsters you believe us to be, then we would have used that information, rather than controlling any retaliation you could make, as we did. We aren't completely unfeeling, simply a bit self-serving, I'm afraid."

"I'm not a fool, Jaci," Richard said then. "Cameron Falladay would have no problem killing a man who threatened his place in the world, or his woman's. We assumed you called this meeting to discuss your demands."

She was in shock. Disbelief and pain were raging through her. This explained so many things, but more than anything it explained Cam's refusal to discuss the pain in his past. Fifteen. Such a vulnerable age anyway, and he had been exploited in one of the worst ways. Exploited and nearly destroyed.

"I didn't call this meeting." She finally shook her head, disbelieving, filled with grief.

Oh, God, Cam. She wanted to rock back and forth in agony. She wanted to race to him, to hold him, to scream in rage that anything so vile could have been done to him.

"What do you mean, you didn't call this meeting?" Annalee straightened and looked to Robert. "We didn't call it."

"No. I called it."

Jaci turned and stared at Moriah in shock. It wasn't Moriah so much that shocked her, as the gun in her hand and the hatred in her eyes as she glared at Jaci.

"Moriah?" Annalee's voice softened strangely, despite the confusion and fear in her voice. There was genuine affection, genuine caring in her tone. "Darling, what are you doing?"

"I called this meeting." Moriah slowly screwed a silencer onto the end of the handgun as Jaci stepped back, shaking her head, fighting to make sense of what was happening. "You see, Annalee, I can't let her tell that nasty Cameron what happened that night. And she will. I know she's going to tell him the moment she leaves here, no matter what you agree to. She told me she would. He might hurt you. I can't let you be hurt."

Jaci's lips parted as she fought to breathe. This couldn't be happening. It didn't make sense. The Robertses had terrified her, brutalized her as a child—hadn't they?

"Moriah?" Jaci fought to believe what she was seeing. Moriah, her face pale, her eyes blazing with madness as she smiled calmly.

"I warned you, Annalee," Richard said then, his voice hardening.

"Yes, you did warn her didn't you?" Moriah cried out then, the weapon turning, centering on Richard. "You've tried to turn her against me the whole time, didn't you, Richard? The poor little crazy girl. You wanted her to leave me all alone. You didn't want us to be happy."

"For God's sake," Richard muttered, his face slack now with disbelief. "Put the gun down, Moriah."

Cam eased himself in position in the doorway behind Moriah. Slipping through the house to the far door hadn't been easy. The apartment was laid out with a series of short hallways, and several crossed each other.

He held his gun at his thigh as he got into position to get a clear sight of the young woman. The psychiatrist's report was right; Moriah Brockheim wasn't completely sane. He could hear it in her voice now.

He couldn't let himself think about the information his brother had heard. Ian and the detective would be in position at the back now, and easing toward the door. He had to take her down before they came in, before they heard as well.

"Moriah, dear, please put the gun down." Annalee's voice was softer, gentler than Jaci could have imagined it would be. "We can discuss this, darling. Jaci is very reasonable, and you know how nice I truly am. Once she sees this, she won't tell a soul. We can convince her."

There was pain and desperation in Annalee's voice, in the sorrow in her face and in her eyes. She truly cared for Moriah. Cared for her. Not as a toy, but as a child, as the little girl Jaci had sometimes glimpsed in the other woman.

"We can?" Moriah whispered hopefully as she turned to Annalee. "Will you tell them, Anna? Will you tell them that I belong with you? Father keeps fighting me. And that stupid psychiatrist won't listen."

"You know I will, sweetheart," Annalee promised,

sincerity as thick as the fear in her eyes now, as she held her arms out to Moriah. "Come here, baby. Let Aunt Anna make it all better. We'll go fix chocolate and talk with Jaci about this, shall we?"

Cam let his eyes flicker over the room, and a second before Richard moved, he knew what was coming. The congressman's muscles bunched and he jumped for the gun.

The soft pop of the gun sent Richard to the floor, his hand clamping over his chest as a glaze of red spilled over his fingers.

Annalee screamed and Moriah turned to Jaci as Cam jumped. He knocked Moriah to the side, grabbed Jaci, and rolled with her, ignoring her cry, pushing her behind the desk as he turned back to the room.

"So protective," Moriah sneered as she regained her footing, turning the gun on him. "You're a gigolo. A man-whore. Your aunt sold your body to dirty old women and you let her. You think I'll let you take Anna from me? You're nasty and brutal and mean. Chase deserves a better brother than you. He always has." She screamed the words, the gun lifting as Cam stared at her in horror.

He had his gun in his hand, staring back at her, seeing the young woman his brother had been so fond of over the years. The woman, so fragile, already broken, her eyes maniacal as her finger tightened on the trigger.

He lowered the gun to shoot to wound. It was a risk. Crazy was fucking crazy, and he knew she would fight to the death to pull that trigger.

As Cam aimed, someone else fired. He watched in shock at the neat, dark little hole in the middle of her forehead, the almost peaceful expression that came over her face before she slumped slowly, gracefully to the carpet beneath her. The pretty white-and-gold dress she wore flowed around her bare legs, her hair feathered over her pale face, and the scent of death and Annalee's quiet sobs filled the air.

Detective Allen was yelling into the radio for backup and the paramedics that were already standing by as he and Ian rushed into the room. The congressman was gasping for breath, and behind Cam Jaci had her forehead against his back. He felt her trembling, a soft sob whispering from her lips as he turned and stared at Chase.

His brother lowered his handgun slowly before turning to Cam, his eyes dark, fury burning hot and bright inside him. And he felt his brother then. Felt that bond tighten as his twin's rage turned on him.

"Your shot went wild, Chase." Detective Allen, portly, breathing heavy, shook his head as he stepped into the room, his dark brown gaze heavy with sympathy as he stared around the room.

"No it didn't, Carl," Chase said tonelessly.

"Trust me." Carl's voice hardened. "My shot took her. Yours went wild."

Cam rose from the floor, pulling Jaci with him, staring at his brother in shock as Chase moved to him.

"Keep your fucking mouth shut, both of you," Chase hissed to Cam and Jaci. "The Robertses can protect themselves. Our pasts stay in the fucking past. Do you understand me?"

Cam shook his head slowly as he stared at his brother's ravaged expression. "What have you done, Chase?"

To himself. He could see it in his brother now, the grief, the pain. He had killed Moriah Brockheim. He'd had no choice. Cam would have taken the bullet and prayed for the best, rather than killing a woman that he knew his brother felt affection for.

"I showed her mercy," Chase bit off, his voice icy. "Start praying I show it to you later."

Jaci moved around Cam as the detective moved to him, her entire body shaking while she moved across the room to Annalee Roberts, where she knelt silently beside Moriah.

Chase was next to Richard, applying a compress to the wound as they awaited the paramedics.

"Bullet was deflected by the ribs. Broken rib, bullet passed out the side," Chase was muttering as Cam caught Jaci's arm, pulling her back to him.

"Don't." She shook her head, her voice hoarse as she stared up at him. "I have to do something."

His eyes were icy. They had been icy, cold, without emotion from the moment she had glimpsed them when he threw himself into the room.

He nodded sharply and let her move slowly away from him.

"She wasn't a b-bad kid," Annalee whispered brokenly. "Even as a b-baby. E-even then, she was so fragile." She smoothed back the long, silky hair from Moriah's face. "Her mother is my stepsister. Margaret is a good woman. This will break her."

Annalee's shoulders heaved as Jaci slowly, hesitantly wrapped her arms around her. Surprisingly, Annalee let her comfort her, and Jaci couldn't explain why she tried, or why the other woman would care. But as she sobbed in Jaci's arms, Jaci had to admit that part of this was her own fault. She had to take the blame for it. She should have told Cam everything. She should have stood her ground, but allowed him to help.

"All secrets are safe here." Annalee lifted her face, her features somehow softer, move vulnerable than they had ever been. "No matter what happens, you'll suffer no more by our hands." She turned back to Moriah and convulsed in sobs again. "This was my fault. Sweet God. So much my fault." She leaned over the girl then, pulling herself from Jaci's arms as she embraced Moriah and sobbed in grief.

"Come on." Cam knelt beside her, watching the other two women with those cold, cold eyes of his. "I'm slipping you out of here. Detective Allen will confer with Roberts before the journalists get here. We don't need to be here."

She shook her head as he drew her to her feet. "But her parents . . ."

"Don't need to know you were here. Now, Jaci. We go now."

He pulled her to her feet and moved quickly to the door of the apartment.

Chase was waiting outside and gave an abrupt nod as they moved to the door.

"Take her down the back stairs. Matthew is waiting for you at the back door. Get the hell out of here."

Jaci moved on autopilot. She could feel the tears still running from her eyes, her body shuddering with shock, disbelief, and so many fears.

She couldn't seem to grasp everything she had heard, everything she had seen. It had happened too fast. It was still happening too fast. Cam's arm was around her waist, pulling her down the stairs to the back entrance and into the limo waiting patiently in the alley.

Matthew was pulling away from the building even before Cam closed the door behind himself. He sat back in the seat and stared across the short distance to her. His face was still hard. His eyes still icy.

Jaci wrapped her arms around her stomach and bent forward, sobs tearing from her. She couldn't handle it. She couldn't imagine ever being the same again, and the terror wouldn't abate.

"Come here, baby." Cam's voice softened, but only marginally.

But his arms wrapped around her and he was drawing her to his lap, wrapping her in his warmth, enclosing her in the protection of his arms.

And all she could do was cry harder. She wanted to tell him how sorry she was, how she had never known Moriah was Annalee's niece. No one she had known had seemed to know. She hadn't heard so much as a breath of that information. She hadn't known.

"You couldn't have known." He sighed against her hair, as she realized she must have been sobbing her thoughts. "Very few people did know, Jaci. Stepsisters. It's not information either family discusses."

There were too many secrets in this world. Too many ghosts in too many closets, and now a young woman was dead; and she could tell, in those few desperate minutes, Cam's world had been changed forever as well.

"I don't know what to do," she cried, her fingers fisting in his shirt as she pressed her head tighter to his chest. "Oh God, Cam, I don't know what to do."

"Don't do anything." He kissed her brow and held her tighter. "Don't do anything Jaci, just let me hold you. For right now, just let me hold you."

CHAPTER
TWENTY-SEVEN

Chase moved back into the study and watched as Congressman Roberts was loaded onto a gurney and investigators moved around the room, securing it.

He was sure that all traces of Cam, Jaci, and Ian had been cleared from the apartment. He and Carl Allen had made certain of it. And if anything showed up? Well, it would disappear just as easily. Allen was a member of the club, and in this case at least, it was a case of the old boys' club. Not exactly legal, but there was no reason to complicate the situation with the lies and half truths they would have to tell.

"Moriah was never stable," Annalee told another investigator from where she sat on the low couch across the room. "She blamed Richard because we wouldn't let her move into our home. She was very dependent on me." Annalee's face twisted in grief as more tears flowed from her swollen eyes. "She was like my child. I loved her."

Chase wiped his hand over his face and turned back to the sight he didn't want to see.

Moriah.

Her parents had hidden her mental problems well. Her psychiatrist, the drugs, the close tabs they had kept on her, kept the truth carefully hidden. Beautiful, fairylike Moriah.

He stepped over to her, sat on his haunches, and stared into her peaceful face. She looked as though she were sleeping, except for the bruised wound in the center of her forehead.

His bullet had struck. Carl's hadn't. Her life had been extinguished before her insanity could destroy anyone else; and she had been determined to destroy Cameron, simply because he protected Jaci. And Cam would have let her, because of Chase.

He had felt that. The torn emotions his twin had felt in that moment. They had been on his face, had twisted across their bond. He would have taken a bullet, rather than see Chase lose someone he cared for.

He *had* cared for her.

He brushed a wisp of hair back from her lips and felt his heart squeeze tight at the memory of his fingers pulling that trigger. Unlike Cam, he hadn't hesitated.

"I'm sorry," he whispered, gazing into her doll-like features as he tried to push aside the guilt and the anger. "I'm so sorry, Moriah."

He pressed his lips together as the leg of Carl's slacks came into view.

"The investigator is finished with Mrs. Roberts. She wants to talk to you before she leaves for the hospital to be with her husband. She's in the kitchen waiting for you."

Carl stepped back as Chase rose slowly to his feet.

"Did you know about her problems?" he asked the other man as he nodded to Moriah.

Carl sighed heavily. "I've had to cover several incidents for her. Her dad's old college buddies with the chief. You don't say no when that happens. Besides, she was a good kid when she wasn't crazy."

Yeah, when she wasn't crazy.

Shaking his head, Chase moved through the apartment and into the sunlit kitchen.

Annalee Roberts sat at the kitchen table. Her face was ravaged by her tears and her pain. He had never liked her, but right now he felt sorry as hell for her.

"Thank you for coming, Chase." Her voice was rough, hoarse from her tears. "I gather you and Cam heard the entire event."

He nodded sharply. He wasn't thinking about it right now. He couldn't. If he was going to hold onto his control and keep from strangling his baby brother, then he had to forget, at least for a little while, the information he had learned.

Annalee nodded slowly. "Moriah's at peace now." She swallowed tightly. "Her parents have feared an episode like this for years. It's why I've been careful to stay away from her as much as possible. She was becoming very possessive of me." Her face twisted with grief.

"She knew about that night with Jaci. Did you tell her?" He needed to know where to place the blame. He had to find someplace for it, to be able to deal with it.

But Annalee shook her head slowly. "I would never have told her. She wasn't strong enough to handle it. Until today, I was unaware that she even knew of the reasons for the animosity between Jaci and me. When she called, she said Jaci had told her, and wanted to meet with us to discuss it." She shook her head as she pressed her fingers to her lips. "Once we arrived she was enraged. She said she had known all along. That she had overheard Margie and I discussing it years before. And that we were to take care of it this time or she would. Sweet God, she told Jaci we had molested her." Annalee broke down again. She lay her head on the table, sobbing pitifully as Chase moved beside her and sat on his haunches by her chair.

"She wasn't sane," he said softly. "You can't blame your-self."

She shook her head in the cradle of her arms. "I blame

myself. I always shall. I tried so many times to help her, to love her, because she was like my own." She lifted her head and stared back at him desperately. "I can't have children. So I loved Moriah like my own child. And I tried so hard to do what was best. All I did was destroy her."

He shook his head and rose to his feet once more. "Her insanity destroyed her, Annalee, not you. Dry your face and go to your husband. You can help *him* now. Moriah's at peace. You don't have to help her any longer."

He walked away from her. He had to. He could feel the rage and pain growing inside him, the pure, fucking fury, a red-hot lance of it driving into his brain, as he thought of the years his brother had lied to him.

Lied to him. To his face, over and over, lied to him.

He left the apartment, feeling something akin to pure, icy, blood fury burning inside him.

Fifteen. That demented bitch of an aunt of theirs had sold his brother to her depraved friends—had somehow forced him to allow her to whore him out for sex. And not once, not one time had he come to Chase. He hadn't asked for his help. He had never goddamned asked him for help.

He bolted out of the apartment house and stalked to the car Cam had left behind. He tried to tell himself his brother was an adult. He couldn't just beat the shit out of him for being a fucking bastard, and not asking for help. Could he?

He slammed the car door behind him and stared through the windshield. Fuck that. Hell yes, he could beat the shit out of him, and that was exactly what he would do.

Jaci forced herself to stop crying before they reached Cam and Chase's home. She dried her face and stayed in Cam's arms—and refused to speak the thoughts on her mind.

When the limo pulled into the garage, she let him lift her from the car, safe in his arms, and she let him carry her up to the apartment. She didn't want him to let her go. She was terrified that if he did, then he would never hold her again.

He got the door open while she kept her face buried in his shoulder. She felt weak. She felt as though she should be on her own two feet, rather than depending on him, but she couldn't. She couldn't let him go. She had to hold onto him.

And he didn't seem inclined to let her go. He moved into the apartment, the door closing softly behind them as he moved to the couch.

"Here." He placed her on the couch, but she didn't let go of him. She couldn't.

"It's okay. I'm not going far. I promise." He forced her arms from behind his neck, pulled back, and turned away. She shivered.

The ice was still in his eyes, despite the gentle tone of his voice, and the sight of it had a shiver racing up her spine.

She couldn't take her eyes off him. She watched him miserably as he moved across the room to the kitchen, opened the cabinet, and dragged out a fifth of whisky and two glasses.

When he returned, he sat down beside her, poured a small amount into a glass, and handed it to her. When he turned to the next glass, he seemed to give it a second thought—then he pulled the bottle back and tipped it to his lips.

He didn't even grimace. Then he lowered the bottle and held it loosely between his thighs.

"I haven't seen you drink whisky since I've been here," she whispered, her voice raw.

She had only seen him drink beer, and he rarely finished those.

He brought the bottle up, tipped it again, and took a long

drink before lowering it and staring at the label thoughtfully. "I used to drink a lot of it." He finally shrugged.
"Sometimes I drank too much of it."

She read between the lines easily. He had been so wild
as a young man, so filled with bitterness and hatred—and
whisky.

She sat the glass carefully on the table before them,
and stared at the amber liquid in it. She didn't want the
drink. She didn't want to dull the pain raging through her,
or the sickness that roiled in her stomach. He had lived
his life, survived it, and now he was being forced to reveal
it. She wasn't going to dull her own emotions, she wasn't
going to dull the love and aching grief she felt for him.

He took another long drink, then set the bottle on the
table.

"The whisky stopped working a long time ago," he finally said. "When I realized it was going to take something stronger to dull the pain, I picked up a pistol, got in
my pickup, and drove out to the most deserted place I
could find at the time."

Her heart leapt in her throat.

"The day you were on the back road of the farm," she
whispered.

He nodded slowly, his lips pursing. "I'd had enough.
Enough sick shame, enough banging my head against a
wall, trying to hide what was happening and trying to
find a way out at the same time."

She couldn't cry again. Not yet. He would stop talking
if she did, and she needed to know, to understand.

"Then you showed up." He reached out and caressed
the dark label of the whisky bottle with the back of a finger.
"And there was this innocent little face and pretty eyes.
And you told me you would take the pain away. I almost
believed you could." He shook his head at the thought.
"You were just a kid, but the only person in that fucking

town that seemed to believe in me, besides Chase. And hell, all he wanted was answers. Answers I couldn't give him."

He pulled his hand back and wiped his hand over his face before he let it hang with the other between his spread knees.

"He loved you," Jaci whispered, "just as I did."

He lifted his head and stared across the room, his expression so distant, his eyes so cold she wanted to scream out at him. She wanted to hit him. Wanted to rage at him for carrying this alone for so damned long.

"I went to the sheriff the next day," he finally said. "You see, Jaci, I almost killed one of those old bitches. They insisted I spend the night, that they lie against me. One night, I messed up. I dozed. And I felt her touch me. The next thing I felt was my hand around her throat."

He looked down at the hand he clenched slowly, then shook his head tightly again.

Jaci had to force back a cry of pain. Eighteen. He had been eighteen. Too young to face such violence inside himself.

"Anyway," he breathed out roughly, "I went to Sheriff Bridges. I told him what happened." He jerked the bottle up, tilted it, and consumed an amount that had Jaci covering her mouth again to hold back a tortured cry.

When he put the bottle down again, it thumped on the table.

"Right after my aunt arrived at the house, she drugged me with some shit. It messed up my head. Made me horny as hell. No matter what she did to me. And she did like to play with those adult toys she had. She pushed as many of them as she could inside me and took pictures of it. Enough pictures, enough poses, that it looked like I was enjoying the hell out of it."

Jaci was going to throw up. She had to force back the

gagging reflex as she thought of the horror, the humiliation he must have felt.

"And here was the deal," he continued. "I could do what she told me to, when she told me to, or she would make sure Chase got those pictures. Chase and every friend I had. See, she wasn't in the pictures. And who would believe sweet Davinda Morris had done something so vile?" His laugh was bitter, furious. "The fucking bitch."

Her soul was writhing inside her, shrieking with pain, as she somehow managed to stay silent. Managed to hold back her screams of agony.

"I went to the sheriff and I made him swear on Dad's grave to keep the secret I was about to tell him. He and Dad were friends." He shrugged again, his voice nearly a monotone, cold and unemotional. "I told him what happened. He came to the house, found the pictures, and forced her to leave. But I had to tell him what happened." His jaw bunched then. "I had to sit in front of a man that loved my father like a brother, and I had to tell him what I allowed to happen. And I saw the pity in his eyes. The pity and the shame. And I swore I'd never see that in another living soul's eyes again." He turned to her, stared at her. "I was a whore, Jaci. For three years. Now, do you feel any better knowing?"

The tears slipped from her eyes. "I love you, Cam. I love you no matter what. I don't pity you, and I don't feel shame. You survived." Her voice broke as she reached out to touch him. His strong jaw, the corners of his icy eyes. "You waited for me." She had prayed he would.

A grimace twisted his face as he turned his away from her again, and he reached for the whisky once more.

"You don't need the whisky." She slapped his hand back. "Does getting drunk make it easier to face, Cam?"

"Getting drunk?" He flicked her a harsh look. "That shit doesn't do anything to take my mind off the fact that

I fucked up," he snarled, that edge of fury showing again. "I fucked up, Jaci. I let her use me, and I was too damned brick-dumb to stop it. And too fucking weak to kill the bitch."

"Try too fucking filled with false pride to live!" Chase's voice was demented with anger, and it echoed through the sudden silence of the apartment as Jaci and Cam both jumped to their feet and turned to him.

And Jaci knew he had heard it all, as Cam stared at the keys in his brother's hands before lifting his gaze to the fire burning in Chase's eyes.

"Find another entrance in," Cam said coldly. "I'm fucking sick of you sneaking in this house and butting your nose in my damned business."

Testosterone and fury filled the air now. Jaci watched the metamorphosis as Cam and Chase stared back at each other, as animosity, anger, pain, and some kind of driving need to smash things seemed to pump up their bodies.

She had heard of the fights these two had as young men. It hadn't been an unusual occurrence to see their faces bruised or to hear that they had fought each other, rather than others.

"Cam." She touched his arm warningly, feeling the bunched muscles and vibrating fury.

He wasn't angry with Chase, not really. He was angry with himself, with Davinda, and with the pride that was so much a part of him. The guilt and the pain had eaten at him for so many years, and now that it was out in the open, she could feel the fight burning between both men.

"Step away from him, Jaci," Chase growled. "You don't want to get between the two of us right now."

"And I don't want you fighting, either," she snapped back at him. "Sit down and discuss this."

Cam's gaze swung toward her, disbelief and astonishment filling his expression.

"Discuss what?" he bit out. "The eavesdropping bastard can't seem to keep his nose in his own business. I'm going to break it for him."

He turned back to Chase, a hard, mocking smile on his face as his fists bunched at his side.

"You two are not going to fight."

"The hell we're not." Cam lifted her and set her aside.

The smile on his face was tight, but something in his eyes caught hers. A lifting of the ice, a resolution. A part of him glorying at the chance to use his fists to pound out the rage inside him.

God, men were so dumb sometimes.

"Chase." She turned to his brother desperately. "Now isn't the time to fight. This is wrong."

"No, this isn't wrong," he snarled. "Wrong was when he kept his yap shut and didn't let me help him. Wrong was leaving me alone and shutting down that bond I needed at the time. Fuck him, Jaci. Wrong was when he ignored the fact that he had a fucking brother." The last sentence was a war cry, as they rushed each other.

Fists, steel hard and filled with male rage, slammed. Chase's head went back with Cam's first blow; Cam stumbled back after a particularly brutal blow to his ribs.

And they were off and fighting. Bar stools slammed to the floor and slid across the hardwood floor as they wrestled each other onto the kitchen island and Jaci screamed as Chase's next punch sent Cam to the floor.

Oh God, they were going to kill each other. Wide-eyed and shocked, she watched them fight as she reached to the table and grabbed the glass of whisky Cam had poured for her earlier.

She took it in one drink and wheezed in reaction. It caused her to miss several seconds of the blood and curses flying around the room.

"Bastard!" Chase cursed, after Cam managed to land another blow to his jaw. "I ought to kill you for that."

"Yeah, for protecting you?" Cam's voice was savage as he dodged a blow to his jaw, but he was a hair too slow to dodge the fist to his hard abdomen.

"Didn't fucking need protecting." Chase jumped at him and the fists were flying again.

Jaci winced and cried out, then she picked up the bottle of whisky and took Cam's earlier example. She lifted it to her lips and drank straight from the bottle.

There had to be a way to stop this. They were going to kill each other. Cam had ripped the shirt off Chase's back already, and his own was hanging in tatters. Both their lips were bleeding, and oh boy, were they going to have some bruises later.

When Chase's fist connected with Cam's face again, she'd had enough. This was ridiculous, she decided as the whisky began to warm her stomach and take the edge off the pure horror of watching these two fight.

There had to be a way of stopping it. Sometime before they killed each other, maybe?

But a little part of her that the liquor had released had to admit it was damned sexy, almost erotic, watching them fight. They were powerful, muscular. Sweat gleamed on broad chests and dampened chest hairs. Blood smeared their faces and their eyes were lit—with savage pleasure. They were enjoying the fight.

There was something they would enjoy just as much, though.

She took another drink of the whisky. Too much. She wheezed and choked as it went down, tears coming to her eyes as she fought to catch her breath.

Okay, that drink hurt. How the hell did Cam do that?

Chase managed to throw Cam into one of the hard

steel beams centered around the room, and at that point she'd enough.

She slapped the whisky to the table and moved to the other side of the couch. The niggling idea moving through her head would never work if they couldn't see her clearly.

She toed off her shoes first and pushed them to the side. She released the button to her jeans, then slid the zipper down, wincing again as Cam slammed his fist into Chase's jaw, driving his brother's head backward.

She was going to kill both of them.

She slid the jeans down her legs, then pulled off the stylish T-shirt she wore. She wore nothing now but the white, lacy panties and the flimsy bra she had put on that morning.

She was unclipping the bra, when a tense silence suddenly enveloped the room.

Jaci kept her smile hidden and her eyes on the little clip of the bra between her breasts. She released it slowly, then peeled the cups away from her breasts before dropping the silken lace to the floor.

She had their attention. It was complete, undivided, two sets of male eyes trained on her, devouring her. She ran her hands up her midriff, then cupped the mounds, her fingers running over her stiff nipples, before she lifted her head and stared back at them, allowing the lust, desire, and the pure love she felt for Cam to show on her face.

They were bruised and bloody—and jerking their boots off.

She lowered her hands, smoothing them over her flesh, down to the band of her panties, where she hooked her fingers beneath the elastic and lace and drew them slowly down her thighs.

She kicked them off as boots thumped to the floor and their hands went to the snaps of their jeans.

Blood smeared their faces. Cam had a cut on his shoulder, Chase's chest was smeared with blood. They looked like warriors—like bad boys looking for trouble; and the effects of that fight had her blood pumping and hunger pouring through her veins.

Conquerors. They could consider this fight a draw, and to the victor goes—well, Jaci. Two victors and the fantasy of a lifetime.

"Would you like to shower first?"

Cam stalked toward her.

"Hmm. Maybe not." Breathing was becoming difficult.

They weren't focused on beating the hell out of each other anymore, they were now focused on her. All that testosterone and need for action swirled in the air around her and left her panting at the knowledge of what could be coming. She could see it in Cam's eyes, this wouldn't be a ménage. In Chase's eyes, she saw the knowledge of that, as he began to move to the stairs. And perhaps there was even a tinge of regret mixed with relief.

"I can't believe you did that." Cam wasn't thinking now, she could feel it. Testosterone filled the air, lust oozed from his pores, as he jerked her into his arms and, rather than moving for the couch, headed for the bedroom.

When he tossed her to the bed, she didn't have time to bounce before he was tearing his clothes off. Within seconds he was covering her, pushing her legs apart, and filling her.

Alone. Staring into her eyes, the bleak shadows that had once filled his gaze had eased, and now, desperate hunger filled his eyes. Emotion. Satisfaction and lust.

"I love you," she whispered, framing his face with her hands and staring up at him as she felt his cock flex inside her. "With everything I am, Cameron Falladay, I love you."

He grimaced, and when he would have buried his head against her shoulder, she pushed him back.

"Watch me," she almost sobbed, "like I watch you. Every second, every emotion. Just like this Cam. Just us."

"Just us," he groaned, moving against her slowly, his cock easing out, then working inside her—filling her, stretching her, taking more than just the lust that rose between them.

"You're always a part of me," she moaned, staring into his eyes, feeling that emotion storming through him, seeing it as his expression tightened, his eyes darkened.

"You've always been a part of me," he told her then, his strokes increasing, pleasure blooming, tightening, taking them higher now, than they had gone before.

The wicked eroticism of the ménages was nice, but this, this deep intensity, the feel of him touching her, hands stroking her . . . his head lowered, his lips engulfing hers, his gaze slumberous, heavy-lidded, as he held hers. This was what it was meant to be. This was what she needed.

Each stroke became harder, faster, until he lifted her legs, pushed them back, and drove into her. And still he watched her. And she held onto him.

"I love you." His face contorted as she felt herself tightening, felt her release nearing. "Always, Jaci. Always fucking loved you."

Harder, deeper, flying inside her, until Jaci felt not just the physical eruptions of release tear through her, but the emotional. As though their souls had merged. As though they had been drawn inside each other even more firmly than before.

Cam drove into her repeatedly, groaning her name, repeating it like a talisman, until, with one last, hard stroke, he buried full length into the gripping depths of her body and filled her with himself. His seed shot inside her, but his eyes never left hers, and she saw the brief moistening of his gaze, the emotion that ripped through them.

In his arms, she would always be safe. But in hers, so would he be.

And when it was over, when the last shudders echoed through her, he didn't move from the bed, he didn't leave her to go to the couch. He pulled her into his arms, tugged the blanket around them, and, exhausted, he held her until his eyes closed, hers closed, and they slept together.

CHAPTER
TWENTY-EIGHT

Cam was asleep in the bed, curled around her, his heavy breathing at her ear, his heart beating against her back. The sun was just peeking through the shades pulled over the tall, wide window behind the bed. Spears of light washed over the room. And Cam had slept with her.

She turned her head slowly to stare at him. In sleep, his features were more relaxed, but still tough and hard.

Smiling, she eased from the bed, holding back a wince at the soreness between her thighs. He hadn't taken her just once through the night, but several times. As she paused at the side of the bed, she turned back to stare at him, love welling inside her, dampening her eyes, and it had her thanking God that she had found him again.

He was arrogant and demanding, dominant and so certain of his own decisions that she was sure there would be times he would make her completely insane.

But he was hers.

Pulling on her robe, she belted it tight, determined not to awaken him. If there was one thing she knew, it was that Cam didn't always sleep well. There wasn't a chance she was waking him up.

Moving quietly from the bedroom, she went to the bathroom, showered and brushed her teeth in record time, then, pulling one of Cam's T-shirts from the walk-in closet, she padded back into the main room.

She was almost to the kitchen island when she saw Chase. He was sitting on the couch silently, dressed only in jeans, his head bent, his hands covering his face.

His shoulders were scratched, his hair mussed, and he looked like a man ready to break from the weight on his shoulders.

She moved silently around the couch, her gaze catching on the whisky that still sat on the table, directly in front of Chase.

His hands lowered from his face and he stared at the bottle as well.

"He's not drank straight whisky since he was eighteen years old," Chase said. "And I've not had a brother since he was fifteen."

Jaci eased herself down on the end of the couch.

"He was always your brother," she said, keeping her voice quiet. "He's just Cam. You have to accept that, Chase. He thinks he has to protect all of us."

He breathed out roughly. "I'd have killed her if I'd known."

Yes, he would have. And they would have both paid for it in ways she knew Cam couldn't accept.

"He would have known that," she whispered.

Chase wiped his hand tiredly over the rasp of an overnight beard and breathed out. The sound was rough and heavy with grief.

"It was my job to protect him."

Jaci shook her head. "You would have done the same thing, Chase. You would have protected him and your pride with the same ferocity. Don't take away from the sacrifices he made. He survived. He made a man's choices when he was no more than a boy, and I won't take that from him. I won't let you take it away from him, either."

"She almost killed him." His voice was hoarse with the tears she knew he wouldn't shed here. "She did kill a part of him."

"Chase, he survived," she repeated. "He's strong and he's honorable. He's your brother and my lover, and he would die for either of us. Do you know how very lucky we are to have him? Just the way he is?"

She knew. She had known men who had charmed lives. Men who had never suffered, never known pain, and they were nowhere near as decent and honorable as her Cam.

Chase's shoulders hunched as he propped his elbow on his knee, his chin in his hand, and stared at the whisky bottle again.

"I want a drink so bad I can taste it." He sighed. "I have a rule. Never before evening. I have it for a reason."

She moved a little closer to him, feeling her heart break for him. She knew he had that rule for a reason. Because for Cam and Chase both, whisky had been a crutch at far too young an age.

"I killed Moriah," he said then. "Sweet Moriah." A bitter laugh left his lips. "God, she had us all fooled, didn't she?"

And she had broken Chase's heart with the decision he'd had to make.

"There was nothing else you could have done. She would have killed Cam, and he would have let her, Chase. He wouldn't have pulled that trigger, because that gun wasn't aimed at you or me. And you cared for her. He knew that."

"Yeah," he said softly. "I cared for her."

And she couldn't help herself. She moved closer to him, put her head on his shoulder, and wrapped her arms around him. After a brief start of surprise, his arms came around her and his hard body shuddered as he buried his head in her neck.

He sat there with her for long moments, rocking her, perhaps because he couldn't rock himself.

Finally, his hold loosened and he set her away from him, his fingers touching her cheek gently before he breathed in heavily.

"Cam slept in the bed," he said then, his voice ragged.

She let a smile tug at her lips. "Yeah, Cam slept in the bed."

He nodded, the movement slow and heavy, before rising to his feet. "I'm going to go shower. I have to wrap this up, meet with Ian and the Brockheims." He shook his head. "Son of a bitch, I hope this day ends soon."

She watched as he moved from the couch to the stairs. He didn't look back, but he didn't have to. She could see the sadness, the sorrow inside him, and she ached because of it.

Cam and Chase. They were so strong, so decent, and parts of them were scarred forever because of the actions of others.

Shaking her head, she turned and moved back to the bedroom, back to her lover. He was sleeping in that big bed without her, and she needed to be with him.

As she turned into the room, she saw that he wasn't asleep at all.

His large body was sprawled out in the center of the bed, the sheet covering nothing but his hips as his powerful arms were folded beneath his head, and he stared up at the ceiling with a frown.

Jaci pulled the T-shirt off and crawled onto the bed, folding her legs to the side as she leaned against his chest, their eyes meeting.

"The bed's comfortable." His voice was soft, reflective.

"It's more comfortable with you in it," she admitted, watching him close, seeing the sadness in his eyes.

"Chase is hurting." He sighed.

"Chase is going to be okay." ˎ

He nodded at that, then turned his head to her, one arm moving from beneath his head to touch her cheek with his hand.

"You didn't get the roses and the candlelight," he said. His voice was regretful, but his eyes were filling with love.

That love swelled inside her. Her Cam. Her warrior. She had him right here where she needed him, and she wasn't letting him go.

"I got better." She smiled. "I got my man."

His fingers threaded into her hair, clenched and tugged until her lips touched his and he smiled. A sexy, wicked smile that tugged at her heart and at her womb.

"You always had the man," he growled, before twisting and pushing her to her back, rising over her, surrounding her with warmth, his gaze sinking into hers, filling her with his love. "Sweet Jaci, don't you know, you always had that man."